PRAISE FOR

the winter

"Confirms that Hetley has created that rarest of gems: a Celtic fantasy worth reading . . . Fans of 'realistic fantasy' authors like Charles de Lint and George R.R. Martin will particularly enjoy sinking their teeth into this gritty and entertaining story."   —*Publishers Weekly*

"Hetley's seamless blending of 'real' and mythical realities is pure magic, every bit as enchanting here as in *The Summer Country*."   —*Booklist*

"A magnificent and powerful work of high fantasy in which alliances change with the wind and nobody can be trusted."
                          —*Midwest Book Review*

"This is adult literature at its finest . . . that rarity of sequels, one that perfectly builds off the previous novel. James Hetley can be very proud of the story he has created."
                          —*Green Man Review*

"Hetley's crossover fantasy series brings into close proximity the fairy and the 'real' worlds as his characters seek a balance between myth and reality. Fans of urban fantasy in the style of Charles de Lint and Tanya Huff should enjoy this well-written sequel."   —*Library Journal*

PRAISE FOR

the summer country

A *Locus* Recommended Read
One of *Booklist*'s Top Ten SF/Fantasy Novels of the Year

"You don't find many books like this, never mind first novels . . . For the jaded reader of Celtic fantasies such as I've become . . . it's such a treat to find a book as strong as this."
—Charles de Lint, World Fantasy Award–winning author of *Trader*

continued . . .

Dragon's Eye

James A. Hetley

▲
ACE BOOKS, NEW YORK

THE BERKLEY PUBLISHING GROUP
Published by the Penguin Group
Penguin Group (USA) Inc.
375 Hudson Street, New York, New York 10014, USA
Penguin Group (Canada), 90 Eglinton Avenue East, Suite 700, Toronto, Ontario M4P 2Y3, Canada
(a division of Pearson Penguin Canada Inc.)
Penguin Books Ltd., 80 Strand, London WC2R 0RL, England
Penguin Group Ireland, 25 St. Stephen's Green, Dublin 2, Ireland (a division of Penguin Books Ltd.)
Penguin Group (Australia), 250 Camberwell Road, Camberwell, Victoria 3124, Australia
(a division of Pearson Australia Group Pty. Ltd.)
Penguin Books India Pvt. Ltd., 11 Community Centre, Panchsheel Park, New Delhi—110 017, India
Penguin Group (NZ), Cnr. Airborne and Rosedale Roads, Albany, Auckland 1310, New Zealand
(a division of Pearson New Zealand Ltd.)
Penguin Books (South Africa) (Pty.) Ltd., 24 Sturdee Avenue, Rosebank, Johannesburg 2196,
South Africa

Penguin Books Ltd., Registered Offices: 80 Strand, London WC2R 0RL, England

This is an original publication of The Berkley Publishing Group.

This is a work of fiction. Names, characters, places, and incidents either are the product of the author's imagination or are used fictitiously, and any resemblance to actual persons, living or dead, business establishments, events, or locales is entirely coincidental. The publisher does not have any control over and does not assume any responsibility for author or third-party websites or their content.

First edition: November 2005

Library of Congress Cataloging-in-Publication Data

Hetley, James A.
    Dragon's eye / James A. Hetley.— 1st ed.
        p. cm.
    ISBN 0-441-01328-7
    1. Maine—Fiction.   2. Vendetta—Fiction.   3. Good and evil—Fiction.   4. Parent and child—Fiction.   5. Conflict of generations—Fiction.   I. Title.

PS3608.E853D73 2005
813'.6—dc22

                                                                        2005048145

PRINTED IN THE UNITED STATES OF AMERICA

10 9 8 7 6 5 4 3 2 1

To Mom, who never got to see these stories,
And to Dad, who never knew they would exist.

one

FEW THINGS IN Stonefort are exactly what they seem.

Daniel Morgan reminded himself of that fact, as he studied the scene in front of him. This was the place. From this distance, it *looked* perfectly normal.

Evening fog rose off cold saltwater, closing in and hiding Daniel's kayak as it bobbed gently in the swells, and the water lay as close to calm as the Maine coast ever got. The tide had just turned to the ebb, leaving a wet line drawn across the coarse pink granite cliff. He sat in his cockpit and thought about geology and camouflage.

Camouflage meant a sea-green kayak ballasted low in the water and a fleece jacket mottled the black and deep brown of waterlogged wharf timbers floating in the tide. It meant greasepaint on his face, a flat black double-ended paddle, and black gloves. Coming in, he'd sculled within yards of a raft of eiders without drawing a blink from the drowsing birds. Whatever gave him the creepy sense of being watched hadn't bothered *them*.

There were things Maine rock did naturally and things it

didn't. Sheer cliffs and offshore ledges were natural. Straight channels tucked behind rough sea-stacks weren't. Neat arch-mouthed caves hidden at the end of those channels weren't.

This place had gnawed at his curiosity, ever since he'd spotted it while tracking down a dinghy that had broken loose. The weathered cracks in the rock, the wind-twisted spruces with their gnarled roots clawing for a hold on the lichen and shreds of soil that escaped the storms, the rock-weed and barnacles below the tide line, all tried to tell him this was a natural cliff. They lied. Men had carved this rock and then gone to a lot of trouble to hide their work. Judging by lichen and trees, the last ring of hammer on chisel had been centuries ago.

The bell buoy tolled from Tinker Ledge, reassuring in its normalcy. He really didn't have any reason to be afraid. Pratts and Morgans had played tag like this for generations. They weren't enemies as such: no blood feuds, no brawling in the streets like the Montagues and Capulets. There were rules.

The two families had even been partners once, but they'd gone their separate ways after a difference of opinion on long-range business planning. Now the two sides kept different secrets, and he couldn't simply walk along the shore and look at something that had caught his curiosity.

Daniel's hand caressed the silver dragon pendant at his chest, welcoming the warmth of the fire-red stone bound in its coils. Even in June, the water carried a winter chill. He noticed a sleek gray head watching him from the water at the edge of the fog, body just awash—seals grew hides for water like this. Humans had to rely on neoprene and Polartec. He'd be so much more comfortable wearing his other skin . . . He shook his head. This needed human eyes, and maybe human hands.

He tucked the warm glow back inside his wetsuit, along with his usual wry curiosity about how it did the things it did. The Dragon hadn't come with a manual. He'd worn it for twenty years now, almost half his life, and it still sometimes surprised him: for example, this ability to see things that had eluded the Coast Guard and a dozen other federal agencies for years.

A flick of the paddle sent him closer to the cliff. The scene fuzzed and then sharpened, as if he'd slipped through a denser patch of fog. "There's a channel here," he said, talking to his left hand inside its splash mitt. "Wide enough for a Novi boat."

A hiss of static answered in his left ear, then a whispered voice. "The charts show solid ledges."

Fifty yards out, you'd never see the overlap in the rocks that hid the channel. Even at high tide, ledges made waters like these a death-trap for anyone without a chart or decades of experience. They meant tricky work even for a narrow sliver of plastic that drew only six inches of water. Daniel would never bring his lobster boat in among these rocks, and there weren't any buoyed traps to show that others were braver or less wise.

He wondered how the Pratts had diddled the charts. Aerial cameras weren't eyes, that they could be fooled by illusions. No matter what the voice in his ear might say: What there *was,* was a path of clear green water about fifteen yards across, zigzagging through the rocks to a turning basin big enough for a scallop dragger—or a smuggler's hot-rod, more likely. That hidden slot back through the cliff to the black mouth of the cave didn't show up on any Geological Survey map, either.

Of course, the Morgan family had a few ancient secrets, too. And ways of keeping them. He smiled quietly to himself.

"I'm heading in," he whispered to his mitt.

"Watch yourself," his ear answered. "The Pratts were never known for being stupid."

"Yeah. Well, Maria would never forgive me if I missed

Gary's party. She's been planning it for months. You know I'm not going to risk her wrath."

"Wrath" was an understatement. Maria's temper was a byword in three counties. The things they didn't tell you, before you took out that marriage license . . .

Daniel sniffed, searching the salt air, spruce resin, and rotting seaweed odors for alien tangs. A faint whiff of gasoline rode the breeze, along with the mustiness of wet rock that never saw the sun. He also picked up the faintest touch of sun-dried hemp, and smiled to himself over the guess confirmed.

"No more talk," the voice added. "Switch code only."

Daniel clicked his answer, short-long-short pulses on the "talk" switch for agreement. The radios operated on unused frequencies just outside "ham" channels, and the odds were very strong against somebody eavesdropping. That didn't mean he could afford the noise of talking on his end.

Delicate flicks of the paddle moved him south, close in along the cliff. He scanned for wires, for sensors, for cameras, for any evidence of alarms. Old habits of the trade—he smiled to himself and shook his head. Storm waves and winter ice would wipe out anything like that, to say nothing of the false alarms a sixteen-foot tidal range would trigger.

The walls of the slot reared up around him, coarse-grained, weathered stone scattered with palm-sized splotches of orange and gray-green lichen. He spotted a single gouge left by a quarryman's chisel, and a patch of discolored mortar that plugged a hole. The cliff face dropped straight down into the water, and he guessed there would be at least ten feet of channel at dead low tide. The smell of gas and marijuana grew stronger.

He sculled around to line up with the cave, keying his transmitter again with a Morse code "285" for the bearing on his deck compass. His earphone hissed "Roger" in reply, the growing static on the FM warning him the stone was shielding his signal. So the radio might not be much use. But then, his little handheld always talked better than it listened.

A single bright scrape marred the entry; someone had gotten careless with a boat hook, fending off. The shadows closed around Daniel, into the total darkness of a cave at night. He dug into his gear-bag, pulled out a headlamp, and put it on. He hated showing light, but infrared goggles gave too coarse a picture for this job, and light amplifiers would need *some* light to amplify.

The beam cut into the darkness, leaving a white shaft of fog like a thin pale ghost questing to right and left. The inside of the cave was rougher stone, chisel gouges and the half-tunnels of blasting holes standing out clearly in the light. This work had been done after gunpowder and iron came to the coast, but before there were enough people to care about the noise.

Daniel crept along, sculling gently while he scanned for alarms. The tunnel curved slowly north—a turn easy enough for any boat that had business being there, but sufficient to shield direct light from the outside. The water lay as still as a millpond, and he heard his quietest paddle-strokes whispering in the silence.

The radio spat static at him, with "distance" barely coming above the squelch. He sent his guess back and received another burst of noise. It sounded as loud as a chainsaw in the stillness, and he killed the volume. From now on, he'd be transmitting blind.

His light swept over a slot in the cave roof and walls, and he studied the bright metal edge it showed. Storm gate, he guessed, stainless steel, something to keep heavy swells out when the Gulf of Maine started getting frisky. He paused just beyond it, thinking about traps. Up to this point, nothing he'd seen could stop him from just sneaking right back out again.

The tunnel opened up into a chamber as wide and high as a barn. The walls seemed smoother here, and natural, as if some troll had blown a bubble in the granite while it was cooling. Water splashed from a spring high up to one side, flowing gently down the rock and into the quiet tide below.

He backed water a yard or two, nerves on edge as his headlamp bounced light across rusted iron overhead. He brought the beam back and steadied it, lighting up an ancient hoist and wooden catwalk high along the wall. Judging by the rotted holes in the wood, nobody had used *that* for fifty years or more. Probably rumrunners and Prohibition. Newer light fixtures also hung from the rock, though, connected by a spider-web of conduit.

Then dark shadows formed into a boat and floating dock, low in the water, new and well-tended. Curiosity sucked him deeper into the cave.

The boat was fiberglass, flat black, long and sleek like an arrow, and bore no name or registration numbers. *Very* interesting. Outside of GPS and radar antennas and a single VHF radio whip, it showed no metal. If the engines sat below waterline, it would have no more radar signature than a chunk of driftwood.

Daniel sculled quietly along it, estimating length and beam and capacity in bales of marijuana or kilos of cocaine. A man could support a very comfortable lifestyle with a boat like that.

Assuming the right connections, of course. Which the Pratts would have. Daniel had seen enough. He spun the kayak with two dips of the paddle and keyed his transceiver again with the code for "leaving."

Lights blazed, blinding him.

He dug his paddle into the water, thrashing through the

glare toward his memory of the exit. Machinery whined, and he heard the rumble of the storm gate closing.

The damned thing would be slow. He still might make it.

A door slammed behind him, and then a single shot blasted and echoed, deafening in the enclosed space. His paddle jerked in his hands. The kayak slewed around and he lost his bearings. He rammed into something, hard and grating on the bow, and that was it. He dropped the paddle and raised his hands.

His eyes slowly adapted to the light. A shadowy figure stood on the floating dock, cradling an assault rifle in his hands. Another sat on a landing by a metal door, rubbing his eyes and dangling night-vision goggles from one hand. Neither of them was actually pointing a weapon *at* Daniel, so he relaxed a touch. He also locked the radio mike on "transmit."

The gunman jerked a thumb at him, waving him back to the dock. Daniel blinked and focused, trying to identify the man. He seemed to be a stranger. Slow strokes of the paddle brought the kayak over beside the float, nothing sharp or sudden to startle the man with the gun.

Daniel grabbed a ladder and twisted through the contortionist's balancing act required to exit a floating kayak. You practically *wore* the damned things rather than riding in them, and you couldn't just stand up and step ashore.

He got a closer look at the gunman. He was definitely not a Pratt, and the Hispanic complexion and features tossed any rules out the window. Daniel shivered with a chill that had nothing to do with the cold water.

The guard must work for the suppliers. Probably Colombians. They had a vicious reputation, the kind of people who gave crime a bad name.

The door clanged again, and Daniel looked up. Three more men had entered the cavern, shadows against the light. One of them had the characteristic short and broad profile of the Pratt family. They started down the ramp to the float, and he got a better view: Tom Pratt, head of the clan, and another two Latinos. Both of the Colombians had pistols out—ugly little Mac 10s, probably full-auto.

Tom shook his head. "Well, well. Look what drifted in on the tide." He grinned, as if the whole scene was a joke.

Take away the guns and Daniel might have laughed. He decided to play along. "Hey, you left the door open."

Tom nodded. Then he turned to the older Latino, a short, thin man with enough lines on his face to suggest that the black hair was a dye job. "How did he get past the illusions?"

"I do not know." His voice had the careful precision of a man who had learned English late but very well. "Is he police?"

That drew a laugh from Tom and the man still up on the landing, the one who'd had the night-vision goggles. Daniel finally identified him as Johnny Pratt, one of the numerous cousins. He now held another assault rifle.

"No," Tom said, still chuckling. "Indeed not. Our cross-town neighbor is the head of a rather ancient clan of thieves and con-men. He's as likely to be nervous of the cops as we are."

He studied Daniel for a moment, head cocked to one side. "It's a pity, him sneaking in the back door like this. That other matter you mentioned, selling some artifacts? Daniel's the man you'd want. I'm sure he could come up with a name or two, people who wouldn't ask embarrassing questions. For a finder's fee, of course."

"That is indeed a shame. Allow me to introduce myself. I am Antonio Estevan Francisco Juan Carlos da Silva y Gomes, at your service. I am a business associate of your neighbor." The old man turned back to Tom. "A thief, you say? Is he here to steal our merchandise?"

"Ah, yes, that is indeed the question." Tom turned back to Daniel. "Just what the *hell* are you doing here, anyway?"

Daniel shrugged. "Curiosity. I saw something that didn't belong, and followed it. I thought it might explain a story Grandfather told Dad."

"I believe," the Latino said, "that you have an English saying about curiosity killing the cat. We have similar warnings in Spanish." He turned to Tom again. "What is this about his grandfather?"

Tom waved it off, like a triviality. "Probably great-grandfather. Our families used to be partners in the import business. There was a small disagreement over policy back in the 1920s, and the partnership was dissolved. No hard feelings on either side."

Daniel snorted. A small disagreement? Granddad hadn't agreed with the Pratts' plan to cut good Scotch with wood alcohol. He preferred repeat customers.

Tom shrugged his shoulders. "A small matter. I still would like to know how he got past the illusions and wards."

"A question that troubles me, also." The older Colombian waved his bodyguard forward. "Please to search him?"

Daniel gauged the distance to the water, and then remembered that storm gate. It must go right down to the cave floor, or it would be useless at low tide. He could hold his breath a *lot* longer than they thought. However, all they had to do was keep the gate closed until they caught him, or dumped a few grenades into the pool. He didn't doubt that they had plenty.

The younger Latino was rough but efficient. He pulled out the radio, the microphone, and Daniel's boating knife. He missed the pendant, and Daniel allowed himself a ray of hope. It might be too small to seem like a weapon, but . . .

"So. A radio." The old Colombian stooped down and poked at it, ignoring the knife. "And to whom were you talking?"

"Nobody. That's a standard marine VHF; I mostly use it for checking weather and stuff like that."

The old man stood up and shook his head. He stepped closer to Daniel, slowly, staring into his eyes. The old man's eyes were dark, deep-set in his lined and graying face, and they seemed like ancient wells with a gravity that pulled sideways on the world.

"You will find it difficult to lie to me. I am a bit of a *brujo,* you see, what you would call a sorcerer. I know things. I know your thoughts. To whom were you talking?"

Weakness flowed over Daniel, as if he had paddled the kayak all day against the tide. He suddenly found it hard to stand, and he forced his knees to hold. His tongue took on a life of its own. "My brother."

The *brujo* held his gaze. "Is this true?"

Daniel's tongue said "Yes" at the same time as Tom Pratt said, "I doubt it. Ben Morgan was lost overboard from a scallop dragger about twenty years ago."

The dragon pendant burned hot under Daniel's wetsuit, and he drew power from it to stand and fight this weakness. The *brujo*'s eyes widened, and he looked Daniel up and down.

"Search him again. Here, I hold your *pistola.* Search carefully." The old Colombian took both Mac-10s and stepped back a pace.

This time, the bodyguard found the pendant. He flipped it out of the wetsuit, and reached to pull it off. Daniel tensed, but the older man grunted and waved the guard back. He handed both pistols to Tom Pratt, and stepped forward to stare deeply into Daniel's eyes. That eerie weakness returned, as if the old man had sucked the strength out of Daniel's muscles and left them filled with water.

"So. Where did you get this little trinket? It is very old, very powerful, yes? It has been in your family a very long time? I think we know how you saw the entrance, how you passed the illusions and the guardians."

The lines around the *brujo*'s eyes were fainter now, and his skin much smoother. The harsh lighting of the cavern must be playing tricks.

Daniel fought back, pulling on the Dragon through its bond with the pendant. He dragged his gaze away from the Colombian, and concentrated on Tom Pratt. The radio should still be transmitting . . . "How did you catch me? Professional curiosity, you know."

"We all have our little secrets. Let's just say that you triggered an alarm, and young Johnny came out to watch you sneaking around. When you turned to leave, he signaled Paco to hit the lights."

And Paco would have been beyond that door, some place already well lit so his eyes wouldn't be dazzled. It was a tidy little trap, proof that the Pratts were everything family lore had said. Daniel hoped that Ben was taking notes.

"*Padrino,* the radio, it is on. It is transmitting."

Daniel jerked his attention away from Tom Pratt. The bodyguard was staring at the handheld, lying on the dock. Its tiny meter showed the steady black band of full output power. Damn. He *would* run into a bunch of thugs who knew something about radio. Where's ignorance when you really need it?

"So!" The *brujo* snatched up the radio, twisted the antenna off, and then swiftly popped the back open and removed the battery. He waved the radio's carcass at Daniel, shaking his head. "This is a shame. This is *stupidity*! Now we must think about your family as well as you. Have you no *honradez,* that you should endanger women and children?"

The words hit Daniel like lead mallets, heavy but no resonance, and left a sick ache behind. *Women and children. Maria. Gary, and Ellen, and Peggy.* Some of the drug bosses ordered whole families killed in their turf wars. Such casual brutality served as a warning to others.

Panic washed over him and died. This *brujo* witchery had

even stolen his will to care. It felt totally alien, totally dead-
ening, nothing like the bright bubbling earth-magic of the
Dragon flowing through the quartz veins and basalt dikes
underneath Morgan's Castle.

The Colombian again stepped closer, bringing that sense
of a cold, black drain with him. His face had lost all its
lines, and he looked no older than forty. The dragon pendant burned with the flow of power. "Tell me again, to
whom were you talking? Give me the name."

Daniel felt as if he was drowning in those eyes. "Ben
Morgan."

"Must be one hell of a radio." Tom Pratt's voice slipped
past the compulsion of the *brujo*'s eyes. "Like I told you, his
only brother drowned almost twenty years ago."

"Muy misterioso." The *brujo* waved his other guard forward. "Diego, remove this delightful little trinket. Then we
shall see what tune the bird sings."

The bodyguard reached for the dragon pendant, and
Daniel braced himself. He'd hoped the Colombian sorcerer
would try to take it himself . . .

The guard's bare hand touched the silver. Power flowed
like a lightning flash, the guard jerked twice, and then he
flopped on the planking of the float. He looked unmarked,
but his eyes were open and sightless. The *brujo* shook his
head, knelt down, and closed the dead man's eyes.

"So many years with me, *macho,* and you have never
learned caution. Or wisdom. I would have warned you if
you had not thought to steal a kilo from our latest shipment." He glanced up at the other Latino, as if he was driving home a lesson that he wanted repeated to others. "It is
true, what the *norteamericanos* say: users are losers."

He stood up and pulled a pair of thin leather gloves from
his pocket, turning back to Daniel. "You will hold very still.
You will give up this thing willingly. You will forget all
thought of resistance."

His eyes drained Daniel. His face was now the face of a young man in full strength, skin smooth and glowing golden. His gloved hands reached behind Daniel's neck and unclasped the chain holding the pendant, carefully avoiding any contact with the silver dragon or the blazing red stone it twined around and guarded.

The Dragon left Daniel, and his knees collapsed under him.

TWO

—⁓—

KATE FROWNED AS the midnight-blue Suburban rolled
past. She wasn't "on duty," but as town constable she was
supposed to keep an eye out for anything odd in the general
small-town humdrum of Stonefort, Maine. She felt a prick-
ling on her skin that forced her to notice that damned car, as
if she was a rabbit under the gaze of a wolf.

Well under the village limit of twenty-five. New Jersey
plates. Windows tinted so black you could have a crowd of
four-eyed Martians inside gawking at the natives and nobody would know. She slouched back against Alice's weathered picket fence and ran her fingers through her buzz-cut
blond hair. The fence complained.

At six foot six and well on the far side of two-fifty,
Katherine Rowley was used to the world complaining about
her presence. Back in high school, the basketball refs had
seemed to think she was committing a foul just by stepping
on the court. Even at thirty-nine, she was broad-shouldered
and more muscular than heavy, her big hands scarred and
callused and missing half the index finger on the left from

years of working as a good-enough carpenter. From a distance, some people even thought she was pretty.

Until they found out she was built to the wrong scale, that is. She straightened out of her "I'm not really this big" slouch and glanced down at Alice Haskell. The contrast between them always made Kate feel even bigger. Small, with dark hair and dark skin from her Naskeag Indian ancestors, Alice looked more like one of those preadolescent gymnasts, something short of five feet and about as much weight as your average chickadee. Kate nodded at the departing wagon.

"Any idea who that is?"

Her friend quirked an eyebrow. "Now you're sounding like a nosy old fishwife."

Kate hooked her fingers into her belt, dropping into her imitation of a Southern sheriff. "It's mah job to know, ma'am. Ahm th' law around this heah town."

Her gaze followed the Suburban around the Stonefort green until the alien vanished toward the waterfront. Something creepy about that overgrown station wagon . . . She wasn't a tourist attraction, that strangers would slow down to stare at her. Besides, New Jersey drivers didn't believe in speed limits.

Kate pulled out a pouch of tobacco and rolling papers, manufacturing a cigarette with unconscious deftness. She lit the product with an old Zippo that had her ex-husband's initials engraved on the side.

Alice wrinkled her nose at the smoke. "You ever going to quit puffing those cancer sticks?"

Kate stared at the glowing end, letting smoke trickle out of her nose. It was her first cigarette of the day, and the nicotine rush gave her enough of a glow that she could ignore the Standard Haskell Healthcare Sermon.

"Probably not."

"Well, toss me that pouch. I need to do a little First People witchery this morning, and you might as well provide the herbs. Could even save your life."

Alice played at being a Naskeag shaman, one of those charming eccentrics you got in small Downeast towns. At least Alice was rich enough to be considered *eccentric,* rather than flat-ass crazy. Kate shrugged and handed over her Bull Durham. Witchcraft was a harmless hobby. The guys at the building site would have smokes, anyway.

"Ain't scared of cancer. I figure I've been playing with the house's money ever since I got knocked off Charlie Guptill's roof and had Dana Peters kill himself on my right front fender, all in one year. If I drop dead tomorrow, that's still sixteen years of clear profit."

"Where's that leave Jackie?"

Kate grimaced. "Don't want to talk about that brat. College scouts are already talking about a full ride just to play basketball, and she won't even dig in to pass tenth-grade English! We had another set-to last night. Damn near grabbed her by the scruff of the neck and booted her over to Lew's house, let *him* feed her for a couple of months."

"Humph! Nine days out of ten, that man ain't sober enough to remember he *has* a daughter."

"He's started AA again."

Alice spat neatly into the bark mulch under her rosebushes. "For the twentieth time. You tell that idiot that his liver is good for about another two gallons of whiskey, max. He can drink it all in one week, or make it last for thirty years. His choice." She studied Kate's face, weighing the familiar symptoms. "You thinking to move back in with him?"

"He gets in a year clean, maybe." Kate stared cross-eyed at the stream of smoke, trying to read the chances of *that* happening. "He's a nice guy when he's sober." Then, defensively: "Hell, he's nice enough blind drunk. Just useless."

"You never give up, do you?"

"If I gave up easy, Jackie would've been born an orphan.

Rowleys don't quit. Grannie told me we've got a town named after us, down near Boston. Consolation prize for making it through those winters back in the 1600s."

"Yeah. And when your ancestors stepped off the boat, mine were standing on that hill over behind Morgan's Castle, bitching about how the neighborhood was going to hell. You won't get anywhere playing that Old Family card around here."

Alice's gaze browsed on the distant view, over the hollow marking the Stonefort harbor and out to the offshore islands fuzzy in the creeping fog. "Look, about that drunk you used to live with. Anytime you get to feeling lonely, you know I've got a lot more bed-space than I need."

Kate considered for a moment and then shook her head. "Never work out. I'd roll over in my sleep and squash you."

"I can remember a few times when being squashed felt awful good."

Those memories brought a faint heat to Kate's cheeks. "Hey, we were seventeen and thought it was cool to sneak into my stepdad's bourbon. I've outgrown both conditions."

"Don't go writing off bourbon. I know Lew sets a bad example, but there are a lot of people who can say no to that third drink. Relaxing your corset a bit can let you breathe."

Kate shook her head again. "Relax your corset too much around here, the blue-noses will ride you out of town on a rail."

" 'Fraidy cat. They let me ride the ambulance, never said word one. Being queer doesn't matter to them when we're delivering a baby in the middle of a run up to Downeast General."

Kate rolled her eyes, carrying on the well-worn banter scripted by the habits of thirty years. "They let you on the ambulance 'cause you're the only RN dumb enough to take the job for free. Beggars can't be choosers." She pushed away from the fence, her mind still half on that dark blue Suburban.

As usual, talking about Alice's homosexuality made Kate twitchy. The small woman had always been quite open about it, and she was the best friend Kate had ever had—a damn sight more reliable than any man she'd known. But Jackie had enough problems without the other kids pasting labels on her, and "butch" would be such an easy one with the genes she'd caught from her mother's side.

"Look, I've got to go. Have to drop some windows over at Danny Nason's project, then play soccer mom. No rest for the wicked."

"That's 'cause you're sleeping in the wrong bed."

Kate grimaced. "Well, thanks for the water." She heaved the five-gallon jerrycan off the ground as easily as another woman would hoist a purse. "The guys all say there's nothing like your spring, best water in town."

Her battered green Dodge truck idled by the shoulder of the road, coughing on about every tenth spark as a reminder why she didn't shut it off unless it was aimed down the slope for a rolling start. Rowley Construction didn't earn enough money to hang her magnetic signs on the sides of anything more reliable. The beast *did* have four-wheel drive, ground clearance for the kind of construction sites she found around Stonefort, and a one-ton payload for a decent pile of concrete blocks and mortar. You take what you can get.

Town constable was ten hours a week, max, and contractor was just another frame of the movie. The concept of "job" barely existed in Sunrise County. What she really had was a succession of ways to pick up next week's grocery money. By local standards, that was doing well. At least she wasn't chasing *last* week's.

By those same local standards, Alice was rich. She worked ER up at Downeast Regional, sometimes two straight twenty-four-hour sieges where she napped on a sofa in the waiting room. On days off, she puttered around her fourteen-room labyrinth of a weathered gray cape, growing

antique roses and incongruous peaches in the teeth of the
Maine winters and torturing innocent juniper bushes into
bonsai.

Kate looked the old Haskell House over with a professional eye, noting the straight ridge line and square gables
that spoke of solid construction well maintained. Fieldstone
foundations rooted on bedrock, bare cedar clapboards protected by a good overhang, a slate roof with copper fasten-
ings that couldn't rust. She'd give strong odds that the lime
mortar in foundations and chimneys was still gaining
strength, more than two hundred years after the first stones
were laid.

Rambling up and over and down the crest of its hill, the
House looked as if it had grown in place over the centuries,
sprouting an ell here and budding out a dormer there like a
healthy plant. Kate felt a kinship with that house that was
stronger even than her bond with Alice.

People had always called it "The Woman's House." It had
been that way since time out of mind, always calling the latest owner "The Woman" as a sort of title. The old pile of
glacier-rounded fieldstone and weathered gray clapboards
was worth maybe forty grand. The ten acres of shorefront
property it sat on would easily bring two million.

Kate shook her head at the contrast. Boston and New
York dollars chased any sniff of saltwater and plunked a
summer house on it. At least the madness paid her heating
bill with a dozen caretaker accounts.

Kate slid behind the wheel, tucking her knees carefully
under the dash and steering column. Danged world didn't
even make *trucks* big enough for her.

Speaking of trucks . . . she ought to run a search on that
Suburban. She flipped her visor down, checking the list of
ten-codes before she made a fool of herself on the air. Then
she pulled the mike out from under the dash. "Five-seven-
seven to Sunrise dispatch."

The radio spat static back at her, with the cicada buzz of the old Dodge ignition. "Sunrise. Go ahead, five-seven-seven."

A sexy contralto: That meant Denise was back on the day shift. "Ten twenty-eight, blue Suburban, New Jersey niner niner eight Charlie Echo Golf."

"Ten four, Kate. New Jersey niner niner eight Charlie Echo Golf. I'll run the tag and get back to you."

Babying clutch and gas and gearshift got her moving without either killing the engine or jerking a couple-thousand-dollars' worth of custom windows over the tail-gate. The cracked side mirrors showed only her normal level of white smoke. She'd heard about life in the fast lane and life in the slow lane. Her own life seemed to tend to the breakdown lane.

ALICE STARED DOWN the road, muttering to herself. Kate's green truck turned right at the commons, opposite to the route that evil blue Suburban had taken. Alice relaxed a touch.

Even *Kate* had felt it—Kate who had all the sensitivity of one of her rough-sawn four-by-fours. About as quick-witted, too, although she wasn't dumb. It just took her a couple of weeks to realize that it was raining.

That didn't stop Alice's heart from jumping every time she saw those lumberjack shoulders. Alice grinned to herself. Flirting with the big moose was always fun. If she ever actually *said* "no," that would be the end of it.

So far, the net result was twenty years of "maybe," hiding behind the face of a straight wife and mother that she maintained for the town and particularly for that mule-headed daughter of hers. But sooner or later, Kate was going to have to come to terms with her feelings. Alice planned on being around when that happened.

There was more to it than sex, no matter how much fun

that was. The House needed Kate. It needed a woman who was physically strong and tough, as well as one who was . . . talented. This generation, both hadn't come in one package.

The Haskell House. The Woman's House.

Alice knew the stories that went back to when Maine was part of the Massachusetts Bay Colony and a century or so earlier. Some of them were even true. Her family had lived on this land before the Pilgrims started hanging and drowning witches down in Salem. The Woman had meant something then, a figure even the white men feared and respected. The House meant refuge for the victims, as well as protecting . . . other things.

She weighed the pouch of tobacco in her hand and then tucked it into the pocket of her denim shirt. Good thing Kate had given the offering freely—even if she didn't believe, that mattered. The spirits that protected this land valued tobacco and enjoyed its smoke. That lummox was going to need some allies, whether she knew it or not.

Alice took one last snip at a climbing rose and gathered up the dead branches from her pruning, humming to herself. The Russellianas had come through the winter better than she'd hoped, and they were the least hardy variety she'd planted. Maybe it was time to push the limits of Maine weather again, see if she could grow those Arethusas that Fosters' advertised.

Roses weren't as tough as they looked. Kate was like that. You'd think you could use her to split rocks, but she broke as easily as any other human. The accident—Alice would just as soon Kate hadn't mentioned it.

Memories flooded through her: Raining, three in the morning, she had been riding EMT on the ambulance and was still groggy from the beeper dragging her out of bed. They screamed to a stop at a high-speed crash, pieces of dark, shredded metal tangled bad enough that you couldn't tell what parts went with what. One driver was dead on the spot, thrown into a ditch like a rag doll. Damn fool hadn't believed in seatbelts. The other still sat pinned in a twisted cage of steel. Alice tasted the reek of gasoline and antifreeze.

She reached through the shattered side window to check for a pulse. She suddenly realized the victim was a woman, and far pregnant. The face was a mass of blood and flayed meat speckled with broken glass, unrecognizable. Damned pickup was so old, it didn't *have* seatbelts or even an offset steering column. Only reason the driver didn't have a horn button sprouting out of her back was that the impact had thrown her across to the passenger side an instant before the front end collapsed back through the firewall. Alice spotted a familiar earring in the middle of the bloody hair and suddenly realized it was Kate's.

They cut the cab to pieces around her and pulled her out. The run to Downeast General took forever. Her heart stopped twice on the way. Alice fed her own life into her friend, keeping the spark alive until the ER doctors took over.

Then she fainted.

That kind of witching carried a cost. Aunt Jean had laid down the law: You could kill yourself, pulling out the life-force and passing it to another. Alice knew that when she gave life to Kate and to her baby, she had probably cut five years from her own.

Kate was worth it. Alice sometimes wondered about Jackie. The twit wasn't flat-out *evil,* not like the aura from that dark station wagon, but she sure wasn't much to brag about. And Kate could never have another.

Alice shuddered and breathed deep of the damp salt air, using the blend of spruce and rockweed to rinse the stink of a hundred car wrecks from her throat. She dumped the clippings into her compost heap, oiled the blades of her pruning shears, and put them away in the garden shed. She stopped off and said "Good morning" to the bees humming around the hives under the apple trees. Routine helped to put memories in their place. She hadn't owned the house then.

She touched the door-post and spoke to her house, a kind of password identifying herself to the small gods living in the timbers and inhabiting the hearths. She always felt more comfortable if she went through the ritual. Otherwise, the walls seemed to be watching. She'd lived here for only ten years, mere seconds as the house reckoned time, and sometimes it forgot that she belonged.

The house rambled long and low above the bay, an organic growth from century to century as generations of Haskell women added on or reworked sections for changing needs. Alice lived in three rooms in the newest ell, the part with indoor plumbing and electricity. The rest mostly just sat there thinking to itself, a labyrinth of rooms small and large, open and secretive, magical and mundane, waiting for whatever call might come. It spoke of shelter against nature and man, a place of solid warmth and nurturing. It sang of harmony.

She checked the venison stew simmering on her big black wood-fired range, shook out some ashes from the grate before adding a single stick of oak, and tossed in a bit of this and that to adjust the seasonings. Days off, she liked to cook things that took a bit of time. They helped make up for the rubber chicken and library-paste potatoes from the hospital cafeteria.

Did she need to do anything? That big Suburban radiated evil, but nobody ever said that the Woman had to fight all the evil in the world. One of Aunt Jean's rules was simplicity itself: Nine times out of ten, the best thing to do was nothing. Alice stood and stared at the wall.

Alice knew damn well, thirty years of practice, just what Kate was doing right now. She was on the radio, running a license check. Never a thought to scanners and the dozens of unofficial ears that heard everything on police-band channels.

The stew could wait. That was the essence of stew. Given the habits of her favorite nosy old fishwife, Alice wasn't sure other things could.

She glanced around the kitchen and "new" parlor, making sure she was willing to have people see the place that way if she never came back up from the cellar. Granted, it wasn't likely, but mistakes *had* caught up with one or two other women in the past.

Everything looked more or less presentable, so she topped off a lamp with olive oil and lit the wick. The house hated the smell of kerosene. It barely tolerated electricity, and insisted on wood heat. Aunt Jean had said that it had sulked for years after they put in plumbing. Opinionated old cuss, it was, just like a cat.

Speaking of which . . . Dixie Bull the Pyrate Queen lay curled up behind the stove, black tail tucked over white nose. Alice reached in and hooked the cat out, scritched her ears, and shoved her out the door. After a green-eyed glare, Dixie fluffed up her fur and plodded over to a sunlit spot in the garden.

That was another of Aunt Jean's rules: "Always put the cat out before you go down into the cellar."

three

—⚹—

ROLLING DOWNHILL AND bearing to the right, Kate passed the picture-postcard Stonefort green, ringed with "stately" homes and the big white Congregationalist church with the classic steeple that was going to fall into the green in another year or so if someone didn't scrape up fifty grand for repairs. Serve them right.

She couldn't go there anymore. Every time she saw the place, she heard echoes from her childhood. "Thou shalt not suffer a witch to live." Congregational churches varied a lot; that was what the title meant. This one had a running war with the Haskell Witches that stretched back centuries. The congregation's elders had a habit of selecting pastors with minds as small and tightly bound as their own. Didn't matter that at least half the congregation would sneak over to the Woman for help if they had a problem.

A left turn ran her past the town dock, the lobster pound, and the small harbor tastefully decorated with white lobster boats, dinks, and a couple of tourist yachts. Kate's stomach did a little roll at the mere sight of the morning chop on the water.

That had been the only job she couldn't hold down. She'd put in a week as "stern man" on a cousin's lobster boat, spending more time leaning over the side and puking than she had in baiting traps. When it became obvious she never *would* get her sea-legs, John had paid her off. He'd added a few rude comments about polluting the bay with all her slightly used breakfasts and lunches.

What he *didn't* say was, his catch of "bugs" had dropped off to nothing while she was on board. He sure didn't need a helper to change the water in his traps. Jonah. Kate and the ocean didn't love each other.

The road took her past the entry to the Morgan place, and she had to slow down because there were cars and pick-ups parked along the shoulder on both sides. They pinched the narrow road down to a single lane. She almost stopped and pulled her ticket pad out of the glove box before she remembered.

Daniel Morgan's memorial service.

Now *that* was an odd one. Not that death at sea was any stranger to Stonefort, but the circumstances . . . No body, and the weather had been calm. The family insisted that he'd been wearing a wetsuit and PFD vest that should have kept his head above water even if he was out cold, and he could swim like a fish. Yet here they were marching grimly along with a memorial when most families would still be hoping the man was safe on some offshore island. They weren't even waiting for the body to turn up in some scallop dragger's net for a regular burial service.

They also kept pushing for a search more than fifteen miles from where his kayak had been found. They said he'd been going out along Pratt's Neck, and the Coast Guard had found the boat offshore on the far side of Morgan's Point. Gear was missing, too, stuff that should have been in his deck bag, and he'd been wearing some valuable jewelry. They managed to imply that *that* was the reason why the body was still missing.

Wouldn't be the first time some boater had changed his plans, but she didn't like to think about people robbing corpses and then hiding them. Not that there wasn't a history of "wrecking" in the town. Something comes ashore, the one who finds it owns it. Poor people living in a tough land were like that, always had been. But the Morgans had money; they'd have paid a hefty reward for the body and anything he carried.

The spruces opened up along the side of the road, and she looked out over the bay. The thrust of a round stone tower dominated the view, weathered granite fifty feet tall and standing on a point of land that itself rose over fifty feet straight up from the water's edge. It always reminded her of photos of Tintagel or some other fabulous sea-girt castle of Ireland or Wales, and it had no business sitting there outlined against the offshore fog.

Morgan's Castle.

Kate had probably heard a thousand tales about it. The one she liked best, because it tied in with the Welsh ancestry of the Morgan name, called it the final home of Prince Madoc of Wales. Problem with that theory was, he'd sailed out around 1170.

The radio woke up. "Sunrise to five-seven-seven."

Kate pulled the mike out again. "Five-seven-seven. Go ahead."

"Ten twenty-eight Blue Chevy Suburban, two zero zero three model, registered Red Bank Delivery, Red Bank, New Jersey. Clean record. What ya got?"

Again, Kate glanced at the ten-codes on the visor: suspicious vehicle. "Ten thirty-nine." Denise was a stacked redhead, and single; *she* could gossip all day and the guys would never tease her about burning up airtime. They'd just lick their microphones. If Kate broke radio protocol, she'd be hearing about it for a month. "I'll be ten seven at the Beech project in about five minutes. Five-seven-seven out." She never had any problem remembering "ten seven;" her radio was "out of service" about thirty times a day.

Hah. Red Bank Delivery: *That* was about as generic a name as you could get. Kate preferred puzzles with a little more meat on their clues.

Like that stark pile of lichen-grayed rock against a gray horizon, set about with a scattering of gray headstones in neatly mowed green grass. It seemed like half the town was out there on the point this afternoon, dressed in suits and sober dresses with a scattering of flannel shirts and blue bib overalls.

The official "Morgan's Castle" legend was that some ancestral Morgan had started to build a private lighthouse, and then the government finally got around to marking the offshore shoals so the tower was never finished. On the other hand, Kate knew that there were a few archaeologists who itched to get their hands on the tower and grounds.

Tough luck. It was the Morgan family graveyard. Had been, for hundreds of years, and no way on God's green earth were they going to let anyone dig it up.

She shrugged her shoulders. That was the rich folk, and the water folk. She was neither. She barely knew the Morgans. Them or the Pratts across the bay. Whatever rumors might wander past when cops sat down to coffee, she'd never had *official* business with either family.

The road wound away from the view and dove back into woods, and she turned onto a gravel driveway that curved inland, climbing rapidly past spruce and pine and tangled close-in underbrush in a series of switchbacks. God help the man who drove the snowplow. But then, the Philadelphia lawyer who owned the place was never here in winter.

"Views." That was the other real-estate agent's catchphrase. If they couldn't sell "waterfront," they'd sell "views." Lawrence Alfred Beech III, Esq., certainly had a view. His front deck looked out halfway to Nova Scotia, across open ocean and spruce-studded straggling islands. The old locals rarely built on such a site. The general feeling was, if you could see the ocean, the ocean could see you. 'Round about January, that clear sweep for the northeast wind lost its appeal.

She wrestled the truck around in front of the four-car garage, faced it nose-down the slope again, and shut it off. The engine coughed, shuddered, coughed again, and finally quit—the old Dodge habit of running on.

Larry Beech had a little "cottage" in the Bar Harbor tradition, eight bedrooms and about ten baths. Hot-tub out on the deck overlooking the bay, sauna as big as her kitchen, home theater to seat twenty—you name it, they had it. Her crew was subcontracting on some renovations, enough profit to buy groceries for her and Jackie for a week. Trickle-down economics.

Charlie Sickles had heard her truck snorting up the grade and shuffled out to help unload. Another thirty years, she'd look like that—gimped up with arthritis and a lifetime of hard labor, sunburned to leather and leaned-down to a stick-figure by age, white hair and missing teeth, still working at seventy because his monthly Social Security check wouldn't buy groceries for a week.

Tourists looked at him and saw a caricature Downeast Yankee. She looked at him, saw the tarpaper shack he lived in with his wife and mother, and paid him twice what he was worth. He stopped, grabbed the tailgate of the truck, and coughed the morning's pack of tar out of his lungs. Someday soon, the lungs were going to come along for the ride. Then she could hire somebody who would pull his weight.

"Hey, Charlie, can I bum a smoke?"

She was just lighting up when the other member of her crew came slouching around the corner, a classic image of teenage rebellion. Jeff Burns was one of those kids who shoved a mass of spiky green hair, nose-ring, and baggy Goth-black clothes in your face and then sneered at you when you blinked. At least she'd made him ditch the baggy clothes when on the job: get a sleeve caught in the DeWalt saw and you could lose an arm. They'd compromised on black jeans and whatever uncensored T-shirt touched his fancy. Today's incarnation was relatively tame: a fake movie logo, SCREW THE WORLD—I WANT TO GET OFF.

Last year, she'd hauled his young ass up to the county jail on a juvie charge of possession and ended up as his de-facto probation officer. Damned if he didn't look like he'd make a carpenter. All she had to do was keep him clean and get some muscle on those scrawny arms.

She parked the cigarette in one corner of her mouth, cuffed him gently on the shoulder, and pointed to the far end of a set of windows. They had a job to do.

LAMP IN HAND, Alice climbed three steps and opened a door into another century. The sewing room and spare bedroom sat waiting—dust covers making ghosts of the furniture, old treadle sewing machine pulled up next to the south window to give enough light for fine stitching. That had been her room for years, whenever she'd visited Aunt Jean. Today it held a chilly memory of winter, and the dead flies of autumn cluttered the floor. The room sneered at her housekeeping and told her to come back with a broom.

The rear hallway was even colder, without south-facing windows for sun and heat, and she stepped back another hundred years. Stairs wound down and to the right as the house hugged the bones of the land. The bare floors creaked, working out frost-heaved kinks under her feet. Out of habit, she checked the brick hearth and bake oven of the old kitchen to make sure the chimney cap still kept water out. The house reminded her that a fire every month or so would be a good idea, just to keep the plaster dry.

A plain board door passed her through the Revolution and into the oldest part of the house. She sniffed a hint of something dead in the winter air that still hid away in here, months after spring had come outside. Through the center hall and to the right, a bat lay in the middle of the parlor floor, mummified by winter dryness. Whitespot. She must have come down the chimney to be close to the spring, sensing her coming death.

Alice toed her friend gently to one side, knelt down, and hooked her finger into a knothole in one of the wide pine floorboards. The trapdoor hinges groaned like they always did, the house complaining that she'd better have something important to justify its waking up.

A steep flight of stairs led into darkness. She followed them down, onto smooth rounded stone that formed still more steps. The warm lamplight poked into shadows, bringing out smooth shapes of granite and dark basalt still showing the scrapes of the last ice age.

"There's funny things in the basements around Stonefort," Aunt Jean had always said. Morgan's Castle, that big old house the Pratts lived in, two or three others in town, all stood where the power of the earth flowed down from the hills and up from the deep stone and met the sea. The Chinese made a science of it, a thing called *feng shui* or geomancy that gave you the rules for fitting your life into the power of the land. Folks in Stonefort had done it just by feel, or maybe chance had put some houses in the proper place and then the power had made those houses prosper.

Then there was this secret, walled in and covered over from the sun and the eyes of men. The spring had always been a woman's place, back when the Naskeags roamed the land. Aunt Jean never *had* explained what kind of deal kept a band of full-blooded Abenaki living peacefully in a community of white settlers. She'd said that was centuries ago, long before Columbus, and when the fur traders came up from Plymouth, Stonefort was already here.

The women's lodge had remained through the centuries and grew into the House. Men had never lived in the house, never seen this cellar. Not that the history was all lesbians: There were tales of men invited to spend the night, and even being seen alive afterward. There had been babies born. Most generations, though, the house and land passed from aunt or great-aunt to niece. The family name passed down on the mother's side, too, from ancient times.

Alice knew men must have held the deed, back when a woman couldn't own property, but no Haskell man ever would have dared do anything with that legal power. She'd inherited it from Aunt Jean and already had a niece lined up to take over forty–fifty years in the future. Haskells liked to keep things tidy.

She touched a thin pine splinter to the flame of her lamp and used it to light three other lamps already sitting in natural hollows of the stone. The flames glinted from the flowing surface of a pool, water so clear you could barely tell the edge. Straight up from the pool, a patch of basalt made black contrast to the pink granite, and a quartz vein split the basalt to a white mound spouting crystal water. The rounded creases of the stone to either side were very . . . feminine.

God, the "boys" on Kate's crew would *die* if they ever saw where their drinking water came from.

Now that her eyes had adjusted to the darkness, Alice could see the beams and floorboards looming overhead, black with centuries of smoke. Someday she'd have to get Kate down here, to check for rot and make repairs—even cedar and chestnut wouldn't last forever. Those stairs seemed to creak more every year.

She puttered through the routine Aunt Jean had taught, checking that the overflow still led water from the pool out through a natural cleft in the stone, to the basin in the *other* cellar that everyone else thought was the real spring. Checking the airflow in through fieldstone foundations to the flue in the old stone chimney, making sure the air stayed clean and dry. Making a mental note that she should bring fresh sweetgrass and sage for the herb bundles hanging from the beams. Routine was safe, and calming.

Then the hair started to prickle on the back of her neck and along her arms. The spring had noticed her. Time to swallow her heart and get to work.

She dipped water from the pool and washed her face, breaking the mirror into a hundred ripples of flashing lamp-flame. Cold on her hands, the water bit her face like fire and left a tingle of power behind. Purified, she gathered shavings of cedar and sticks of fine-split apple wood from small hollows in the stone, laying a tiny fire at the base of the stone chimney. Small as she was, even *her* hands could span the blaze and snuff it out. It was enough.

"Stone of the sun, water of the sky, air of the sea, I ask you to bless this house."

Fine tendrils of smoke rose up, aromatic, and seemed to defy the draft by seeking out each corner of the hidden cellar. The sense of power increased, as if Alice had woken something deeper than the spring.

The flames glowed green and orange, from trace minerals or from spirits dancing on the blackened wood. She added sweetgrass and studied the glowing tangles of ash it left behind; she added sage and watched each leaf dissolve into a skeleton of fiery veins. Fire wove its hypnotic spell.

"Stone of the sun, water of the sky, air of the sea, evil has come into our land." She felt the slimy touch of the gaze be-hind that black-tinted glass, the weight and pull of the deadly power riding in the dark car. She fed her memories into the flames, watching them flare into cleansing smoke.

The pencil-thin sticks had burned down to a red glow, waiting. Alice took out the tobacco pouch and emptied it into her right hand.

"Wind of the west, I call to you. Watch over my friend." She scattered a pinch of tobacco into the coals. The glow sent blue smoke spiraling up, straight to the chimney flue and into the sky.

"Wind of the east, I call to you. Watch over my friend." A second pinch of tobacco followed the first.

Aunt Jean had made her stand outside in the cold, one January evening, watching the thin tendrils of smoke rise up from the chimney. Each puff had trailed off to its compass point, defying the icy northwest wind and logic.

"Wind of the south, I call to you. Watch over my friend." A third pinch. "Wind of the north, I call to you. Watch over my friend." A fourth.

She poured the remaining tobacco from the palm of her right hand. It cascaded into the coals in a shower of sparks.

"Spirits of the earth, spirits of the water, spirits of the sky, I send smoke to you. I send sweet smoke to you. Guard this land. Guard the people of this land. Guard the giver of this gift. Guard us against evil. Make the sun shine into darkness, make the wind sweep the air clean, make the waters wash away the stains that lie on the land. Guard us against evil."

The smoke closed around her, tight and suffocating. Her heart thudded in her chest, and she felt the whole weight of the house pressing down on her shoulders. Power tugged at her and tested her, prodding for lies.

Those New Age kiddies with their lilac-tinted Wicca nattered about threefold payback if you worked evil with your power. As if power would do something *it* didn't want to do. Alice gasped for air and felt sweat pouring down her back. The powers of this spring guarded their strength carefully. She pushed the limits by protecting Kate. If they thought she was being selfish, protecting her lover rather than the community . . .

The vise around her chest backed off, and she could breathe again. She hadn't crossed the line.

As always, the fire had burned to ash, and the ashes were cold. She never knew if that meant the heat had been sucked out by the power, or that she'd waited somewhere outside of time while she was tested and entropy did its thing.

She stretched the tension out of her shoulders and washed sweat from her face. The water felt like water now, cold from the earth, not liquid flame.

There were other things that needed doing, safer things. She gathered ashes from the fire, a small stone from the pool, herbs, the breast-feather of an eagle, a bone whistle the length of a child's finger, and put them in the empty tobacco bag. She plucked a hair from her head, wrapped it into a circle, and added it. The bag now carried all her magic bound to power from the spring. If she could get Kate to carry it, it would stand guard. Or maybe Alice could tuck it under the seat of the truck.

She touched ash to her wet forehead and cheeks, marking them with straight dark lines. She swept the small hearth with a wild turkey's wing, gathering the remains of her fire into a small pouch sewn from birch-bark. The house and the spring demanded neatness.

She blew out all the lamps except the one she'd brought and topped up the ones that needed it from oil kept in the cellar to absorb the power. And then she climbed back up the stairs, and let the trapdoor thump back into place, and breathed a sigh of relief. She was still alive.

Always put the cat out before going down to the spring. Then she won't starve if you don't come back.

Her shirt stuck to her back and belly, and she could smell her fear in the sweat. She slid the dead bat into the birch-bark pouch, blew out the lamp, and headed back through the centuries for a hot bath and a good stiff shot of whiskey.

four

—✦—

GARY STARED DOWN at the slab of pink granite set into the spring-lush sod by his feet. The stone stared back at him. IN MEMORIAM, it said, in fresh-cut letters as sharp as a knife. DANIEL L. MORGAN, it said. 1964–2004, it said. It didn't bother with months and days.

It didn't mention that June 7, 2004, had been the day before Gary's graduation. It didn't mention that Gary had walked down the aisle in the Stonefort Consolidated High School gym the next evening, not knowing whether his father was alive or dead.

There'd been TV reporters sticking microphones into red-eyed faces, the whole instant-news thing of pathos or bathos or whatever the proper term was, the class valedictorian bravely carrying on while the search continued for his missing father. More at eleven. He'd come within an inch of breaking one reporter's arms, shoving a camera up another's nose. It would have been so *easy,* with the things he'd learned in the dojo.

Then a switch had clicked somewhere in his emotions,

and he'd detached from the whole scene. The switch was still off at the breaker box, power disconnected. That detachment had carried him through today's swarm of mourners and relatives, the endless line of faces of people that should have been important to him. They weren't.

LOST AT SEA, the stone added. There were a lot of those scattered in the neatly mown grass on Morgan's Point: stones without the gentle mounding of dirt filled back in over a coffin, or the ancient graves with a slight hollow where the soil had settled down into the space left when coffin and body had rotted to dust. Stones remembered storms and reefs and boats that had simply vanished. On some of the older ones, LOST AT SEA was all you could still read.

The stone next to Dad's echoed it. BENJAMIN S. MORGAN, 1961–1984. The lines bracketing the name and date were identical: another memorial, to another Morgan lost at sea.

People were scattering now, drifting slowly back to the house, back to coffee, sandwiches, and quiet condolences. Gary thought he probably should join them, show how he was able to act like the man of the family now. He didn't want to. He wanted to stand out on the end of the point and scream hatred at the sea.

The sea was a thief.

Gary shoved his hands into the pockets of his windbreaker. The wind was cold off the water, damp with offshore fog, and it stank of rotting seaweed. It stank like a grave.

His jaw clenched, and he stalked across the grass until he reached the tip of Morgan's Point, the strip of salt-burned grass right above the surf. He stood in the shadow of the stone tower and tried to make tears come. He couldn't cry. He was too angry. Nobody had ever told him that grief was rage.

Words choked his throat. He stared down at the cold gray indifferent swells rolling in under cold gray fog. He wanted to scream at the sea, curses and blasphemies, and then his father's voice whispered out of the damp wind, words from Gary's first morning as stern man on Dad's lobster boat.

"Never curse the sea, Gary. Never curse the wind. You'll only hurt yourself. The sea made us—made the Morgans, made Stonefort. Without the wind and sea, we wouldn't even be here. Remember that. Whatever the sea takes from you, it's worth the price."

His father's voice stole the rage from Gary and left grief behind. His knees folded under him, and he slumped down to sit on cold stone and stare out at the endless rows of wave after wave after wave flowing in from the fog to hump up and smash against the rock. They blurred as if the fog was condensing in his eyes, and he finally wept. The foghorn out on Tern Rock moaned in sympathy.

The fog slipped in to blanket the point, creeping across waves and rocks and up the cliff to turn the world gray. Gary waited, searching for the courage to go back to the house, back to his mother and his sisters and the quiet swarm of cousins. A hand fell lightly on his shoulder. "He was a good man."

Gary jerked with shock and looked up into a face that was vaguely familiar—a man, older than Dad, with the slim build, gray eyes, and sharp nose of the Morgans. One of the cousins, then, but the older generation. Gary couldn't put a name to him.

"That's another Daniel Morgan you're sitting on, son. Daniel John, 'Old Daniel' they called him. Commanded a sloop under Saltonstall in the Revolution, had to burn it when the whole fleet retreated up the river from Castine and got trapped. Never forgave that idiot from Boston, swore he'd get the value of his ship back by fair means or foul." The man chuckled. "He did, too."

Gary looked down at the stone. It was marble, not granite, and the salt air and the centuries had eaten the carved words into gibberish. Whoever this stranger was, he knew the family history.

Then Gary blinked with shock. The tower loomed dark in the fog behind the man, and its door stood open. All he could see from here was a black hollow and stone walls at least six feet thick. But he'd never even seen that much before, never been inside the heavy iron-studded oak door that didn't show a lock or latch.

"Too dangerous," Dad had always said. "The old dump is falling down." Gary had climbed the walls once, fifty feet straight up, when both Mom and Dad were gone for the day. At least the roof was solid—solid enough to hold four bronze cannon in black iron carriages. He'd found another door up there, set into the battlements, again solid oak without a latch and just as immovable. With that taste to sweeten the mystery, Gary had pestered Dad a dozen times, a hundred times, but the answer had always been the same.

Another figure formed in the mists, turned into Mom, and then stalked forward radiating anger at the stranger. "You *bastard*! You *dare* to show up now!" She made one of those Italian gestures she'd learned from her quarryman grandfather, the uppercut fist and hand slapping biceps that nobody would ever translate for Gary. The meaning was pretty clear, though. Then she emphasized it by spitting on the ground between them.

"Maria . . ."

"Crawl back under your rock and leave my son alone!"

"He's Dan's son, too."

Gary blinked at the name as much as at the sudden storm of rage. After all, that was Mom, Melodrama Incorporated. But nobody ever called Gary's father "Dan." It was always "Daniel," even from close family friends.

"Damn you, the boy is only seventeen! Leave him be!"

Gary stood up, trying to force his mother and this

stranger to talk *to* him rather than *over* him. His mother ve-
toed that by pushing him back down to sit on the head-
stone. When she was mad, she gained about a foot in height
and fifty pounds of muscle.

The stranger shook his head. "He's almost eighteen, and
he needs to know before he goes off to college. You know
Dan was going to do it this weekend. Now he can't."

Gary's mother bit her thumb at the man. "Screw you and
all the Morgans and all the ships you rode in on! Choose
someone else!"

Gary stared at his mother in shock. She'd always had an
explosive temper, but she never used language like *that*. He
tried to stand up again, and again she forced him down with
her hand on his shoulder. It felt like the tower itself sitting
on him.

The stranger shook his head again. "You know it doesn't
work like that. I didn't choose Gary. Dan didn't choose him.
The Dragon makes the choice."

"You can take that Dragon and shove it where the sun
don't shine! If anything happens to my child, I swear I'll
kill you!"

"Maria, you know I wouldn't do this if there was any
other way. He *has* to know."

Gary's mother spat again and muttered something in
Italian. Then she shot the horned fist at the man and stalked
back into the fog. The stranger stared after her, a peculiar
mixture of humor and pain twisting his face.

Mom wasn't holding him down anymore, but the shock
kept Gary glued to the tombstone. "What was *that* all
about?"

"*That* was something from before you were born. She's
never forgiven me. Probably never will."

The tone grabbed Gary's attention, and he studied the
man again. He had the family's dark brown hair, graying at
the temples, and Dad's jaw as well. Definitely one of Dad's

cousins, then, and he must have grown up in Stonefort if he knew both Dad and Mom before they were married. But Gary *still* couldn't come up with a name.

"I'm sorry; there are just too many people around today. Who are you?"

"I'm Odysseus, boy. I'm the wandering old sailor returned from looting Troy. I'm battle-scarred and gray-bearded and full of sneaky plans. You've wanted to see the inside of that thing?" He grinned, showing gold caps where two side teeth had been broken, and waved at the door of the tower.

He hadn't answered the question. Still, Gary found himself trusting the man. For all Mom's venom, she *had* gone off and left the two of them alone. But *God,* she was acting weird. Weren't widows supposed to cry? All *she* did was throw things and yell at people over the phone.

"Dad said it was dangerous."

"So 'tis, boy. The fruit of the Tree of Knowledge is *always* dangerous. You go in there, you'll never be the same again. The Dragon might eat you." He mimed crocodile jaws with his hands, and backed them with an expression of mock horror.

The hair prickled on Gary's neck. Dad had been like that, over-the-edge comedy at times that drove Mom up the wall. Then he'd start to cackle like a madman and juggle stuff grabbed up from Mom's collection of Venetian glass. Dad's hands were quick like lightning, always snatching the delicate glassware back from the edge of disaster.

"Myths don't eat people."

"Myths?" The man threw a pose of injured dignity. "There's a *real* dragon under that tower, boy. Been there for centuries, just lying in wait for innocents like you. Every generation, some young fool comes along and pokes at it. If it wakes up grumpy, it eats you. Butter it up nice, and you walk away with all the gold and rubies you can carry. Want to take a chance?"

Gary shook his head in disbelief. Dragons. Gold. Rubies. Bullshit. He *did* want to see the inside of the tower, though. "What's this Tree of Knowledge bit?"

"Oh, that's the Dragon's specialty. It tells you things. Things about yourself, things about the Morgans. Confucius say, 'Self-knowledge is greatest treasure.'"

He'd switched to a singsong parody of a Charlie Chan movie for the last bit. Then he swung into the spiel of a sideshow barker. "Great Dragon sees all, knows all, tells all. Learn your fate and fortune, just ten cents. One thin dime, one tenth of a dollar! Step right up, ladies and gentlemen."

Again the stranger sounded just like Dad. Stuff like that drove Mom crazy, but Dad would only laugh. Said if she didn't shut up, he'd run off someday and join the circus. Gary's eyes stung with new tears. He swallowed the chuckle that had been bubbling up his throat.

"Does your Dragon know what happened to my father?"

The man sobered and stared deep into Gary's eyes. "Yes, it does, boy. You can go in there and learn, or you can go back to the house. Just one thing before you choose: Once you go in, you can't back out."

He paused, making sure Gary knew this *wasn't* the clown speaking. His mannerisms were so much like Dad's the resemblance was eerie. "It's a one-way trip, boy, and you can die taking it. Dan didn't think you would. But it's possible. That's what has your mother spooked. If she wasn't so damned mad, she'd have hugged you and cried before she let you try it."

Gary stared at that arched stone opening into darkness and mystery. The tower called to him. A shiver ran down his spine and tingled in his fingers. The strange man faded from his thoughts. Gary stood up, slowly, as if he was stalking a wild animal and didn't want to startle it. If he moved too suddenly, the door might jerk closed before he got there. Then he'd never learn the secrets, never find his father.

But his father was dead.

"Son, you'll need this."

The words pulled his attention back to the stranger. The man tossed him a pocket flashlight, one of those magnesium things like a scaled-down version of the four-cell weapons the cops carried. The black finish was worn to bare metal in spots, as if it had seen many years of use.

Gary glanced from the man to the flashlight and back again. "Aren't you going to show me around?"

The man shrugged. "Nope. I ain't invited. This is a private tour, just you and the Dragon. Good luck."

He looked as if he really meant it, as if Gary needed all the help he could get. Gary nodded his thanks and then turned back to stalking the door.

He'd always thought the door was ancient, just like the tower was so obviously ancient, weather-beaten, and stained with lichen. But when he looked at it closely, he found the worn oak face was just a veneer over something that looked like it belonged on a bank vault, thick black steel with bolts that retracted into holes bored into the stone. The inside face was blank, though, just like the outside. Those bolts must be controlled electrically.

Electricity? He glanced around the inside face of the wall and found a switch. It worked. Bare incandescent bulbs lit a circular room about thirty feet across, empty, with stone walls and a ceiling of age-blackened wooden beams and planks about ten feet above a stone-paved floor. A steep stair curved up along the far wall to a closed trap door, and a hole underneath showed stairs down into darkness. Both stairs were carved granite, without handrails, and the treads had been hollowed out by centuries of feet.

Dad had said the place was falling down. Instead, it

looked as solid as the rock it sat on. Gary tested the stairs with his weight, and then climbed up. The trap door didn't stir when he set his shoulder to it, as if it wasn't just locked, but had furniture sitting on it or was nailed shut. So this private tour must be down, rather than up?

Damp air rose out of the lower stair, and the lights only showed the first few treads. Apparently the power didn't go down there. Gary checked the flashlight and then climbed slowly down into the darkness.

Stone masonry lined the first few feet, and then the walls changed to chiseled rock. The ceiling hung low over Gary's head, as if the people who had carved this passage had been shorter than his scant six feet. Now and then rough stone brushed his hair, and he had to keep swinging the light down to check the worn stairs and then up to watch that he didn't bang his head. Down, and down, and down the stair led, curving around in a spiral as if it followed the walls of the tower overhead.

He looked back and turned off the flashlight. The curve had blocked all light from overhead. He stood in velvet blackness, damp and slightly cool, feeling the air washing back and forth past his face. It was almost as if the tunnel was breathing.

Maybe this coiling tunnel was the Dragon that strange man had named, the one that Mom had cursed. Gary switched the flashlight on and started down again.

The stairs vanished into a pool, nothing more than a flat surface of water that rose and fell maybe a foot with a pulse like waves. The flashlight showed more steps leading down, down, down under the water into a black hollow beyond the dropping roof of the cave. A dead end. Just *how* was he supposed to go on with this so-called quest? He switched off the light again, listening. Water trickled in the darkness, thin streams flowing from cracks in the bedrock. A slight hiss and suck timed the rise and fall of the water. Nothing else—apparently the Dragon wasn't talking.

His eyes started to invent lights to fill the total darkness. Most of them swirled around as he glanced to right and left, but one stayed still. The faintest glimmer of light teased him, underwater, showing around the curve of the tunnel. It seemed to pulse like a heartbeat.

So there was something farther on in the tunnel. Daylight? A lit chamber guarded by the water?

Gary knelt on the last dry step and reached down to the surface. The water felt cool rather than cold, nothing like the icy shock of the bay even in late summer. The water tasted of salt, though, so it *did* connect with the sea. The pulse must come from swells, somewhere out beyond the rock.

Was he supposed to wait for the tide, or swim?

He remembered that the tide was near dead low. The stairwell walls had been damp for about the last ten feet. He could swim, or he could go back.

Cave diving? The YMCA scuba teacher had said that was the most dangerous diving there was, even worse than wrecks. It was too easy to get lost or turned around, too easy to get trapped. Anytime something came between you and a straight rise to the surface, you were asking for trouble.

This tunnel was different, though. It was just one passage, and if you followed the ceiling and your bubbles upward, you'd get right back where you started. It wasn't *too* dangerous, and it was the only way to go any farther.

He stripped off his clothes, piling them on the last step above the damp zone. The water wasn't any colder than the pool at the Y. He pushed gently down into the underwater tunnel, swimming sidestroke and keeping one hand on the ceiling so he wouldn't bump his head or lose his way.

The light grew from a faint glimmer to a definite glow ahead and around the curve. He'd been down maybe fifteen seconds, swimming carefully, and he knew he could free dive for over two minutes. Going back would be faster. He was still well within safe limits.

A spark showed around the edge, and he felt the ceiling rising into an open chamber. The light was on the *left,* up near the ceiling; the way out was *that* way. Gary fixed the map in his head as if his life depended on it. The spark grew into a glowing dot and then into an oval, shading from green through yellow and into red as he swam closer and water no longer filtered the light. It looked like an eye staring back at him. Half a minute down, look around and then go back for air.

He reached out carefully and touched the glowing red oval, afraid it would be burning hot. It was comfortably warm instead, like touching a cat that had been sitting in the sun. The stone walls to either side felt the same.

<Gary!>

He jerked back. He bumped his head against the stone ceiling, and blinked against the stars that shot through his sight. The red glow was still there. He reached out again. The stone felt warmer this time, as if his touch had wakened something.

<It's Dad, Gary. Tell Ben they gave my Tear back to me and I can talk again.>

Dad! Gary's thoughts spun around in confusion. *Where are you?*

<Don't worry about that, boy. Ben knows. Just be careful and get on with your test. Tell Mom I love her.>

Who's Ben?

<He'll tell you. Forget about me and swim, you idiot!>

Gary's chest felt tight, maybe half a minute of air left. Time to hurry back, grab another breath, rest.

A ruby drop split from the eye, almost like a tear, and Gary followed it down. It drew him, wiping thoughts of air from his head. The pressure in his lungs grew, but he had to have that glowing gem. He twisted after it, snatched it, and tucked it into his mouth to keep his hands free. He started up.

The eye was gone. The light was gone. He'd spun around in his dive and couldn't tell which way led back and which led deeper into the tunnel.

His lungs burned.

five

—⁓—

KATE WRESTLED THE truck around in the school parking lot, backing and turning and babying the clutch, until
she had the nose pointed downhill and she could safely shut
off the engine. It coughed into silence, and a swarm of ban-
shee shrieks rode over the echo of the last backfire.

Why couldn't girls learn to *yell,* for God's sake? Why
couldn't they learn to *cheer*? Instead, they squealed when
they got excited, and girls' sports ended up sounding like
mayhem in a pigpen.

The fog was moving in again, damp gray wisps blotting
out the spruces over on Morgan's Point, so Kate hauled her
jacket out and shrugged it on. June could still feel like early
spring in Stonefort. She scanned the field and scoreboard,
trying to figure out which side had been making all that
racket. Stonefort led Edgewater by a run in the second, with
Stonefort's red jerseys coming off the field and slapping
high-fives right and left. Must have been a close out or a
good play. She hoped Jackie hadn't done something spectac-
ular and she'd missed it.

"Soccer Mom," she'd said to Alice, but that was a generic title. It was spring and the game was softball, with Jackie playing third base where her reach and strong throw simply *murdered* right-handed pull hitters.

Kate reminded herself to lock the cab of her truck. Besides tools and the radio, it held all her "cop" stuff—badge and ticket book and the old Browning automatic that Grandpa had "liberated" from a dead Nazi near Remagen. She tended to be careless about locks, but there were just too many kids around the school for her to take chances.

The Stonefort field was short on bleachers, so Kate strolled over to the bank off the left foul line. She picked a patch of grass and sat, choosing her spot mainly to inconvenience the kids trying to sneak a cigarette out behind the scoreboard. Not that she hadn't done the exact same thing when she was their age, but it hadn't been illegal then. Now it was.

That's what she did, mostly. Town constable was a set of official eyes wandering around, someone who noticed if you looked like you were up to no good. Kate was the officially sanctioned town gossip and busybody. Serious crime was a job for the sheriff or the state patrol.

A thin man climbed down from the bleachers and headed her way. Now *there* was your typical "bad element." She ticked off the description as he walked over: five foot ten, about one fifty-five, scraggly-bearded, with a dark ponytail pulled back and braided with feathers like some kind of Cheyenne warrior, grease-stained denim jacket hacked down into a vest with a skull patch on the back and big Harley logo, pack of cigarettes rolled up into the sleeve of his T-shirt, tattoos up one arm and down the other. He looked as if he should be holding a placard with a set of numbers in front of his chest.

Instead, Bernie Peters was one of the sharpest narcs she'd ever met. He had a daughter on the Stonefort team, a senior with grades a *hell* of a lot better than Jackie's. She played second base. He walked straight over to where Kate was sitting.

"Heard you calling in a tag this morning."

"So?"

"Leave it be."

Kate cocked her head to one side. "Says who?"

Bernie pulled out a cigarette, then offered her one.

She shook her head. "I ought to write you up for smoking on school grounds."

He blinked, then slid the smoke back into his pack, unlit. "Look, the Godfather says to stay clear of that car."

That was a cop in-joke. "The Godfather" was Bernie's boss at the Maine Drug Enforcement Agency.

"You got reasons?"

"Enough. Stay clear of the Pratts, too. There's a connection."

"You guys gonna make it worth my while?"

"We'll see about it. No promises." He smiled and shrugged.

"Okay, just *be* mysterious. I'll be a good little girl. Just tell me where I'm not supposed to be and when I'm not supposed to be there."

Bernie nodded and headed back toward the bleachers. Just as well she'd sat by herself—she'd have a hard time explaining *that* conversation to the clam-digger on the street. Bernie had been a state cop for years, before he went "bad." He still worked for the governor, though—MDEA, usually undercover.

So the MDEA was running a case that involved the Pratts and that big blue Suburban? And they wanted Kate Rowley to keep her oversized elbows out of it? Well, at least she understood now why that car had slowed down this morning. Checking out the opposition.

While she'd been talking with Bernie, the first Stonefort batter had taken two strikes and then popped out. Jackie was due up next, and the catcher walked out to the mound for a little chat with the pitcher.

Kate knew what *that* meant. Jackie had the highest count of walks in Eastern Maine Class "D" softball.

The catcher walked back and set up far enough away from the plate that Jackie would have to jump halfway down the first-base line before she could hit a pitch. Kate grinned—one practice game, her daughter had done exactly that and whacked the ball over the right field fence.

Four straight balls and Jackie trotted down to first base. Business as usual. She took her lead and started taunting the pitcher, trying to force an error on the pick-off move. The next girl up was Jean Bouchard. Kate knew the coach kept tearing his hair out, trying to teach Jean to bunt without popping the ball up. No such luck. So she'd be hitting away.

Sure enough, Jean took a big cut at the first pitch and sliced a grounder toward third. The fat ball died in the grass, forcing a hurried throw to second. Second base scooped the ball out of the dirt and spun for the throw to first for the double play. Jackie slid into her, feet high, and knocked the Edgewater girl halfway into center field. Her throw went high, up the bank and into the spectators, and Jean took second on the error. The Stonefort girls were squealing and bouncing around again. They had a runner on second with two out, instead of the end of the inning.

Then the cheers died. The Edgewater girl stayed down, twisting around on the grass and holding her leg. Her coach ran out on the field, and the trainer, and her teammates clustered around. The field ump had Jackie by the arm and was pointing toward the gym, toward the lockers. She wasn't just out; she was out of the game. She slammed her batting helmet down in the dirt and dropkicked it clear to the right foul line. And Jean was trudging slowly back to first, head down.

Dammit, that was a legal play! See it in baseball all the time!

Kate found herself halfway out on the field before her brain caught up with her feet. She'd *sworn* to herself that she wouldn't take that Soccer Mom bit all the way, yelling at umpires and coaches, cussing the kids and parents on the opposing teams. She veered to the right, to meet Jackie when she came off the field. Kid could use some friendship, right about now.

The Edgewater girl was up again, limping around, apparently going to stay in the game. Now *she* was arguing with the ump, waving at Jackie, waving at the bench. Looked like she thought the take-out play was clean.

Kate stopped for a moment and shook her head. Of *course* that kind of play was against the rules in girls' softball. Got to protect the little darlings. Just like Yogi Berra said, it was déjà vu all over again. A moose like Jackie committed a foul just by being born.

The moose was filthy, coated with dust all down one side and sweaty from running. Kate started to put an arm around her shoulders, then backed off when she saw the angry shrug coming. Teenagers were a prickly crew, especially in public. Hormones.

"Tough call, kid."

"That . . ." Jackie bit back whatever she was going to say, and threw up a wall of sullen silence.

"Get yourself showered and changed. We can talk about it later."

"Nothing to talk about. That Edgewater kid took a dive, just trying to get me thrown out. Faking hurt. Stupid little pimple-faced twink. No guts."

The game resumed behind them. Stonefort's next batter hooked a double down the right-field line, runners on second and third with two out—Jean couldn't run fast enough to make it home ahead of the throw. Jackie didn't even look. If she wasn't in the game, it didn't matter.

Kate followed her daughter toward the gym. "Just

change up. We can watch the rest of the game or head home. Your call."

"Nah. Jean's got her dad's car. Bunch of the guys are headed over to Michael's house after the game. You stay if you want."

Typical reaction for a sixteen-year-old girl: "Back off!" As far as Jackie was concerned, Mom's function was a source of food, a roof now and then, and money for clothes. Companionship and advice didn't figure into it.

Then Kate replayed her daughter's words. Michael. That would be Michael *Pratt,* Tom's younger son.

Oh, shit! *Good ol' crack-buster Bernie just warned you off the Pratts and that damned Suburban, and your pea-brained daughter hangs out with that crowd!*

Kate fumbled around in her makeshift operator's manual for a teenaged girl, trying to come up with words her daughter wouldn't just filter out and ignore. "Jean only got her license last week. I don't think it's safe for you kids to be riding around with her. She needs more practice."

"Mom, it's *only* five *miles*! We'll be back before dark."

"Are Michael's parents home?"

"*Jeezum,* Mom, how would I know?"

"Well, I don't think you girls ought to go off with a bunch of guys and no adults." Kate knew she was tiptoeing along the edge of a teenager minefield. But Bernie would skin her alive if she mentioned anything about drugs. She could lose her badge, or worse.

"*Mom-mmm!*" Jackie pulled the word out into the eternal wail of an outraged daughter.

They'd both stopped in the middle of the parking lot, working into the roles of an industry-standard generation-battle. Kate shifted her focus. "Look, they had that crash over in Merritt Falls last week. Six kids in a car, driver like Jean, a six-pack of beer passed around. Kid missed the curve and wrapped his mother's Buick around a tree. You can see why I'm worried. We don't need any more funerals."

"Mom, Jean's smarter than *that*! And nobody in our crowd drinks or does drugs. They don't even *smoke*!"

Like hell they didn't. Kate fell back into Protective-Mother mode. "Why don't you kids come over to our house?"

Oops. She'd said the "K" word. She felt the tension escalate.

"*Moth-errrr!* You don't need to watch me every *minute*!" Then Jackie switched on her "cat" look, the one Kate knew meant something nasty and devious was coming. "And you don't need to worry about me getting pregnant or catching VD or something. They taught us all about that in Freshman Health." Her daughter paused with that cutting, calculating smile. "I guess they didn't have that class when *you* were in school."

Oh, hell. "I don't know what you're talking about. We knew about sex. We knew about contraception."

"What happened, then? The rubber busted? I can count up to nine, Mom. I know my birthday. I know when you and Dad got married. I'm smart enough to do simple subtraction, Mom."

"You *know* you were premature. You *know* about the accident. I had an emergency C-section and we both nearly died. You've seen the scars."

"Yeah. Nine-pound, two-ounce premature baby. That's pretty advanced for a sixth-month fetus, Mom. Freshman Health teaches you things like that. I bet you were in labor before the accident. I bet Dad was too drunk to drive you to the hospital. What happened? You have a contraction when you should have been watching the road?"

Kate wanted to snatch her only child up by the neck and strangle her. That whole scene sounded like the girl had scripted it out and memorized the lines, like she was writing a goddamn play. Why couldn't the kid be smart where it *mattered*? It sure didn't help things that she was right on every count.

Maybe Dana Peters *had* run that stop sign. She still should have seen him. She still might have stopped in time if her damned belly hadn't thrown a riot.

"Jacquelyn Eileen Lewis . . ." Kate bit her snarl off and turned away before she did wring her daughter's neck. She and Lew *had* wanted children. They just hadn't planned on getting married until they could afford it. Then she'd turned up pregnant and they'd moved their plans ahead a year. They'd *wanted* Jackie, God only knew why.

She turned back, to tell her daughter that, to try and calm things down and work out some way to keep the kid away from the Pratts. The parking lot was empty. Jackie had gone into the locker rooms to change and probably would hide out there, safe from her mother until she could slip away with her friends. She'd gotten just exactly what she wanted. Somehow, she always did.

Dead end. All Kate could do was hope it wasn't a permanent one.

Drugs. Bernie and the Pratts and the MDEA. Probably Feds, too. Kate walked slowly back to her truck, softball game forgotten. The drug boys wanted her to keep her nose out of their investigation. Well, she wouldn't use the radio, and she wouldn't knock on any doors. Listen, yes. Watch, yes. Young Jeff might know something—he'd been in the drug scene before she busted him. And she might ask a Morgan or two. The way the last week had gone, it sounded like they might be willing to say a few things about the Pratts.

No way in hell could she ignore this if Jackie was involved. She'd been a mother a lot longer than she'd been a cop.

Damned brat.

Kate climbed into the cab of her truck, buried her face in her hands, and cried.

SIX

—⁓—

BEN STARED AT the surface of the pool. It surged gently to the beat of the surf outside, a dark pulsating mirror for the single light on the cavern wall. He checked his watch again, compulsively. Two minutes. Amazing how long two minutes could be.

Maria *would* kill him. With another woman, that could have been random noise or exaggeration. Not Maria. She'd never bought into the whole Morgan thing. She'd refused to enter the tower, refused to accept the family history, lived an armed truce with Dan in order to give young Gary a father's name. Now some of the chickens were coming home to roost. Why did everything have to happen at once?

Where the *hell* was the boy? Two minutes ten seconds. As soon as Gary had entered the tower, Ben had zipped in through the back way and up to the security boards. He'd clicked his watch when the boy took his last gulp of air and jackknifed down into the water at the base of the spiral stair. Showed up perfectly on the IR cameras upstairs, that hot body against the cool damp granite and even colder seawater. The affinity was there, the mark was there, the call was there. Kid wasn't a failure, not like Ben.

This inheritance thing sucked.

Primogeniture, male succession, the need for the Change and the Dragon's Tear—the whole thing sucked. It trapped Maria where she was, ignored Ellen and Peggy, left the whole Family resting on one set of shoulders in each generation just like some feudal lord. Somebody needed to persuade the Dragon that they lived in the twenty-first century, the United States.

Two minutes twenty-five. Dan should be the one sitting here, sweating, feeling the chill of the rock and regretting sins long past. *He* was the one who heard the call. The Dragon chose *him*—she could damn well keep her promises. Why force the reject to chew his nails and break bad news to a mother with a temper like Maria's?

The water surged against the pulse of the waves, a body forcing its way through the narrow channel beneath the surface. Gary's head popped up, and gasping breaths echoed through the silence. Ben sighed his relief, gulping in salt air heavy with the damp mustiness of stone. He'd been holding his breath nearly as long as the boy had.

As the *boy* had. He hadn't changed.

Gary's arms swirled the water with a lazy sidestroke, as he caught his breath. He grabbed the rock ledge and pulled his dripping body out of the pool, spat something into his left hand, and swiped hair out of his eyes. The kid shouldn't have been able to do any of those things. Seals don't have arms.

Dammit, he had the mark—had the slight webbing between his toes and fingers, not enough to notice unless you looked for it. He should have been able to change. Dan's Tear had glowed when the boy was born, showing that the Dragon recognized Morgan blood—no matter how he'd come by it. The Dragon had told Dan it was time.

Ben tossed Gary a towel and some clothes. The boy

crouched on the rocks, panting. He seemed oblivious to the small cave and the sloping half-tide ledges spaced neatly for a seal's body.

"Alive. Dad's alive," the boy whispered. He stared up at Ben, willing the words to be true.

How on earth did he know? Ben nodded. The boy dried himself and dressed, keeping one hand closed. Ben wondered if he'd hurt himself during the dive.

The boy seemed to be slowly coming to grips with his surroundings. He glanced up at the arched stone ceiling overhead, clear of any tide, studied the dark well of the water he had come out of, noted the shadowy stairs that led up from an alcove on the back wall. He finally turned back to Ben. "Dad's alive? Really?"

"Yes."

Gary's knees folded under him, and he sagged down to a seat on the ledge. He closed his eyes, slowly shook his head, then rubbed his face with one hand. Ben avoided noticing the fresh wetness.

The boy looked up at him. "Where is he? How do you know?"

"Dan? The Pratts have him stashed away somewhere. We were hoping you'd be able to help us get him out." Hoping he'd be able to follow into that cave and figure out where it led, figure out what had gone wrong and avoid it. Hoping a selkie could sneak in where a kayak got caught. "How? We have ways." *Yeah. Sometimes that damned Dragon even condescends to talk to the failures.*

"Does Mom know?"

"Yes. That's one reason why she's acting the way she is. Your sisters don't know, and you can't tell them. They're not old enough to act a part."

The boy stared at Ben, studying his face again. "Who *are* you?"

"Ben Morgan."

"What caused that fight between you and Mom?"

Ben winced. "Son, that was a long time ago. She'll tell you if she thinks you ought to know."

The boy blinked. "Wait a minute . . . Ben Morgan? Uncle Ben? Dad's brother? You're dead!"

"Not quite."

"But I saw your stone."

"You saw Dan's, too. Just because something's carved in granite doesn't mean it's true."

"Dad's alive." The boy looked stunned—too many punches to the head in too short a space of time. If he found out just *why* Maria went through the roof when she saw Ben and Gary together, the kid would *really* have a bad day. The boy shook himself like a wet dog, blinked, and then extended his left hand. "What's this thing?"

Gary opened the fist, the one he'd kept closed since coming out of the water. A crimson light glowed in the middle of his palm, achingly beautiful. Ben's heart skipped a beat, faltered, and then started thumping. It wasn't possible. The boy had failed. He hadn't changed.

Why had the Dragon given him her Tear?

At least that explained how he knew Dan was alive. The Dragon acted as a bond between each of her Tears, as if they all were still parts of her. Family legend said that a glowing egg of crystal fell from the sky and talked to men, back in pre-Christian Wales. Ben wasn't sure how much of *that* he believed. *It* had struck a bargain with the ancestral Morgans. For whatever reason, *it* wanted to see the world through human eyes. If Morgans carried it wherever they went, it would give them certain powers.

"What is it? That's a good question, boy. Take it into a gem shop and ask someday. One expert will tell you it's a ruby, another will say it's garnet, a third will say tourmaline or rosy quartz. Seems to depend on what they expect to see. What it *is,* is a piece of a living thing. Always keep it near you. If it is separated from its chosen human for more than a day or two, it starts to die."

At least the Tear gave Ben something to do, to keep his mind off the problem of Gary's failure. He pulled a small jewelry box out of his pocket and opened it to spill a cascade of silver into his other hand. Shaking out the tangle revealed a silver chain and one of the ancient pendant dragons the Morgan family had hoarded since the beginning of time.

"Isn't that Dad's?"

"There are five of them, and they're all a little different. I don't know that more than three of them have ever been in use at once. Right now, yours and Dan's are the only ones. Put your Tear in the center."

Gary reached out slowly, as if he was reluctant to lose touch with his gift. The stone glowed like a liquid flame, and then quivered for an instant before reforming into a faceted gem clasped in the jaws of the twisting silver dragon. The whole pendant glowed for a few seconds and then faded into a mundane piece of antique jewelry instead of magic on a silver chain.

Ben jerked his mind away from the stone's sorcery and from thoughts of what might have been. He reached out and slipped the chain over Gary's head, allowing his hands to rest on the boy's shoulders a second longer than necessary. He was alive.

"Can you tell me what happened down there?"

"I climbed down the stairs and came to the water. You know all this? You've been there?"

"Yes."

"I saw a light underwater and dove in. The light came from a red ball, like an eye, set in the stone. I touched it, and Dad talked to me. The glowing thing gave me this piece of itself. I ran out of air and almost got trapped before I saw the light from this cave. Did you pass the same test when you were young? Did Dad?"

"We both tried it. I never saw the Dragon's Eye, and never got a Tear. Dan saw it, the Eye wept for him, and something else happened as well. I'll show you what he said about it in the family records. As far as I know, this is the first time that a Morgan has been given a Tear without this other thing happening afterwards."

The boy looked puzzled. He had cause, but Ben figured reading Dan's words would have more effect than a tale told by a stranger that the world thought was dead. The fact remained that something more than usually strange had happened down in the Dragon's lair, something outside the centuries of Morgan experience.

Ben gnawed at his lip. Morgans tended to be pragmatic types, more like technicians or engineers than scientists. They worked within their heritage, applying it to problems rather than stretching it. They used the Dragon without having to understand just what she was. To the best of his memory, none of them had ever dug into magic theory. If they had questions on metalworking, or computers, or archaeology, they went to experts. Now he needed to find a consulting wizard.

He winced at the thought. The only person he knew fitting that title had a sharp memory, an even sharper tongue, and an older sister who had been damned attractive twenty years ago. That was the problem with coming back to a small town—everybody lived in each other's pockets.

He wondered what Lainie was doing these days.

Still, maybe it was time to have a talk with the Wicked Witch of the East. Black Alice probably knew more about the powers than anyone else in Maine, and the Morgans had a long history with the Haskell Women. Not friendship, exactly—those dykes weren't friendly with *any* male-dominated group. But the families had worked together many a time, and had a mutual respect. And Alice could keep her mouth shut when it suited her.

Of course, she'd probably gaze into her crystal ball and come back with some smart-ass comment about women's lib, about why couldn't Ellen and Peggy take this same test. And maybe she'd be right. Damn that Dragon.

First things first. Gary needed to learn a little family history before he'd be ready to talk about the kind of things Alice might know, answer the kind of questions she was liable to ask. Ben waved a hand toward the other stairway, the tower's "back door." "Seems to me you asked for a guided tour. This part I *can* show you, if you're still curious."

"There's more?"

"Yep. Now it gets interesting."

Ben led the way. This stairway was much steeper than the other one, almost a ladder in a shaftway through the granite, and he was always glad of the iron rails bolted into the stone on either side. Out of long habit, he ducked each light globe as he passed it. A hollow thump and mutter of pain told him that the boy hadn't. Ben stopped and glanced back with a sympathetic smile.

The boy rubbed his head for a few seconds, then stopped and ran his hands over the granite walls, stopping at a patch worn smooth by generations of shoulders. He leaned forward and gauged the wear on the steps, then shook his head as if he didn't believe what he saw and touched.

"How old *is* this place?"

"This stair? About five hundred years, five-fifty, something like that. I'd have to check the journals. The upper stair is as old as the tower, maybe six-fifty or seven hundred. The spiral stair, the one you went down, that's older still."

"That's . . . that's not *possible.*"

Ben shrugged. "I'll show you the records. It's just as well Dan made you study Latin, though. Most of the stuff before about 1600 was written by the family priests."

"But . . . the Pilgrims didn't land at Plymouth until 1620."

"Yeah. And when they landed, they found some Wampanog Indians that spoke English right back at them. Wasn't us, but folks had been sailing back and forth across the North Atlantic for centuries. Columbus got here before 1500, and he was a latecomer."

Gary blinked and shook his head. The poor kid was giving his disbelief circuits a serious workout. Ben turned back to the stairs and headed up. A few minutes of climbing brought them to a cramped landing and two level passages. One of them led straight ahead into darkness. Ben pointed down the one that led to the right.

"That one's fairly recent, dug about 1800. It goes to the old mausoleum in the graveyard—that's how I got down to the pool before you did. There's a slab in the back that opens if you do a few things outside before you open the door. I'll show you when we leave."

"Where's the other one go?"

"That was done when they built the tower. It used to go all the way across the road and into the forest, back exit in case of a siege. We had to close the far part off when the county road went through. Now it just opens into a dry well inside that big lilac thicket out by the driveway."

The upper stairs led off to the left. It had been recut a few generations back because the wear had gotten dangerous, so the steps were smoother. Ben straightened up, the muscles in his back glad of the improved headroom. The air smelled fresher, too, with the circulation from the two side passages. They started climbing again, through bare rock and then into tight dry-stone masonry where the stairway started to curve to the left. His shoulders brushed the stones on either side. It was a good thing all the Morgans tended to be slender.

"This top part is actually inside the wall of the tower. The rooms are a few feet off-center. We came up opposite to the door, and we'll end up next to the landing of the old inside stairs. These stone treads balance the cantilever of the ones inside. They closed *that* stair off about the time your Pilgrim latecomers showed up down in Massachusetts."

They'd reached another landing. The stairs continued up, but Ben pushed a worn tapestry to one side, opening the way into a circular room the full width of the tower. Other tapestries draped the walls, and scattered down-lights turned the space into a dim treasure-house full of glittering reflections. Gold gleamed, silver shone, gems and paints lit fire in pools spotting the gloom.

"Wow! What *is* this place?" Gary panted a little from the climb, still recovering from his dive. Or maybe it was shock.

Time to get back in character, now that he could relax a touch. "Aladdin's cave, son, Ali Baba's lair, the Dragon's hoard. The fairy tale promised you rubies and gold, and the genie always delivers." He bowed the boy through the door, with an elaborate flourish as if he swept the floor with a plumed hat.

Ben didn't expect any scrap of attention for ten minutes, minimum. The family had always kept a few things in the tower, treasures that damp and salt air wouldn't hurt. That habit dated back to the time when you kept your wealth only by standing over it, sword in hand. He'd spent the morning moving the other stuff in before going down and opening the door. It was all part of the ritual, the secrets you learned when you came of age.

But the boy hadn't changed. He hadn't found the Dragon's Eye and been trapped. He hadn't come within an inch of drowning and felt the Family's twisted genes kick in and warp his body into its selkie form in order to survive. He'd failed. The Morgans were left with nobody to follow Dan.

Gary turned from side to side, eyes wide, cataloging the treasures lying on stone or on burlap sacking spread on pedestals, set into the masonry niches and hanging from the walls of a single circular room the size of a small house. Ben absentmindedly picked up three Lalique crystal paper-weights and started juggling them while he watched.

A true teenaged male, Gary ran one hand along the green barrel of a bronze six-pounder cannon and then reached for a seventeenth-century ceremonial sword, French, all gold and gems and a blade almost as dull as a Congregationalist ser-mon. Kid showed some sense, though—he didn't touch the steel, and he wiped his hand again before picking up a stack of Maria Theresa thalers and examining them. He stared at a flint Mayan sacrificial dagger that Dan hadn't found a buyer for, but again he didn't touch it, just jingling the old silver coins from one hand to the other.

He put the coins back in their silver bowl and stared at things for a minute. Ben could almost hear the cash register ringing as the boy totaled up the scene.

"This stuff belongs to us?"

"Yep."

"It's all real?"

"Ayuh."

"That painting—that's Picasso, isn't it? And the one next to it is Gauguin?"

"Yep." So those art-history lessons had took. No need to tell him that the good stuff was mostly failures, things that you couldn't sell, sometimes couldn't even hang on the walls of your own house because they were all too well known. A copy of that Picasso was considered the real paint-ing, and this one had been labeled "a clever forgery," un-sellable. Granddad had painted the other one, and *he* damned well had known which one was which. However, the so-called experts had the final say. That Gauguin, the guy who'd commissioned the theft had tried to cut his price after Dan had already lifted the painting. After all, the Mor-gans couldn't sell it anywhere else . . .

Gary had stopped in his prowl around the room. He tilted his head to one side, studying a mannequin covered with charcoal-gray velvet. The featureless head bore twin diadems of woven gold, intricate pendant earrings, and a wide gold necklace hung with patterned plates. Brooches and bracelets lay on more velvet at the base.

"I've seen this stuff before. A photograph."

Ben grinned. Dan had told him about the boy studying Homer in his senior World Lit course. "Priam's Treasure. Guy named Schliemann dug that up, in a place called Hisarlik in Turkey. He thought it came from the Trojan War. He was only off a thousand years or so."

"But . . . Mrs. Allen told us he took it back to Germany, and the Red Army looted it at the end of the Second World War. Disappeared for about forty years, but it's on display in Moscow now."

"Copies, son, really *good* copies. If somebody ever analyzes the metal they've got in the Pushkin Museum, the alloy would match a South African Krugerrand."

"How on earth did it end up here?"

"Well, this Greek billionaire didn't think his people's heritage belonged to either the Russians or the Germans. He paid for the copies and the substitution, back before the Kremlin even knew what they had in those Nazi crates. Too bad he died before he could enjoy the loot."

Or before he could pay us, either. Of course, Dad never told that old buzzard that the stuff really *belonged to the Turks. The customer is always right.*

"Where'd we get all this stuff?"

"It's simple, son. We got it the old-fashioned way. We stole it."

seven

—m—

DANIEL GLANCED AT his watch: 8:37 P.M., in this cave that didn't have days or nights. He was surprised that they hadn't taken the watch away from him, to add to his isolation. Maybe they were still in the "good cop" phase. He'd like to encourage such behavior. Up to a point.

Antonio looked very sleek tonight. Daniel had thrown away the rest of that caravan of names, mainly because stringing them together granted the thug more status than he deserved. They also seemed more suited to silver hair and the wisdom of old age, and didn't seem to fit a man who grew younger every day. Today he looked more like a Tony.

Anyway, the Colombian looked like a well-fed cat staring at his favorite catnip mouse. "I wish you to tell me some things." The cat spread his paws in a gesture of friendship, but claw-tips still peeked out from the fur.

"There are two women, one very large and blond, one very small and dark. I see them together. Who are these?"

That one was obvious. "Alice Haskell and Kate Rowley. Alice is the small one."

The Dragon's power allowed Daniel to deflect some of the questions, answering them with half-truths and evasions. Not straight-out lies, though, and this Colombian had a knack for asking the right questions. Besides, he could get that information from the Pratts. Daniel saved his weapons for more important battles.

"Which one of these is the *bruja,* the witch?"

Now *that* was a peculiar question. Anybody who knew enough to ask it should already know the answer. "Alice."

As interrogations went, these sessions seemed almost friendly—no rubber hose, no truth drugs, not even a hard chair and bright lights in Daniel's face. Yet. The *brujo* had even returned the Dragon pendant, when some of its peculiarities started to show. So far, all Daniel had to face were long and very polite sessions of questions, and a maddening lack of will to resist them. He intended to keep things neighborly for as long as possible.

"The small one, not the large?" The *brujo* paused and his eyes focused beyond the granite wall. "And yet it is the blond goddess who smells of flint and lightning. I think I will continue to examine that link in the chain. Weakening one weakens both." He spoke quietly, as if thinking aloud. Then he shook himself and came back to the cave. "Most curious. Tell me, what are the powers of this Alice?"

"Damned if I know. She's a nurse, rich, queer, got a tongue that could flay an ox at a hundred yards. Purebred Naskeag Indian. The Haskell Women have been around this area since Noah stepped off the Ark. They aren't mean, but if one of them tells you to do something, you do it. People avoid crossing them."

"Crossing? Oh, yes, angering. This word you use, 'queer,' it means something other than strange?"

"Homosexual. In this case, Lesbian." The *brujo* had gaps like that in his vocabulary, places where the idioms didn't work.

"Ah. The large woman, this Kate, then she is the small one's lover? What is her work, her family, her personality?"

"Town constable, works about fifty part-time jobs, divorced, one daughter. Nice woman, not as dumb as she looks, but she *can* be a severe bitch if she thinks you deserve it. Tossed a man halfway through a wall once, busting up a bar fight."

The man's eyes narrowed, and he tilted his head slightly as if mentally adding up his data. "This daughter, she looks like the mother? Large, and blond? A young woman?"

"She's in high school, can't remember what grade. Not quite as large. Hair a little darker, honey blond instead of straw."

"And the mother's associates, these many jobs she holds?"

Daniel couldn't figure where this was going, but it seemed harmless enough. After all, smart drug smugglers wouldn't attack a cop. Drew too much heat. And Tom Pratt knew all of it, anyway. "Kate runs a contracting business, odd jobs and renovations, serves as caretaker for a bunch of summer places. She did some masonry work for us, and I think she did some carpentry for the Pratts. Small crew, two helpers. One's an old coot named Charlie Sickles, the other is a kid she picked up out of juvenile court. Don't remember his name."

The Colombian nodded, pausing, pushing his lips in and out in thought. His eyes seemed to lose focus, freeing Dan's mind for a moment. Not that he could act on that freedom: His cell was carved from solid granite and the steel door was firmly bolted on the outside. He doubted if attacking the *brujo* would have any good results. And then there was the closed-circuit TV camera in one corner of the ceiling, God's omniscient eye.

Just like the interrogation, the cell could have been much worse. It was warm and dry, with lights Dan could control and a comfortable bed. He doubted if it was originally intended as a cell—they gave him a chemical toilet and water in jugs, for example, and the room wasn't vented so he could still smell the last five meals. He guessed it had been some kind of storeroom in a former life. They trusted him with an electric heater to fight the chill of the stone, evidently sure he had no thoughts of suicide. The only thing really wrong with the place was that lock on the outside.

And the Colombians on the other side of it.

Tom Pratt had spent too much time with those Colombians. The Pratts had always been *Stonefort* smugglers, members of a tight-knit community that closed ranks against outsiders. That was how Stonefort survived.

Now the old rules were dead. Tom had joined with an outsider against his own neighbors. The *brujo* was the kind of man who took what he wanted. He wouldn't mind using torture and murder to get it. He dominated the Pratts. Tom had become either too ruthless or too scared to argue.

Daniel wondered where the cell was. A blackout separated this room from the floating dock—they could have moved him miles away while he was out. The solid walls were the same pink Stonefort granite, so he hadn't been moved off the island.

So he couldn't tell Ben, or now Gary, where to look for him. Best guess would be somewhere under the Pratt compound, still in the smuggling tunnels.

Antonio came back from wherever his thoughts had taken him. "So these two women are lovers. It is open? They do not try to hide their love?"

Daniel scratched his right ear and grimaced. "I don't think they've ever posted a notice on the town hall door. They don't live together. But it's common knowledge around town, been twenty years or so. Nobody cares, if that's what you're asking. You can't blackmail them."

"This Viking goddess, she also likes men? She has been married?"

"Town gossip says her marriage broke up over booze, not sex. I know I've seen her truck in front of her ex-husband's house at four in the morning."

Antonio's eyes narrowed. "And the daughter, she and the mother do not get along? Like all children, she wishes to rule her own life before it is time?"

Daniel shrugged. He didn't know the family that well.

The *brujo* smiled gently as he studied Daniel's face. "You wonder why I bother with these things, why I ask you questions my associates can answer. These things help me to know how you act when you are telling truth. They give me, what is the word, a *baseline* to tell truth from lie."

That didn't sound good. Time to grab the bull by the horns. "When are you going to let me go?"

"You have something I want. We can discuss your future when you give it to me."

"It wouldn't do you any good. You saw that it started to die when you kept it."

"*Idioto!* You think I want that foolish bit of silver? No. As I have said, I want the power behind it. Now, tell me where your brother lives, this Benjamin Morgan who died twenty years ago."

The compulsion blossomed into something squeezing Daniel's chest. Sweat beaded on his forehead. He clenched his teeth, trying to keep control of his tongue.

He lost. "I don't know."

The Dragon turned chilly against the skin of his chest, not the cold of the *brujo* pulling power from it but a sense of separation blocking Daniel's own connection with it. It felt as if the pendant had changed into a piece of jewelry instead of a living thing.

The *brujo* cocked his head to one side. "You truly do not know. What you do not know, you cannot tell. Very wise. Perhaps. Who else knows you are alive?"

Daniel gave up on his jaw and clenched his fists instead.

He drove his fingernails into his palms, concentrating on the pain. Maybe pain would draw his focus away from those hypnotic eyes.

"My wife. My son." The words felt like they had been torn out of Daniel's throat.

"You can talk through that interesting jewel?"

"Sometimes."

Again the *brujo* seemed to study Daniel's soul. "Sometimes? You do not seem to understand this thing you have. Curious. You could do so much more with it than that."

Talking through the Dragon didn't seem to bother the *brujo,* or even come as a surprise. He nodded as if he followed Daniel's thoughts.

"Perhaps you should tell this ghost of your brother to make himself more visible, more solid. That would save me the trouble of having other members of your family become dead. I mean truly dead, not this game your clan seems to play with the government. Maria, I believe she is called? And Ellen, and Margaret?"

Daniel felt the blood drain from his face, and spots danced in front of his eyes. He blinked until the small room came back into focus.

The *brujo* smiled at him, almost sadly. "You seem surprised. My people have learned how to be ruthless, you know. We have had excellent teachers, from the days of the *conquistadores* and even earlier. It shows in our national character. What do you call them in English, the Shining Path? The *guerrilleros* know: Kill everyone in a village, and the next village over the hill is most generous with their food and shelter."

"But I can't give you what you want! The Dragon only speaks to Morgan blood. You saw what happened when a stranger touched it!"

Now the *brujo*'s smile turned mocking. "I saw what happened when you set a trap. I let my man walk into it because he was cheating me. The rest of my men know what that meant. But I would not try to take this thing by force." He shook his head, emphasizing the point.

"I know more about these things than you do. I have the tales of my people, the wisdom of my Master's centuries. I know how to have a thing such as this accept a new friend, watch through new eyes, recognize new blood. If you give it freely, your family will live. Your choice is how and when I get this thing, not if. Your choice is whether your family lives or dies."

Daniel grimaced. "And when we give you the Dragon's Eye, tell it to recognize your blood, then you kill us anyway. I've heard about the way you Colombians do business."

"*Colombians?* Ai! You *norteamericanos!* Always you make the large pot of stew, mixing everyone into one lump. I am Peruvian. My men are Peruvian. The Colombians are trash. They are cowboys, they are gangsters. They come from the swamps and still smell of the mud."

"I'm not sure I can see the difference. Drug bosses don't have a reputation for honesty."

"*Es verdad.*" The *brujo* sat thinking for a moment, then nodded. "There is one other thing that I am not, my men are not. We are not *Dons.*" He said the word with an overlay of acid that turned it into a curse in Spanish. "We are Inca, and we have pride. We do not carry the blood of liars and thieves and rapists in our veins. When I say I will do a thing, I do it."

Daniel blinked. He studied the face in front of him: broad and round, brown skin, smooth cheeks and chin even though the hour was late. That was not the face of a Spanish *hidalgo.* So much for snap judgments and stereotypes.

"What happened to *Don* Antonio Estevan Francisco Juan Carlos da Silva y Gomes?" Daniel rattled the lengthy name off with the correct Spanish pronunciation, feeling inordinately proud of his memory, and tried to dip the *Don* in the same acid the *brujo* had used.

"A name and a passport for which the original user had no further need. You may call me Tupash if you wish. It is close to the pronunciation of my name in Quechua."

"Inca, Spanish, it makes a difference? I'm supposed to trust you more because you descend from people who practiced human sacrifice?"

The Peruvian shrugged. "That was done rarely, only in times of great crisis. The sacrifices were condemned criminals or volunteers. We were not like the Aztec, piling up a mountain of corpses to make the sun rise in the morning. This remains—the blood of Viracocha and Manco Capac flows in my veins. I do not lie, and when I say a thing, I do that thing. Ask your Dragon to look into my heart and tell you what it finds."

Daniel nodded, thinking. At the least, pretending to go along would buy him time, buy Ben and Gary time to figure out an escape. "How do you know so much about the Dragon? I've never heard of anything else like it."

"These things, they are very old and very secret. I tell you what I know to show my trust, to show how much you can gain if you trust me. Great power is there for the taking. I know how to use it. You have forgotten."

A wry smile twisted Daniel's face. "Trust? And here I thought you were gloating like a villain in a cheap movie."

"I wish you would not think of me as a villain. I came here as a businessman, trading a product your people want. Your family is not troubled by laws. Neither am I. Laws are made by others, to be obeyed by others. I offer you wealth and power, security, peace. Give me this thing and your family will prosper. Refuse me and your family will die. But you have no reason to refuse."

"Perhaps I prefer to keep the power in my own hands?"

"You do not hold it now. You do not know *how* to hold it, or you would not be here."

"Perhaps I would prefer that no one held it?"

The *brujo* shook his head. "I *will* hold it. Now that I know that it exists, where it exists, it will be mine. I say again, I know how to reach this thing. Think of how your gem turned dull, away from your touch. Think of your Eye itself, with no Morgan blood left living. A year, two years, it will seek another ally. I will be there."

Any delay helped Ben, gathering the ideas, the bits and pieces of information he needed to make one of his plans. Ben *always* figured something out. Just give him time. Daniel glanced up at the TV camera. "What about the Pratts?"

The *brujo* waved his hand at the box on the ceiling, and the light under its lens winked out. "They have no part of this. Drugs they can have, as before. Drugs are cheap. The power? That will be mine, and also yours. If you are vindictive, they can be destroyed. I wish to make a deal with you, and they can be part of the price. But you do not seem that kind of man."

The arguments made a perverted kind of sense. Morgans had worked with many allies over the centuries, some far worse than a South American drug lord. They'd sold looted art for Mengele, Cambodian artifacts for the Khmer Rouge. The *only* rule had always been the good of the family. This man had the power to end the family, and the will to do it, and a reason.

He nodded slowly, warily. "I need to believe we can trust you. Why do you need us, if you can simply take the Dragon without my help?"

"I tell you these things because I want to be your friend, your partner. That is why you still live. I have no need of corpses. Corpses have no value. Clever minds have value. Clever minds are very rare, and ones with the skills of your

family are even rarer. I need you. Can you believe this, trust this? A single man does not use power such as your Dragon offers. That kind of greatness calls for an army, and an army needs many generals."

His words were seductive. Daniel wondered how much of that was hypnosis and how much the power of the arguments themselves. He'd always sensed that the things the Tear gave him—the ear for truth and lies, the ability to hide in plain sight, the mastery of locks and hidden places that seemed to run in his family—that all these things barely scratched the surface of the Dragon.

The selkie change, that was something separate from the Dragon. Morgans had changed their skins since before time began. So far, the *brujo* hadn't asked any questions that hinted he knew about that. Daniel had no plans to mention it.

He grinned at the *brujo,* at Tupash. "I think you don't want to wait a year or two before you get this power."

The man laughed quietly and clapped him on the shoulder. "This is also true. I am an old man, older than you can guess. I have learned patience, but I have also learned that Death does not wait forever. He took my master after many years, and someday he will catch up with me no matter how far I run. I have better things to do than sit in a damp cave, staring at your Dragon and waiting for her to change her mind."

"What *is* the Dragon's Eye?"

"According to my master, these things are part of many myths. Toltec legend speaks of Quetzacoatl's Egg, in words very like your description of your Dragon's Eye. My master thought the Hebrews carried something similar in their Ark, hiding it from unclean eyes and calling on its power to destroy their enemies. That is how desert nomads would use such a thing, not hiding it deep in the earth as you have.

"The Inca had one. The Child of the Moon they called it, and they kept it in a cave in the heart of Machu Picchu.

It glowed with a silver light. My master said Pizarro took it and sent it back to Spain, and it vanished from history. It is thought that one of his priests called it a thing of the Devil and threw it overboard from the ship." The *brujo* shrugged and spread his hands, palm up, as if commenting on fanaticism.

So there had been others, maybe still were. Daniel tried to wrap his mind around the concept.

One thing still bothered him, and if Tupash was feeling chatty . . . "Why are you here?"

"Ah. This is interesting, yes? As your neighbor said, I have some artifacts to sell: very old, very strange, perhaps very valuable. I looked among my associates for someone to point the way, someone with the right connections. The name of your neighbor seemed to glow on the page. I think that now I understand why."

"I need time to think about this."

The *brujo* nodded, stood up, and walked toward the door. He turned back, with a sad smile. "Certainly you may think. I would not think long, if I were you. Consult your watch. In two days, people start to die. People important to you. I think your darling wife might commit suicide from grief. So think hard."

Daniel shivered.

Tupash nodded again when he saw Daniel understood. "Talk with your brother. I can offer him many interesting cities to be dead in. I do not recommend telling your loved ones to flee. They would not get far. We can be good to each other, or I can be very cruel. The choice is yours."

The ice left Daniel's pendant at the same instant as the bolt clanged home on the far side of the door. He glanced up at the corner of the ceiling. The little red light on the camera glowed back at him.

eight

—ᴧᴧ—

SOMETIMES YOU JUST had to be firm with the House. Aunt Jean might have complained about the old shack's attitude when she'd installed the indoor plumbing, but Alice had absolutely *no* interest in returning to the outhouse-and-kitchen-pump days. She toweled her hair and ran a last swipe down her body, wallowing in the warm tingle of a soak in the spring's water—a soak in the spring's water *after* it was heated, with lavender bath oil, in a civilized tub. It sure beat the hell out of scrubbing down with lye soap in the screened garden pool out back that once had served for baths. *Brrrrr . . .*

Brrrrr. Brrrrr.

Damn. That wasn't shivering in sympathy; that was her pager. Alice snatched it up, read the code, cussed, and started grabbing clothes. Ambulance call.

Whyinhell did people *always* decide to dial 911 when she was in the tub? Autopilot routine swapped her yard-work clothes for the blood-and-guts crash suit and EMT jacket, flipped the damper on the kitchen stovepipe to put dinner on hold, grabbed her roadkill bag, and dumped Dixie Bull out the side door to shake her ears in irritation and lick a paw to show proper feline disdain. Alice slammed the door behind them, touched the door-post for luck, and hopped into the old Subaru.

Rossini's *Lone Ranger* overture rang out in her head, more accurately known as *William Tell*. She floored the gas pedal and spun out of her driveway in a four-wheel drift—first man to the ambulance shed got to *drive.*

Two minutes later, she skidded into the lot at the town garage. Irv Watson's pickup sat by the side door, so she pulled over to the left, clear of the ambulance and fire bays. By the time she was parked and out of her car, the overhead door was rising and she heard the growl of the diesel ambulance. She'd lost the race.

He paused just clear of the door and had the heavy rig rolling again as soon as she'd dumped her EMT bag in back and grabbed the seatbelt buckle. She flicked switches for him as he swung right onto Main Street, activating the lights and the bee-boo of the electronic siren.

"What's the call?"

"Dead call, 3930 Sunrise Lane."

She punched the street and address into the mapping system and watched the software bring up a route on its display. The GPS woke up, as well, but that wouldn't matter unless they ended up *way* out in the puckerbrush on some unnamed tote road.

"East on 176, then left on Salt Hay Road. Remember that blind corner beyond Gooding's Hill."

"Roger that, good buddy."

She caught her breath and settled into the shotgun seat, letting the distinctive ambulance reek of diesel and disinfectant kick her brain into overdrive. Dammit, this was what kept her on ER shifts in spite of the hours, this adrenaline rush of life-or-death.

Irv's eyes flicked right and left, checking the idiot quotient at each driveway and intersection as he accelerated. His glance rested on her wet hair for an instant. "Caught you in the shower?"

"Every frigging time. Phone seems to be wired to my plumbing." Of course, the pager system was radio rather than telephone, but so what? The principle was the same.

Funny thing was, the phone system actually *had* a wire clamped to the pipes in her cellar. Kate swore it was a ground lead and totally harmless, but Alice doubted that. The phone was just too satanic.

A "dead call" was shorthand for a 911 call with nobody talking on the other end. It was the same sort of gallows humor that had them calling burned corpses "Crispy Critters" and crash victims "roadkill." Anyway, when they rolled, they never knew for sure whether "dead call" meant a heart attack, a robbery in progress, or a kid pressing the wrong button on a memory dialer. It could make for an interesting morning.

"3930 Sunrise" didn't ring any bells with her—they'd renamed and numbered just about every side road in town a year ago, nailing down addresses for the enhanced 911 service. She checked the mapping system. For all its cutesy suburban sound, Sunrise Lane had been "Fire Road 13B" in its previous life, a two-rut gravel path that wound past old trailers and scattered shacks up to an abandoned quarry. Most of the "houses" wouldn't pass muster for decent chicken sheds.

"Right at Mason's Mill Road."

"Got it."

Alice noticed an echo from their siren and leaned forward to scan the mirror on her side. A white car with flashing blue light-bar rounded the previous turn, and Irv slowed down. The sheriff's cruiser whipped out around them and then skidded back into their lane to avoid an oncoming car. His right-side wheels kicked up dust from the shoulder, pelting their windshield with gravel, and Irv tromped his brakes and started cussing about lead-footed county Mounties.

She jerked another look at the side mirror, her stomach sinking. That car going in the other direction—it was the big blue Suburban from the other day, the one that had threatened Kate. What were they interested in, out this way?

Irv swung the ambulance off the paved road and onto gravel, following the dust trail of the sheriff's deputy. Alice grabbed the side grip and held on against the sway and bounce of back roads. They could go slower on the way out, if the patient needed smooth more than he needed speed. Another turn, and Irv dropped into low for the climb. Sunrise, AKA Fire Road 13B. They passed two crapped-out trailers and two startled faces, then a shack you couldn't give to a porcupine, but it had smoke coming out of the rusty stovepipe—scenic Maine coastal cottages.

They turned again, past "Sickles" on a weathered pine board, and skidded to a halt behind the cruiser. Alice killed the siren but left the lights going. The place was just another shack, looked like three rooms or four and a lean-to shed with the roof caving in, and the outhouse still had a clear path showing it was in daily use. The deputy was headed toward the side door, right hand near his holster. Good news—they could let the man with the gun go in first, to find whatever he found.

Alice didn't recognize him. Kate had said there was a new guy on the force, straight out of the Criminal Justice Academy. He played it by the book—knocking on the door, standing carefully to one side in case some drunken citizen decided to pump a few shotgun shells through the unpainted wood, and then testing the knob. It wasn't locked. Alice would have been surprised if it was.

The deputy cautiously stuck his head inside and yelled,

then vanished through the doorway. He reappeared in seconds, waving them in. Alice and Irv grabbed their bags and ran, and she shifted into her controlled-speed mode where she did everything precisely but without a wasted second. The things she did could kill people if she did them wrong, but they'd die on their own if she did them too slowly.

The entry stank of poverty: boiled cabbage, rotting potatoes, rancid bacon grease, damp wood and plaster. Generations of stale tobacco smoke overlaid the other smells, making them even fouler. An old man lay on the kitchen floor, next to the dangling phone. His eyes were open but fixed, not a good sign. She checked for a pulse, for breathing, she touched his eyelid. Nothing. His skin felt cool already. She grabbed eye protection and snapped on a pair of sterile gloves.

Irv had started to set up for CPR. Alice glanced at her watch—fifteen minutes since her beeper signal, allow another minute or two for the dispatch. Too damn fast for the man to feel like that, even if he'd died the instant he finished dialing. Someone else had placed that call. She glanced up at the deputy.

"Check the rest of the house."

CPR started, Irv leaning on the victim's chest in a steady rhythm. She marked the time, then set up the plastic airway and started to share breath with a corpse while she dug out a preloaded hypo. Natural division of labor—small as she was, she had to work too hard to move a man's ribcage, even with her full weight.

She'd spell him, though. Or the deputy would—CPR was part of cop training. The ambulance really needed a three-man crew, minimum, but Stonefort couldn't swing it all the time. Guys had to dig clams when the tide called, or pull their lobster traps.

"You've got some more customers."

The deputy had reappeared in the doorway. Alice

grabbed her bag and chased him through the house. Now the air smelled like a bad nursing home—unwashed bodies, cheap disinfectant, and aging bedpans. The front room had been turned into a sickroom, and an elderly woman lay on the bed, eyes closed, no visible breathing. Another gray-haired woman lay facedown on the floor beside it.

Both bodies were cold, even through the gloves. She moved one hand, then another. Semistiff. Rigor was setting in on both bodies. Both corpses.

Sickles. Alice remembered the name-board out by the road and finally matched it up with a face. The man on the kitchen floor had been Charlie Sickles, Kate's sometime carpenter. She'd met him once or twice, remembered he had a wife and old mother at home, both ailing. Just seeing the name hadn't meant much: There were about as many Sickles families in Sunrise County as there were rabbits.

She looked up at the deputy. He stared back, no clue about the random thoughts zipping through her head, wondering if there was a hope here, the way she'd paused.

She shook her head. "Not a chance." Then she started linking things, back to business. "Guess is, the old woman died in her sleep. From what I've heard, she was over ninety. Younger woman had a bad heart herself, emphysema, lifetime smoker: died from the shock of finding the body. Man came home, found both of them, and tried to call for help. Don't think we can revive him."

The deputy nodded. "Looks like. Still have to have an autopsy. Unattended deaths. I'll call for the medical examiner." He spun on his heel and headed back out through the house to use the radio in his cruiser. Probably the handheld on his belt wouldn't work this far from base.

Something still didn't add up. Alice remembered the feel of the old man's skin, much too cold to have died ten or fifteen minutes ago. She touched the inside of her wrist to the woman on the floor. Cold—colder than room temperature, impossible as that seemed.

She'd felt that cold before. It didn't really have that much to do with temperature. The bodies felt as if not only the people had died, but all their cells and all the bacteria in their guts and even the mites living on their skin and hair. These bodies were more dead than dead.

Aunt Jean had called it *chi,* stealing a term from Chinese lore in her eclectic way. Life force, or energy. All of the *chi* was gone out of these bodies. They felt like the rabbits Aunt Jean had bought and used to teach the draining witchery. Used on meat animals, the "spell" was no more evil than any other form of slaughter. Alice had to learn to take energy before she could give it out to others. *Chi* had to balance, just like any other form of accounting. Nothing ever came from nothing.

They'd eaten rabbit stew for the next three days—Aunt Jean wasn't one of those vegetarian witches. As she used to say, "Everybody is somebody's lunch." Like all the Haskell women, she'd been buried unembalmed in a plain pine box, to move on through the stream of life.

Alice shook herself out of those thoughts. Another siren moaned to silence outside, the fire department crash squad. Now they'd have some muscle to move the man. She glanced at her watch again, automatically. Eighteen minutes since the beeper woke up.

Back to the kitchen, check again for a pulse in a gap of Irv's chest-pressure sequence, snap decision balancing the man's age against zero response to CPR.

Prep the hypo, inject. "One milligram Epinephrine." Announce all medication—keep both partners working on the same page.

No response. She caught her partner's eye and shook her head. "Flatliner."

He nodded, agreeing, but kept up the rhythm. EMTs and RNs didn't have a license to declare people dead. They'd hauled cold meat before, once saw it warm up again into a young wife and mother. That sort of thing was enough to give you religion.

The door was too narrow for the gurney. They loaded him into a Stokes basket they carried for wilderness rescue, then *still* couldn't make the turn in the little mudroom between kitchen and shed. Finally cleared out a window with a fire axe and pulled him out that way.

Alice cornered the cop for an instant, first free breath she'd had since they'd hit the site. "Why'd you pass with a car in your face? Damn near ran us into the ditch and didn't save ten seconds!"

The deputy turned white with the memory. "I *looked*! I *swear* the road was clear! Damn truck must have pulled out of a driveway!"

Truck? "Take a look when you go back. No driveways between Felt Brook and that turn."

Alice finally slowed down enough to actually notice the guy. He'd just been a mobile uniform outside her focus, but now she realized he was kinda cute in a steely-jawed cleancut Mountie sort of way—big and young and solid, hadn't had time to work up a belly and go soft from too much time in the cruiser and too many donuts on night patrol.

They had the man strapped to the gurney now, loading him in the back, CPR continuing. Irv climbed in, along with Ed Guptill, another EMT from the fire squad who hadn't been on call so they hadn't waited for him at the garage. Alice slammed the doors behind them. Twenty minutes from the pager's beep. Adrenaline junkie.

She hopped up on the driver's seat and ran it forward enough so she could reach the pedals. Irv was about a foot taller than she was, and *he* wasn't tall. She hit the siren again, hauled the wheel around, and jiggered twice before getting the rig aimed back down the driveway. Damn good thing the bus was automatic and had power steering.

The cop was stringing yellow tape around the shack, protecting evidence. Too bad they wouldn't find any.

Out the gravel road, past more curious faces. Alice kept a lid on her lead foot, cruising around potholes rather than crashing through them. Irv and Ed weren't strapped in, and some of the stuff in the back had sharp edges.

"Hey, Irv! What'd you see when that deputy cut us off?"

He grunted. "Damn fool swung out," grunt, "pulled up," grunt, "damn near took our," grunt, "bumper off cutting," grunt, "back in." He grunted again, the CPR chest massage. "No need."

Ed must be doing the breathing, two-man routine. She pulled out onto the pavement and goosed the ambulance. *This* was where the fun started. Her personal best was the full ton, a hundred, but Irv claimed he'd hit one-twenty once—weather clear and track fast. Probably downhill, too. 'Course, you needed to be careful about that stuff. Heavy as the rig was, you didn't want to have to stop or turn in any hurry.

"Did you catch the license of that car?" Failing to yield to a siren could cost that Suburban a few hundred bucks.

"What car?"

An electronic voice mumbled in the back, the hopped-up AI defibrillator warning everybody to stand clear so it could calculate and time a charge. She missed the pop of the capacitors firing, lost in the rattle of loose gear as the ambulance wallowed over a frost heave. She slowed up a tad, knowing the man in the back was truly dead and she couldn't justify risking three other lives to rush him to the ER. Even if it *was* fun.

Irv had never even seen that blue Suburban. The deputy hadn't seen it until they were nearly head-on, and he thought it was a truck. That was some powerful mojo.

Mojo that had killed a man and two women. Mojo that threatened Kate, if Alice had correctly read the malice in that slow pass of the Suburban. Mojo that might be attacking Kate, cutting away her friends and crew and leaving her to stand alone, as well as sucking *chi* from dirt-poor throwaway old people whose deaths would be written off as "natural."

Alice swung the ambulance north onto Route 17, headed for Downeast General. Damn good thing tourist season hadn't hit full stride—all those Massachusetts and New Jersey rubberneckers could add half an hour to the run. She cranked the diesel up to eighty and watched two cars dive for the paved shoulders of the road, heeding her lights and noise.

How the hell do you hide two tons of Chevy metal? That was a trick Aunt Jean had never taught. Time to consult with the House, interview a ghost or two. Two women dead and a third threatened? The House didn't like that sort of thing.

She crested the hump of the bridge and saw the long straight stretch they called Daytona Speedway, just resurfaced last fall. The needle edged past ninety, and the road was clear.

She'd kicked in over ten grand of Haskell money when the ambulance squad was rebuilding this yard-sale special. Stonefort's normal ER run was over fifty miles—a little speed could make the difference between life and death.

Right.

Damn, driving fast was fun!

nine

—ɯ—

BEN MORGAN PERCHED in one of the crenels on the
top of Morgan's Castle, feeling like the vulture of doom. He
ran his hand over the cold green barrel of a bronze cannon,
fiddled with the wooden tompion that sealed its muzzle,
and stared out across the point and the countryside. The air
was still, the fog gone, and rare June sun warmed the stones
of the tower, creating an idyllic landscape totally at odds
with his mood.

The gun was loaded—up until Ben's "death," the family
had fired a salute each Fourth of July, and Dan still replaced
the charge each year. Ben could pull that wooden plug, un-
seal the touch-hole, prime the gun, and fire it. Damned
thing would probably put a six-pound cast-iron ball right
through the Congregational church roof. The noise and destruction might make the day look better.

He was getting nowhere. Dan still languished in du-
rance vile, the Coast Guard had *no* intention of running a
detailed look at that stretch of Pratt's Neck seashore, and
discreet hints through third parties to the DEA still pro-

duced no inclination to search and seize anything in the Pratt compound. Where the hell was the law when you really needed it?

Four cannon lurked up here on black iron carriages, invisible from the ground, guarding the points of the compass through stone crenellations, and they spoke of a Morgan past that was rather more violent than recent generations. If you took up certain slates on the deck, you'd find waterproof covers protecting the base-plate for an 81mm mortar and threaded sockets for mounting the tripod of a 106mm recoilless rifle. Those were more recent Morgan contributions to coastal defense against Russian submarines or the ruthless hordes of invading Canadian tourists. The mounts had been there for decades, never needed, waiting patiently.

Neither the ancient nor the modern weapons had enough range to touch the Pratts, six miles or so across the bay. It was probably just as well—Ben didn't need that temptation. There were aiming tables, though, down in the cave that housed the actual weapons, with range and azimuth plotted for damned near anything within 10,000 yards. Morgans had even joined the army to learn how to handle the weapons and pass that knowledge down.

Weapons. They were tools of desperation, and Ben felt desperate. He'd scouted the edges of the Pratt domain, probing for weakness, and found damned little. Without the power of the Dragon backing him up, he didn't dare to push it further. Maybe Gary could reach that necessary extra step.

The boy was learning fast. Dan had dangled hobbies in front of his nose: karate, scuba, ham radio, a knack for intricate mechanical models that was perfect preparation for locks and security systems—all the tangled skills a kid needed to grow up to be a Morgan. To grow up to be a selkie and a thief.

Sooner or later, though, the boy was going to start asking

questions, and Ben wasn't sure he had enough answers. Questions about Maria and Dan, for example. About the Dragon. About morality.

He stood up and stared down the four tall stories of the tower, fifty feet, at the ranks of gravestones and memorials: seven hundred years of Morgans. They'd come close to ending more than once before. He didn't know if the other guardians of the line had felt this helpless. Somebody had always managed to pull a hat out of a rabbit, though, make that little twist that preserved the line. Maybe this time Maria had supplied the new blood that would save the old. Or maybe not—Gary hadn't changed.

Ben turned and opened a worn oak door set into the curving stone wall. Cool air flowed out, musty-damp with the salt air rising from the Dragon's Pool far beneath his feet. Ben smiled wryly to himself: time to put on the jester's hat he hid behind when dealing with his audience of one. He spiraled down through darkness, one hand on the wall and feet searching the edges of the worn stone steps. They had never run power up this far—didn't want any chance of light showing from an abandoned tower.

He passed the fourth floor, storage and a bed he sometimes used, and turned off on the landing of the third, into warmth and light and the smell of electronics. The family had divided this level into four rooms at the same time they'd blocked up all the windows and arrow-slits, back around the turn of the century. The entry quadrant was now surveillance, rows of monitors and little indicator lights slaved to a set inside the main house. Ben picked up a slice of cold pizza and settled into the swivel chair at the focus of the desk.

Anchovies. The kid *had* to like anchovies on his pizza. Ben shook his head as he chewed on spicy shoe-leather.

He glanced over the board automatically, reading the green lights of the daytime system and the reds of the infrared and starlight cameras off-line until nightfall. Everything read "normal." No calls logged, in or out, no unusual traffic on any of the scanner channels.

The monitors read "normal," too, including the road out front. There'd been a car parked out there yesterday, hung around for maybe half an hour, a big blue Suburban with smoked glass and New Jersey plates. Ben had watched it the whole time, an itch he couldn't scratch. When it had finally pulled away, he'd felt as if the sun had come out again.

Maria was weeding her kitchen garden. Ben reached for a joystick and zoomed the camera in, wondering just how much she knew about the systems that guarded her house. That outfit of halter top and tight shorts . . . damn, she was still a fine-looking woman. He shook his head and zoomed back out to the wide-angle view. If only that damned Dragon had decided otherwise . . .

Drop it.

He wiped pizza grease off his hands, stood up, and stepped through the right-hand door, into the room that served as a clean workshop and library. Gary looked up from the workbench where he was disassembling a complex keycard lockset. He had his mother's eyes, eyes with questions in them.

Well, it was about time.

"How did our family turn into robbers?"

Ben shook his head. "Thieves. There's a big difference: Robbers take things while the owners are right there, and usually threaten force. Thieves just take things, and try really hard to never *see* the owners. If anybody ever sees you taking the loot, you've made a serious mistake. In fact, if you do it right, they'll never even know the stuff is gone."

"You mean, like all that gold from Troy?"

"Exactly." Ben grinned. "You know the real beauty of that job? If somebody ever *does* notice, they'll assume the fakes are for display only. That the real stuff is in a vault somewhere, safe. Museum people exhibit replicas all the time—no worry about some weirdo smashing the case and stealing something irreplaceable, or destroying it."

"Uncle Ben . . ."

"*Arrgh!*" Ben threw up his hands in mock horror. "Don't call me that! I may be your uncle, and my name may be Ben, but I *don't* sell rice!"

"What *do* I call you, then?"

"Just 'Ben' will do fine. If you're so overwhelmed by respect for your elders that you have to make it formal, 'Mr. Morgan' will also serve."

The boy grinned. "Okay, *Mr.* Morgan. You didn't answer my question."

Ben waved at a shelf of leather-bound books. "Well, son, you've been reading, but you haven't had time to wade through five hundred years of Latin. *Bad* Latin. So I'll give you a capsule history of the Morgan clan, as it applies to a cultural predisposition towards kleptomania."

Gary removed another screw from the cover-plate of the lock, exposing circuit boards and solenoids and springs. The boy frowned and scratched his head, giving Ben only half his attention. Mechanical puzzles fascinated him. That ran in the family.

Ben settled into a chair and picked up an amethyst geode that served as a paperweight in the chaos of the workroom. He stared into the purple depths as if seeking inspiration, and then waved his free hand over it like a Gypsy fortune-teller consulting her crystal ball.

"The mystic stone sees all, knows all. Once upon a time, in a faraway land, there lived a Handsome Prince. His name was Madoc ap Owain Gwynedd, Madoc son of King Owain of Wales." Ben paused and grinned. "We aren't descended from him, so don't go giving yourself airs.

"King Owain went and died, as all men must. Now, Prince Madoc had a couple of older brothers who both wanted to rule the land, and they both pestered him for support. He got bored with the situation and thought life would be easier—and perhaps longer, as well—in some other place. Sailors told tales of a western land found by some fool Norseman named Leif Ericson, and how wonderful it was, full of trees and green grass for grazing and grapes for wine—mighty attractive to a fairy-tale prince tired of politics. So Prince Madoc went sailing, sailing, sailing, over the western sea."

Young Gary rolled his eyes, perhaps tired of the fairy-tale format or just asking Ben to cut to the chase. Ben wrinkled his nose at the interruption.

"Okay. In or about the year 1170, some Welsh guys sailed west and found land. They expected to—it wasn't any mystery. They looked around and decided there were some prime house-lots going begging. They came back. They gathered some settlers, and sailed out, and were never heard from again. That would have been the end of it, because the Welsh still ruled their land and were happy in it. But this guy called Edward came along and decided the English really owned Wales, and proceeded to prove it with steel and fire. That changed the picture considerably."

Gary put the lock down. Apparently he thought this was worth his *full* attention. Ben smiled inwardly, feeling his way to a relationship with this boy he'd never dared to meet.

"Okay. Edward the First of England was a nasty man. He went around destroying castles, killing local chieftains who wouldn't lick his blood-spattered boots, and filling the Welsh countryside with his Norman cousins. In 1282, the last independent ruler of Wales died in battle, one Llewelyn ap Gruffydd. A bunch of his subjects, including the ancestral Morgans, had had enough of the thieving English. We packed up and left."

"And sailed off to join Prince Madoc's colony?"

Ben looked up from the depths of the geode. "Nope.

Never found him. There are legends that he settled down in Alabama and had all sorts of trouble with the local natives. No, our revered ancestors poked around here and there, Newfoundland and Nova Scotia and such, until they turned the corner and sailed up the Gulf of Maine. Morgans always *were* a picky lot. Us and the Dragon, who had some pretty solid notions of what she wanted."

Young Gary lifted his eyebrows at this. "Let me get this straight. They had the pick of the whole East Coast of North America, and they chose *this* poverty pocket? I mean, Sunrise County is a nice place, but there was lots of land with real soil and timber and a climate that doesn't have frost nine months of the year."

Ben put the geode down and stood up, swapping the stone for three screwdrivers that he flipped from hand to hand like juggling clubs. It was another family trait, busy fingers that seemed to work independently of the mind. Gary was fiddling with the lock again, even though Ben knew the boy was listening.

"Think about those legends I just told you. What happened to Prince Madoc? What happened to the Vikings a couple of centuries earlier?"

"They fought with the Indians?"

"Yep. Even the Vikings got their butts kicked, in spite of being rough and tough and hard to diaper. Steel swords and axes weren't enough advantage. They pulled out and moved back to Iceland. Madoc disappeared without a trace. We're still here."

"So the Morgans and the Dragon were looking for friendly Indians?"

Ben flipped an underarm toss with a double turnover and caught all three screwdrivers in one hand. He bowed to his audience. "Give the boy a kewpie doll. The Naskeag Indians were an oddball lot, matriarchal and matrilineal, and they wanted stuff we had. Iron-making, glassblowing, sea-faring, and fishing, you name it. Our revered ancestors struck a deal, and settled, and all was right with the world for about three hundred years. Then the snake wormed his way back into the Garden of Eden."

"The English?" Gary offered.

"Yep, the damned English. *Again.* They finally got the balls to do what everybody else had been doing for hundreds of years—sail across the great northern ocean. They stepped off the boat and started right in where they'd left off in Wales, claiming they owned everything in sight. Didn't matter one whit to them that people already lived here. They stole it."

He waved at the horizon, and then pointed to the door and the stairway. "Climb up to the top deck and look around. Everything you see used to belong to us and to the Naskeags, all the way to Naskeag Falls and beyond. All of Eastern Maine and half of New Brunswick thrown in, plus a chunk of Nova Scotia. Only way we could hold on to this tower and the point, we stole it back from some blueblood in London who'd never even laid eyes on it. The damned English king had given *our* land to him."

"And that justified our stealing other stuff?"

Ben grinned. "Makes a hell of a good rationalization, don't it? But it did teach us that it's hard to prove clear title to wealth in this wide world. Think about that Trojan gold. Can the Russians really claim they own it? Could the Germans? Did digging it out of that mound at Hisarlik give Heinrich Schliemann the right to steal it from the Turkish government? Who *really* owns it? We *possess* it, and that's the only claim anyone else could make."

"Were we always thieves instead of robbers?"

Ben grinned and shook his head. "Remember that gravestone you were sitting on, when you first met me? Old Dan Morgan and that ship he lost for the cause of freedom? It was a privateer—a twelve-gun sloop that could outrun anything it couldn't outfight.

"I don't know if you've ever heard the definition of a privateer, but it meant a pirate with a license. Governments used to license private vessels as warships to attack enemy commerce, issuing papers they called 'Letters of Marque.' Capture an enemy ship, you could make a hell of a profit—the ship and cargo were yours to keep or sell.

"Old Dan sailed first for the English, against the French, and then for the Continental Congress against the English. In neither case did he ever bother much about what actual flag his victims flew. He wasn't the first Morgan who sailed as a pirate, and he wasn't the last one, either. You can get away with a lot when you've got a whole town ready to swear you were in port when some ship disappeared."

The boy grinned like he didn't mind having a pirate or two in his family tree. Then he frowned. "But we don't still do that, do we? We don't kill people?"

Ben hesitated, ran both hands through his hair, and then settled on a wry shrug. There was no point in sugar-coating life. "Son, we do whatever needs doing. That Trojan gold—we worked with the Moscow Mafia on that job, and some bent KGB *apparatchiks*. They tortured and killed three clerks, covering their tracks. That's the world the KGB lived in. We didn't tell them to do it, but there's blood on that pretty jewelry."

Gary swallowed and stared at his hands, as if he expected to see bloodstains.

"Son, I can just about guarantee murder was done for that gold, long before we ever heard of it. Wealth is like that. Some guy once wrote that all property is theft. I wouldn't go quite that far, but an awful lot of ownership traces back to a man who was handy with sword or gun.

"Those pots you helped me unpack yesterday—they'd

been stolen twice before we got our hands on them, and the first time was grave-robbery from national monument lands out West—and those *lands* were stolen from some Navajo or Hopi band. Whoever rightly owns those pots, it sure wasn't the guy we took them from."

Gary nodded and then wrinkled his nose at the lock in his hands. "How *do* you open this darned thing, anyway? Some kind of electronic reader to pick out the code?"

The puzzle-solver mentality showed through again. Ben laughed. "The easiest way is with the keycard. 'Social engineering.' You usually can get your hands on one through bribery, blackmail, or plain and simple theft. Barring that, what would you hit if you drilled in about three-quarters of an inch below the center of the 'R' in Renwick?"

The boy checked. "Looks like the positive terminal of a solenoid."

"Bingo. Feed a twelve-volt DC lead through the hole, touch the negative to the lock plate, and you're in."

Gary put the lock down again. He glanced vaguely off into a corner of the room as if thinking, and then focused those eyes, Maria's eyes, straight on Ben's face. "Why are you dead?"

Ben sighed. "Long story, son. There are three basic reasons why Morgans vanish. First, you make a mistake. If it looks as though one of us is going to get caught, we fake a death. It's simpler than getting convicted and less painful than being hung. No Morgan has done jail time in two hundred years.

"Second, ever since the government started to get real nosy, we've found it useful to have some people who don't exist—Morgans who pay cash for everything, who have verifiable fake ID, who can't be traced by any record. We started it back in the Civil War, when Lincoln decided to draft men into the army. Old Ephriam Morgan said he didn't want the expletive-deleted government to ever be able to put their slimy hands on every member of the family or every dollar we owned."

Gary chuckled at that, and nodded. Looked like Dan had laid some groundwork there, a little Libertarian political philosophy.

"Finally, the Dragon has some medieval notions about how the world ought to work. Primogeniture wasn't really a Welsh concept, but neither is she. Anyway, the oldest son rules the family, inherits the title and the castle. Doesn't matter if he's a drooling idiot or thinks he's an eagle and has to be forcibly restrained from trying to fly off the castle roof, he's The Man.

"Well, the old way of dealing with that was to cull the litter of pups, kill off the runts and defectives until the fittest son *was* the oldest son. Back around Ephraim's time, we went soft. These days, if you are deemed unfit to wear the crown, you disappear. The Dragon rejected me. I fell overboard and was lost at sea."

Gary stared at a pile of books shoved to one corner of the workbench. "Dad wrote about that. Crazy stuff, myths or songs or science fiction. People don't change into seals."

"Believe it, boy. Polish up your Latin and check some of the older journals. I failed, and Dan passed. That meant he got to be the big cheese. The Morgan."

"Is that what happened between you and Mom? You had to 'die' and leave her?"

Damn. Ben had thought he'd hidden how he felt about Maria, and he'd hoped the kid was too young to know how tightly linked love and hate could be. "Close enough. And if you mention anything about this to your mother, I'll strangle you."

The boy nodded.

Close enough, Ben thought. *Only thing was, son, you got the sequence reversed. I was already 'dead' when I met your mother, so I couldn't marry her whether I wanted to or not. The man she thought she loved didn't exist.*

ten

—⁕—

ALICE WAS PLAYING her Piaf CDs again. That was a bad sign. Kate glanced down from her scaffolding on the highest gable of the old house. Alice was just standing there, a foreshortened figure in an oversized man's dress shirt and faded jeans, staring glumly at a stunted juniper in a stoneware pot. Kate shook her head and went back to chipping dead mortar off the chimney stones.

You could judge Alice's mood by the music she chose. Loreena McKennitt and Tori Amos helped settle her mind for witching; J. S. Bach at the keyboard meant she was trying to disconnect from a long day in the ER; Cream or Hendrix were for manic laughter and cartwheels across the lawn. She had a sound system Jackie would kill for, speakers about the size of a small truck and an amplifier that required the electric co-op to kick in a standby generator. Crank up the volume and she could shatter windows clear across the bay.

When Alice pulled out the Little Sparrow and started whispering to herself in French, Kate knew she was seriously depressed. This morning she was repotting a bonsai to the background of *"Non, Je Ne Regrette Rien"*—about as bad as it could get.

Kate picked up a stone, checked the number she'd scrawled in pencil on the backside when she'd chiseled it loose from the chimney, and verified the location on her detail photo. This job was finicky, historic preservation, putting each piece back where she'd found it. When she finished rebuilding the chimney, she intended it to look *exactly* the same as when Abigail Haskell first set the stones over two hundred years ago.

Same materials, too. The lime mortar had a consistency all its own, greasier than Portland cement. Kate set the stone, worked it into its bed, and tapped it down with the heel of her trowel to drive out any air and seal the bond. She checked against the photo again, gauging the mortar line and fit against the adjacent stones. This chimney was going to be here for a while; she might as well take the time to get it right.

She paused for a moment, resting the ache in her left arm, and gazed out at the bay. Pretty as hell. Deceptive as hell. Just this morning, it had swallowed Maria Morgan and spat back a drowned corpse. No mystery hung over that one—suicide. Kate shook her head and turned back to studying stonework.

Maine winters took their toll. Water trickled into any crack, even soaked into the face of the rock if you made the mistake of using sandstone. Water crept in wherever it could, froze and thawed, split the bond of the mortar joints or the rock itself, levered chunks out of the chimney, set them teetering loose for wind or gravity to snatch and dump down through the attic into your lap while you sat eating supper. Kate tooled the joint to drain, to shed water, guide it down to the lead flashing and onto the slates of the steep roof.

She flexed her arm again, measuring the pain against remembered hurts. It barely made the scale. The *mental* pain, though, ranked up next to the crash, or falling off a roof.

Jackie. Motherhood. Where the hell did I go wrong?

Kate shook her head. She didn't want to think about that. Sure didn't want to *talk* about it. Back to stone—she understood stone. Two more to go. These were the long capstones, the full width of the sides and at least a hundred pounds each, flat tops and dished bottoms to settle in with a locking wedge that the sea wind couldn't nibble loose. Glacial rocks these were, gray chunks of the Canadian Shield hauled down to the Maine coast during the last ice age.

Kate muscled each into its own bed, making sure she relied on gravity to hold the masonry rather than the glue of the mortar. Mortar only sealed the work. The stone had to stand on its own, or time would tear it down.

She finished the chimney with a mortar wash across the top, thick enough to hold together and beveled to shed water so it couldn't pool and seek the cracks that would form with summer sun and winter ice. Lime mortar healed itself that way, water leaching lime from each side to flow and seal the cracks, just like building stalactites in a cave. She'd mixed the mortar for the top courses a little rich for that reason, an extra measure of the burned seashell powder slaked with water from the cellar spring.

Kate stepped back to the edge of her scaffolding, tilted her head, and compared the chimney with her photos. She climbed around, carefully, all four sides—identical to the pictures. Only then did she allow herself to sit, and think, and admire the view.

The house sat in the heart of Stonefort, the focus of the rounded hills and ever-changing bay. Alice nattered on about *feng shui*; Kate saw it more as organic growth. The house, the deep indigo of the bay with whitecaps showing in the morning breeze, the fresh spring greens of the hills—

there was no way they could be other than they were. God had built the house when She sculpted the land.

Every time Kate worked on this house, it tried to seduce her. Each project was a lesson, each part was the way it *had* to be. It wouldn't permit her to make a mistake, use a wrong technique or material.

So much for mysticism. Kate shrugged, loaded her tools into a white plastic bucket, checked the knot on the rope, and lowered them to the ground. The leftover mortar followed in another bucket. Cleanup time. Once again, she flexed her left arm, judging the constant ache against her memory. She hadn't stressed the stitches.

She backed her way slowly down the ladder, checking slates and flashing as she went. Keep an eye on a slate roof and it would last forever.

Down in the side yard, Alice was still torturing her bonsai, still listening to Piaf's whiskey-voiced ballads about faded love and the Paris street-people. Kate walked the ladder away from the eave and laid it down carefully. "Okay, Lys, that's done. I'll leave the scaffolding up until I come back for the acid wash. Give the mortar a chance to cure for a couple of weeks before I clean off the slop. Good weather for it, cool and damp."

Her only answer was a grunt. She glanced over at Alice, saw the small woman studying bare roots and snipping here, snipping there. A redwood box waited, lined with green copper, half filled with dirt and surrounded by selected rocks and clumps of moss. Alice was building a new setting for a tiny tree older than she was—some of her bonsai were well past the century mark.

Kate shook her head, concentrating on rinsing the last traces of mortar from her trowels and pointing tools. She glanced up at Alice. "You know, watching you do that gives me the willies. I see you persecuting those poor plants and wonder how they ever trusted you with a nursing license."

"Huh?"

"For a healer, you sure can be sadistic."

Alice shrugged and brushed potting soil from her hands, the job done. "That's part of medicine. Sticking needles in people, forcing them to strip naked in front of strangers, feeding them measured doses of poison—you don't want to even *think* about tracheotomies."

Kate went back to washing tools and buckets. She thinned the leftover mortar into a soup of lime and sand, then dumped it on a patch of garden dirt that Alice had said was too acid. Everything worked together. Too bad the rest of the town couldn't say the same.

"I'm just glad you didn't try pruning *my* roots to keep me small. You're like that Procrustes guy in Greek myth, cut people's legs down until they fit his bed. No thanks."

Alice shrugged off Kate's attempt at a joke. "Speaking of cuts, you going to let me take another look at that arm?" She rinsed her hands with the hose, then shut off the water. Kate grimaced and rolled up her left sleeve, revealing white gauze from just above her wrist to just below the elbow.

"*Some* people have enough sense to rest a day-old wound." Alice picked up the same surgical tools she'd just been using to snip juniper roots and delicately cut the bandage off Kate's arm. Peeling back the gauze revealed a slash about four inches long, neatly stitched, with the yellow of iodine mixing into the bruising of trauma. One stitch showed the red of fresh bleeding, but Alice nodded faint satisfaction.

"You'll live." She rinsed and dried her hands again, pulled a pack of sterile gloves out of her bag, and rolled them on through the peculiar gymnastics that never touched the outside surface with unclean fingers. Deft hands patted fresh antiseptic along the wound, ripped open sterile pads, and wrapped a new bandage into place. "You check your shot records like a good girl?"

"Yeah, tetanus booster just last year. The knife was clean, anyway."

"Ain't no such animal," said the nurse who had just been using her EMT bandage scissors for garden work. "Still wish you'd taken that to the ER or walk-in clinic rather than bringing it to me. Get me in trouble, playing doctor without the proper sheepskin."

"You know they've got rules about knife and gunshot wounds. I'd just as soon not write this up."

"Well, she's your daughter. Just remember, my malpractice insurance doesn't cover this."

The CD player swung a new round of French melancholy into position and started playing. Kate wrinkled her nose. "Hey, what's bugging you, anyway? Whole damn morning, you've been looking like a candidate for a suicide watch."

Alice tossed used bandages and gloves into her burn pile. "Look, I've had four patients die on me in the last week, and your daughter tries to gut you with a switchblade. I think I've got a right to be depressed!"

"I *told* you, she wasn't trying to hurt me. I just got careless taking the knife away from her."

"Bull. Kid carries a switchblade in her backpack, I'd question her motivation. You ready to talk about it?"

"No." Kate didn't want to even *think* about it, but the Haskell Witch had special rights.

"Okay, maybe." Kate shook her head and settled her bulk onto a garden bench. The bench complained, and then didn't even notice when Alice perched lightly on the other end.

"She's taking English again, summer school, making up that failed class. She *still* isn't working at it. She said something, I said something, we started yelling at each other. *You* know."

Alice made a noncommittal noise, nodding for her to go on.

"I grabbed her backpack from where she'd dumped it, going to pull her books out and wave them at her, throw them at her, something. I dunno. She screamed at me, snatched it back. Next thing I knew she had this knife in her hand. After I'd gotten it away from her and broke the blade off, she noticed the blood and turned white as a sheet. She didn't mean to do it."

"Yeah. And Dixie didn't mean to kill that chipmunk she left on my pillow this morning. Just sorta happened. You seen the kid since?"

"No. I think she skedaddled over to Lew's, looking for a bomb shelter. Another day or so, I *might* not bust her head before I say 'Hello.' Yesterday, I was too pissed to even call and check on her."

"Quick question: Did she take the backpack with her?"

"Yeah."

"Shame. I'd like to sneak a look inside. I've got a nasty suspicion that knife wasn't all she wanted to hide from you."

Kate closed her eyes and sighed, sagging against the bench. "I try to avoid thinking about that. You're probably right."

"You want the name of a good treatment center or a shrink?"

"Can't afford it." Kate slammed her left fist on her leg, then groaned as the pain slashed up from her forearm. "Dammit, Lys, it's all my fault, anyway. Lew got fired for showing up drunk at work, we got divorced, I spent ten, fifteen hours a day working to meet payments on the trailer and keep us fed. Never had any time for her. If I'd moved in here like you offered, she wouldn't have had a ghost for a mommy."

"Bull. That kid tried to kill you before she was born. Been a downhill slide ever since."

Kate trembled on the edge of losing it. She'd been holding it in, being strong. She'd played that role for too many
years to give it up and throw hysterics. "Lys, what am I going to *do*?"

Alice made a face. "Change the locks on your doors and
send a note to Juvenile."

"Can't do it. You've never been a mother."

"Don't think I missed much, judging by what I see
around town. Cancel that. Caroline always was a good kid."

Caroline was Alice's niece, twenty, likely the smartest
kid ever graduated from Stonefort schools, and the next designated Haskell Witch. The contrast with Jackie couldn't
be worse. Kate grabbed hold of her emotions with both
hands. If she didn't change the subject damned fast, she was
going to be all over the place and Alice would have another
patient for the funny farm.

"Hey, patients . . . you said you'd lost four *patients* this
week. What gives? I haven't heard anything."

"Charlie Sickles and his family. Maria Morgan."

Kate grimaced, reminded of Charlie. She was going to
miss the old fart. Not that he'd ever earned his pay, but he'd
been so *real*. He'd been an anchor and a touchstone, reminding her that Larry Beech and his type were empty shells.
Charlie *was* Sunrise County. Or had been.

"Patients? Every single one of them was dead before you
pulled up in the meat wagon! Saw the M.E. report on Charlie and the others yesterday, straightforward, natural causes.
Maria went and drowned herself, jumped off that damned
point at high tide in her nightgown. You gonna take the
blame for *that*?"

"I knew people were going to die, Kate. I tried to protect
them. I tried to protect *you*. It didn't work."

And suddenly tears glistened on Alice's cheek. Kate felt
like the earth had cracked open at her feet—Alice was invin-
cible; she had a core of case-hardened steel. She *couldn't* cry.

"How the hell can you protect a three-pack-a-day smoker from dying of emphysema? And God appointed you guardian to a whacked-out Italian widow who wanted to join her husband in the Big Sleep?"

Alice shook her head. "Maria wasn't a widow, and she knew it. She had no reason to kill herself. There's evil walking around this village, Kate. I feel it, but I can't see it. I'm trying to fight it, and I'm losing. People are *dying*!"

Kate made a soothing mommy-gesture, and suddenly Alice was in her arms, in her lap, just like Jackie at age seven with a skinned knee, crying on her shoulder. Alice was still small enough to fit. Kate smoothed her friend's hair, rubbed the back of her neck, made soothing noises, hugged her. That's what mothers did.

The sobs stretched on, softened, quieted to a slow murmur—Alice whispering something she didn't want the world to hear. Kate felt the tears soaking hot through her work shirt. She bent down and kissed her friend on the top of her head, just like she was a child. Alice's hair smelled like fresh hay with a touch of lilac.

Kate kissed her again, on the ear, and then on the side of her neck against the pulse. Suddenly, she was *very* aware that the body pressed against her was no child and it had been a *long* time since she'd shared a bed with anyone. Alice lifted her head from Kate's shoulder, inched back far enough to study her friend's eyes, and blinked.

"You serious?"

Kate paused for a moment, then answered by pulling Alice into a long kiss that melted the pain out of her arm. Damn, she tasted good. Twenty years of caution vanished downwind. Small hands roved over Kate's body, gentle but insistent. She trapped one and pressed it against herself.

A timer started beeping from the kitchen window. Kate winced at the sound, then remembered Alice setting it before she started work on the bonsai. The small woman pulled back, cussed, and then wrapped her arms around Kate even more fiercely than before.

The beeping rose about ten decibels in level, and Alice broke their clench. She climbed down from Kate's lap, breathing hard, her dusky face flushed.

"If I was even five years younger, I'd toss that damned thing in the bay, haul you inside, and lock the doors. I must be getting old." She elevated both her middle fingers to the sky in a gesture of defiance.

"You know, sometimes I think God really *does* hate queers. I finally reach the moment I've been dreaming of for twenty years, and I've got a client due in ten minutes. Can I take a rain-check on this?"

Kate couldn't trust herself to speak. She nodded, reluctantly, smoothing down her hair and catching up on oxygen. She'd better leave: Whether or not she believed in witchcraft, they sure as hell didn't need an audience.

At least she didn't have to worry about lipstick on her collar. Neither of them ever used the stuff. She checked to make sure all her clothing was in place. She filled the plastic buckets with her tools, took two steps toward her truck, and turned back. Alice was standing in the door, a brown waif with smoldering eyes. Somehow her shirt had come undone, and the bra under it.

" '*C'est l'amour,*' " Kate quoted from the Piaf album still playing.

"Tell me about it."

"Don't let me go back to being stupid, okay?"

"Not a chance."

Kate concentrated on turning off the fire under her boiling hormones. She loaded her tools in the back of the truck. Climbing into the cab, she ran her fingers through her short hair again and checked the mirror for any traces of passion other than her flushed cheeks. She pulled out a pack of cigarettes and lit one, taking a long drag and savoring the smoke. Did that tradition hold for lesbians, too, a cigarette after sex?

She turned the key in the ignition and listened to the starter whine uselessly. Just a little something to bring her back to earth? She slipped the brake so the truck could roll a couple of feet and rotate the flywheel. The starter worked, this time, the pinion catching the ring gear once the chipped teeth were past, and the old junker coughed to life.

She flipped a mental coin: head over to Lew's and see if she could catch Jackie by surprise, or go straight home and hope the silly kid had finally gotten brave enough to show her face. This time, Kate promised herself, she'd keep her temper lashed down tight if it took half-inch steel cables.

Home, she decided. Get rid of some work-sweat, some splashed mortar, Alice's tears, and the little smells of her aborted entry into the world of the sexually ambivalent. If Jackie hadn't come home, and the twit wasn't at Lew's either, and he was sober, Kate just might end up staying awhile. She had some residual urges she needed to work off.

She didn't think that was infidelity. Alice knew she still liked men. It wasn't as if they'd said vows or anything.

And then she heard Alice's voice again, whispering clearly in the back of her brain. "Maria wasn't a widow, and she knew it. She had no reason to kill herself."

What the hell was *that* supposed to mean?

eleven

—⟋⟍—

BEN MORGAN PULLED a John Deere hat down on his brow and looked away from the road, turning slightly sideways in his pickup cab as if reading something on the seat beside him. He carefully avoided eye contact with the driver of that old Dodge stake-bed. "The wicked flee where no man pursueth," he quoted to himself.

No reason to suspect Ms. Town Constable Rowley would recognize him after all these years. Even if he *had* played basketball against her one-on-one in driveway games. And lost.

Still, he was nervous. He'd rather volunteer for a root canal without novocaine than face the current Haskell Witch. He'd brought along a sweetener that *might* blunt her tongue.

Alice always had been too damn smart. She didn't have to be so hard-edged about it, though. Lainie had been just as smart or smarter, but she hadn't felt the need to prove it all the time. Maybe that was one difference between straight and lesbian. Lainie and Lys, Elaine and Alice, an alliterative study in contrast.

He pulled into the driveway next to the old Haskell place, grateful that tall hedges screened the side and rear of the house and whatever heathen rites and goings-on that the witches wanted to hide. The rusty GMC pickup was about as anonymous a vehicle as you'd find in Sunrise County, one of a few thousand clones gradually discarding bits of themselves on the roads and trying to evade the state inspection, but he still didn't want to park it anywhere noticeable. That had been the story of his life for twenty years—keep a low profile.

He picked up a shoebox from the seat next to him and automatically headed for the side door, following generations of feet. Front doors had always been ceremonial doors in Maine, only used for weddings and funerals. Some of them hadn't been opened in a hundred years. Daily life came and went by the kitchen. Even cats knew that. A long-haired black and white specimen appeared from nowhere, ignored him, and stared at the door. He shrugged and knocked.

The old door opened, and the cat sauntered herself inside with the air of the undisputed owner. Ben was left facing the small dark-haired woman on his own.

She stood in the doorway with her hands on her hips, looked him up and down with a critical eye, and shook her head. "Laws a mercy, Miz Scarlett. Look what the cat done drug in. If it ain't God's gift to Sunrise County women." She stepped back from the door and waved him in.

Ben obeyed. He'd *hoped* Alice wouldn't recognize him, but that had been a feeble chance at best.

She tilted her head sideways, studying his face, and then pointed toward a couple of Eames chairs in the parlor, elegant pieces of modern sculptured leather and wood that still seemed to fit the ancient house. So did the music she had playing softly in the background, something vaguely Celtic with an insistent beat.

Mischief twitched her lips. "You want something to settle your nerves? I remember Lainie said you were partial to rum in various disguises."

"Yeah. You got anything resembling a daiquiri?"

"I think the bar can handle that."

She paused on her way to the kitchen, pulled a blued-steel pistol out of the back pocket of her jeans, clicked the safety on, and tossed it casually on a leather ottoman that matched the chairs. Ben twitched at the sight. Reflex identified the gun as a Walther TPH automatic, a miniature of James Bond's famous PPK, only a .22 long rifle cartridge but deadly at close range.

Ben hated guns and studied them only out of self-defense. After all, people kept them as a protection against thieves.

Alice noticed his reaction. "Hey, you called, you gave me a name I didn't recognize, and the old verbal stress-meter said you were lying. What's the point of being a witch if you can't live to a ripe old age and frighten the kids at Halloween?"

She vanished into the kitchen, leaving him to wonder about the ways of witches and bitches. He took a deep breath to calm himself, the herb-smells of the kitchen blending with old wood and beeswax to waken memories of visits long ago. His mother would bring over a couple of lobsters or a loaf of home-baked bread; "Aunt" Jean would swap them for a jar of honey or a bag of apples from the orchard out back. Then the women would sit and gossip for half the morning while Dan and Ben got into mischief in the ancient place.

It still felt the same, even though Aunt Jean was dead ten or fifteen years. The house didn't change. *Alice* must have changed a bit, to fit in so smoothly. After a few quiet clinks and gurgles, she returned and handed him a cold glass. He traded the shoebox for it. "That's your fee, whether you can help or not. It needs to go home."

She set herself in a chair and the box in her lap, lifted the lid, and pulled out wadded tissue paper. He saw the faded yellow of corn shucks, and then she hastily repacked and covered the box and whisked it away into the older part of the house. He sipped the daiquiri. It tasted wonderful.

She came back, shaking her head. "Where'd you get that?"

"Private collection. It wasn't the item we went for, but it didn't belong there."

"Uh-uh. I know some people who will be very glad to have her back where she belongs. Thank you for keeping her covered." She settled down in the other chair again, the one next to the ottoman with the gun on it.

He nodded. "So, it's genuine?"

"Oh, yes. Not one of the tourist replicas. Couldn't you feel her power?"

Ben relaxed a notch. "I don't know about power. That's your territory, not mine. I just felt it wanting to come here."

She sat quietly, studying him. "Well, you going to talk about it?"

Ben stared at the drink in his hand. He found it hard to start. These were secret things, ancient things, crazy things, and the Alice he remembered had a very low bullshit threshold. Besides, he was afraid of her. He looked up, straight into a sardonic smile.

She shook her head. "Look, I interrupted some serious business for you. Shit or get off the pot."

He had to chuckle at that. "Yeah. I saw her leaving." He still couldn't find a place to start on this tangled thread. There were things he wanted to keep out of it.

She started drumming quietly on the side of her chair, matching the quiet music, and then chanting with the beat.

THIS I TELL YOU.
THE SEA PEOPLE CAME ON THE SOUTH WIND,
THE WARM WIND,
THE SEA PEOPLE CAME IN THEIR GREAT
SWAN CANOES.
THE SEA PEOPLE CAME IN THEIR GREAT
SWAN CANOES,
THE SEA PEOPLE CAME FROM THE LAND OF
THE DAWN.
THE SEA PEOPLE BROUGHT THE BRIGHT EGG
OF THE DAWN,
THE EGG OF THE DAWN IN THEIR GREAT
SWAN CANOES.
THUS IT IS SAID, FROM MOTHER TO MOTHER,
THUS IT IS SAID SINCE THE DAY OF THE
DAWN."

South wind? Oh, yeah. You had to go around Nova Scotia and turn north. Simple geography, but Ben had always visualized his people sailing into the bay out of the rising sun.

She broke off. "Your family keeps records scribbled on parchment. Mine has a verbal history. That sounds a hell of a lot more impressive in Naskeag, and it scans better, too. I doubt if you're prepared to listen to twenty or thirty hours of it, though.

"I think you'll find it easier to talk if you realize that I already know the weird parts. That's what witches *do,* you know. It's our job description. Your family and mine have been intertwined for nearly a thousand years. You're probably more'n half Naskeag yourself. Ever try to grow a beard?"

Ben rubbed his chin, ruefully. He could get by with shaving twice a week, but he'd never thought about what that meant. Sixty, eighty Welsh men and women, even twice that, alone in a wild land far from Europe? That gene pool wouldn't last long, wouldn't stay pure in the five hundred years between landing and the coming of the English. Trading and fishing voyages couldn't tip the balance much.

She grinned. "Works both ways. The Naskeag language is probably about as much Welsh as Abenaki. Nobody's noticed because nobody has been crazy enough to look."

So he started talking, and for the first time Ben could remember, Alice Haskell actually kept her mouth shut. He tried to tell things in some kind of order, but he kept skipping back and forward with connections and she either nodded politely to show she followed him, or raised her eyebrows in silent question when she didn't. Most of all, she *listened,* and he remembered that his image of Alice Haskell was more than twenty years old, an image of a rebellious hellion of a younger sister always jealous of Lainie's interest in men.

His thoughts ran in parallel with the story, wondering what changes old apple-dumpling Aunt Jean had worked on this woman seated across the room. He could almost see the old witch as a ghost image around Alice, the soft round woman with thinning white hair and deep-seamed mahogany face a quiet presence that had both awed and comforted him from his earliest memories. The power of Stonefort sat here, in this room, in this house. It always had. Now the power listened, and he found he no longer feared it.

Finally he ran out of words, and looked plaintively at the bottom of his glass. Alice took it, made clinking noises in the kitchen, and returned it full. While she was gone, he checked his watch and was surprised to see that he'd lost an hour somewhere in the telling.

She sat quietly for a few minutes, weighing his story, her eyes focused on the far side of the kitchen wall. Then she came back, and he felt as if her gaze pinned him to the chair. "So Daniel warned you. What went wrong? What happened with Maria?"

A woman had died. *That* was the important part. Daniel

and Gary were secondary. He remembered where he was sitting. The Haskell house was a *woman's* house, a woman's fortress.

He shook his head. "We've got alarms, I was out all night prowling the grounds, there's other stuff I'm not going to tell you about unless you've got that famous 'need to know.' She was fine last night. This morning we found her floating off the point. I guess this *brujo* that Dan told me about is for real."

"How are Gary and the girls taking it?"

"Rough. Gary knows Dan is still alive, and he knows we're in a fight. He's not too bad. Ellen and Peggy are still in shock."

"Okay. Item one, we get the girls over here. You can take care of young master Gary however you want, but Ellen and Margaret sleep in this house, stay on these grounds. I'll follow you over there and bring them back myself. I don't care what you tell them. Nobody has ever harmed a woman in this house. Nobody ever will."

Her tone sent icicles down Ben's back. The room seemed darker and colder, suddenly, and the doors and cupboards were watching him with unfriendly eyes. He remembered legends of the Haskell Women. He sipped the fresh drink in his hand and wondered if there was a slight bitterness that he hadn't noticed in the other one.

"Um . . . Ellen's twelve. Peggy is eight. Are you sure it's a good idea for them to live in this house?"

She glared at him, glared at the thought hidden under his question. "You know, if I wasn't a *particularly* softhearted and forgiving type of witch, you'd be hopping around in the grass and going '*gribbit*' right about now. There's a hell of a big difference between a queer and a pedophile."

She took a couple of deep breaths as if she was counting to ten in Naskeag. "If they're straight, they'll stay straight. If one of them turns out bent, don't blame me or the house. I don't run classes in beginning and advanced lesbianism."

She paused again, and a speculative look flitted across her face. "I *might* teach them to be witches, though. Is that better or worse?"

Ben kept his mouth shut. Anything he said at this point would only get him in deeper.

"Item two," she went on, "is Daniel tough enough to last it out? It's awful damn noble to say we can't let this Evil Sorcerer get his hands on your Dragon. Oh, yeah, there are lots of bad things he could do with it, starting with world domination and the destruction of modern civilization. Problem is, that doesn't weigh too heavy when you balance it against the safety of your children."

Ben sat and thought about it. "Dan sounded really rocky when I told him about Maria. Not that their marriage was close. But I think he'd *give* this Peruvian spook the Dragon if it wasn't so damn obvious that he knows more about it than we do. What Dan'd try to do, he'd try to set up some kind of trick or trap. Now he doesn't think that would work and he's desperate. I'm not sure what he plans to do."

"Ugh. You tell Daniel Lewellyn ap Morgan something for me. I'll cut off his balls, mince them fine, and fry them in fish oil for Dixie's dinner if he dares to give that Dragon's Egg to his frigging *brujo.* The bastard gets that kind of power, we'll *all* be gone to shit."

Now *that* was the Alice Haskell he knew and loved. "What about Gary and the selkie change?"

"Sorry, we don't do skin-changers—that's not a Haskell thing. We like ourselves the shape we are. There's a guy I know up near Katahdin. His family's into that scene. I'll send him an e-mail, see if he has any suggestions."

"Huh? You're talking as if this was vanilla stuff, post a question on the Internet about how to set the timing on a '72 Chevy truck."

"Believe me, Greg knows the selkie change is possible. He's a werewolf. Not the fantasy novel kind—he's a totemic shaman shape-changer, becomes a silver wolf when he wants to. It's something his family has done for generations—learned it from some cousins of ours."

Ben just sat there, his jaw down somewhere around his chest. For an instant, he wondered if Alice was pulling his leg. That was the kind of thing she'd do, the Alice he remembered from twenty years ago. Then he read her face again and decided she was dead serious.

"You've got a whole computer *network* for this crazy shit?"

She threw back her head and laughed. "Man, there's *always* been an underground, shamans and witches and such. Somebody knows somebody else with the Craft, with the Blood, with a voice from the oracle or the house snake or the spirit drum. With the Internet, I can toss a question out and get parallels and suggestions from frigging Siberia, from the Outback, from Kalahari Bushman witch doctors.

"Thing is, it's private. It's still underground, organized into cells like a terrorist conspiracy. I know Greg. Aunt Jean knew his father and his grandfather. He's genuine, vouched-for, got a pedigree. Anybody *he* asks will have the same credentials. And everything is encrypted against snoops. Your secret is safe."

Ben felt light-headed, either from the daiquiris or the swirling changes she threw at him. Things he'd thought were deepest, darkest secrets seemed to be common gossip in the village. Things like . . .

"You didn't seem surprised that I was alive, that Dan was alive, just that I came to ask for your help. I mean, after all the history between us."

"I told you, we've watched your tribe for centuries. Witches see things. There's a way Morgans behave for a real death, and a different way they act when one of you needs to vanish. Don't panic—only people with good eyes and long memories could ever put two and two together and come up with five Morgans instead of four."

"Lainie knows? How's she doing?"

"*Elaine* is doing fine." Her emphasis made it clear she didn't think he had any further rights to the familiar form. "She knows. Got herself a husband, a *reliable* man you never met, and more children than I can keep track of." She paused, as if calculating something. "Caroline is doing fine, too."

Ben racked his brain, but he couldn't remember a girl-friend named Caroline. His blank face must have been a dead giveaway, because Alice nodded with a wry smile.

"Your daughter."

Ben felt as if she'd picked up that damned pistol and shot him in the gut. The Dragon had made her decision, and he'd had to disappear. That had left a number of things hanging in midair. Elaine had been one of them.

"I never knew. If you'd told Dan . . ."

"Humpf. Yeah, you Morgans have a *real* attractive way of dealing with that sort of thing. No thanks. We've never made a habit of naming the father of a Haskell child. Caroline's a Haskell, not a Morgan. We take care of our own."

"Look, if I can pay for school or something . . ."

Alice choked back a snort of laughter. "She's got a full scholarship out in Arizona, studying anthro, working on her doctorate before she can get past the bouncer at a bar. For her Ph.D., she's doing fieldwork in the pueblos, trying to trace the woman's side of the mystical tradition back to the Anasazi. Maybe she can pick up some secrets from the women's kivas before she settles down here. She's my heir."

Ben blinked, trying to shake off three fast jabs to the chin. First she told him he had a daughter he never knew, then this daughter was some kind of genius, *then* this un-known addition to the Morgan family was the next Haskell Witch. He was glad he was sitting down.

She watched him work through all that, then nodded. "You want to pay something to soothe your conscience, pay forward. Send some of your ill-gotten gains up to the rape crisis center in Naskeag Falls, or the Domestic Violence Project. Sell off a few of those Mimbres pots you nabbed to build a homeless shelter. Whatever will help you sleep at night."

Damn. This woman knew *far* too much about Morgan family business. But then, as Alice had just pointed out, Elaine and . . . Caroline . . . weren't the first mixing of Welsh and Naskeag blood.

Alice nodded as if reading his mind. "You guys want a place on the tribal register? Gets you all sorts of preference on government contracts, you know—a minority-owned business is clear points ahead on a competitive bid. Then you guys could subcontract for the CIA."

She paused, and a distant expression crossed her face as if she was listening to something far away. Then she came back from wherever it was, and Ben saw the old wicked Alice-gleam in her eyes.

"You know, Romeo, Caroline has the same percentage of Morgan blood that Gary has. I think you need to meet your instant daughter. I think your *Dragon* needs to meet your daughter."

Ben swallowed. He knew what kind of response his words would trigger, but he had to say them. "The Dragon only works with men."

"Well, now," she drawled. "Ain't that a shame. Ain't that a frigging Medieval *shame.*"

twelve

—⚉—

"AUNT ALICE, ARE you *really* a witch?"

Alice studied the child sitting across the table from her. At eight, Peggy's beanpole figure was still essentially neuter, a scrawny stick topped by perpetually tangled short dark hair and a fair and freckled face. Her older sister took off in the other direction, olive skin and shoulder-length hair just a shade darker than honey blond, on a body that was starting to develop curves. With their mixed ancestry, appearance was sort of random chance. They both showed promise of being really cute, though.

"Well, perhaps I'd better find out just what you think a witch *is* before I admit to being one or not." She pushed the basket of fresh-baked whole-wheat rolls over to Ellen. The twelve-year-old had been eyeing them, and a belly full of good food was well known for easing grief. "Let's do a little Socratic dialog here. I'll ask you some questions while you work on that chicken, you'll answer them, and we'll find out whether I'm a witch or not. And don't talk with your mouth full."

Aunt Jean had taught her to *never* dumb her language down for kids. These two were a bit of a surprise, anyway. She'd ask them to choose the music for dinner, and they'd put their heads together and ended up with Gregorian chants. Ellen had said she thought they were "way cool."

Alice scooped up a forkful of homegrown peas and let the monks fill the silence at the table. She found it amusing that Peggy was asking the questions, but Ellen seemed to be more annoyed by having to wait for answers. They were a little young to have worked out tag-team interrogation already. So far, moving the girls to a new and exciting place— the *witch's* house—seemed to be helping them.

She swallowed. "So. What makes you think I might be a witch?"

"Oh, *everybody* says you are." Peggy made a very superior eight-year-old wave of dismissal. It was *obvious*.

"Everybody says. Let's see now." Alice turned to Ellen— it was time to make her join in on this. "You call me 'Aunt Alice.' Am I your aunt?"

The older girl started to speak, caught herself, swallowed, and followed the piece of buttered roll with some milk before answering. "No. We just call you that. It's, like, being polite."

"So putting a label on someone doesn't mean that label is true?"

Both girls nodded, their mouths busy again. Alice shook her head, mentally, ruefully. If she only could get *that* message nailed down and glued in place on a global scale . . .

"Next question: What is a witch?"

Alice figured *that* one would be good for a few slices of honey-glazed chicken. She'd made the girls do most of the cooking, just supervising, and had made the menu decently complicated to force them to think of what they were doing rather than what was being done to them. Ellen had turned out to have definite potential with spices—just *precisely* enough ginger in the glaze—while Peggy thought knead-ing the rolls was more fun than Play-Doh. More squishy, and they smelled better.

They all chewed for a while. Finally Ellen put down her fork. "Well, there's, like, this girl in school who *calls* herself a witch . . ."

"Who?"

"Andrea Messer."

Ah. Leah Messer's kid. "And what does she do to be a witch?"

"She's always wearing like these long black dresses and a black beret and *way* too much makeup and *reaalllly* strange jewelry. Like, crystals and crescent moons and five-pointed stars? She sits in the shadows and, like, stares at people?"

Well, anybody who'd use scented candles for a ritual *would* have a child like that. And as for skyclad dances under the full moon, well, whatever turns you on. As far as Alice was concerned, that didn't work in Maine—you'd either freeze your butt off or get eaten alive by bugs.

"Any evidence of witchery?"

"Well, like, she weirds everybody out, you know. There's this *thing* in the corner, like, it's *staring* at you. Creepy."

"No pimple-faced boys turned into frogs? No poisoned apples for the fairest in the land?"

Ellen giggled and shook her head. Alice looked over at Peggy. "How about you, Margaret Morgan. What's your definition of a witch?"

"Somebody who cooks up potions in a big iron pot and flies around on a broomstick and tricks children into eating gingerbread houses?"

"Well, you helped sweep all those dead flies out of the old parlor so you could sleep there. Did that broom show any evidence of aeronautical experience? Any FAA registra-tion numbers or radar transponders?"

"No."

"You girls have known me since forever. Have you *ever* seen me wearing black?"

"No."

"You cooked dinner. Did I show any tendency to shove either one of you into the oven?"

Now *Peggy* giggled, exactly like her older sister, quietly, with a hand over her mouth and shoulders quivering. She shook her head.

"Well," Alice went on, lowering her eyebrows in a sinister fashion, "I *had* been thinking of baking gingerbread tomorrow, with lemon sauce. Am I going to get a label slapped on my forehead?"

This was skirting the edge. Ben had said they both loved gingerbread, but Maria had used to bake it for them for a special treat. It could be comforting, or it could set off the waterworks.

Now the giggles were broadcast in stereo. Alice breathed a sigh of relief. She was still feeling her way along with these two, trying to get into their heads enough to help them.

Witchcraft, at least as the Haskell Women knew it, was nine parts practical psychology to one of magic. The earth magic, the spring's magic—that was real. However, it mainly defended, healed, and preserved. It was an inner magic, a female magic. She'd need something more masculine and aggressive to fight this little war Ben Morgan had dumped in her lap. Something like Kate's . . .

Meanwhile, the plates were empty, and nobody seemed to be looking around for more. Time for the next step on her program.

"Now you kids wash up. I've shown you where all the stuff goes, and I'll dock your pay if you break anything."

Ellen glanced at Peggy. "But you're not paying us *anything*."

"Be a shame to start out in the hole, wouldn't it?"

Alice lit an oil lamp and headed for the old part of the

house. The girls had thought it would be *cool* to sleep in the seventeenth century, with oil lamps and a fireplace for heat, surrounded by all the ghosts of Haskells past. Alice had kept her mouth shut about her reasons. She threaded her way through the halls and stairways into the oldest parlor, the room located right over the spring.

It waited, ready: futon mattresses on the floor, comforters, pillows, the neat piles of clothing they'd brought over from Morgan's Point, two threadbare teddy bears. She'd see what they thought about the seventeenth century after being stuck with chamber pots at night—and emptying them come morning.

Alice checked the shutters again, heavy oak planks inside and out, none of those newfangled slatted things that wouldn't stop a burglar or a bullet. They were barred on the inside, and the walls were also solid oak over a foot thick. This part of the house had been built like a fort, for good reason. There were still a couple of British cannonballs buried in the old logs, somewhere along the bay side and underneath the clapboards. Kate would know where to find them.

She knelt down on the hearth, struck a match to the kindling, and watched flames nibble their way into the maple and birch she'd laid there earlier. Murmuring an invocation in Naskeag, she scattered herbs over the growing fire. Sweetgrass first, that was purification. Rosemary followed, for the traditional remembrance, then sage and juniper and bloodroot to stand guard. Tobacco summoned the winds, to hide the children and bring them news.

Alice felt a brief chill, wondering if the kids were *really* strong enough for the summoning she planned. She stared at the flames for a few minutes, drawing calm from them and from her bond with the spring below her knees.

She glanced at her watch—almost ten. They'd eaten late because of the turmoil of moving. Even nearing the first day of summer, the sun had set. Time for tired kids to head for bed, with a little bedtime surprise.

Back through the centuries to the kitchen, Alice found Ellen standing in the middle of the floor, hugging Peggy. The smaller girl wept slowly, quietly, her face buried in her sister's shoulder. Ellen's face also shone with tears. She noticed Alice hesitating in the doorway.

"Your pot scrubber," the girl explained. "It's exactly like Mom's. Even worn the same way."

Damn and spit. She'd taken the chance with gingerbread and won, only to get tripped up by a two-buck scrubbing pad. Alice tiptoed her way into the room and a tentative three-way hug. Their body-language accepted her as a substitute mommy. Alice felt the House enfold them all, offering strength and solace. Gradually, tense muscles relaxed.

They separated. Peggy wiped her face with her sleeve and offered a red-eyed, rueful smile. "I think I want Barney Bear."

Alice glanced around. The children had finished washing and drying. The room was neater than *she* usually kept it, and they'd even folded the dishcloth and hung it right. If they'd done all that while crying, they were stronger than she thought.

Alice handed one lamp to Ellen and picked up another for herself. "Bedtime, girls." They didn't protest.

The fire had taken the chill off the room, with the fast-burning birch already settling into coals and the rock maple still holding firm. It made a perfect focus for dreaming, and Alice settled down on a cushion in front of it. The girls hesitated for a moment and then snuggled into a sandwich close and warm on either side. She slipped an arm around each and started chanting softly in Naskeag, speaking to the waters of the land.

The power of the spring rose around her, lifting the hair

on the back of her neck and forming goosebumps on her arms. She felt Ellen shiver, and then Peggy, so both of them had *some* sensitivity. Quick sideways glances showed that both were staring into the flames as if hypnotized.

Alice changed her chant, speaking to the winds, sending them searching. She formed an image of Daniel's face in her mind and placed it in the heart of the fire, building his features out of the purple and blue of the hottest flames against a background of red and orange. First Ellen gasped in shock, and then a minute or so later Peggy turned rigid and held her breath.

So Ellen truly had the power? Alice had suspected as much, but hadn't been sure. Maybe the "aunt" was more than just politeness.

The power flowed through her, into the image flickering in the fireplace. She needed more than sight. Chanting to the bones of the land, chanting to the rock, calling again on the waters of the earth to flow and channel and mingle their messages, she built ears.

Daniel's image noticed them, jerked with shock, and smiled tentatively. "Ellie? Mouse?"

Peggy twisted to bury her face in Alice's shoulder, nerve broken by the fire's whispery voice speaking her dad's pet name. Alice hugged her, rubbing gently on the back of the child's neck and flowing peace through the palm of her hand. Ellen just shook her head in stunned acceptance.

Alice forced herself to speak, knowing it could shatter her magic. "Daniel, can you tell us where you are?"

The image flickered, but then it firmed. She guessed he'd pulled strength from his Dragon to add to the power of the spring.

"I'm underground. I'm still on the island. Girls, trust Aunt Alice. Do *exactly* what she tells you to do. She'll keep you safe."

Alice felt the strain burning through her, as if another

power wrestled with hers. Daniel's face danced again and almost dissolved into mere flames. Peggy turned her head sideways, sneaking another peek at this impossible thing that was happening.

Daniel's face glanced to one side, as if he was being watched. "I love you, girls. I'll try to come back to you, but if I can't, remember that: I love you, and Mommy loved you. Trust Alice."

A log split in the fire, and the face vanished in sparks. Both girls jerked and slumped. Alice felt sweat trickling down her back and damp under her arms, and an odd coldness spread from her belly as if she'd swallowed ice.

Peggy burrowed into her arms, weeping softly again. Alice held her and wondered if she'd done the right thing. Children could be so fragile. Tears dampened her own cheeks, and she stared into the dying fire that was just a fire. The child quieted and gradually sagged into sleep.

A soft hand touched her arm. Alice broke out of her drowse and saw Ellen smiling sadly in the red glow of the coals.

The girl leaned forward and whispered, "You really *are* a witch, aren't you?"

"Yes, Ellen, I am."

"And that was magic?"

"Yes."

"Is Daddy alive? Gary said something and then slapped his hand over his mouth. I kinda guessed."

"Hush, love. Don't wake your sister. Yes, your father is alive. Don't tell Peggy yet."

Ellen's fingers bit into Alice's arm. "Did Mom and Dad have another fight?"

Oh, *God*! "No, this doesn't have anything to do with that. It isn't anything you children did, either. Your father is being held prisoner, and it hurts him terribly to be away from you. Now you keep this a deep dark witchy secret and help me get Peggy into bed."

Alice laid Peggy down on one of the makeshift beds, gently unwrapping thin arms from around her neck. She slid the screen across in front of the fire, checked the oil in one lamp, and turned its wick down to a nightlight glow before tucking it into a safe niche in the stone over the mantle.

Soft rustles behind her back spoke of clothes and sheets and young bodies. When she turned back, Ellen had already changed Peggy into ridiculous bunny pajamas without waking her and was just slipping into her own top. Alice snuggled a worn bear into Peggy's arms, smiling gently when she saw how the patterns of threadbare backing matched the child's clutch. The second battered friend already lay next to Ellen's pillow, outgrown comfort suddenly necessary once more.

Alice tucked sheets and comforters around both girls and kissed both gently on the forehead, murmuring a Naskeag blessing. She checked the shutters again.

"Aunt Alice?"

Alice turned back at the door.

Ellen offered her a wan half-smile. "Thanks. I love you."

Alice smiled her care back, pulled the door closed, and quietly set the latch. Now the spring could work more healing while they slept.

She'd told the girls to call her if they woke in the night, and they'd seemed to think she would listen through some ancient magic. Her real tactics were a little cruder. She planned to spend the night sleeping in front of their door, and anything that wanted to get at them would be coming through her first.

She left the second lamp sitting on the floor—she'd be running short of hands on the return trip. Threading back through the dark hallways by memory, she ducked into the newest part of the house and up the stairs into her own bedroom. What with one thing and another, she hadn't had a chance to gather the tools for this particular witching.

Poking through a storage space tucked in under the cape's steep roof, she collected a sleeping bag and Aunt Harriet's old pump shotgun, a trench gun from the Great War complete with bayonet lug. Her bedside table contributed a four-cell Mag-Lite flashlight guaranteed to blind a burglar at twenty paces.

She also picked up the Walther and tucked it into her hip pocket. Two spare magazines helped balance the load on the other side. Kate said to always carry a backup. Alice jacked the action of the shotgun open, fed birdshot shells into the long magazine and the chamber, and checked the safety. Birdshot would be deadlier than buckshot or slugs at the ranges found inside a house. She'd seen the results in the ER.

Downstairs, she checked the cookstove, the doors, and Dixie's water dish. Then she retreated through the centuries, latching and locking each door she passed and setting an oaken bar across the last and oldest one. The house had been built for a defense in depth.

Alice spread her sleeping bag on the floor and squirmed into it fully clothed, nose wrinkling at the musty smell from years of storage. She hadn't used it since Girl Scout days: good thing she hadn't grown an inch since then. She blew out the lamp and felt down along her side for the flashlight, checking it again. The light glowed orange through layers of fabric and stuffing. A quick touch verified the icy slick metal of the shotgun lying next to her.

Stars glittered through the small window at the end of the hall, dancing in the old warped glass when she moved her head, and an owl hooted down near the shore. A loon answered from out in the bay. Those were the only sounds that passed the walls, as if the house had transported her and the children centuries into the past.

Alone. She *needed* Kate for times like this, needed her strength and toughness. Alice shivered inside the sleeping bag, the fabric still cold against her skin.

She'd called in to the hospital and the ambulance squad: a family emergency, she had to go out of town. True enough, and they could juggle the rosters for a few days. After that, it was the girls or the job. She knew where that choice led. No matter how much she loved her job, she didn't have to work. That's what all that Haskell money was for.

She *did* have to serve.

Damn you, Kate, I need you here!

The loon called again. Alice wiped cold tears from her cheek.

The girls were so *young.*

thirteen

DANIEL STARED AT the blank section of stone. It had formed a misty hole like a whirlpool, shadowed, framing faces glowing as if in firelight: Alice, small and round-featured and dark, framed by Ellen and Peggy. He'd smelled smoke, sharp and fragrant of birch and herbs, and their images had wavered in a heat-mirage. He'd chosen his words carefully, with a thought to the monitor camera and probable microphones.

Now they were gone.

This wasn't speech forming in his head, the conversation with Ben or Gary through the Dragon's power. He had felt the difference. The Dragon was tight and hot and focused, while this other thing was cool and spread throughout the stone itself. When the *brujo* had sensed it, tried to grab it and twist it to his use, it had slipped through his fingers like water or the wind.

Daniel sat and stared at the wall. It stared back at him, coarse pink granite with the faint ripple of tool marks and scattered glints from embedded mica. It felt cold and rough under his hands, and the touch of it made him ache to run his fingers through the warm softness of Mouse's tangled curls. The sense-memory made his eyes sting for a moment. He shivered.

What was Alice doing? She always had at least three reasons for anything she did. Showing magic to the girls, that would be one of them. Get them used to the fact that strange things happened, that magic happened, that the funny woman who lived in the funny house they used to visit on autumn afternoons was a real, certified witch and could protect them.

Showing Ellen that her father was still alive, that could be a second reason. He could feel his daughters' reactions through the link. Poor little Mouse had just thought her eyes were playing tricks on her imagination, but Ellie *believed*.

But what other reasons did she have? To let him know his daughters were safe, were hidden in the Woman's House and beyond the reach of the *brujo*'s slimy touch? That couldn't be it. She must know that anything she showed Daniel, the *brujo* would find out. Alice was too devious to give away information so cheaply.

Women moved to the Haskell House as a last resort. It was the final break, the step that announced everything to the scandal-wagging tongues of small-town life. No woman ever went back to the violent husband, no child to the abusive parents, after she moved in with the Haskell Witch. They all moved on, not back. Was *that* Alice's message?

Daniel stood up and started pacing. He glanced at the videocamera, at the malevolent red glow of the little light under the lens. He hesitated by the electric heater, stooped down, and plugged it in. He squatted in front of the gray box, warming his hands, smelling the dry reek of dust baking off the glowing coils. Get the watchers used to certain actions; get them to ignore things that proved to be innocent, again and again. The first time he'd unplugged the heater, one of the guards had been inside the door within five seconds.

The heater made this humming noise, he'd explained. Even with the thermostat turned off, there was this humming whine. It annoyed him. He'd demonstrated, and the guard heard the whine, and nodded, and left Daniel with tacit permission to plug and unplug the unit whenever he damned well pleased.

After all, a grown man couldn't commit suicide by sticking his fingers into a wall outlet. He'd have to strip the wires bare and grab one lead in each hand to force the current through his chest. That took more time than he'd have, and even then a 110-volt household current probably wouldn't kill him.

No, Alice wasn't telling him he was an abusive father. Moving the girls to the House was a signal. Showing the girls to him was a signal. She wanted him to know how serious the problem was. That and her message through Ben, they said the same thing. Desperate times call for desperate measures.

The *brujo* must *not* get the Dragon.

There was another reason why children, girl children mostly, moved into the Haskell House. They were orphans.

People died. Stonefort people lived hard, working the woods and waters and rocky fields of a hard land. Down through the centuries, women died in childbed, men disappeared at sea, horses bolted and dragged farmers to their deaths. Children stayed behind, alone, helpless.

Stonefort had never had a town farm or an orphanage. The Woman took care of waifs and strays, found relatives or other families to take them in, supported them if necessary, guarded their lives and any property coming to them. People who took in a child from the Haskell Witch considered her offer a kind of blessing. Legend spoke of one family that had an orphan child taken back again: They left town, root and branch, after a year of shunning.

Daniel rubbed his hands in the warmth of the heater. The chill of the stone cell had settled in his belly, and the cold damp musty smell reminded him altogether too much of the family crypt. Alice's message had been for *him,* not just for the girls. She'd been reminding him that the world thought he was already dead.

He wrinkled his nose in disgust. He didn't like to think he was a coward. Of course, marriage to Maria was a form of cowardice. He'd done what had to be done, what the family needed. Not what he knew was right. And what had it gotten her? Wealth, yes, and a jump three levels up in the social register of Sunrise County. But Daniel agreed with the Bible: "Better is a dry morsel with quiet, than a house full of feasting with strife."

Well, she had peace now. Whatever Father Henderson might think, Maria's God knew her death wasn't suicide.

The door clicked behind his back, deadbolts drawn and latches turned. He'd expected it, expected the grumpy face of the Peruvian *brujo.* Daniel had no secrets here. He stood up and faced the Inquisition.

This time Tupash was not alone. Two squat bodyguards followed him into the room, brown impassive men about as wide as they were tall that reminded Daniel of Chinese movie thugs. The *brujo* shook his head. "You do not seem to take me seriously. Or perhaps you did not love your wife so much that her death was a problem for you?"

Daniel winced inside; that cut too close to home. He had nothing to say, so he said nothing.

"There are perhaps others who are more dear to you? Your daughters, perhaps? Moving them to this Witch's House was not wise. All you have done is widened the danger. An innocent woman must now die, an outsider to this test of strength. And I believe she is important to your little village? Irreplaceable?"

The *brujo* studied Daniel's silence. "You seem to place

great faith in this *bruja* and her *casa*. My associates, your neighbors, they have told me tales of her and her line. These women are strong, but they have never faced such a test of power. They protect and heal, but only against nature and normal men. I am not a normal man."

He paused, considering options. "The house is wood. Something as simple as fire, perhaps? Would you like your daughters to burn to death? A clinging fire like napalm or phosphorus, eating into their young flesh?"

Again, Daniel felt the vise closing in on his chest, forcing words out of his throat and over his tongue. "That house won't burn. Witch-hunters tried to burn them out, back in Colonial times. Five ministers up from Boston, five graves over in the churchyard, burned themselves to death one at a time. Still true: Thirty, forty years ago, some damn fool tried to firebomb the place because his wife left him. Didn't even kill the grass."

The *brujo* tilted his head to one side, considering. "It is kind of you to tell me this. I hate wasting time and effort. So I will set another scene. One small woman and two powerless children, what can they do against men such as these?" He gestured at the bodyguards.

Daniel swore to himself, wishing he didn't know so damned much about the Haskell house, wishing he hadn't spent so many afternoons climbing apple trees and poking around in dusty attics. He fought to hold his breath, control his tongue, but the *brujo* just lifted one eyebrow and Daniel's resistance vanished. "Men can't even get inside unless a woman lets them in. Witchcraft. Game we used to play as kids—we'd try to open the doors and windows. You can open them from inside, but from the outside they stick shut. Only a woman can open them from the outside. And we were guests, invited."

"Very good. You are most kind to tell me this." Again the *brujo* sat quietly, pushing his lips out and in as he thought.

Daniel couldn't even read any irony into the *brujo*'s voice. The man spoke as if he was getting a briefing from a spy or trusted aide.

"Windows can be broken. So can doors."

Daniel shook his head, after another brief struggle. "Kids played baseball in the yard, largest open space in the village. Never broke a window. I hit a ball straight at one, once, thought I'd die. The ball curved away."

"And the doors?"

"Solid oak, three inches thick. Not just locks—barred on the inside."

"Very interesting. I would like to talk with this Haskell Woman, study her family and her art. It is a shame. But a woman can enter, you say, someone this Alice knows? Or perhaps something else, something that is not an *hombre*? Something that is not even human?"

Daniel's head nodded itself, a traitor. Birds had gotten in, and bats in the attic. One summer there'd been a swarm of bees in one wall, and Aunt Jean had let them stay. She'd given Ben a garter snake that wintered in the cellar, after making him promise to care for it and let it go before fall.

The *brujo* studied Daniel's face. "I do not understand why you make this so difficult. I offer you riches and power, and you refuse. You think of suicide. That would be a mistake, *compadre*. Then you could not stop what happens. My associates tell me that family is everything to Morgans, much more than God or country. Can you desert your family like that? Can you expose them to such danger?"

The bastard kept trying to shove guilt down Daniel's throat. "Blame the victim," as if *he* controlled the situation. Daniel's fingers twitched, and he imagined wrapping them around that lying throat and squeezing until guilt or innocence no longer mattered.

Tupash lifted one eyebrow. "I dislike being so crude. We should be friends, business associates. But you persist in being stupid. Consider these men." The *brujo* waved at his two bodyguards, standing like chunks of rock to either side.

"Your Maria found a quiet death, a gentle death. I saw to it myself, that she did not suffer. Your children, that will not be gentle. These men are animals."

Daniel glanced from one to the other, wondering if they understood English. His question must have flitted across his face, for the *brujo* nodded.

"Yes, they understand. They believe I have just complimented them. It is a *macho* thing." One of the bodyguards smiled faintly and nodded. The other remained impassive and watchful.

"I have need of good men," the *brujo* continued. "I need you and your dead brother, and other members of your clan. But I also need *bad* men, and these men are very bad. They enjoy causing pain. And I believe they like little girls. What are your daughters? Eight years old, and twelve? Twelve is a little old for Jago's taste, but I'm sure he'll do the best he can. I believe that they could make the pain last for a week or more, before death comes to set your children free."

"I. Can't. Give. You. The. Dragon." Daniel had to force the words past his teeth, past his rage and fear.

"On the contrary. You cannot keep me from taking it. All you can control is the things I do to get it. Think about your daughters, so young and sweet and innocent. Think about this animal on my right, the one who so enjoys small girls. He likes to take them in the rear. The normal orifice he reserves for other things. When they finally stop moving, he kills them. Can you condemn your daughters to such treatment?"

Daniel spun on his left foot and kicked at the bastard's knee. He thought he'd moved fast, he thought he didn't telegraph the attack, but the nearest bodyguard simply turned and scooped the kick out of the air with one hand, lifting and pulling until he stole Daniel's balance. Daniel landed in a break-fall, curling and rolling, but the other bodyguard took one short step and planted a kick in his belly as he came to a crouch. Daniel collapsed back to the stone floor, curled around pain and empty lungs.

He lay there, gasping, waiting for more kicks. They didn't come. He finally uncurled enough to look up at the *brujo*.

"These men may be animals, but they are *skilled* animals. They are very good at what they do. All of my men are very good at what they do. That is why I wish you to join us." He turned toward the door, then turned back with a gesture to his bodyguards, inviting them to feast. "Do not break anything. He must be able to speak, to hear, to see at least with one eye. No permanent damage: He is valuable to me."

The animal on the left nodded, as if he was in charge. Daniel tried to roll away, but the other one moved faster, kicking to his back. Fire lanced through his kidney, and he flopped back to the floor. Other blows—kicks and punches and stiff-fingered jabs—probed nerve points and muscles. They struck slowly, scientifically, allowing him to feel each strike, allowing pain to ebb and flow instead of numbing him with a deluge. Each time he clawed back to control of his body, they struck again.

He started to fade, welcoming the darkness. The blows stopped. The two men stood over him, studying him, weighing how much he could take. They hadn't broken a sweat—even their hair looked smooth and fresh from the comb. The leader tilted his head to one side and lifted his right foot.

Daniel cringed away, into the other man's toe. The blow lifted under his armpit, sending sparks down to his fingertips and leaving the tingle of numbness behind. He flopped forward, into another kick that punched in just under his ribs and stunned his diaphragm. He curled around the fire again, gasping for air. Something blurry formed in front of his eyes, a face seen through tears. The face nodded—detached, cool, scientific. It withdrew and vanished. Daniel heard the door click and slam, distantly noted the rattle of the bolts.

He lay on the cold stone, coarse grit biting into his cheek. His ragged gasps slowed and deepened, finally bringing air into his tortured lungs. The fire of the blows died to embers. Feeling oozed back into his right hand, with the pins and needles of returning circulation. He concentrated on that, on wiggling his fingers and flexing his elbow. By focusing on that, he could force the rest of the pain down into a dull ache.

He straightened out, uncurling and sagging onto his back. Feet worked. Knees worked. Hips, shoulders, elbows, neck—all the pieces worked. The animals had obeyed the *brujo*'s orders. Nothing broken, nothing torn. One tooth felt loose, but he'd had worse before and it had settled back onto its roots. He swallowed blood.

Peggy. Ellen. Those animals.

You've got to trust Alice, he reminded himself. *The house is strong. The house protects itself, protects the women living in it. Alice is strong.*

But he'd given so much of that strength away. His memory was a traitor. He reached up and clutched the Dragon, the pendant with its crimson tear, drawing power to ease his pain. He could hand that over to the *brujo,* give the bastard the Dragon's powers. Then Ellen and Peggy would be safe.

All he had to do was take the pendant off and give it to the man. Ellie would be safe, Mouse would be safe—even Alice would be safe to come after Daniel and make good on her threats. He'd rather face her wrath than have Ellie and Mouse in the hands of those two thugs.

You've got to trust Alice. You've got to trust the Haskell House. No woman has ever been harmed in that House.

He forced himself to his knees, still clutching the pendant. It gave him the strength to move. He huddled over the heater, soaking up the warmth it offered to fight off the chills of shock and fear.

The pendant lay in his hand. He slipped the chain over his head, to free it. The red stone glowed at him, a living thing that felt his mood and read his thoughts. It seemed to approve of them.

"Our Father, who art in heaven . . ." Prayer seemed necessary. So many faiths thought you achieved heaven by dying with your prayer on your lips and God in your heart. Into thy hands, O Lord, I commit my spirit. Shema Yisrael, Hear, O Israel, the Lord our God, the Lord is One. Allahu Akhbar, God is most great.

That red stone was Daniel's link with Ben and Gary, the source of treason, the source of salvation. It was a piece of his soul, had been for twenty years. He couldn't imagine life without it. Most likely that wouldn't be a problem.

He kissed it and tottered to his feet. Spots swam around his head, and he staggered against the wall of his cell. The beating had taken more than the Dragon could give back. He slumped back down again, leaning against the stone, holding on to the metallic conduit connected to the wall outlet.

Trust Alice. Into Thy hands, Lord . . .

His left hand unplugged the heater. His right hand wedged the pendant in between the prongs of the plug, with the Tear right in the center. He jammed the plug back into the socket before he could change his mind.

Electricity flashed, blue against the red fire of the Tear. The silver dragon glowed orange and then white before splashing molten sparks down the wall. The Tear shattered into a thousand fragments.

The Dragon clutched his heart in her talons.

fourteen

—⁓—

KATE BACKED HER truck up the driveway, set the brake, and switched off. The clunker clunked twice, backfired, and shuddered to a stop. Another day, another twenty-five cents. Before taxes, that is. At least bashing out walls with a sledgehammer and wrecking bar helped take her mind off things.

She glanced at her watch; she'd put in at least twelve hours actual job time. Nearly eight in the evening, and she'd left the trailer before six that morning. She climbed down from the cab and stretched her aching back. And the arm still worked, too.

They'd been hauling trash to the landfill all afternoon, a couple of tons of scrap lumber and busted-up sheetrock, and without a dump bed on her truck she'd had to lift every ounce of the damned stuff at least twice. Time for a long, hot shower and another night spent staring at the ceiling, wondering.

Maybe Jackie had come back. Maybe Alice had left a message. Kate wasn't sure which mystery troubled her more. Jackie had never been gone this long before—two days was her max, before she ran out of money and her friends' mothers got tired of feeding that gaping mouth. Alice, now, Alice wasn't answering her phone or pager, and *that* was something new. The hospital said she was on "family emergency leave."

Kate trudged up the path to her trailer, automatically noting the crazy angle of the front steps and the gouged siding on the mudroom she'd tacked on when she bought the place. Both injuries were the calling card of a drunken pass by Lew's snowplow. That had been three winters ago, and she still hadn't found the time to set it straight. The cobbler's children went barefoot, and the contractor's house was the last one fixed.

The mudroom door stuck, heaved out of square by ten years of frosts and thaws, and she whacked it open with her hip and shoulder. Anyone who didn't know her, know that door, would have thought it was locked and bolted. Security system, Downeast style.

She stepped through another door into the trailer itself, into the combined kitchen/dining/living room with its worn, thirty-year-old vinyl flooring, cheap cabinets with the printed wood-grain wearing off, and yard-sale furniture. "Jackie?" Silence answered her, not even a chirp from the answering machine. Damn. She'd left a message for Alice two days ago, made Kate wince to think about it—full of adolescent gush and babble, the sort of thing you'd like to pull back and edit or totally erase five seconds after you hung up. No wonder Alice hadn't answered.

But Kate *needed* to talk to Alice, about that message and other things. And she needed to do that talking at a safe distance. The cop job said so.

"Jackie?"

The only noise was the creaking of the undersized floor joists as she walked around. The silly brat would have to come up for air sometime. Lew hadn't heard from her, either, though the way he'd been drinking lately, their daughter could have vanished into one of his blackout periods.

Kate checked the answering machine, anyway. After all, the beeper could be broken. Nothing. She punched up Alice's number on the phone and listened to the ringing and the ringing and the ringing. Her answering machine never came on the line. That meant the message tape was full. No e-mail on the computer, either, a four-year-old machine that Alice had given Kate with the free choice of keeping it or hauling it to the dump.

Shower first, supper later: She had to keep her priorities straight or the leftover pizza would taste of sheetrock dust. Construction work was filthy work, the main reason she kept her hair cut short. Kate unlaced her steel-toed workboots and then peeled off her work shirt and jeans and dumped them next to the washer on her way to the bathroom. Not that it was a long trip—a twelve by forty two-bedroom trailer was small enough that you couldn't cuss a cat without getting fur on your tongue.

A white rectangle hung on the corkboard in the hall, folded paper with a blank outside. Jackie? Alice? Kate wiped her hands on her panties and pulled the paper down. Jackie's writing stared back at her from the inside, a short note.

I'm staying with some friends, and I'm not coming back. Just stopped by to pick up my clothes and things. Don't bother trying to find me. I know the law, and I'm old enough to live on my own.
If you want to be a real bitch about it, I took some money. So you can have me arrested. Think about it real hard before you try, because I took your gun, too.

No signature, but Jackie didn't need one. She never *had* learned to write well, and her printed scrawl still looked like she was in fifth grade. Kate's eyes blurred for a moment. She leaned her forehead against the wall, wadded the paper into a crumpled mass, and dropped it.

Damn. Damn, damn, damn, damn, *damn!*

Then she knelt down, the vinyl floor cold and gritty under her bare knees, and carefully unfolded the note. She smoothed it out again, delicately, like she was smoothing Jackie's hair under her hands. She read it through again. Money. Kate had kept a few hundred in cash tucked behind the fridge in the compressor coils. That was the "absolute desperation" fund, and she guessed Jackie was absolutely desperate. She shook her head. The kid wouldn't be going to the Youth Center for *that.* It was only money.

Gun. When Jackie was a kid, Kate had kept all the guns locked up. Now she was a teenager, rapist bait alone in the trailer most days, and knew how to shoot. Kate had trusted her to know *when,* as well.

Kate stood up again, opened the hall closet, and fumbled back in the shadows. Her fingers closed around a cold steel cylinder, the barrel of the Mossberg riot gun. Somehow, she hadn't thought Jackie would steal *that* one. Too hard to hide in a backpack.

A few strides took her into her bedroom at the end of the hall, and she pulled the top drawer of her dresser open. The Colt still lay there, .44 magnum Anaconda with an 8" barrel that she'd bought used from Bernie after *twice* having to put down injured moose when they'd argued with local cars. The old Browning just hadn't been up to the job; the second time took three shots with that puny 9mm cartridge to kill the critter.

So what had Jackie meant? Hoping against hope, Kate swung the other bedroom door open. Chaos: clothes hangers scattered on the floor, closet open and drawers open and nothing left but the stuff Jackie had outgrown or scorned, posters gone from the wall, boom box and CDs gone. She must have brought her "friends" along to carry all that junk.

Numbed shock carried Kate back into the kitchen, and she slipped her hand behind the refrigerator to find dust and bare metal where the money should have been. But what was that bit about her gun? Then she noticed the box of empty cartridge brass on the counter.

Qualifying. She'd been out to the county range yesterday, annual firearms recertification. Then she'd brought the Browning in, cleaned it, and left it sitting on the counter with the two spare magazines and a fresh box of shells. Forgot to put it back in the truck this morning.

Stupid. Stupid, stupid, *stupid!* And Jackie had practiced with that ancient chunk of Nazi steel. Kate had taught her. A woman should be able to defend herself. Jackie and Alice used to compete against each other, out on the range— they'd both been about the same size, then.

Kate leaned her forehead against the cold metal of the refrigerator, trying to soak the numbness through into her brain. Her pulse pounded against it, and she swiped wet grit from her cheeks.

Jackie. Her baby. Gone.

She picked up the phone again and speed-dialed Lew's number. It rang and rang, then broke off with the clunk and rattle of a headset knocked off the hook. She heard music in the background, sounded like Hank Williams, and the too-loud chatter that was alcohol talking.

"Wha?"

"Lew?"

"Yeah."

"It's Kate. You seen Jackie?"

"Oh, hi, darlin'. Nope. Haven't seen her for a month. She late getting home?"

Month, hell. Jackie had spent two days over at Lew's

place just last week, throwing a hissy-fit. Kate had chewed her out and grounded her for driving a motorcycle without a license. Typical teenage hormone spiral.

"Lew, she's been gone for three days now. I've called you every day. Be sure to let me know if you see her anywhere."

"Sure, honey. Hey, come on over. We're having a bit of a party. Old friends."

"No thanks. Been busting my butt all day, just want a shower and some food." She hung up before he could turn on the charm.

She tried Alice again, listening to the phone ring and ring and ring. No ice storms in June, so the lines wouldn't be down. Then she called two other friends, places Jackie sometimes went, parents of kids Jackie hung out with. No news. She stared at the phone, thinking about the one place she *hadn't* tried.

One of the Pratt boys owned that motorcycle, frigging Japanese crotch-rocket that could do over a hundred-twenty and reach that speed in about five seconds. "But, *Mom,* I've *got* a driver's license!" A car license, yes. Not the special motorcycle license Maine required, for good reason.

Thing was, if Kate called the Pratts and Jackie *was* there, life could get damned sticky. The kid was right. State law, she was old enough to leave home. Smart enough, mature enough—those weren't legal concepts. The law talked about concrete things, like age. Jackie was over sixteen. That was old enough.

Tie that in with Bernie's little tidbit about the Pratts and drugs, you had a can of worms. Jackie hadn't been using drugs—God knows, Kate had learned the symptoms. But the twit had been too protective of that backpack. Was she carrying for someone else? *Selling?*

Kate pulled the refrigerator door open, operating on automatic pilot. The pizza had vanished. Probably the toll charge for Jackie's moving crew. She grabbed some three-day-old bean salad and wolfed it down. Questions popped up in Kate's mind, and she whacked each one on the head with a six-pound hammer before it had a chance to get awkward. Then she wrinkled her nose. The power of a mother to rationalize . . .

"Users are losers." Jackie didn't just parrot that catchy little phrase; she loaded it with enough contempt to drench a brushfire. Kate grabbed that assurance with both hands. Whatever ways Jackie had found to screw up her life, doing drugs wasn't one of them.

A quick shower and clean clothes, and Kate was out the door. She left the truck, walking slowly back to the center of Stonefort and the small cluster of shops that passed for a business district, half on foot patrol and half looking for her daughter. She looked in at the video rental, checked the arcade with its flashing game machines and random electronic explosions, walked through the pizza shop and checked each booth for a large blond girl trying to make herself invisible.

There was still enough light for her to see into the cars cruising back and forth from the town landing out to the town garage, identify the kids and twenty-somethings looking for some fun in the least-likely town in Maine. No sign of Jackie.

Twilight settled over the green commons in the center of the village, and the thumping car stereos faded away as their owners headed home or out to the abandoned quarries for a little beer and sex. Lights switched on, both the few streetlights the town was willing to support and the spotlights bathing the front and sides of the white clapboard Congregational church. Such a quaint New England scene, it looked like a tourist postcard.

She wandered over to the church. She hadn't been inside in years, uncomfortable with the face of stern piety and self-righteousness, comparing the pronouncements of her neighbors against the reality of their actions. Cop work showed you the darker parts of people's lives. The pastor abused his children. The choir director had a ten-year affair with his lead soprano. Three deacons had been linked to arson at the local boatyard, but nothing could be proved. A fourth's stern-man had gone missing at sea, two weeks after a fight in the local bar. A woman was involved, married to still another pillar of the church. *Peyton Place* lived on.

The smells of wax and dust and old wood woke up memories: hymns, drowsy sermons, the congregation rising and sitting and bowing in prayer, communion, marriages, baptisms, funerals. She stood in the back of the dim sanctuary, staring the length of the center aisle at the pulpit and the dull brass of the organ pipes, lights glowing through the stained glass windows to either side, four windows each. Two panels dedicated to ancient Morgans glowed on the right; two facing windows weighed in for the Pratts on the left. Three of the four other families identified by discreet bronze plaques had vanished into the churchyard.

But where was God? She walked slowly down the aisle, listening for the white-bearded patriarch that ruled this house. He declined comment. She sat in the first pew on the left, staring up at the austere white pulpit and choir rail, thinking of the cold shoulder they offered—no cross or crucifix or statue of a comforting Mother Mary, no bright Byzantine icons and incense, not even a candle.

This faith was abstract and sere, a winter religion for a winter land, and it refused to coddle the believer. Predestination loomed on the horizon. God had known the verdict of damnation or salvation for each soul, before the firmament was brought forth and the sea divided from the dry land.

Why was Jackie predestined to be a loser? Kate had *tried*. She'd tried to stay with Lew, because the kid needed a father. She'd stayed friendly with the damned sot even after the divorce, and never said word one against him in Jackie's hearing. Only criticized the booze, not the man who drank it. She'd given Jackie every minute and dollar she could spare from the struggle to make ends meet.

The pulpit remained empty. It spoke a sermon, older than the timbers holding the roof overhead: Nothing you do can stand against the Will of God. He set the course of your life at the same time that He set the course of the stars in the heavens, and nothing that you do can change either by an inch.

Kate turned her back on the pulpit, twisting around in the pew to look up into the shadows of the balcony. Her blurred eyes tried to force a straw-yellow head into those shadows, a child whispering with her friends under cover of the hymns. The dark pews remained empty. She stood up and walked back up the aisle, past the wine-red wood of the seats spaced out by the white tombstones of the pew dividers. Her footsteps echoed against the hard cold walls of the sanctuary.

The evening fog was sneaking in off the bay, clammy, rank from the low-tide seaweed and mudflats. Halos formed around the streetlights and stabbed out from the rare passing cars. Kate shivered. It was a bad night to be alone. Maybe she'd go over to Lew's, after all. If she wasn't up for a party, she could turn it into a wake.

She felt coldness over her shoulder, and looked back. A big car rolled by, scrupulous about the twenty-five limit, and she recognized that dark Suburban from a couple of weeks ago. New Jersey plates, 998 CEG, Red Bank Delivery—the car Bernie had warned her away from. So it was still in town, still wandering around like the Grim Reaper drumming up business. To hell with it—that was Bernie's problem. He owned it free and clear.

Larry's Bar blinked its Michelob sign at her, a neon glow through the thickening fog. The bar was the other linchpin of Stonefort social life, the one she hadn't bothered to check because Larry knew damned well how old Jackie was and he *always* carded. But maybe one of the good ol' boys would have heard something from a friend-of-a-friend.

Wednesday night, the bar was damn near empty. Larry stood behind his beer taps, polishing glasses, and Clyde Abells was setting up nine-ball breaks on the old pool table. Andy and Jenny Beals had the entire row of booths to themselves, taking a well-earned vacation from five kids. So much for collecting gossip.

Clyde refused to meet her glance, but she'd be willing to bet he hadn't hit Ginny since their little "discussion" a month or so back. For a moment, Kate considered picking up a cue and whipping the peckerhead's ass at a couple of games of straight pool. He'd probably turn nasty and give her an excuse to punch him out. Maybe that would make her feel better. It wouldn't help her find Jackie, though.

She pulled a twenty out of her back pocket and tossed it to Larry. "Jim Beam. Double. When that's empty, give me another."

"Problems?"

"Nothing that getting blind drunk will solve, but I'm going to try it anyway."

He chewed on that for a moment, studying her face. Then he held out his palm.

She shook her head. "You don't need the keys. I walked. Sleeping it off under a bush on the commons won't kill me."

"Your choice." He shrugged, turned, and poured bourbon over ice. It looked more like a triple to Kate, but she wasn't going to complain. It would take several of those to have any effect with *her* body mass. She collected her glass and picked a stool at the back corner of the bar, one where she could keep one eye on Clyde and the other on the front door. Then she started studying ice cubes.

She was working on the variable melting-rate of her third set of cubes and considering a visit to the unisex sanitary facilities when the door opened. A stranger entered, male, slim, and medium height, and slid into a stool near the front with easy familiarity. Larry nodded as if the guy was a regular, and started pouring a drink without waiting for an order.

The stranger looked vaguely familiar, darkish skin under the bar lights and an apparent age in the twenties. Then Kate nodded to herself—racial resemblance. He looked a bit like Alice, with the rounded flat features and glossy black hair. Indian. Or Native American, or First People, or whatever the "politically correct" title was this week.

He accepted his glass with a nod, handing over a few bills. He moved gracefully, a little like a cat, and was far from the worst male specimen she'd seen in the last month or so. The resemblance to Alice sure didn't hurt.

Then he met her gaze. He turned to the barkeep. "Who is this goddess with the golden hair?"

Larry blinked, probably having to reset his worldview to fit the concept of Kate as a goddess. Before he could answer, the stranger picked up his drink and moved down the bar to sit one stool away from Kate.

"Allow me to introduce myself. I am Antonio Estevan Francisco Juan Carlos da Silva y Gomes, at your service." He winked. "But you can call me Tony."

The room temperature seemed to shoot up about ten degrees, all of a sudden.

fifteen

—◊—

DIXIE REFUSED TO go outside. She backed away from the open door, arched her back at the night, and hissed. From a cat that hated the litter box, that was a Portent. Alice shook her head. She closed the door without showing herself against the light, and replaced the heavy bar.

Sparks crackled in the kitchen, and she grabbed her shotgun. Smoke curled out of the toaster oven. An instant later, fire spat from the back of her microwave. Alice strode over to the electrical panel, opened it, and flipped the main breaker off. The refrigerator died, and silence replaced the Japanese Koto from her CD player. The warm yellow glow of oil lamps remained.

She tucked the shotgun back into a corner, picked up her fire extinguisher, and squirted yellow powder here and there. She inspected the scorched outlets and the wires leading from them. Both smoked quietly and stank of burned insulation.

She glanced over at Ellen and Peggy, where they sat in the new parlor. They stared back at her with wide eyes, silent, staying out of the way and waiting for her to tell them what to do. "It's okay, girls. Just a problem with the old wiring. I've shut off the power, so there isn't any danger." None from the power, anyway. From what caused the overload? That was another matter.

She dug a screwdriver out of a drawer. Removing the outlet plates showed her cracked plastic and melted metal. She squirted the extinguisher into each box, then pulled the ruined outlets to check the wiring. At least *that* looked okay. Everything was cooling down, probably safe. Have to get Kate over, though, make sure everything checked out before she installed new outlets, maybe even pulled new wires through the conduit.

Dammit, stop woolgathering!

The pigs had been playing with her. She knew that. They could have attacked anytime from that first evening on, but they wanted to wear her down first. Even a witch needed sleep. But they didn't understand the House all that well. Killing the power just made it stronger. Alice could feel the old place heave a sigh of relief, ridding itself of those conflicting magnetic fields and nasty humming machines.

Still, she considered the refrigerator, wondering if just *one* live circuit would be safe. Then she shook her head. Time to find out if that super-duper Energy Star insulation was worth the cost. It should be able to hold food safe for a day or two. Beyond that point, she'd definitely have more important problems.

Just on the outside chance . . . she picked up the phone. Still dead. They'd cut the line, sometime between her call to Caroline and her attempt to answer Kate's message. That had been three days ago, the opening shot of this war of nerves. Such a nice, subtle signal that was: "We know where you are. We know the girls are there. Have a nice day."

She remembered the ice storm three years back—power and phone lines down all over the county. Anybody calling on those dead lines would hear a ringing signal but never get an answer, just like there was nobody home. Only way you could find out otherwise was to drive out to the place and check. You'd think the phone company could work out some way of telling a caller that the line was out of service.

She'd tried a cell phone once. The House didn't like it. Either that, or this corner of Stonefort was a dead spot on the coverage. The pager worked fine, but that was receive-only.

Phones—that message from Kate had been sweet. The only thing wrong was the timing. Alice had shut the tape off when it got too graphic for young ears, then had played it through the next morning before Ellen and Peggy were up. And by then the damned phone was dead. Talk about star-crossed lovers . . .

Dixie consented to use the cat box, then glared at Alice for making such an indignity necessary. The cat had her own ideas about what was important in this world, and a witch-war didn't make the list. Humans should settle such things without disturbing her routine. She stalked off into the older part of the house, twitching her tail.

"Okay, girls. Bedtime."

That roused a groan and a great pouting of lips. She'd been telling tales of the house, to an appreciative audience. Of course, in the stories she told, the good guys always won.

"Tell us one more, Aunt Alice." Peggy had needed the stories more than Ellen had. She'd understood less of what was going on.

Ellen got that crafty look again. "Are there any stories of the witch helping *men?*"

Alice shook her head, but weakened. She'd never make a good mother, able to make rules and stick to them. "Okay, one more. Yes, the *House* sometimes helps men. We help good people who can't find help anyplace else. People who have to live in fear, for no good reason. What sort of man might fit that description?"

Again, it was Ellen who first found voice. "There's this boy in school, everybody calls him a fag. Or there's Mikuma—he's some kind of refugee from Africa. Kids pick on him, even though he's kinda nice. But he's black, and he doesn't speak English very good, and kids keep calling him a terrorist or a raghead because his folks pray funny."

"He's probably a Muslim, a follower of Muhammad. But those are good choices, Ellen. One of the men who stayed in this house awhile, over a hundred years ago, was black. He was an escaped slave named John. Nobody gave family names to *slaves,* and he refused to use his owner's name.

"Anyway, he came to Stonefort late one night before the Civil War, traveling by the Underground Railroad. Do you know what that was?"

Ellen nodded. She must have been through the Black History Month programs. Peggy looked puzzled. "Is that some kind of subway?"

Alice jumped in before Ellen could put her expression of scorn into words. "No. The 'railroad' was a metaphor, a figure of speech. The Underground Railroad was a network of people who were opposed to slavery, opposed to it strongly enough to break the law and help slaves escape to Canada. They hid runaway slaves, helped them to travel, gave them food and clothes and money, sometimes traveled with them as if they were slave owners."

Peggy nodded understanding, so Alice went on. "There was a law back then, the government had to send escaped slaves back to their owners. The police had to help recapture the runaways. Somebody knew that John had come to Stonefort, some idiot who thought black people were animals that could be bought and sold. So the police looked all over town, searching people's homes and barns and such, looking in all the boats in the harbor. But they never looked in this house. Everybody *knew* a man couldn't be hiding here. This was a *woman's* house."

Alice paused, and smiled. "Remember, always be careful about trusting what *everybody* knows. That table over there, the maple one? John made that, while he waited for a chance to move on. He was a skilled man, a cabinetmaker and a good one, but some people *knew* he wasn't even human. You've been eating supper from his gift, his skill offered as thanks for common human kindness.

"He stayed here for two weeks, hiding, working on that table. Then one night old Ephraim Morgan rowed John out to the schooner *Sally Ann* and took him across to Nova Scotia. So your family had a part in the story, and you should be proud of them. Now get ready for bed."

They pouted again. Ellen looked cheated, as well. "But that story didn't have any *magic* in it."

"No, it didn't. But you will find, young lady, that ninety-nine times out of a hundred, you don't need magic to do what's right. Remember that."

And then there's that hundredth time, she reminded herself. She watched as Ellen filled the portable lamps and lit them. She gave the girls as many chores, as many *responsibilities,* as the situation allowed. They needed them. Work could be a great healer.

Once again, they walked back through the centuries to the oldest core of the house. This time, Alice purified the fire and set her guards with the girls watching—burning the sweetgrass and the sage, the juniper and the bloodroot, offering tobacco to the winds and to the ancestors. She moved slowly through the ritual and said the words, watching Ellen out of the corner of her eye. The little minx was memorizing every syllable and gesture. Well, nothing ever said the Haskell Witch couldn't have *two* apprentices.

The girls undressed for bed. This "motherhood" thing was a challenge, instant children eight and twelve years old, *fragile* children who'd lost father and then mother in a space of days, for a lesbian who'd never felt the nesting urge. Alice went with the example of her sister and the raucous brood *she* still was raising. Learn from the pro. Eight and twelve, that would be closest to Jen and Lisa. Alice helped Peggy arrange her blanket and pillow on the futon, carefully keeping her back turned on Ellen—at almost the same age, Lisa was so shy of her changing body that she wouldn't even undress in front of her own mother.

Alice tucked Peggy in with a motherly kiss on the forehead, patted Ellen softly on the head, turned down the lamp to an orange glow, and shut the door behind her. She heard the bar thump home, the deadbolt click, and then the rustle of sheets as Ellen got into bed.

She rested her hand on the oak planks of the door for a moment, offering a silent blessing for the children. Then, aloud, "And remember, don't open the door even for *me*. Not without the password. If you hear noises, or something tries to open this door, get down in the cellar. Understand?"

Muffled giggles came through the door, followed by a faint "Yes, Aunt Alice." They must have been thinking of the password, to find something to laugh about.

Alice checked her weapons and flashlight again and slipped into her sleeping bag. Before she blew out the lamp, she studied the single unshuttered window at the end of the hall, high and too narrow for a man to pass through quickly. A web covered it, hand-spun of milkweed floss and spider-silk and hung with three wing-primaries from a peregrine. She'd left that one opening deliberately, trapped with the strongest soul-catcher she could weave. Dixie settled down into a miniature sphinx by her head, also staring at the window and the stars beyond. Apparently the cat knew more than she was telling.

There was that phrase from AA that Lew Lewis pasted on the bumper of his pickup and then ignored: ONE DAY AT A TIME. Well, she had to take this one night at a time. It wasn't a matter of vampires dying if touched by the sun, or the powers of darkness waxing stronger in the wee hours of the wolf. Still, she knew the first attack would come at night, in the dark, when she couldn't see, when she was sleepy, when the irrational and the impossible gained strength in human minds. Just make it through, one night at a time.

And Caroline might show up tomorrow. It depended on schedules and reservations and flying standby and possibly renting a car and driving straight through from Boston. Or Amtrak, into Boston again. Maine didn't have any passenger train service. Whatever worked. Then there'd be two witches to guard the children. Then one of them could stay home and the other could go out and find Kate and get the phone fixed. Then Alice could sleep.

She blew out the lamp, and waited.

Shattering glass woke her from a drowse, and she heard Dixie's squalling battle-cry. One hand found the flashlight while the other groped for her shotgun. She flipped on the light, fiercely bright in the hallway, and slid it away so that anybody shooting at the light would miss her.

A dark mass oozed through the high window, tangling the soul-catcher and dripping to the floor. Dixie slashed at it with her claws, bit, and spat something out before diving back in. Alice aimed higher and cut loose with the shotgun. The blast and recoil dazed her for an instant, and then she saw the darkness reform like a column of ants. It rolled over Dixie, and Alice couldn't fire low without shredding her friend.

She blasted it again, higher up, and saw bits fly loose like smoke. The old pump gun roared a third time, tearing through the window and chopping the mass in half. She untangled herself from the sleeping bag and staggered to her feet. Part of the thing was still inside, writhing around the corner into the back hall. Alice scooped up the flashlight and held it far out to one side, inching forward. Then she heard the creak of hinges.

Shutter. She braced the shotgun on her hip, stepped around the corner, and fired blind. The recoil knocked her back against the wall. *Too damn small for this,* she thought. *Need Kate.*

Blood spattered along the plaster, and she saw a human leg jerk back through the window. The dark snake shattered into a thousand bits and Dixie snarled in triumph. Alice staggered to the window, her head still ringing from the shotgun blasts. A shadow retreated across the back lawn, limping, and she fired once more. The shadow fell and then rose, slowly.

She let it totter away into darkness. Bodies could be such inconvenient things to explain, come next morning. And given what she knew of shotgun wounds, that shadow only had about two days left to live. She'd loaded other things besides lead pellets into those shotgun shells, nasty things that Winchester or Remington had never dreamed of.

She pulled the outer shutters closed, latched them, and then the inner ones. Kate could replace the glass. Same with the high window in the back hall. With the house secure again, Alice pulled fresh cartridges out of her pockets and shoved them into the magazine. She turned and stared at the plaster in the hallway, pockmarked and shattered by shotgun pellets. More work for Kate. Drifts of dead leaves covered the floor, with a mixing of grass and dirt. Golem. Her enemy had shaped that thing and sent it into the house, knowing the house would let it pass. It wasn't a man.

A pale thing fluttered in her soul-catcher, a large moth caught in a spider's web. Dixie sat on the floor, glaring at it between bouts of washing her paws and trying to groom dirt out of her long fur. Alice studied the thing carefully for a minute, judging angles, and then wrapped it in the tangling threads without ever allowing its struggles to touch her. It *probably* wasn't dangerous, not by itself, but she didn't feel like finding out the hard way. It was too ugly.

Then she carried it back to the new kitchen and the banked fire of the cook stove. She lifted a burner lid, stirred the coals, added alder wood split small for a fast blaze, and laid the thing on the fire. It shriveled and smoked, giving off an acrid stench like burning hair. Alice heard a low growl behind her and turned to find Dixie glaring at the stove with her fur all on end. Something screamed in the darkness, down near the water, a long scream a long time dying into echoes.

The stench vanished up the chimney, and the house relaxed around her. She knew she'd just killed a person—a man, to judge by that scream—and the thought didn't bother her a bit. That one wouldn't leave a corpse behind. A scorched patch down near the tide line, maybe—the laws of similarity and contagion could be rough on the neighborhood.

Two down. The one who'd limped away wouldn't have been the life-force for the golem. Neither of them would be the enemy sorcerer, worse luck, but at least he was short a couple of tools. Alice used a poker to break up the shriveled bits of her soul-catcher and the soul it had caught, until everything had whitened into ash.

It was a shame about the peregrine feathers. They were hard to come by.

Alice walked slowly back into the heart of the House, breathing deeply and shaking out tense muscles to discharge the adrenaline from her fight. At each door, she reset the bars that defended the passage within. She didn't bother to rig a new net at the window. Her enemy wouldn't try the same attack twice. Instead, she finished reloading the shotgun, laid it down, and tapped softly on the parlor door, shave-and-a-haircut pattern.

"Little pig, little pig, let me come in."

Footsteps creaked up the basement ladder, and she heaved a sigh of relief. The girls were okay, and they *had* retreated to the spring when all hell broke loose. The house would have protected them, down there, even if the men had gotten past her.

A voice slipped through the door, tentative, "Not by the hair of my chinny-chin-chin."

"Then I'll huff, and I'll puff, and I'll blow your house down."

The lock clicked, and thumps announced the removal of the bar. Alice had thought that such an idiot sign and countersign would be the safest—even if the attackers had managed to force her to tell, one way or another, they probably wouldn't have believed her.

Alice pushed the door open, slowly, not wanting to startle the girls. Ellen stood by the open hatchway, biting her lip, with a smaller shotgun in her hands pointing *almost* at the door, and Peggy's head just showed above the floor. Smart kids. Brave kids. Alice smiled her relief.

Then her arms were full of girls, hugging, and she felt both of them trembling. "It's okay," Alice murmured. "It's okay. Dixie and I scared them off."

No need to mention dead men, or provide any other food for nightmares.

Dixie scalloped around their ankles, demanding a reward for *her* part in the battle. Ellen stooped down and picked the cat up, scritching ears and snuggling until Dixie started to rumble a purr. Peggy stopped sniffling and Alice wiped the child's eyes. "You're safe now." *Until the next time.*

Something rattled the outer shutter of the window, a gust of wind or prying fingers. A dry, hard touch scraped across it like the bare ice-stiff branches of winter, and then it rattled again. Both girls jerked in fear.

"It's okay," Alice explained. "Just a tree limb."

Except that there wasn't a tree or bush within reach of that window. The girls didn't need to know that, though. At least not until the sun was shining.

sixteen

—〰—

NIGHT AND FOG hung close over the bay. Gary blessed the fog. He was scared, no way around it. The cold, dark, salty cotton wool helped to calm him. He slipped between sheds on the old dock—the battered, rotting work-boat dock covered with rusty gear and fish gurry that the New York yachties thought looked so quaint from their safe distance upwind on the transient moorings.

With weathered gray wood all around him, gray decking underfoot, gray jeans and turtleneck and watch cap and gloves, the night and fog would make him damn near invisible. Besides, then he could blame condensed seawater for the dampness in his gloves. It *wasn't* his palms sweating.

Still, it was an exciting kind of scared. He'd felt like this the first time he'd shut off the car lights out at the old Stanford quarry and slipped an arm around Sue Hemming. Scared, yes, but certain that something *very* interesting was on the horizon.

The old dock was rough under his feet, planking splintered from decades of storms and heavy use. He slipped his feet over the surface and felt for each step—folks left trap buoys and lobster crates lying around, and if somebody had decided to dry and mend a net . . . His nose told him the blur to his left was the bait shack, rank with the memory of the tons of herring and alewives that had passed through on their way to lobster traps and swordfish downriggers.

The dock looked different at night, almost sinister, something out of a forties spy movie with Bogart meeting Bacall to pass along the plans for the coastal forts. Gary must have been down here a thousand times, meeting Dad's boat, loading, unloading, mending traps, finally climbing aboard to work his saltwater *bar mitzvah* as stern man, a *man's* job in a man's world. But this time, at this tide, he had no legal business.

A shot echoed across the bay, muffled by the fog. Gary ducked behind a stack of lobster crates. Another followed, and then two more—the last one louder, as if the shooter had moved. He straightened up and wiped his forehead with the back of his sleeve. Night hunters. The deer eat your peas, you eat the deer. Simple equation. In Sunrise County, even the wardens didn't pay much attention. People lived too close to the edge. They'd nail you if you tried to sell the meat, but turned a blind eye to a man who needed to feed his family.

He trailed his fingers along the weathered cedar shingles of the Stinsons' net shed. Perly Stinson was almost eighty, hands knotted up with arthritis, hadn't set a net or trap in years. No sons. Another five years, ten years, heavy snow would cave in the roof or a northeaster would swipe a wave over the dock, and the wreckage would join the driftwood on the cobble beach. Nobody else would use the shed, though. It had been in the Stinson family since God was a baby.

A "mailbox," Ben had called it, a blind drop just like in the spy movies. One man would leave something, another would come along an hour, a day, a week later and pick it up. They never saw each other. Kept the right hand from knowing what the left hand was doing, or who the left hand was. Couldn't both be caught in the same raid.

The door was just where it had always been. Jumpy as Gary felt, he wouldn't have been surprised if it had moved or hidden from him. He tapped the switch on his radio, alerting Ben.

The earphone hissed back at him. "All clear."

Ben had chosen different radios, UHF bands, on the off chance the Pratts would be listening on the one they'd got from Dad. And he had to keep transmissions short so a scanner couldn't lock on. The terse sentences and voiceless coded signals only added to the whole *nacht und nebel* atmosphere.

Now was the point where it got interesting, just like seeing if Sue would swat his fingers off the top button of her blouse. Which she hadn't. Instead, she'd started working from the bottom up while he fumbled from the top down, and their hands had met in the middle before parting on separate scouting missions.

Focus, dingleberry! He pulled out a thin probe of spring steel and slipped it into the padlock, then fitted the flat torque lever into the remaining slot. According to Ben, the main problem with *this* lock would be age and corrosion. You couldn't really twist harder on picks, like you could with a key. A little spray can of WD-40 had joined the kit, just in case.

The probe slid in and out of the key slot, riding over the pins. He could feel each one yield a smidgen. Steady pressure on the torque held them down until he could push them further. The gloves made things harder, even as thin as they were. But somebody else had used this lock recently; it didn't turn as hard as he'd feared. It snapped open, and Gary pushed on the door. It swung away from him, silently. They'd oiled the hinges, too.

The inside of the shed was pitch black. He tapped a code

on his radio, updating Ben. A single click came back as an answer. Gary slipped inside and pushed the door nearly shut. Then he pulled out his penlight and looked around. His heart thumped, and the wavering shadows thrown by the flashlight all looked like cops or drug-runners. He tried to swallow, but his mouth was too dry.

This was the first thing he'd ever done that was flat-out *illegal*. Nothing like running a stop sign or swiping a throat-burning swallow of Dad's vodka. Illegal entry was a felony. Heck, possession of "burglar's tools" was one, too. So why did he feel like Sue had just slipped her hand inside *his* pants?

The net shed looked almost exactly as it should: the dusty, rusty, spider-webbed remains of generations of working watermen. Coils of pot-warp and rough-carved buoys hung from nails, a rotting fyke net mounded one corner, broken traps waited for repairs that would never come. His eyes caught one oddity, though. The floor was clean. No dust, which meant no footprints.

Now to see if Ben's grapevine knew what it was talking about. "Third bait-bucket on the left," it had said. Gary lifted an old oak-slat lobster pot down, then another. The nets of both parlor and funnel had rotted as thin as cobwebs, and he handled them gently so as to leave no trace. Then he looked into the wooden tub. Three plastic-wrapped foil packages winked back at him in the glow of his flashlight.

He picked one up and slipped it into another plastic bag, to protect him from any leakage and also avoid contaminating the evidence. It was heavy, over a pound, and hard-soft like an unopened sack of brown sugar. He tucked it into a shoulder bag, replaced the old traps, and tapped another code on the radio: "Heading out." The earphone clicked an "all clear" back at him.

He turned off his flashlight. He stepped through the door and into the dark fog. He pulled the door shut and made sure the lock was set in the hasp and staple. If he got caught now, he was in *real* trouble.

So how come it felt as good as that first time out in the quarry with Sue?

GARY STUDIED THE green lines on the oscilloscope screen. He turned a knob clockwise, then counterclockwise. The square peaks and valleys of the dual traces merged and separated. They matched perfectly. He'd checked it three times now, and they'd matched perfectly every time. Nerves.

He glanced up at Ben. "It can't be this simple."

His uncle shrugged. "What's so complicated? You've got a remote control. It transmits. The car receives. The code matches. The system turns off. Those are all simple declarative sentences, no subordinate clauses or conditional wishy-washy ifs, ands, or buts. One of the rules of the game says that what one person transmits, another can intercept and decode."

"But that isn't a security system."

"Every security system ever invented has a weak spot. Sometimes it's a physical flaw, sometimes it's a bypass, sometimes it's a human with a taste for something you can offer him. That was true when you had an Australopithecus with a sharp rock guarding his tribe's dead warthog, and it's true with the most sophisticated computer lock ever made. All any security system ever does is raise the cost of admission."

Gary looked down at the remote control on the workbench. The "cost of admission" in this case just meant buying a duplicate unit from a dealer up in Naskeag Falls and reprogramming it to the frequency and code they'd intercepted. It still seemed too easy.

Ben must have read his thoughts. "Locks and alarms are aimed at amateurs. Take a step back from the problem and look at it. That car has eight big panes of glass. You want to get into it, all you need is a rock. Sure, the alarm will go off.

But you could steal anything inside and be gone in a matter of seconds. It just takes a little planning and nerve. We're going to the trouble of matching the security because we don't want them to *know* we've been there. Not till it's too late."

Ben had a small circuit board in his right hand, a couple of IC chips and input-output networks on a square of green board about an inch and a half across. He rolled it across the backs of his fingers like a parlor magician doing coin tricks with a quarter, then made it vanish. It reappeared in his other hand. Ben leaned forward, reached over to Gary's ear, and pulled a duplicate out of thin air. "Two for the price of one."

By now, Gary was getting used to Ben's antics. He just shrugged and passed his uncle another breadboard assembly of chips and dangling wires. It looked more like a bunch of dead bugs soldered to a maze of copper Egyptian hieroglyphics than a working circuit. Ben plugged wires into the board in his right hand, connected up a speaker and battery, and pushed a button.

"Red Subaru station wagon," the flat tones of synthesized speech repeated. "Maine plate ten-three-five-seven-Victor, Stonefort Commons ten A.M. Storage compartment over left rear wheel well."

Gary frowned. "And that's enough to bring the cops?"

"Special DEA hotline. They only give the number out to undercover agents and trusted informants. They'll be there, with bells on."

"Why use the voice circuit?"

"Every call is recorded, with caller ID logged. Don't want to give them a voiceprint. I'll use a pay phone over in Alder Mills when you give me the signal."

"Aren't we taking a chance, saying where the car will be?"

Ben shrugged. "The guy has been there every morning for a week—shows up between nine-fifteen and nine forty-five, leaves about ten-thirty. Cup of coffee and a Danish, sits there and reads the Naskeag Falls paper. If he doesn't show, I'll file an amended flight plan for him."

Gary still thought it seemed unnecessarily complicated. "Why didn't we just tell the cops where the stuff was?"

"Three reasons. Nobody would ever believe old Perly Stinson knew anything about it. The stuff didn't belong to the Pratts in the first place. And if we work this right, we can get both the cops *and* the other guys down on Tom Pratt's ass."

"Who *are* the other guys?"

"I don't know. I don't *want* to know, and neither do you."

"What's in the package?"

Ben grinned at him. "Same answer."

Gary wrinkled his nose. He was curious and had his suspicions about both questions. Like, Ron Pelletier and his French Connection. Heroin. However, those were minor worries.

"Have you heard anything from Aunt Alice?"

"No. She asked me not to call—I think she's scared of a tap on her phone. She's supposed to be out of town, rather than hiding in the cellar." Ben didn't look as if he was happy with his own explanation.

"What about Dad? Have you heard anything from him?"

Now Ben looked definitely sour. "Not a peep, son. That damned Dragon won't even say 'Good morning' to me. I'd hoped *you* would have some word."

Gary fingered the pendant at his chest. It felt dead. *Something* had happened, a couple of days ago. The Tear had broadcast rage mixed with a pain like burning. Then it fell silent and cold.

"Nothing." He didn't want to think about what that might mean.

* * *

THE OTHER JOB had been about as safe a burglary as you could find. Gary knew that, *had* known that in spite of what his sweaty palms had tried to tell him. It had been a perfect place to start.

This one was dangerous.

He stared into the darkness, breathing slowly, working up his nerve. Mom was dead. Drowned. No matter what the police thought, she *hadn't* killed herself. Gary had pushed himself through the shock and tears and into a quiet, deadly rage. Ben had told him the red Subaru had something to do with her death. The car was tied to the Pratts. And they damn well *knew* the Pratts were holding Dad. Now Gary could fight back. This might be dangerous, but it was *important.* He could do it. He switched off the headlights and climbed out of Dad's car.

The fog had thickened in the past three hours, but it didn't help much when your target sat right under a monster mercury-vapor yard light. It didn't help much when that yard light sat twenty feet off Highway 178, the closest thing to a main road in the town of Stonefort. Now that same fog was a problem for him rather than for his target. He couldn't see oncoming cars. He couldn't see some dippy insomniac out walking a dog at 3:00 A.M. He couldn't see some crazed drug-runner sitting in an upstairs window with an AK-47, just daring somebody to touch that car.

Walk like that dippy insomniac, he reminded himself. *Walk like you don't care who sees you. If you sneak up on the car, you'll look suspicious. Next time, borrow John Thompson's Brittany spaniel for the night, as camouflage. Or Hillary Denton's brain-dead Newfie hound.*

Just his luck, either one of them would get tangled up with a skunk at the critical moment. Scratch the Newfie, for sure. At least once a month, you could smell that idiot dog's nighttime adventures on Hillary when she got on the school bus the next morning.

He walked through the shadows toward the buzzing yard light, senses twitching. The air smelled dank and earthy, losing the salt and seaweed this far from the shore. He heard every drip from the trees and bushes, every "greep-greep" from the frogs or toads or whatever the hell made that noise. Maybe bugs. Something feathery touched the side of his neck, and he swatted it.

The hum of tires rose out of the background. He glanced around, picked a thick tree ten feet off the road, and became a shadow. *Keep your face turned away, the white would show up. Don't move—movement catches the eye.*

The car whooshed by, tunneling the fog with its headlights, neither slowing nor flashing its brake lights. Gary found he could breathe again. He studied the retreating trunk and roof. No light bar, no lettering: not a cop. It vanished into the night, pulling the red glow of its taillights in after it.

He shifted the satchel from his right shoulder to his left. Over a pound, he'd guessed. More likely a kilo. He wondered if it was heroin or cocaine or some recreational wonder-lab nose candy. PCP. Ecstasy. Whatever it was, he was carrying enough to stone all Sunrise County and half of Atlantic Canada. It might be the price of Dad's freedom, if he could ever get through this crazy night.

He stepped away from the tree, nerves settled enough for him to move again. The tire hum died nearly to silence. Then it blossomed again—fast, insanely fast, driven by the snarl of a high-powered engine. High-beam headlights tore through the fog, with a flashing blue bar above them. A siren blipped a warning, and the cruiser roared past before Gary even saw it. Another siren chased it, and he managed to move back into the woods in time.

This time the lights flashed red. Stonefort ambulance. Must be another drunken smash-up on Route 1.

Well, at least now Gary knew where the night deputy was. He swallowed his heart and blinked the flashes of red and blue out of his eyes. That Subaru wagon still lurked under the yard light, fifty yards away. Ben had scouted it out. No dogs, the man rented from a relative of the Pratts and lived alone, he kept regular hours. Whatever he did for the drug-runners, it wasn't pushing dime bags on the street corners.

Do it!

He concentrated on each step, striding along like he owned the road. Confidence. At twenty yards, he triggered the remote. The car beeped softly back at him. Either he'd disarmed the security, or the guy hadn't bothered to set it and Gary had just *armed* the system. He couldn't remember whether a single beep meant "armed" or "disarmed." He felt brain-dead, just like Hillary's Newfie.

Set the satchel down beside the rear wheel, in the shadow. Crouch down, so your own shadow is just a blur against the back of the car, hidden from the house. Fish out the picks, the different set for a two-sided key. Grit your teeth and touch the lock.

Nothing happened. The alarm system *was* off. He slid the pick into the lock, set the torque lever, and started probing. He had to slip two sets of pins for this lock, and he'd never done that well in practice. The gloves bothered him, and he started to pull them off in irritation. Then he remembered what he was carrying. This car was going to get a *lot* of attention if things went right. *Any* set of prints would attract unpleasant questions.

He backed up and started over. *Reset the torque, this time from the top because those pins seem easier. Move the probe in and out, keeping steady pressure. Patience.*

The lock clicked and turned. He was in. The latch was under the license-plate holder. He pressed it, and the tailgate lifted. As Ben had predicted, the dome light didn't go on—the driver kept it off, so he wouldn't be seen getting in and out of the car at night. Thank God for small favors. Gary found the built-in storage compartment over the left rear wheel. He flipped the switch on his penlight.

The compartment was full. Two quarts of oil, a box of flares, battery jumper cables, blankets—this driver didn't trust the back roads in winter. The compartment under the floor held tire chains, a come-along, and towrope. "Be Prepared." Frigging Eagle Scout in the drug trade.

Gary tried the compartment over the right wheel well. It held spare gloves and a ski hat, but there was enough room for his package. He slipped it out of the satchel and the extra plastic bag, wedged it in carefully, and set the plastic catch holding the cover panel.

God, he was glad to be rid of that thing. It was probably worth fifty grand wholesale, or twenty years in federal prison—whichever came first. He backed out of the car, lowered the rear gate, and pushed it closed.

It wouldn't latch. He leaned on it, and it still wouldn't click shut. Every time he let go, the damned gate started to wheeze open. Gary looked around, hands sweating again. Ben had said the guy slept in the front upstairs room, maybe thirty feet away. The sirens had probably woken him up.

He gritted his teeth, raised the gate, and slammed it shut. It caught. He crouched down in the shadow and waited forever, expecting house lights or a shout, expecting shots or sirens or a cold voice telling him to stand up slowly and keep his hands in view. After a few minutes of pins and needles, he pulled out his picks again to set the lock. It went faster, the first thing that had gone right since he'd left the tower. He slipped back into the shadows, remembered the empty satchel, and returned for it. Then he had to turn back again. He'd forgotten to arm the security system. It beeped at him, a quiet series of three electronic blips.

Fifty yards down the road, he took a minute to catch up on his breathing. A pickup rolled by in the fog, cruising in no particular hurry, two heads scrunched close together in the cab. That same twitching high flooded through Gary, even better than after the job on the dock.

I've done it!

A hundred yards farther and he turned off onto the woods road where he'd parked Dad's car. He unlocked it, slid into the seat, and sat shivering for a minute or two. He'd actually *done* it. Now the cops would *have* to search the Pratt place.

Ben was waiting. Gary pulled a microphone from the dash, switched on the radio, and checked the soft green glow of the frequency readout for the third or fourth time. Pulsing the mike switch changed the setting to another frequency, also correct.

"Done," he transmitted. "*Right* rear. Repeat, *right* rear."

Was that too long? How long did it take for a scanner to lock on?

"Roger."

The digital clock said 3:45 A.M. And the car even started. Gary pulled out on the highway and headed for home, switching his worries to skunks or deer in the road, hidden by the fog. He wondered when he'd be able to get to sleep, with all the adrenaline flushing through his veins.

I've done *it!*

seventeen

—⁓—

CAROLINE HASKELL SHIVERED and cranked the rental car's heater up another two notches. She fantasized the headlines: PROMISING YOUNG ETHNOLOGIST FOUND FROZEN IN DITCH. She reminded herself that this was normal weather for coastal Maine; she'd be lucky to see seventy at high noon on a clear day. The sun wouldn't be up for another hour or so, and the fog added a bone-deep chill she hadn't felt in over a year. PRODIGY PH.D. CANDIDATE DIES OF HYPOTHERMIA. Two days ago, the temperature in Phoenix had hit a hundred and eight. Arizona did that kind of thing in June.

Or was it three days? She'd lost track. It had taken a day for Aunt Alice's message to reach her out in the canyonlands. Then half a day for the minimum ritual to avoid offense and make it possible for her to come back to her research. Pack the essentials, three-hour drive through shimmering mirages to the airport, check in at the counter for the electronic ticket she'd *thought* she'd booked on the Internet. Then find out a Bermuda high had locked in storm patterns across the Midwest and canceled half the flights.

She ended up about two hundred down on the waiting list. "Lady, you can't *get* there from here."

Then she'd waved her magic wand—the famous Haskell platinum Visa card with the bottomless credit limit. She'd had to damn near *buy* the flaming plane, but a charter company could be bribed to route her up to Idaho and into Canada damn near to Hudson Bay before dumping her in St. John. Then back across the border and smile sweetly at the nice customs man so he'd ignore the strange stuff in her baggage.

When Aunt Alice says "Jump!" you ask "How high?" on the way up. So much for the notion that First People didn't like to hurry.

So here she was, still with corn pollen smeared on her forehead and Oraibi grit behind her ears, driving through cold pea soup. Fog swirled through the beams of her headlights, a gray blankness bordered by the ghostly white and yellow lines on the asphalt. They were the only proof that there actually *was* a road out there somewhere. Green numbers glowed on the dashboard, informing her that it was 3:25 in the morning.

The subtext to *that* was that she hadn't slept more than four hours a night in the last three days. There'd been an all-night ritual in the kiva and then climbs up three separate sacred mesas under the scorching Arizona sun, puffing and sweating behind the tiny, frail-looking figure of Grandmother Walks-with-the-Moon. If you wanted proof that the old ways gave you strength, that gnarled brown chunk of walking mesquite spoke volumes.

Caroline eased back on the accelerator. If she wrapped this Canadian Plymouth around a tree, she couldn't help a bit with whatever crisis Aunt Alice had cooked up in her crock-pot. The message hadn't said; Aunt Alice had known the words would pass through about five mouths before they reached Caroline's ear, so it had been phrased in innocent-sounding code. But the key words had been "come" and "danger" and "power." And to Aunt Alice, "come" meant "yesterday."

Finally, a white patch loomed out of the fog and resolved into the sign announcing the Stonefort turnoff. Well, that was a good news/bad news joke. The good news was, she had less than twenty miles to go. The bad news was, now she was leaving Route 1 and the road would go to hell. Sunrise County ranked at the bottom of state highway priorities. No money, few voters—even the tourists rarely drove this far past Bar Harbor and the Boundaries of the Known World.

She gritted her teeth and aimed her Avis special down the narrow, twisty asphalt. Ghostly trees closed in on either side, and she concentrated on keeping in the middle of the corridor. Trees, rocks, the small bridges over streams—all blurred into a tunnel in the fog of the night and her sleepy brain. She stopped at the first tidewater bridge and rolled down the window, hoping the wet breeze would clear her head. The heavy reek of the mud flats told her the tide was out, and she sucked it in like a cold beer after a long day under the desert sun.

The smell of home. Arizona had a haunting beauty all its own, but it was too damn dry. Mostly rock and sand and dust. She yawned, rolled up the window, and drove on. Too late in the night to get philosophical.

A dark lump in the road firmed up and became a porcupine waddling myopically in search of his next pinebark meal. She slammed on the brakes and shook her head as the critter ambled diagonally out of her headlights. Damned animals were *sure* nothing in the whole wide world could threaten them inside that wall of quills. Sort of the attitude you'd get about the House.

She blinked, rubbed her neck, and sat for a minute. Highway hypnosis. She hadn't seen another car in half an hour. This section of road didn't even have power lines, much less houses. She flipped the radio on, searching for some heavy metal or even lovesick cowboys singing laments for their lost hound dogs—anything to insult her ears and rile her brain into wakefulness. All she found was talk radio and some NPR thing with new-age saxophones whimpering against the rush of surf. She flipped it off, knuckled her eyes, and headed down the road again.

Three roadkill skunks and ten miles later, she passed the town garage ghostly in the murk and sodium-vapor lights. Left turn, right turn, coast down one hill and halfway up another, left turn again, and the fog relented enough to show her Aunt Alice's rosebushes. Gravel crunched under the tires, and Caroline finally set the parking brake. *Done.* And she was alive. Awake, even. *Well, almost.*

The House was still standing. She looked it over in the glare of her headlights. No visible damage. All the shutters were closed, and the kitchen door gave out that "fortress" feeling that said her key was useless. Well, Caroline had slept in a car more than once before. Right now, the idea seemed damned attractive.

She reached to switch the lights off. A shadow moved, around toward the front of the House. She slipped the brake and backed up slightly, turning, throwing on the high beams. Dixie? It was a low lump, too small for a man, too large for a cat. She thought of raccoons or bear cubs sniffing for garbage.

The shadow dissolved.

Seeing things. Sleep deprivation.

She rolled down the window and sniffed. She wrinkled her nose. Aunt Alice never kept garbage around that long, and something really nasty had burned somewhere upwind. Trouble, right here in River City. Something was rotten in the state of Denmark. Caroline knuckled her eyes again, blinking sleep away.

"Come" and "danger" and "power."

She'd left the Glock back in Flagstaff—airlines took a dim view of 9mm semiautos, and the Canadians were even worse. Still, she had other weapons, ones more fit for a witch's war. She scrounged around in the dusty backpack she'd tossed in the backseat.

Sage. Finely powdered ochre, with just enough bear-grease binder to stick to her skin. A shallow pottery bowl decorated with black and vermilion geometry, *without* the deliberate errors that broke the power and made tourist-ware safe to sell. A small fan of golden eagle feathers for the power of the sky.

She dabbed ochre on a fingertip and painted herself, working with the rearview mirror and the dome light of the car. Now lightning zigzagged down each cheek and the back of each hand. She felt coldness there, and then fire as the symbols pulled power from the air of her land and from the waters deep below. She coated the palms of her hands and then lit a smudge of sage leaves in the bowl.

Wafting the smoke in front and to each side with the eagle fan, she opened the door and climbed out. She felt the darkness draw back into the night as she chanted quietly, her thoughts switching seamlessly to the guttural syllables of Naskeag.

Smudge the air in front, to each side, behind. Walk slowly, walk calmly, walk in beauty with the world. A sacred way I walk. A sacred song I sing.

First the left palm on the left door-post, then the right palm on the right door-post. Clear prints of the sacred ochre. Tell the lodge that I am here, tell the lodge I am a friend. Smudge the sacred smoke to left and right, drive evil from this House.

A sacred way I walk. A sacred song I sing. Sacred waters give me strength.

"Wear this sacred pollen in beauty," Grandmother Walks had said. "Wash it into your sacred waters. It will tell them where you have been. It will tell them what you have learned. Our blood speaks to your blood. We are sisters."

The power of the spring had brought her inside the kiva, brought her inside the sisterhood of the Turtle Clan. Her brown skin hadn't been enough to bridge the gap, climb the walls around the sacred rituals. Grandmother Walks had felt the power of the spring running deep in Naskeag blood. Grandmother Walks had let down the ladder so Naskeag blood could climb up and enter the ancient stone houses, so that Naskeag blood could climb down into the secret heart of the kiva and listen and learn.

Caroline ignored the shadows within the darkness, walking down the path to the small backyard pool, the overflow from the spring. She set the smudge bowl between two moss-furred stones on the sunrise side and placed her hands on the damp rock. The spring read the ochre on her hands—read the message older than the Naskeags, reaching back to the Red Paint People before the dawn of time. The spring knew she was here. She bent down and splashed coldness on her face and over her hair, washing Oraibi grit and Oraibi pollen into the waters of her spring. The spring knew where she had been, knew what she had learned, knew the message from the People she had visited.

She felt the darkness pull back into the gray of first light. The watcher wasn't afraid. It felt *puzzled,* as if she added a new variable to the equation and forced a change in plans. The darkness was a chess master, mapping out moves five layers deep, and any new piece on the board required study. The darkness could afford to wait and come back a second time or a third for whatever it wanted. It left her with the sense that tonight had been a probe testing the guardians of the House.

Caroline rocked back on her heels, drawing strength from the icy water dripping down the back of her neck. Now that the House knew she was here, she didn't need a key to get inside. There were ways, open to her and to Aunt Alice but no one else. She sniffed the air again, sitting upwind of the sacred smoke from her bowl. The air told her of rotting garbage, burning meat, a whiff of gunpowder smoke. Aunt Alice didn't like surprises, and she was too damn quick with that old shotgun.

Caroline yawned deeply, nearly dislocating her jaw. The House would talk to Aunt Alice, come morning. Out beyond the fog, the sky brightened in the east. The party was over for the night. She slopped some of the spring water into her bowl, mashing the sage ashes into a paste. Suddenly feeling as if her twenty years had been multiplied by ten, she straightened up slowly, joint by joint, sleepwalked back to the car, and painted guardians across each window. Finally, she slumped into the backseat, pulled her sleeping bag over her body, and locked the doors.

SOMETHING WAS RAPPING, tapping, tapping, at her chamber door. Caroline felt like telling Raven to stuff his pallid bust of Pallas where the sun don't shine. Ethnographic nightmares were bad enough without E. A. Poe sticking his thumb into the pie.

She pried an eye open. A dark shape blurred into focus against the light. Face. Too pale for an Indian. Caroline fumbled her hand out to thump against the car window, her skin brown against the glare of early morning fog, at least three shades darker than the face.

Aunt Alice. Caroline's brain fuzzed, and she blinked repeatedly. Aunt Alice was full-blood, while Caroline was half white-eyes and always *had* been paler. Dramatic evidence that Indians *do* tan. Arizona sun contrasted with Maine winter.

She yawned and fumbled for the door handle, yanked twice, remembered to unlock, and tried again. She unfolded herself from the sleeping bag and a backseat that was too small for a five-eight woman. *Drive a car like this, you're better off a midget like Aunt Alice.*

The midget stepped back from the door swing. "Where the hell you been?"

Typical Aunt Alice. Caroline yawned again. "You want the full list or the summary?"

Her aunt looked like hell: hair draggling around every which-a-way, raccoon eyes from lack of sleep, a reddish lump on her forehead. So the crisis was real.

Alice turned away toward the kitchen door. "Forget it. Canadian plates, I can guess enough. You couldn't get a seat. Bet you drove all night, too, and damn near ended up in a ditch."

Caroline tried to rub some sense into her brain. She grabbed her backpack and suitcase, slammed the trunk, and followed her aunt toward the house. Alice stopped and traced a finger over the red handprints on the door-posts.

"The house would have preferred sweetgrass."

"Have to restock; used it all up out on the mesas. Besides, I've mostly been working with sage."

Alice nodded and stepped into the kitchen. "Go with what you feel comfortable with." She pulled a couple of chairs back, moving quietly, and sagged into one. "Keep the noise down. I've got a couple of guests that didn't get much sleep last night."

"They're not the only ones." Caroline ducked into the small john off the kitchen. Cars lacked certain basic amenities for an all-night accommodation. When she came back out, feeling pounds lighter and much more comfortable, Alice had brewed a pot of coffee. Boiled coffee, made up on the wood stove, it would be strong enough to stand a spoon up straight. Caroline thought that *might* serve to keep her eyes open. For a few minutes. She poured a mug and let the heat seep into her hands.

Her aunt seemed to be studying the mug in her own hands. "I'd hate to put a crimp in your creative solutions to adversity, but you could have waited in that airport for ten–twelve hours and been on the ground in Naskeag Falls yesterday morning. 'More haste, less speed.' Weather changes, you know. Airlines adjust schedules. And then there's Amtrak, or a bus. Think ahead. Think things through."

Caroline blinked. "I'd have been bored out of my skull."

"You'd have been *here,* when I needed you."

Another typical Aunt Alice bit. She kept nagging about impulsive actions. Caroline changed the subject. "So what hit the fan this time?"

"Morgans and Pratts at each other's throats."

"*Again?* Oh, shit. Why don't you let both sets of idiots kill each other off?"

"There's some kind of Inca *brujo* involved, too. It gets complicated. And don't talk about your father like that."

"Old Ben? According to Mom, he can't think straight if there's a woman within three miles. Anyway, he doesn't even know that he *is* my father."

"He does now."

"Why? Ain't that against company policy?"

"He needed to understand some things." Her lips quirked, and her eyes narrowed. "Besides, I remembered your mother's tastes. And yours."

"Oh, *hell.* I don't need *that* complication. You might as well tell me about it."

Caroline sipped coffee, letting the heat and the caffeine and the words wash through her, feeling the House adjust to her presence and feed its own peculiar energy to her. The tale seemed to soak in without passing through her ears, in a state of half-drugged hyperawareness like a vision quest.

Links formed with memories, faces floated past in the shadows of the kitchen—even smells she'd forgotten, of rugosa roses in the garden at Morgan's Castle and playing baby-sitter for two small girls. She blinked and shook her head at the mention of the soul-catcher and the wood stove. She'd never seen *that* side of Aunt Alice before.

And that brought the tale up to this morning, plots within plots within plots. "Shit. Peggy and Ellen. What do you want *me* to do? I'm just the lowly apprentice."

"Couple of things. You can stand watch, so that I can get some sleep. You can go out and get fresh groceries and call about the phone, while I hold the fort. And you can take notes while I do a Seeing. I need to know just what I'm up against."

Caroline winced. She stared pointedly at the lump on her aunt's forehead. "You up to that?"

"This?" Alice traced the spot with one finger. "Damned shotgun kicks like a mule. Caught me off balance and I bumped my head on the wall. And Seeing works better if you're short of sleep. That helps disconnect your back-brain from the Critic and lets your soul slip out through the crack between them."

"Hey, it's your life." Caroline shrugged. "I could stand inheriting a few million right now. Sell this dump, get me a nice place in Hawaii where I have to climb a mountain if I want to see snow, lie out on the beach all day and ogle the surfer dudes . . ."

Her aunt's hand twitched, and Caroline ducked a clout to the ear that never came. Naskeags had great patience with children, but sometimes she pushed the edge a *little* far. The Haskell money and the House were a tribal trust fund administered by the current Witch, not personal wealth. Caroline had been talking white-man trash, as if she stood apart from the web of clan and kin that bound her to the whole Stonefort Tribe. She finally let the wicked grin escape onto her face.

Alice looked like she'd bitten into a lemon. "I swear, Caroline Haskell, some days I come *this* close to handing you back to Lainie and telling her to try again. Or maybe I should have taken the turkey-baster route when I was young enough to handle babies. You've got too much Ben Morgan in you to make a decent Witch."

"Okay, okay, you're fine, I'm fine, no problems. I just don't want to lose my favorite aunt. When do you want to do the dreadful deed?"

"Your *only* aunt."

"Yeah, well that, too. I just remember what I felt like after the peyote circle. Dogshit in the hot sun just about covered it."

"Sounds close. As for when, right now looks good. I don't want Peggy and Ellen watching this."

She unlocked a cupboard at the end of the kitchen counter and pulled out a lab balance, several jars of powder and liquid, and a leather-bound notebook that had seen better centuries. Caroline could see brown stains on age-yellowed paper, with darker brown ink spider-webbing its way across the pages. Scribbled notes crowded the margins in purple or black—the Haskell Grimoire, three centuries of distilled witchcraft. She felt the House centering itself, ready for any attack, like a kung fu master rising up on the balls of his feet.

"Five grams of dried Amanita muscaria powder. Ten drops of nightshade extract."

Short of sleep as she was, Caroline couldn't help herself. "Fillet of a fenny snake, in the cauldron boil and bake."

Alice looked up from the counter and glared at her. "Shut up, or I'll make *you* drink this muck."

"Eye of newt and toe of frog, wool of bat and tongue of dog . . ."

"Look, *Ellen* wants to learn this stuff. Do *you*?"

"Okay, okay. I'm shutting up now. But why are you going with this cookbook stuff rather than chants and drums and dancing like they do in the kiva?"

"Because your great-great-great-et-cetera-aunt Hepzibah

learned it from a European witch, that's why. And don't bother to memorize these proportions. They'd be wrong for your body weight, anyway. Start at the low end of the scale and work up to an effective dose."

Caroline watched as her aunt added a dash of this and a smidgen of that, each time referencing a line in the old book. The end result looked like pond slime and smelled about as bad. Alice glared at the mug, shuddered, and tossed it down in one long swallow. Then she rinsed out her mouth with straight whiskey and spat the results in the sink. Lab balance, jars, and book went back into the cabinet. Alice locked the door and pocketed the key.

She stepped over to the china/junk cabinet built into one corner and took out a chunk of deep green crystal, trigonal gem-grade tourmaline almost the size of a football that had been in the family since the end of the last ice age. She set it on the kitchen table, sat down in front of it, and blinked. "Remember, take notes. Ask questions. Odds are, I won't remember half of what I see. And if anything happens, wake up the girls and head that car back to Canada."

Caroline nodded.

She waited. She waited some more. Fifteen minutes ticked by on the wall clock, sliced into seconds by the pendulum. Twenty. Alice grunted and shook her head, lost in the depths of the crystal. Caroline chewed on her pencil and fidgeted.

"Anything happening?"

"What?" Her aunt just stared into the green stone.

"You're supposed to be Seeing. Looking for the Pratts' *brujo*. That Peruvian spook Ben told you about."

"*Brujo*. Spanish noun, masculine gender. Sorcerer, magician, wizard."

"Don't bother with the definition; I've got a perfectly good Spanish-English dictionary. You're supposed to be looking for the *man,* not the flaming *word*!"

"He's with Kate."

"Huh?"

"I can't see his face. He's smallish, well-dressed, Latino or Native, but I can't see his face. Fog."

"Where is he? What are they doing?"

"Kate's trailer. At the door. Kissing good-bye."

"Look at his face. Describe it."

"Fog. Nothing but fog."

Tears streaked Alice's face, and her eyes were closed. She sagged back in the chair, asleep. Caroline picked her up like a child and carried her featherweight aunt upstairs to bed.

Cool it with a baboon's blood, then the charm is firm and good. Well, that *gave us the square root of minus one. Does that mean this Peruvian is stronger than we are?*

She stared down at her sleeping aunt. *Great. Now* I've *got to stay awake.* She stretched, unkinking her shoulders again. *How much coffee is in that pot?*

eighteen

—⁓—

KATE CRAWLED OUT from under the truck and stowed the ratchet drive and sockets in her toolbox, leaving everything tightened down after the final DC smoke test. She stretched the kinks out of her shoulders and glanced at her hands with a wry smile, counting new scars in the making—not a Jergen's ad, by any means, blackened nails, missing fingertip and all. This had been a two-knuckle job, replacing the battery and the starter.

She shook her head as she stepped back inside the trailer to wash up. Those replacements had *not* been in her budget. The starter was a junkyard special, pulled off a wrecked truck of the approximate year and tested good, but she couldn't dodge the cost of a new battery. Damned truck *had* to start, February cold or not.

The soap stung her scraped knuckles, and she cataloged the damage. Right thumb was the old bolt twisting off, whacking a knuckle into the rear engine mount. The one on the left was the sharp lip of the oil pan nibbling away while she tried to hold the replacement starter with one hand and align the bolts with the other.

Scars on top of scars on top of scars. That was the story of her life. Some of them were physical—like her hands, and her belly from the emergency C-section. Others were mental, like Alice on top of Jackie on top of Lew Lewis falling off the wagon. Again. Gossip said Caroline Haskell was suddenly back in town, proving that Alice was *there* but not answering messages. So Kate had made a damned fool of herself. *Again.*

Then there was that other thing gossip reported. If Kate went over to talk to Alice, smooth things out face to face, her Town Constable hat might have to officially notice the two orphan minors living with a woman who was not their relative. The DHS frowned on stuff like that. Adoptions and fosterings were supposed to be formal and blessed by tons of Official State of Maine paper—not a traditional specialty of the Haskell House. So far, nobody had asked embarrassing questions.

Well, Alice Haskell could go screw herself. The whole lesbian thing had been her idea in the first place. Antonio, now, *he* looked intriguing. Smooth, well-mannered, gallant, and darkly handsome, even if he did come well short of her shoulders. She hadn't finished up her plan to drink Jackie down the drain. The rest of that night *had* been kind of vague, though. She'd never met a man with that kind of charisma before. When you focused on him, the rest of the world got blurry.

Come right down to it, he could be as potent a drug as the bourbon he'd replaced. No aftereffects, though. That had helped considerably when she'd had to take a sledgehammer to some stone patio walls over at Larry Beech's place the next day—not a job you wanted to tackle with a hangover already banging away on your head.

He'd said to call him Tony. That seemed out of character to Kate, as if Louis XIV had asked her to call him Lew. Antonio Estevan Francisco Juan Carlos da Silva y Gomes was a born aristocrat. His family probably had a silver coat of arms tucked away somewhere on the wall of a castle in Spain.

She dried her abused hands and headed back out the door. Work called, and she had to earn that battery back. She climbed up into the truck, ducking and shoehorning herself into a space meant for someone six inches shorter and about a hundred pounds lighter. The starter just whined at her, as its recycled pinion gear found nothing to crank. Easing the brake with clutch engaged rolled the truck forward a foot or two, and the starter locked into the few teeth left on that stripped ring gear that she didn't *have* to replace. Yet.

She contemplated the cost of junkyard flywheels and where she could steal the day or so necessary to pull the engine. Really should replace the clutch, pressure plate, and throw-out bearing at the same time, though. Those would have to be new parts. That exercise in fiscal folly carried her across past Morgan's Point and out into the realm of Philadelphia lawyers who didn't know or care how much a new starter for a Mercedes-Benz might cost. Of course, Larry Beech didn't keep a car long enough to *need* a new starter.

Alice might have a ton of money, but she sure didn't make it obvious that way. Her Subaru had more than 200,000 miles on it, rusted fenders you could throw a cat through, and foam rubber leaking out of the upholstery. When a Haskell threw something out, you *knew* it was junk. Not like Larry Beech, replacing a hot tub because the whirlpool pipes needed a dose of Drano. Not like Jackie, who wanted to dump their old computer because "that hunk of junk" couldn't handle downloading music files.

The road blurred in front of Kate, and she pulled over to the shoulder. *Jackie.* Why couldn't the little twit have waited another year or two? Didn't she have enough of an example staring her in the face, her mother living from hand to mouth because *she'd* dropped out of high school and run away from home when *she* was seventeen? Kate had come home from that state championship game, punched out her stepfather for razzing the coach, and left. Then she'd had to get a job down at the cannery, and never graduated.

Alice's sardonic voice echoed in Kate's ears: "Those who fail to learn the lessons of history are doomed to repeat them." It'd been meant to describe politics and nations, but it damn sure could be applied to individuals.

Jackie, Jackie, Jackie, the voice in her head keened. Still no word. Kate couldn't put out a Missing Person on the twit, official, not with the gun and the money missing. All she could do was ask around, friends and cops and kids she knew, and nobody who knew anything was willing to talk.

She slammed her fist into the dashboard. The truck lurched with the impact, and she rubbed her thrice-abused knuckles as she counted the dents in the cracked vinyl padding. There hadn't been anywhere near that many before she'd found her daughter's note. She fumbled for a cigarette and her old lighter, retreating into smoke as an excuse for smarting eyes.

Alice would stare into that lump of tourmaline of hers and claim to nail Jackie's young butt down to within a yard, sure as hell. Probably toss in some sidelights on just how many cornflakes the kid had poured into the bowl that morning and whether she'd changed her underwear. But Alice wasn't returning calls, and one thing Kate shared with Jackie and a long line that allegedly traced back to Plymouth Rock: the Rowleys had a well-deserved reputation for stiff necks. The next move was up to Alice.

Stiff-necked, yeah. The only way Alice got you to take that com-

puter was replacing it and pretending she was going to throw the old one on the dump. Damnfool woman offered to buy you a truck about five or twenty times, said it'd be an "investment."

Lay it out in black and white like that, it looked like a bribe, almost prostitution. "Sleep with me and live like a rich woman." But Alice wasn't like that, at all. She was just too used to having enough money. It changed the way you saw the world.

Kate stared at the smoke rising from her cigarette. It went up straight, not jiggling back and forth. Her hands had calmed down enough to find a gear. She wiped her eyes and pulled back out on the road, switch-backing her way up to Larry Beech's place.

Jeff's mountain bike leaned against one of the garage doors. So her "crew" was here already. He'd bought the high-end bike used, well-tended, and it made a hell of a lot more sense than any car the kid could have afforded. Just keep his toolbox on the truck as well as hers. He was starting to use his brain instead of frying it with chemicals. Another year and she could kick him out of the nest, ready to fly free.

Why hadn't it worked with Jackie? Mother-daughter thing, instead of mother-son? Would father-daughter have worked out better? Might the little twit have made it if Lew hadn't kept diving through the neck of a bottle?

Her sometime-punk assistant sauntered around the corner of the garage, swigging a bottle of soda. His T-shirt-of-the-day was a flat black, red-lettered editorial proclaiming DEATH: ENJOY THE RIDE. Maybe that was a music group.

And then she remembered that Charlie wasn't going to gimp around the corner after him. Damn. She'd never realized how much she'd counted on him. And now he was dead. Damn, damn, *damn*.

She'd woken up last night, black thoughts in the hour of

the wolf, and wondered just what she'd done to piss God off. Alice. Jackie. Charlie. Isolation.

She grabbed hold of herself and put her "boss face" on. "Jeffy-boy?"

"Yo!"

"You get those flagstones set like I told you, over on the side patio?"

"Yes'm, boss-lady. Want to check it out?"

"Take your word for it. That's done, then we'd best get the new tub leveled and nailed down, ready for Perly to hook it up. He told me he can come out tomorrow."

Kate grabbed her four-foot level from the gun rack of the cab, Jeff hoisted his toolbox and work belt out of the truck bed, and they both headed around to the south deck. Mr. Philadelphia Lawyer Beech had decided the view was better there and thought nothing of dumping ten grand for the change. Now he and his trophy wife could bask in the afternoon sun rather than greeting the sunrise with a hot, relaxing soak and a little cuddle in the clean sea breeze. *The rich are different from you and me.*

Except for Alice—she wasn't.

The new tub was set flush into the deck, six feet deep and damn near big enough for swimming laps. Jeff crawled under the redwood deck and fitted a wrench to one jackscrew. Kate squinted at the bubble of her level. "Up a turn or two." The bubble shifted. "Up two more." It shifted again. "Got it."

She heard him setting the lock nuts and whacking the strut a couple of times to make sure the jackscrew base was firmly bedded. Good kid, paid attention to details. Then she heard scuffles and muttered cussing as he started worming his way around to the second strut, dodging the boulders under the deck that had dictated just *exactly* where the tub could go. Jeff was down there because he was the designated gopher, yes, but Kate wouldn't have fit anyway. Sometimes, scrawny was an advantage. She shifted her level to another side of the tub.

"Hey, Jeffy-boy. You hear anything about Jackie?"

Silence. Then he started crawling again, without answering.

"Jeff?"

He stopped again. "Miz Rowley, you *promised*."

When she'd hired him, he'd been worried about her being a cop. There'd been a long talk, both of them sitting out on rocks and staring in different directions down the bay, and she'd finally agreed that she could be two people. The contractor wouldn't ask questions, and the cop wouldn't do construction. As far as either the contractor or the cop knew, he'd been straight since then. But she wasn't supposed to ask.

"Jeff?"

"Yo."

"I'm her mother, Jeff," she went on softly. "This isn't cop stuff."

Silence reigned for a minute or two, and then she heard the clinking of his wrench on the second jackscrew. "Down half a turn." The bubble shifted.

His voice filtered up through the redwood decking: "Pratts."

She swallowed. *Suspicion confirmed.* "Down another half." The bubble shifted again, a bit past level. "Back a quarter." The bubble jiggled to dead center. "On."

He set the lock nuts and tested the bearing, again, then squirmed on to another support. Damned tub was big enough, it had three a side, and they all had to be set firm or the fiberglass would break when you loaded it with a few tons of water. She kept an eye on the bubble, but Jeff seemed to have a deft touch with the wrench. He set up jackscrew after jackscrew, and the level barely quivered.

"What's she doing, Jeff?"

She could hear him puffing as he crawled around the far corner, but he didn't answer. Kate moved the level again. The bubble stayed centered.

"I need to know, Jeff."

"Miz Rowley, I want to keep working for you."

Kate blinked. "Jeffrey Burns, I ain't the kind of boss to fire a good worker because he tells me something I don't want to hear. Not long as it's true."

He set one jack and moved on to the last. She heard the scratch of the threads as he turned it down, and then the slight hum of the rod as it took load. She didn't even bother to look at the level; Jeff was tuning those jackscrews like a fiddle.

The sound stopped. Then she heard a quiet shuffle, as if he was rolling over on his back and looking up through the slats of the deck. "Miz Rowley, I haven't had anything to do with the Pratts since you busted me. I'm done with that. But back when I was doing stuff, I didn't need to worry about where to get it. Just ask Jackie. She never carried stuff, she never sold it. But she always knew where I could get it. I ain't the only one she told." Then she heard the wrench again, tightening the lock nuts.

Damn. Damn, damn, damn, damn, damn. Worse than an addict, worse than a street pusher—Jackie was a frigging dope *dispatcher.* The girl's voice echoed in her mind, heavy with scorn: "Users are losers." *I've raised a frigging vampire.*

She stood up, fumbling a cigarette out of the pack in her shirt pocket. Her eyes were burning again. "You get done down there, come back up and trim out the lip of the tub. Use the table saw and rip the stock you need out of the scrap decking we pulled up. Try to keep all the fresh edges hidden—that way the wood'll match." She lit her cigarette and wandered off, half blind to the world, shaking her head. *Jackie, Jackie, Jackie. Where the hell did I go wrong?*

Complications Jeff didn't know, stuff that hadn't hit the papers yet, might not even be on the streets. Bernie the Narc had called, professional courtesy, they'd had a tip . . .

If the little twit had been at the Pratts' when last night's raid went down, why hadn't Kate heard by now? Should have been a phone call from the jail, hours ago. Should have been *something.* She paced out to the driveway, turned back onto a flagstone walkway, lit another cigarette, and paced some more.

A muttering came over the salt breeze, breaking into her thoughts as it grew deeper and louder. *Harley,* she thought, *out on the point road. You can tell one of those hogs five miles away.* The rider downshifted for a curve, and then again. The rumble faded and then grew again, swelling up through the spruces. She dropped the butt end of her smoke and ground it out on the flagstones, shredding the paper and tobacco until they disappeared. Couldn't do that with filters, but she'd always figured that if she was going to take a shot of poison, she'd take it straight.

A Harley, coming up the driveway—that would be her favorite undercover ex–state trooper. Maybe Bernie had word on Jackie and had brought it in person, to soften the blow. Scars on top of scars on top of scars.

He pulled up about six feet away and studied her with a peculiar expression on his face, the big V-twin thumping away. Then he busied himself with shutting down his hog and leaning it over on its stand.

He stepped off and straightened up, staring out over the trees. "What am I going to do with you, Rowley?"

Kate gritted her teeth, wondering what the hell was so bad that he was avoiding her eyes. Had some damn fool started shooting? Nothing on the cop radio, no ambulance calls . . .

Hot metal ticked between them, cooling, like the motorcycle was a time bomb. Finally, he shook his head. "You're not stupid enough to do it."

"Huh?" Brilliant repartee, but she didn't have a clue what he meant.

"You're not stupid, and I don't think you're a crooked cop. If I did, I'd be talking to Her Royal Highness instead of you."

Bernie didn't think much of the Sunrise County District Attorney. The woman had bungled a couple of important cases, year or so of good work trashed and two real hard-asses back working the streets.

Kate decided to just dig out the splinter. It hurt less in the long run. "She's not really a bad kid, Bernie. Maybe getting busted will straighten her out. It worked for Jeff. What's the bail?"

"Bail?" He snorted and shook his head again. "Ain't nobody going bail, Rowley. That's why I'm here."

Kate blinked. "Didn't you guys get the warrant?"

"Oh, yeah, no problem with the warrant." He spread his hands. "A kilo of pure heroin is pretty solid 'probable cause.' And we tied the car in with somebody visiting at the Pratts, so's we were golden. The boys went in last night, just as planned."

"And?"

"Nada. Five MDEA agents, ten deputies, and a snoop from the Feds. Two sniffer dogs. The place was clean, the people were clean, and there was Tom Pratt as smooth as goose-grease but with this shit-eating smirk when he thought you weren't looking. The agent in charge came back and damned near tore me a new asshole, he was so mad."

"You weren't there?"

"Damn straight. Tom Pratt and his cocaine cowboys get my face on their security cameras, I might as well retire. I'd rather sit back and let the uniformed boys take all the glory."

Back to that damned splinter. "Was Jackie there?"

"Funny you should ask. My boss *really* had a burr up his butt about her. Mouthiest little so-and-so he'd ever seen, came *that* close to hauling her in for interfering with an officer. Only thing that saved her, Tom Pratt had one of those Latino cowboys put a hammerlock on her before she got her ass in a sling."

Bernie was still staring out at the treetops and the bay. What the hell was going on?

"Talk to me, Bernie. You've got something else. I smell it."

He turned around. "Smell? That's an interesting choice of words. Those dogs alerted all over the place. People, closets, cellar, the garage, you name it. Funny thing is, that little beagle Jerry Thompson runs is trained *real* good. Fifi was wagging her tail for coke, not heroin. And we didn't find a gram of the stuff."

"Shit."

"Yeah. They knew we were coming." Bernie wrinkled his nose, as if *he* smelled something rotten. "Thing is, there's this professional courtesy bit. I told *you* there was a raid going down. Your turf, and all that. Then the boys waltz in and find your daughter on the scene. Looks bad. Thing looks worse, I warned you off that big-assed New Jersey Suburban and our boys say you've been seen in a bar with the owner. Seen kissing him good-bye at the door of your trailer, next morning. Tell me what this looks like, Rowley."

Kate's belly did a flip-flop. "Owner?"

"Yeah. 'Red Bank Delivery' belongs to a string of dummies that belong to one Tony da Silva, AKA 'El Indio.' Different string of dummies own that Subaru wagon we busted with the smack. All leads back to the same place. Talk to me, Rowley. Tell me I'm wrong."

But Antonio was so *nice* . . . "I never saw him with the car. You never told me who owned it, and I didn't check any further. You told me not to."

He glared at her. "You've been told now, Rowley. I can't tell you how to run your love life, but da Silva got that nickname from an old Clint Eastwood Western. Movie character was a whackjob, killed for kicks. You're out of the loop, Rowley. No more professional courtesy."

Kate squeezed her eyes shut. She couldn't make Antonio's face fit the mobster template. It didn't work. She shook her head. "I didn't tell him, Bernie. I didn't tell *anyone*. I haven't even *seen* him since you told me about the raid."

Bernie swung his leg over the Harley and stood there, straddling the seat. "Yeah. That's the word I had from the guys watching him. That's the only reason I'm here rather than up at the DA's office, Rowley. Thing is, you've got a telephone. Watch yourself." He kicked the machine to life, shutting off any reply.

She watched his back retreating down the drive. The beat of the Harley faded and then roared again as he hit the main road. Kate just stood there, chewing on her lower lip and trying to settle the pain in her belly, as the rumble faded back into the sigh of wind in the spruce trees. She lit another cigarette, counting what remained in the pack. Five left. Have to stop off at the store on the way home.

Antonio. "El Indio." Cocaine and heroin and Jackie and a drug raid on a house that was almost clean. Now her cop job was in the shithouse, as well as her family life. But Bernie wouldn't have told her anything if he thought she was a bent cop. The pieces didn't fit together.

"Miz Rowley?"

Jeff had appeared around the corner of the garage, sometime during her thoughts. He wouldn't meet her eyes, either. She wondered how much he had overheard.

"Miz Rowley, word on the street is, that smack was stolen. Part of a shipment for Boston. Folks had this turf sliced up, see. Running coke and grass was one group, smack was another, meth and ecstasy and angel dust they bought in from a third. All nice and peaceful. Now the smack boys want a piece of the cocaine group. No more Mr. Nice Guy. Thought you might want to know."

"Jeff, please pass the word along. Tell Jackie she can come home, anytime. No questions. No yelling. Just come home." Kate realized that she was crying again and didn't much care if he saw.

He nodded and vanished around the corner, leaving her to her pain, leaving her to wonder what had forced him to break his silence.

Oh, shit! *Jackie in the middle. With that damned gun.*

Alice, and Jackie, and Charlie, and now Bernie. Kate felt like somebody was following her around, cutting every connection that gave her strength. Was Jeff going to be next?

nineteen

—◊—

As NEAR AS Ben could figure it, ounce for ounce Alice Haskell *had* to be about the nastiest woman walking God's green earth. She had some kind of game going, rubbing his nose in the powers of the all-knowing, all-seeing Haskell Witch and all the secrets the Morgans had *thought* they'd kept for centuries. And the worst was, she knew that he knew that she knew that he knew that he couldn't go anywhere else for help. He had to swallow it.

That woman should have been drowned at birth. Hell, he'd had a chance himself, when she was six or eight and fell off the town dock. But no, he'd *had* to jump in and pull her out. Might be the stupidest thing he'd ever done.

As penance, he was waiting in the deepest, most secret chamber of the Morgan tunnels, the chamber of the Dragon's pool, under fifty feet of Maine granite, breathing clammy salt air, watching the tide ebb in the black water and leave a wet line on the coarse pink stone. "The Dragon needs to meet your daughter," that damned woman had said. "She's got as much Morgan blood in her as Gary has."

Okay. That was bad enough—bringing a woman to the Dragon, bringing a Haskell Witch into the heart of the Morgan secrets. Then she'd told him Caroline wouldn't need a guide. The girl would meet him at the pool. "Oh, and bring young Gary along," Alice had added. "Caroline will have a message for him."

So Alice knew the tunnels and the chambers and the secret entrances. Hell, as far as *that* went, the damned witches might have their own private door hidden behind the deceptive stone walls of some side tunnel. One even *he* didn't know about.

He'd set Gary to studying the alarm system, a training exercise to keep him out of trouble. Now the boy was slipping along one wall of the cave, staring at a motion sensor and occasionally sticking out one hand and waving it. Sometimes the little red LED flashed; sometimes it didn't.

He turned to Ben and shook his head. "Don't the sensor specs give a wider detection angle than that?"

Smart kid. "Yeah. I set different trigger thresholds on the indicator and on the alarm relay."

"So somebody could think he wasn't setting off the alarms, but you'd actually know he was there?"

"That's the general idea."

"You're not very nice."

"It's on the Morgan coat of arms: 'Never show 'em all your cards.' Of course, that's a paraphrase of the original Latin."

"I never knew we had a coat of arms. Shouldn't it be on a shield over the door, or carved into the mantel over the living room fireplace?"

"Think about it."

The literal translation was "I know more than I say." That attitude had served the family well, down through the centuries.

Ben glanced over at the doorway leading to the stair tunnel. No sign of Caroline. He wiped his hands on his cargo pants and cussed silently, wondering why he felt so nervous. He'd never seen this daughter of his—being dead meant he couldn't spend much time in Stonefort, where people had long memories and might ask embarrassing questions.

Gary had probably seen her at school, but the difference in ages meant the boy couldn't connect her name with any memory of a face. There was a white square with NO PIC-TURE written over her name and accomplishments in the old school yearbook.

He wondered for a moment if the Haskell Witches actually *could* be caught on film. The list of activities had been interesting, though: a whole slew of academic honors, then Drama Club, Latin Club, Chess Club, Math Team, Cross-Country Team, and Girls' State. The final entry had made him smile—Juggling Club. He wondered where she had found time to breathe.

Ben pulled three golf balls out of his thigh pocket and started juggling them, just to give his hands something to do. There was a complicated pattern, "Mel's Mess," he was trying to get nailed down from a written description. Parts of it didn't seem to make sense. The concentration helped to quiet his twitchy feeling about this whole daughter/witch thing. Alice Haskell could give lessons to Niccolo Machiavelli.

Now the boy stepped out from the wall and danced slowly across the cave floor, eye on the sensor light. Ben moved back to make sure he and the juggling balls were out of range. The light stayed off as Gary slid closer, flowing through the positions of one of his karate forms.

"Slowly," Ben prompted. "Smoothly. Move slow enough and you can walk right by that kind of sensor. Just remember, there are systems that can tell if a new object is in the field, even if it doesn't move. They work with passive sensors and line-of-sight, or aggregate echo count. Always know what you're dealing with."

Ben checked the tunnel mouth again and she was there, five feet inside the cave of the pool, watching them, with the Morgan gift of never being noticed until she wanted to be. Tight black jeans and RED POWER! T-shirt, she was Lainie made young again: thinner but broad-shouldered and sinewy with exercise, burned dark from the Arizona sun and with glossy straight black hair that seemed to glow under the cavern lighting. Ben's breath caught in his throat. God, she was beautiful.

He glanced back to Gary. The boy looked like somebody had whacked him between the eyes with a baseball bat: instant love, or probably lust would be more accurate. *This could be a problem.*

Ben's hands had kept up the three-ball pattern, operating on reflex programming while his brain and hormones tripped over each other. She smiled, nodded a greeting that included both men in some private joke, and then she stepped up in front of him, snatching the balls one after another in a perfect steal. She continued the flow he'd started and then elaborated with underarm tosses to each side, reverse catches, and some kind of behind-the-back routine he'd never seen even a professional attempt.

Through all that, she stared at Ben's face and ignored her hands, as if memorizing every pore of his skin. Then she glanced back and forth between him and Gary. She nodded again, as if checking off a guess confirmed, and Ben felt cold sweat on his back. Those eyes, those gray Morgan eyes, looked as if she saw *much* too much.

"Gary," she said, and her low voice raised goosebumps on Ben's arms. "Aunt Alice says she talked to her shape-changer shaman. They think you might be too good a swimmer. This never happened before because a lot of local sailors never learned to swim. Certainly not state champions."

She glanced at Ben, and he nodded confirmation. With the water temperatures off Stonefort, the cold could kill a man within minutes. If you went overboard, you were dead. Why prolong the agony? Survival suits had changed that, but most working boatmen were still poor swimmers.

"Anyway," she went on, "his family uses an ordeal drug in their initiation rite. It forces you into total terror, and you find your totem animal and shape-change to escape. You may need to be actually drowning before the selkie change can happen. He added a warning: When you change, remember to change back."

Then she tossed the balls over her shoulder to the boy, one at a time, and he caught them and habit continued the motion into a cascade. *Just one big, happy family,* Ben thought. *All Morgans together. Time to put the troupe of jesters on the stage.*

Time to take control of the situation, rather, or *try* to. "How'd you get in?"

"Back door. Climb down the cliff by the bald-headed spruce, cram yourself into a crack in the rock, sit down, and slide feet-first under a ledge. Pull yourself in using handholds in the ceiling. Helps a lot if you aren't too fat. Take the first right and third left once you're in the tunnels and you're at the head of the stairs."

Gary caught all three balls in one hand and glared at Ben. That was an entrance the boy didn't know about. Never show 'em all your cards.

Ben's rage boiled over. "You *mind* telling me just *how* you know about that route? This is private property. Always has been, always will be. People who don't belong here end up *dead!*"

She shook her head. "I belong here. My people have *always* belonged here. Naskeags helped dig these tunnels. The workers told their Woman, the Woman wove the knowledge into a chant, and the chant was passed down through the generations. Then some Aunt wrote down the lore so there was no chance of losing it from one generation to the next.

You want to kill it off now, you're going to have to track down a secure server on the Internet and five backups in five different locations. Aunt Alice told you what witches do. We remember. We always remember. That's on *our* coat of arms."

So she'd been listening, long before he'd noticed her. Before she'd *allowed* him to notice her. Gods above and below, what a Morgan could do with her abilities. And she was just an apprentice Witch.

What a Morgan could do . . . "Any chance your lore has the layout of the tunnels beneath the *Pratt* compound?"

That drew a sharp glance from her Morgan eyes. "I don't know. They aren't part of the tribe, aren't 'white Indians' with the long bond we have with your family. But they might have hired local labor. I'll have to check with Aunt Alice. My passwords won't work unless I'm prepared to say she's dead."

Ben's head spun with the implications of what she'd said. He had to assume she meant to reveal the things he gleaned from her words. He had too much respect for Alice and any heir she'd choose to think otherwise. *Damn the woman!*

He wasn't sure *which* woman he meant to damn. This daughter of his could be just as exasperating as her aunt. Maybe it came with the territory. Then his lips quirked into a wry grin. "Daughter" didn't mean much in this context. Her genetics might be half Morgan, but her attitudes were pure Haskell. If that damned Dragon had let him settle down with one woman, things might have been very different. Lainie had been *years* before Maria.

Ben gritted his teeth and tried to get a hand on the slippery situation. "Okay, you're here. What was so important that your pain-in-the-butt aunt . . ."

She wasn't listening to him. Neither was Gary. They were staring at each other, but it wasn't the drooling lust he'd seen before on Gary's face. It was the look of two people who were listening to the same voice, a voice Ben couldn't hear. The Dragon was speaking to them.

And he was locked out. Whatever the Dragon was saying wasn't for *his* ears. She rejected him. She always rejected him.

Gary shuddered and then reached up to his throat and touched his Dragon pendant. He loosened the chain and lifted it over his head, so that the crimson glow of the Tear rested in his palm. He took a slow step toward Caroline, extending and then withdrawing his hand as if he was reluctant.

Ben froze. They *couldn't* . . .

Then he stood between them. "*No!* That thing can *kill* a stranger!"

Caroline shook her head. "I am *not* a stranger."

<Stand clear.> The Dragon's voice echoed in his head, as if she'd spoken aloud in the cave. <She has challenged me for the right.>

His daughter reached out, palm up in a demand for the Tear. "I *have* the right!"

Ben pushed her hand aside and crowded Gary away from her. Pain in the butt or not, he was not *about* to let this new-found daughter commit suicide.

<You cannot stop this. Stand clear.>

Gary and Caroline glowed with a red aura, and Ben's eyes felt scratchy as if he had gone three nights without sleep. His hands flopped to his sides, useless, and then he lost control of his knees. Pain lanced through his head. He was looking up now, from a seat on the floor, and he wondered if he had just had a stroke. He couldn't move.

Caroline reached out again. Gary clenched his fist around the Tear, trying to obey Ben and protect the girl, fighting against the Dragon's will. Then his fingers unfolded, one by one. The stone blazed in his palm. When Caroline took it, Ben could see the glow clear through her hand.

The crimson blaze spread up her arm, as if she was turning into a human torch. She screamed once. Then she started chanting in the gutteral syllables that Alice used, that Aunt Jean had used when she was wafting herb-smoke in one of her Naskeag rituals. The fire spread until her eyes glowed and her body was a single flame.

Her voice rose until she was almost shouting. Then she screamed again and collapsed to the floor, a loose doll discarded after playtime. The Dragon was done with her.

Ben moved a hand, then a leg. He crawled across the rough stone floor, twitching as he regained control of parts of his body. The air smelled of lightning and seaweed and sweat. Gary lay in his path, limp, eyes closed. Ben couldn't remember a Morgan *ever* giving up his Tear—not in the tales, not in the journals. If that damned witch had killed the boy, Ben would kill *her.* That was one bit of tribal crudity the family still practiced. No one killed a Morgan and lived. The Pratts were going to find that out, sooner or later.

Ben's hand tingled all the way up to his elbow, like he'd whacked his funny bone, and his head throbbed. He steadied the twitching and reached out to lay a palm on Gary's chest. The shirt moved under his hand—the boy was still breathing. His heartbeat felt strong and steady.

What about Caroline?

The girl lay beyond, crumpled facedown on the cave floor. Ben forced himself forward on hands and knees, one leg dragging. He wondered what the Dragon had done to *him,* to keep him out of the fight.

Her smooth black hair glistened in his eyes. He touched it, remembering the caress of Lainie's hair under his hand, remembering the fresh-hay smell of her. *Damn that Dragon!*

Her hair was damp. A drop of sweat beaded and then ran a track down to the tip of her nose, crossing one eyelid without drawing a blink. He was afraid to check for a pulse or breathing.

She sneezed.

He jerked back. He felt curiously reluctant to touch her, as if she might break.

She pulled her hands in and pushed her shoulders up from the floor. She sneezed again. "Typical bunch of men. Don't you ever *sweep* down here?"

The Tear glowed in her hand, smoldering like a banked fire. She stared at it, shaking her head as if wondering if it was worth the price. She grunted and shoved herself up and backward to squat on her heels, squeezed her eyes shut, and then shifted her gaze to Ben, blinking and squinting as if she found it difficult to focus. "You okay?"

Control returned to his body. He nodded and then staggered to his feet, looking down at her, and then offered her a hand to help up. She glanced at the Tear again. That "listening" look crossed her face. She spread the chain, slipped it over her head, and tucked the silver dragon down inside her T-shirt. Then she took Ben's hand and pulled herself upright. Both of them swayed with the effort.

Ben saw her gather herself together and draw strength from some deep reserve. She straightened up and blinked three times, shaking her head like she was shaking off a physical blow. Then she narrowed her eyes, wiped sweat from her forehead, and quirked one corner of her mouth into a wry attempt at a smile. "I need to talk to you," she said. "Alone."

With that, she turned and staggered over to the stair tunnel, expecting him to follow. Ben glanced at Gary. The boy looked like he was sleeping. He'd keep. Might as well do what that damned Haskell Woman expected. Trying otherwise was like Canute ordering back the tide.

She stopped at the first landing, leaned on the wall and panted for a moment, and then turned aside into a chamber where generations of Morgans had hidden things, thinking they were secret. The sharp odors of grease and solvent overpowered the smell of damp stone. She wrinkled her nose and gestured at the stenciled green packing cases. "Thinking of starting a private war?"

Ben had been cleaning up the mortar and recoilless rifle: wiping off the preservative grease, mounting sights, and swabbing the bores. Some of his recent dreams tended to get violent.

He shook his head. "Contingency plans."

She nodded. "Aunt Alice asked me to remind you of what happened to that British sloop back in 1814. Any of those shells come near the House, she says you can squat down in some deep, dark corner, tuck your head between your knees, and kiss your ass good-bye. Her words, not mine."

Ben grimaced. More joint family history—in the War of 1812, the British had fired on the town, burned a couple of shacks, and laid siege to Morgan's Castle. Two cannonballs had hit the Haskell House. That night, the British sloop blew up in the harbor, a fire in the magazine. At low tide, you could still see rotten planks and ribs in the salt mud where they'd beached the hulk and let her burn herself out. Without the ship's guns to back them up, the surviving Royal Marines had decided that a strategic withdrawal was a good idea.

"You tell your aunt that if she keeps on being such a pain, I *won't* blow her house up. What I'll do instead, I'll toss her headfirst into that frog pond behind the place. She hasn't grown an inch since the last time I did it."

That drew a weak smile. "Can I watch? From a safe distance? Anyway, that isn't what I wanted to ask. Are you ever planning to tell Gary?"

That chill ran down his back again. "Tell him *what*?"

Caroline wrinkled her nose. "Hey, I take after Mom, not Aunt Alice. I think boys are *way* more interesting than girls. I was giving Gary the old Haskell look-over. You'd have to score him at least a nine on the cuteness scale, and I was thinking that cousin isn't all *that* bad, you know, not like *real* incest. 'Specially with birth control. And he's past the age of consent. But it's a little worse than cousin, isn't it?"

She mimed a Mall-Rat flip of her hand and tipped her head to one side. "Sex with your half brother is, like, *so* redneck. You know, all those, like, inbred hillbilly families that don't have the brains to wipe the drool off their chins?"

Damned Haskell Witches. Half Morgan or not, this one wasn't any duller than the rest of them. "I *can't* tell him. It isn't my secret to tell. With Maria dead, the only one who can tell him is Dan."

She shook her head, turned, and vanished into the darkness of an unlit tunnel. Ben frowned. Just to add insult to injury, the little lights on the motion sensors refused to glow. She was moving too damn fast to get away with that.

Then that soft, sexy alto came out of the shadows and ran ghost fingers down his spine, so much like Lainie. "She hasn't rejected you, Father. The Dragon looked into your thoughts and found something worth much more than another tribal chieftain with a strong sword-arm. You rule the Morgans more than Daniel ever did. You *plan* what he tells them to *do.* She made you hide because you are priceless, not worthless."

twenty

—◊◊◊—

GARY LAY ON the cold stone, aching. He couldn't muster the strength or the will to move. The cold and the ache, those were as much in his heart as in his skin and muscles and bones. The stone was cold enough, yes, and damp, and hard where it bruised his back. And the floor *was* dusty, as she'd said, with the dust of centuries in this deep place. But he'd catch royal hell if he dared suggest that she could clean it up if she found it so damned offensive.

The cold and the ache, those came from loss. He hadn't known what the Tear meant to him until the Dragon had told him to take it off. First he'd feared that the Tear would kill this girl with the raven hair and gray eyes and a face that had struck him dumb. Then he'd feared it wouldn't.

She'd kept it, and lived. And a part of him had walked out of the cave and vanished up the stairs.

The cave had strange acoustics. Parts of it echoed and passed sound around like the "whispering galleries" in old buildings, in domes like Saint Paul's and the Capitol. Some places you could hear a pin drop in a room far away, and then move six inches and never hear a shout.

She was speaking. She was moving, and snatches of words came down the stair to him: "... tell him ..." "... cute ..." "... worse ..." Some of Ben's words filtered down, as he moved or turned or followed: "... secret ..." "... Maria ..." "... Dan ..." They made no sense, no sense at all.

But one phrase reverberated in his ears, and it made altogether too much sense: "... half brother ..." *Whose* half brother had been lost in the echoes, but he thought he knew.

That opened a can of worms, and he wasn't sure which way they slithered. Who was his *real* father? Who was his *real* mother? Was he a Haskell or a Morgan? Did that explain why he couldn't do the selkie change? Did that explain why he didn't look all that much like Daniel Morgan, or like his sisters? He did recognize *her* face, with its overlay of what he saw when he looked in a mirror. "... half brother ..."

Endless questions. And from what he'd heard, the Haskell *men* never amounted to much, rare as they were.

He opened his eyes and stared up at the rough stone ceiling. You could still see the tool marks in the granite after all those centuries. He visualized the red glow of the Dragon's Eye, under cold water just a few yards away. "Why did you give me that thing and then take it from me?"

<The Caroline is strong. There is crisis. Strength must meet crisis.> The Dragon's voice was calm and analytical, like a computer.

"And I wasn't strong enough for you. Because I'm not *really* a Morgan."

<The Caroline is strong. Your strength has not been proven.>

So maybe he could earn the right to another Tear—Ben

had said that he remembered three in use at once. But how? Morgans had a test, which he had failed. Did the *Haskells* have a test, for proving strength?

<The test remains the same. The blood remains the same. The bond with the Caroline is through the father, not the mother.>

So he did not need to speak aloud. The Dragon read his thoughts, as well as placing her own in his head. But *Dad* was Caroline's father? But Ben had said . . . Gary's thoughts whirled in confusion, until he finally came up with one soap-opera script that fit. Ben must have been covering up a family scandal, Dad cheating on Mom. Suddenly all the fights made a kind of sense.

"So I *am* a Morgan?"

<The promise was given and accepted. For as long as Morgan blood shall live, I only talk to Morgan blood.>

Gary's thoughts edged around a black pit in his mind. He *had* to know, but he couldn't force himself to ask straight out. "Do you speak to any other Morgan?"

<The Daniel no longer touches me.>

The pit reached out and sucked him down into searing emptiness. His father was dead. Gary squeezed his eyes shut, tensing his whole body against tears and a scream of rage that clawed at his throat.

<The Daniel lives. The Daniel has broken his bond with me, protecting Morgan blood.>

Relief washed through Gary's body, and he sagged back to the floor. For days now, they'd felt nothing, heard nothing. He would glance at Ben and shake his head. Ben would look back and shake *his* head. Neither dared to speak the words—the continued silence meant that Dad was dead, but saying it out loud might be the black magic that made it true.

Dad was alive, but still held by the Pratts. Ben couldn't find a safe way into their grounds or tunnels. They'd tried tricking the DEA into searching, and the best drug-sniffing dogs had failed. And the one way they *did* know about, the sea cave, was a trap. Gary couldn't use that unless he learned to change. Ben had failed the Dragon's test, and Gary had met only one part of it. Now the Tear had passed on to Caroline and the Haskell Witches. Could *Caroline* change? Had she inherited *that,* as well?

Gary shook his head and forced himself to move. With Daniel gone and Ben "dead," Gary was *the* Morgan now, the way the family journals used the name: the oldest male, the head of the clan. The Morgan didn't quit. He might die, but he didn't quit. Morgan blood *never* abandoned Morgan blood. The Morgan had to save his father or die trying.

The Morgan gritted his teeth and stood, swaying, his vision spotted with black and silver dots. He felt like he'd just finished his black belt test, or crawled out of the water after a ten-mile swim. He'd finished both on sheer determination, all strength and stamina drained.

Swimming. Caroline had tossed a comment about the selkie change into that mix, words Aunt Alice had passed on from somebody she knew. Gary was too good a swimmer. The dive hadn't pushed him past his limits into unknown depths.

Depths. Gary stared at the black water of the Dragon's pool. He stripped off his shirt. The buttons were hard, his hands shaking. T-shirt and shoes, pants, socks, underpants— he stood naked and shivering, blinking with exhaustion. He had to lock his knees in order to stay upright. *Anything* now would be pushing past his limits.

He'd been wading through those dusty, musty journals, slowly, abused Latin irregular verbs and bastardized declensions and all. So far, he'd found two more mentions of the change, two more cold, hard eyewitness descriptions thrown in the teeth of impossibility. "What I tell you three times is true."

He staggered three steps to the water, each move a battle. He stopped at the edge. He'd never feared the water before, perhaps a gift of his Morgan blood. Now the slow, dark heave of it looked menacing.

If he stared at it any longer, he'd back down. Remembering *why* he was diving, he didn't take a breath before plunging in head first, and shock nearly drove the remaining air from his lungs. The water had seemed almost warm, the time he'd dived before. Now it felt like it had flowed straight from the Arctic.

Darkness welled up and swept around him. He forced himself down into the freezing water, searching for the red gleam of the Dragon's Eye. The walls, the floor, the ceiling all turned black as he swam beyond the last reach of the cavern lights. He followed the rough walls by touch, then rose to crawling upside-down along the ceiling.

His lungs burned. His eyes sought phantoms of red among the yellow and white sparks dancing across his vision. His head broke water, into blackness.

Gary sculled around until he found stone steps, crawled up onto them, and crouched there, gasping. He was in the tower stairway, the way he'd come in the first time. The Dragon was hiding from him.

Caroline's words echoed in his head: "Total terror." "You may need to be actually drowning before the selkie change can happen." He hadn't pushed far enough. Yet.

He sculled back out in the icy pool and dove again. He followed the rough stone downward, swimming slowly, scanning the black water for any gleam of red. His head buzzed, and lights danced in front of his eyes again, but they were white or yellow. A mosquito whined in his ears, growing to a rushing roar like a jet engine. Silver light flooded the tunnel. He turned over, lazily, and looked up at the mirrored ripples of the inner pool.

He couldn't take a breath. That would be cheating. He

had to go back down. He rolled over again and stared at his hands, floating loose in the water. His fingers and toes tingled and then went dead. They belonged to somebody else, and he had to pull the puppet's strings just right.

Something grabbed him and he fought it, twisting away and shoving. He wasn't done yet. He hadn't changed.

It pulled him up into warmth and dragged him across coarse stone, the rough surface tearing fire from his skin. Something forced air into his lungs, warm damp air from warm lips, and pressed against his chest in a familiar rhythm. CPR. Lifesaving class.

He swung out, blind, struggling against rescue. He had to dive again. Coughs spasmed out of his lungs.

Rough hands spun him facedown, pinning him to the stone. Warm breath panted in his ears, followed by gasping words. "What the *hell* do you think you're doing?"

Gary found enough air for words. "Got . . . to . . . dive. Got . . . to . . . change."

"God damn Alice Haskell to *hell* for a meddling *bitch*!"

The voice and the attitude had to be Ben. Gary relaxed and quit struggling. He had lost. He couldn't force himself to dive again. Pressure eased on his back, and he retrieved his arm from the *chi na* lock he hadn't realized his uncle knew. Gary shook his head painfully. There was so *much* he hadn't realized.

"I've got to try it." He coughed again, pain shooting through his chest. "I've got to get another Tear. You heard what she said. I need to be really drowning."

The hands turned gentle, twisting Gary's shoulders until a face swam into view. "It isn't worth it, boy. It isn't worth risking your life. You've passed her test once. There's no need to do it again."

Gary stared up at Ben's face, blurry through fatigue and dripping seawater. It was Caroline's face, underneath the age-lines and stronger jaw, Gary's own face crowned by graying hair. Funny he hadn't noticed it before. But like Ben said, people mostly see what they expect to see.

Dad screwing around with Elaine Haskell, that wouldn't have been a scandal. Haskell women did what they damned well pleased, always had. That wouldn't have started the endless fights. Ben had said Caroline was twenty. Best Gary could remember, that meant Dad and Mom hadn't even met when Caroline was born.

"*You're* my father."

GARY SHIVERED. DRIED, dressed, wrapped in a blanket, and sitting in front of an electric heater, he still felt groggy with cold. He handed an empty mug back to Ben. Back to his *father*.

They hadn't talked, coming up the stairs into the tower. Gary didn't have the strength to connect words in a row. Ben probably had his own reasons for keeping quiet while he kept the boy moving, wrapped him in warmth, and brewed the coffee.

His father took the mug, poured another dose of inner heat, and hesitated. Then he shook his head. "To hell with doctors and their sage advice." He reached up into the cabinets that lined one stone wall of the room, pulled out a bottle, and topped off the mug. Whiskey fumes spread over the aroma of fresh-brewed Sumatra gold. "The Irish know what a man *really* needs at times like this." He poured himself a drink, as well, and didn't bother to add coffee to it.

Then he sat down and stared at the wall, at a point somewhere ten feet beyond his son. Minutes seemed to pass while they both sipped at their mugs.

"No, Gary, I'm not your father. I'm just a man your mother knew, seventeen, eighteen years ago. Your dad is the man who stayed around to change your diapers. Genetics doesn't have a damn thing to do with fatherhood."

He went back to staring at the wall. After a while, he got up and refilled his mug with whiskey, and added straight coffee to Gary's. Then he settled down to wearing a hole through solid granite with his eyes.

Finally, he sighed. "You've figured out the basics. Might as well give you the whole story, so you can keep your mouth shut down the road.

"I was taking some courses at the university up in Naskeag Falls. Good deal for everybody involved—I got the education, this numbskull hockey player got the credits, and the university got a conference championship while not *officially* knowing a damn thing was going on. One year they even made it to the NCAA finals. Everybody's happy." He took another swallow of whiskey.

"Then I met Maria. One thing led to another, and the name I was carrying wouldn't have passed muster for a marriage license. The family could have cooked us up some papers for another life, but by that time your mother wouldn't have married me if the Pope had presided at the ceremony and we'd given her the State of California as a marriage price. That woman had a temper, and she could carry a grudge from here to Pluto without ever breaking a sweat."

Gary winced. Yes, he could imagine that. He had no trouble visualizing the entire scene, complete with textbooks instead of expensive glassware raining down on Ben's head and bouncing off the walls.

"Abortion?" Ben shook his head. "Not for Maria—she was a straight-arrow Catholic, even in bed. That's what got us into the mess in the first place."

He emptied his mug, refilled it at the cabinet, and then brought the bottle with him when he walked back to his chair. "She wouldn't even meet me after that first explosion. I'm surprised it didn't show up on the seismographs there at the university. So Dan carried messages between us, sort of like a second setting up a duel. We were going to pay for everything, have the baby—have *you*—handed over to Aunt Jean and then be adopted by one of the cousins. That's how Alice knows all about this mess.

"But Maria said we owed her a *legal* marriage license with a *legal* name and a child raised as a full-fledged unquestioned Morgan with all the rights and appurtenances thereto. Dan liked her and thought he could make a go of it. Sex ain't rational, boy. Always remember that. Sometimes they got along fine. You wouldn't have two sisters if they hadn't. Call it fifty-fifty, heaven and hell, and no possibility of divorce. That was Maria, nothing in between. Sometimes I purely *hate* that Dragon."

Ben stared down into the amber depths of his mug and shook his head. "Now you know more about your parents than any person ought to know. I hope you've got the decency to never breathe a word of it to Peggy or Ellen."

Gary forced himself out of his chair, still clutching the blanket tight around his shoulders. The coffee had given him false energy, and the dose of whiskey had shot it straight into his legs. He couldn't sit, even though he couldn't really stand, either. The dark passages pulled at him, offering time and space to think.

"Sit down, boy. You're in no condition to go for a hike."

Gary looked over at his father. "What am I supposed to call you?"

"Same as before. Just 'Ben.' And living or dead, Dan is still 'Dad.' He's earned it."

"Dad's still alive."

Ben's hand jerked, splashing whiskey. He stared at his mug for an instant, blinking, and then solved *that* problem by gulping the rest of his drink. "You sure? You talked to him?"

"The Dragon told me. He broke his bond with her, to protect us."

"I didn't know that was even possible. Did she say how?"

"No."

"If he broke his bond, how the hell does she know he's even alive?"

"She didn't say. It *felt* like she would sense an empty space, after all those years of contact."

"Damned *women*! That Dragon is worse than Alice Haskell!"

For a man with such a passion for women, Ben sure seemed to have mixed feelings about them. Gary added that to his long list of puzzles. He needed peace to chew on them and time to try and digest the strange meal of this day. He tugged the ancient oak door open, staring down into the darkness of the stair.

A hand fell on his shoulder. Ben stared into Gary's eyes, shaking his head. "Be careful, boy. Alice and her friends don't know everything. We can't afford to lose *you*."

Gary thought about the icy black water of the Dragon's pool. He shuddered. But that was the only choice he knew.

As if reading Gary's mind, Ben shook his head again. "Don't do it, boy. If you die, we'll *never* get Dan back. Promise me you won't go diving down there again."

The Dragon had hidden from him. She demanded strength and proof. Slowly, reluctantly, Gary nodded.

"I promise. I won't dive in the Dragon's pool."

Ben let him go. Gary climbed slowly down the stone steps and took a tunnel at random, letting the dark and silence soak into him. He needed to be alone to chew over the things he'd learned. Dad alive, Ben actually Gary's father, Caroline his sister—his head spun.

No, he wouldn't dive in the Dragon's pool. He'd already proven there wasn't any point to that.

But a man could come *out* of the Dragon's pool without diving *into* it. The tide had to come from somewhere.

twenty-one

—w—

ALICE STARED AT her computer screen without seeing it.
Ben had posed a pretty problem with that question about
the tunnels under the Pratt compound. Haskell chants and
Haskell records mentioned them, but no specifics. Naskeags
hadn't been involved in carving them. The Pratts had
brought in hard-rock miners and quarrymen in groups of
two or three, housed the men away from the village,
shipped them home when the work was done. Or maybe
dumped their bodies in the bay with waste stone chained to
their ankles. There had been dark speculation on that, back
in the 1800s and again during Prohibition.

But she had other ways of finding out.

Her computer got bored with her and switched over to
Caroline's latest screensaver, a sign that announced I ATE'NT
DEAD in scraggly letters floating slowly from corner to corner across the monitor. A high-pitched peeping from her
left also reminded her to get back to work, demanding pay-
ment for services rendered. She picked a mealworm out of

the cup on her desk and tossed it toward the ceiling of the parlor.

Scarface launched herself in a flurry of wings, trapped the mealworm in midflight, performed two neat barrel-rolls in the process of transferring her snack from wing membrane to mouth, and swooped back to hang upside-down from her curtain valence. The bat groomed herself contentedly.

Big brown bat, *Eptesicus fuscus,* dark brown fur as soft as velvet and black wing membranes that had the touch of warm silk. Scarface was the matriarch of the colony since Whitespot had died over the winter. Alice couldn't cure herself of naming the colony's spokes-bat, even though it was the colony that was the true unit.

Just like with the beehives out in the apple grove, bodies might be born and die, each living but a short time, but the colony was nearly immortal. Scarface's ancestors had lived in the house's attic since the first rafters cut off the sun. Long exposure to the spring had made the colony members some-what . . . *different.* Besides keeping the bugs to a tolerable level, the little night-fliers had other uses.

Alice twitched her trackball to wake up the computer and then entered a few more figures. She probably had the only 3-D CAD program in the world that used bat wing-beats as a unit of measurement. The wire-frame model on her screen sprouted more yellow lines, a tunnel leading from the red of a metal door. Ten beats across, fifteen high, a hundred long, all mapped out in terms of a tiny spy flying in the dark. Three additional red rectangles spotted the walls of the cave, hard smooth echoes that were the way a bat would "see" connecting doors.

Amazing how much knowledge you could tuck into half an ounce of body and a brain a little larger than a BB. Bats had a spatial memory that defied logic. Their sonar tracked gnats through starless night, mapped textures, guided swoops and rolls between trees while avoiding thorns that could shred delicate wings, brought the bats straight home across miles of countryside to a roost opening smaller than Alice's hand.

"Is that where they're keeping Dad?"

Alice jumped slightly. She'd nearly forgotten about Ellen sitting in one corner of the parlor, quietly cringing away from the "Eeeuw, ick!" factor of mealworms and bats. The girl would have to learn to deal with worse than that if she really wanted to be a Witch.

Besides, bats were delightful creatures once you got to know them. It was a damned shame there were so few in Maine. You'd think with all the bugs there would be more, but it was the killer winters and lack of natural caves.

"That's one of several possibilities. My little friends wouldn't know your father if they heard him, but *something* was breathing inside that middle door."

Ellen looked dubious. She probably still thought bats were horror-movie vampires or would get tangled in her hair.

Alice decided it was time for another lesson. "Come over here. You won't believe in this stuff unless you see how it works."

The girl looked like a doe caught in the apple orchard—twitchy and on the edge of running, but severely tempted. She sidled toward the desk, carefully keeping Alice between her and the bat.

"Be calm. Do your breathing exercises. You'll never be able to rule the universe if you can't control your own heartbeat."

Ellen closed her eyes and relaxed, nodding her head slightly with her heartbeats as she used them to time her breathing. Alice could *see* the child's face relax as she emptied her mind.

"Now lift your right arm. Hold out one finger, as if

you're pointing with it. Keep your thoughts on your breathing. Keep your thoughts on your heartbeat. If any distractions cross your mind, watch them calmly as they float from darkness into darkness and leave you centered. Think about your breathing. Think only about your breathing."

Scarface tilted her tiny head sideways and then dropped from the curtain in a whir of wings. The colony had learned, over generations, that a human standing like that meant free food. An instant later, the tiny bat hung from Ellen's finger, folding those silken wings around her body.

The child was a natural. She didn't twitch a muscle. Alice could remember the first time Aunt Jean had taken her through this exercise. First she couldn't clear her mind enough, then the prickle of tiny claws had made her jump and the bat had tumbled away with an angry chitter. It had taken Alice three days to turn into a decent perch. She'd been too twitchy at that age. Caroline had needed three tries, in one day.

"Keep your eyes closed. Think only about your breathing. Empty your mind. Build the room around you. Place me in your thoughts. Place the windows in your thoughts. Place the fireplace in your thoughts. Concentrate on your breathing. Concentrate on your heartbeat."

Alice was leaping ahead, skipping steps. The House seemed to press her with a sense of urgency. Ellen needed to have faith in these things, needed to believe them *now.*

"How far am I? What direction?"

Tension flickered across Ellen's eyelids and then calmed away. She kept her breathing regular and slow, her eyes closed. Scarface cocked her tiny head toward Alice. "Two. The small sun is *there,* in the right eye."

"How far to the fireplace and the chimney flue? What direction?"

"Ten. To the stone face and down."

"Open your eyes."

Ellen did. Her glance darted to the tiny bat hanging from her finger, and she started to tense.

"Think about your breathing. Concentrate on your breathing. Feel your finger. Tell me what you feel."

The girl calmed again. Then she giggled. "It *tickles*!"

Scarface unwrapped one wing and started to nibble gently at the membrane, grooming, as if she was *trying* to look cute and harmless. Alice could almost see the wonder spreading across Ellen's face, looking at this tiny mammal with the bright eyes and pointed ears and soft short fur.

"Those numbers you gave me, those were beats of her wings, how far she'd have to fly. The small sun is the floor lamp in the corner. That's how a bat measures her world."

"*Her* world?"

"You'll learn to feel the difference. The females are smarter. Now take your left hand. Move it slowly, don't startle her. Rub gently across the top of her head. She likes that."

The bat leaned into Ellen's finger like a cat accepting an ear-scratch. The tiny pink tongue flicked out, tasting her new friend. Scarface cocked her head again, and peeped gently.

"She'd like another mealworm. Then she needs to sleep."

Judging by Ellen's face, that was asking a lot. She set her jaw and reached gingerly into the cup on Alice's desk. Her hand jerked back and then reached again. She scrunched her eyes shut, concentrated on her breathing exercise, and pulled out a single mealworm. She reached blindly over to her other hand, offering the pale, squirming grub.

"Just toss it up in the air. She prefers to catch her food on the wing."

Ellen's hand jerked upward, and the bat swooped after her prey. The girl wiped her hand on her jeans, shuddering.

Still, she smiled as the tiny body looped through the air and then disappeared up the chimney.

Another movement caught Alice's eye. She glanced out the window, then did a double take and grinned like a maniac when she saw that familiar bulk striding up the driveway. *Kate!* Now she could get those wires checked out, rather than cringing every time she flipped the breaker on for a few hours. Get the broken plaster and glass patched up. Damned telephone company had said it would be a week before they could check out *their* lines. Maybe Kate could fix that, too.

And there was some *other* unfinished business, too. She found herself smoothing her hair and straightening her blouse.

She remembered Ellen. That kid already knew too much for her age. "I'm through here. Why don't you go help Caroline and Peggy clean up in the old house? Then you can both go down in the cellar and talk with the spring."

The girls could feel the health and power of the women's waters. They loved to sit in the dark, mysterious cellar with the lamps turned down to an orange glow, dreaming of brown-skinned women and the strength of the House. It was a natural refuge to them, healing the scars and pain they'd suffered in the last few weeks.

Ellen vanished like smoke in a breeze. Alice smiled, then caught herself primping again. *Silly schoolgirl.* Besides, there was no point in camouflage. Kate knew what she was getting.

Alice headed toward the door, trying to hold her grin in check. Funny she hadn't heard the truck, though. The big oaf must have walked, five or ten miles. That was the kind of thing she'd do, rather than spar another round with her damned junker Dodge. But would she let Alice invest in a new truck? No way.

Kate was stubborn as a mule and dumb as a stump. Numb as a hake, but good with her hands. All those Downeast clichés. Alice was blithering to herself. Dumb or not, it was good to see the big moose. Kate might know what she was getting, but then, so did Alice. She didn't care. Near as she could tell, love was like that.

The house felt skittish, and the side door stuck when Alice went to open it. Damned if the old place wasn't getting jealous. And then she was face to face with Kate, smiling tentatively, wondering how to tell her friend that the silly babble of that phone message had been cute. Cute was *not* an attribute you normally connected with Kate Rowley.

Kate just stood there, impassive, with her traffic-cop face on. Alice felt her smile die. She stared for a moment, waiting for the mood to break, and then stood aside to wave her friend through the door. "Come on in. Don't just stand there with the rain dripping on your head." No matter that the sun was shining out of a cloudless sky.

Kate lumbered through the door, walking even larger than usual. She brought the smell of fresh dirt and old leaves with her, probably off a cellar hole at another construction site. She glanced around the kitchen, taking in the oil lamps and the smoke stains by the counter outlets.

Alice felt a chill run through the house. Something was wrong.

"Alice Haskell, I have a court order for the custody of two minor children. Are Ellen Morgan and Margaret Morgan in this house?"

Alice swallowed acid. Kate knew her face too well for her to make a lie stick. Maybe Caroline would hear, would tuck the girls in the hidey-hole. Even with all her work around the place, Kate didn't know about *that*. Nobody but the Haskell Witch or her designated heir could open it.

And Kate had come for two children without her truck? Stall. "Where's this court order?"

"Are Ellen Morgan and Margaret Morgan in this house?"

Something was *very* wrong. "Show me your court order. Come on, Kate, you know the rules."

"You don't deny that Ellen Morgan and Margaret Morgan are here?"

"Kate Rowley, I'll deny that the sky is blue and the sun rises in the east until you show me a warrant 'particularly describing the place to be searched, and the persons or things to be seized.' Fourth Amendment to the Constitution of the United States, adopted December 15, 1791. Cut the crap!"

Alice backed into the room, away from Kate, toward a certain corner of the kitchen. Laws didn't matter, friendship didn't matter, *love* didn't matter. She had a blood oath to obey.

Kate towered after her, striding forward, her head brushing one of the lamp globes that dropped below the beams of the ceiling. Damned moose *always* forgot to duck. Alice felt as if she was shrinking, the difference between their sizes growing until she was a mouse in front of a cat.

"Kate, get out of here!"

"You invited me in."

"And now I'm inviting you out! Unless you have a warrant, *get the hell out of my house!*"

She remembered flashes of her Seeing, flashes of Kate with the faceless man who was the enemy. She backed up again, her voice rising to a scream. "Show me the goddamned *warrant*!"

Her hand groped around behind her, in the corner next to the counter. It found cold metal, and grabbed it. The shotgun lay heavy in her hands, and they took over from her mind. They jacked a shell into the chamber and pointed the worn metal cylinder at Kate. *"Get . . . out . . . of . . . here!"*

She felt like a zombie, her own hands taken over by the House. The House thought Kate was a puppet ruled by the

Peruvian *brujo*. Kate sneered and shoved the shotgun to one side, her hand sweeping on to knock Alice sideways like it was brushing off a fly. The big woman shouldered her way past to the parlor door. Alice stumbled back and smacked her head on the corner of a cabinet. Stars and tears filled her eyes. She lined twinned shotguns up on the back of twinned heads. The safety clicked off without any help from her.

"STOP, DAMMIT!"

Kate took another step, through the door into the parlor. The shotgun bucked and Alice fell backward. She watched as she fell, deafened and horrified. White and red and gray chunks burst from Kate's head, floating forward and up from the shattered skull like some gruesome slo-mo of a movie finale.

ALICE BLINKED. THE cracks in the ceiling looked like a map. Southern U.S., perhaps, with Florida pointing to the right. That old grease stain was Cuba. Have to get Caroline to wash the ceilings, patch them, paint them. That was what apprentices were for, wasn't it? No, Kate would do the repairs, the painting.

Coolness touched her brow and then moved on to dab at the side of her head. That woke pain. She tried to grab the cold thing, push it away, but her hand missed.

"Don't try to move."

"Kate . . ."

"Just keep quiet."

"But I shot . . ."

Alice forced herself up on one elbow. Caroline blocked her view of the parlor. The shotgun lay to one side, an empty shell casing next to it on the floor. She couldn't remember pumping the action after firing. Reflex.

Powder smoke and sewage fouled the air. Bodies usually stank—God knows she'd handled enough of them, between the ambulance and the ER. "Death with dignity" was just a catchphrase for people who'd never seen the real thing.

She forced herself to roll over and climb the cabinets, knob by knob, until she stood swaying with both hands braced on the counter. Closing her eyes seemed to help. That way, the world stayed still around her. The parlor door waited. One hand after another, she worked her way along the wall and reached the door casing.

Alice opened her eyes. The parlor stood in front of her, looking exactly as usual except for a patch of shattered plaster showing through the wallpaper and a drift of leaves and dirt across the oriental rug. *Another goddamn golem.* She slid down the doorframe and sat, leaning on the wall and with the wood trim digging into one shoulder blade.

Golem. Her fingers toyed with the mess on the floor. *Golem, not Kate. And I invited it through the door. Broke the wards. Just like a man, thinking with my gonads.* She worked her way along the wall, using it to anchor her world. A wisp of gold caught her eye. She teased it out of the mess: a lock of blond hair, fine and short.

Kate's hair. Alice remembered the soul-catcher and the stove. She *still* might have just killed her friend, her love, her almost lover. It all depended on the spells the *brujo* had used, how he'd gotten the hair.

There wasn't enough of a mess on the floor. Kate was a big woman, should have left a big mess. Where was the rest? Alice shook her head, ignoring the pain, trying to clear her thoughts. Black jeans walked across in front of her, and she followed them up to a dark face and black hair.

Caroline.

"What the *hell* are you doing out here?"

"*Trying* to keep you from hurting yourself worse than you already are."

Ice settled over Alice's heart. "Where are the kids?"

"Old parlor."

Alice forced herself off the floor, clawing at the hands that tried to hold her down. They battled to a truce, Caroline tucking her smaller aunt under one arm and shuffling gently through the maze of the old house.

"Wartime, they'd shoot you for leaving your post under enemy fire. Your job is to protect the girls, not play nurse to a dumb old woman."

The old front door stood open, dead leaves on the threshold. The old parlor door stood open. The room was empty, the trap door to the cellar and the spring still closed. Caroline heaved it open, but silence greeted them. The girls were gone.

Black and white fur stirred behind the door and formed a cat shape. Alice pinched her eyes shut, forcing her brain to work. She looked again. Dixie struggled across the floor, scratching with her front paws only. Alice knelt down, reaching out to touch the third guardian of the House. The cat licked her fingers, feebly. Touching delicately, probing, feeling beyond the evidence of her fingers, Alice found numbness instead of pain. The backbone took a sideways jog just behind Dixie's shoulders. Blood and scraps of flesh dirtied her claws.

Some of the attackers had been human. They would find that those battle-scars did not heal. They would find that those claw-marks festered deep and drew death into the flesh. Alice found herself chanting quietly in Naskeag, setting the winds to smell for that flesh and blood, setting the waters to deny them cleansing, setting the earth to search them out and track them and drag them under to a coward's grave.

Alice rocked back on her heels. "Pratts. The damn fools *dared!*" But it must have been that Peruvian. Tom Pratt would know better. His family had lived here long enough to know what it meant to attack the House. She'd teased Ben about it, banter within the family, but everyone in

Stonefort knew. Attacking the House was a messy form of suicide. She'd killed two men a few nights back, reinforcing that lesson.

Alice reached out to Dixie again, gently. She laid her hand on the cat's head, smoothed the forehead fur, scritched behind the ears, and then sighed. She *hated* doing this. Dixie licked her hand again, gently, as if the cat asked her to do what she must do. Alice moved her hand to feel a heart beating fast under her palm, laboring, weakening. She closed her eyes and harmonized that pulse with her own, two beats to one.

Polarity, she thought. *My hand is cold. Warmth flows from one body to another. If you make your hand hot, you are giving life. If you make your hand cold, you are drawing it away. The gifts of life and death are two faces of the same coin. My hand is cold.*

Warmth flowed into her hand and up her arm. Dixie lay still, eyes open but unseeing.

"Farewell, pirate queen," she whispered. "May the sun of the summer lands warm your fur."

Alice sat quietly, letting the shape of the cat dissolve into a blur of tears. She heard Caroline closing the old front door, the hinges groaning with unaccustomed use. *Front doors are used only for weddings and funerals.* The House would have tried to jam the frame, but there was a limit to what it could do if its guardians failed.

The latch clicked. The bar thumped back into place. *Locking the barn door behind the horse-thieves.* The defenses were designed to keep enemies out, not in. That damned golem had opened it from the *inside*.

Caroline returned, radiating grief. *So young to find out that witching can be a war instead of a game.*

There was a thing Alice had to do. Best get it over. "Remember what we are. We protect the spring. We protect the House that guards the spring. We protect any person who is granted refuge in the House. Those are our duties. Not a

damn thing in there about rescuing a dimwit aunt who believed her heart instead of her eyes. I screwed up. You were
the second line of defense. You failed your duties. You failed
those children."

She watched each word lash across Caroline's face like a
whip. Tears streaked the poor child's face, but a lesson
earned through pain would likely be remembered. Steel was
born from iron only through fire.

Alice dropped her gaze to the limp pile of fur on the
floor. Chewing out Caroline didn't really make her feel any
better. The poor girl hadn't let that *thing* past the door. No
way around it, *that* was the mistake that had cost Dixie the
last of her nine lives. *So much for the myth of the all-knowing,
all-seeing Haskell Witch.*

She gathered Dixie's body into her arms, caressing the
still-warm ears. She staggered to her feet. Her head spun, and
she blinked three times before the room stopped moving.

"Okay. Now we go and get those girls back."

twenty-two

—⁓—

KATE EASED HER truck ahead in the line, squinting into the low morning sun. Damned Detroit refugee from a scrap-heap wanted either to stall or chew on the virginal white ass of that yuppie Miata in front of her. Either way, she'd jam up the works. Fifteen cars and two trucks still waited to roll aboard the ferry—a normal morning load for the island loop in June.

Compare that to, say, January, when they might cancel the run for three days straight because nobody wanted to play dodge-'em cars with the sea ice and the storms. Maine in summer and winter were two different worlds. The islands used to have a thriving year-round population. In the last decade or so, they'd turned into ghost towns from October to May.

She stared ahead at the *Governor Chamberlain,* wrinkling her nose at the squat, rust-streaked black hull and dirty white superstructure. Just looking at the damned boat made her seasick. However, a friend of Larry Beech owned a summer place out on Ayers Island. That was how she got most of her work, "friend of a friend" referrals, and she couldn't afford to break that chain. It kept her fed.

If the damn fool wanted to pay her fifty bucks an hour to puke her guts out, Kate was game. It was a time-and-materials job, charge from the minute she stepped out of her door until she got home again—she couldn't argue with that. Besides, she could stand to lose a few pounds.

She'd left Jeffy Boy behind for this job, said she didn't need him. True enough, as far as it went. But she didn't want to find his body sprawled under a ladder, or floating facedown in the tide like Maria Morgan. Kate was sure someone had been following her around, and she didn't think it was one of Bernie's friends.

Speaking of cops . . . she reached under the truck's dash and pulled the microphone from its bracket. "Five-seven-seven to Sunrise dispatch."

Static answered her. The line inched forward another car length, and she tried again. Maybe she'd been hidden in a radio shadow. "Five-seven-seven to Sunrise dispatch."

"Sunrise. Go ahead, five-seven-seven."

Webber's voice rasped, still on the fringe of radio coverage. He was filling in at dispatch after totaling his cruiser. Nice guy, but he *shouldn't* have been going that fast on the Beaver Cove Road.

Well, he'd have another month to meditate on his sins before the cast came off. The tree had come out of their meeting in much better shape. She keyed her mike again. "I'll be ten seven on the *Chamberlain* to Ayers Island. Out of service until Tuesday's evening run gets in. Five-seven-seven out."

"Roger, five-seven-seven. I log you off-duty on Ayers Island until next Tuesday. I'll have five-one-eight swing through town a few times to show the flag."

Kate left the radio on, keeping track of the slow flow of traffic reports and gossip of a county that stretched over a hundred miles from end to end and mustered only about twenty thousand people. She was next on the ramp, rolling down past the high tide line and across the metal grating. As soon as her tires touched the ferry's deck, she could feel the slow heave of the *Chamberlain* and her inner ear started to send alarms straight to her belly. She gritted her teeth, parked the truck, and set the brake. As always, switching the ignition off was a gamble. She *did* have a winch on the front if she couldn't move the beast any other way.

She climbed down from the cab and tried to ignore the growing rebellion in her stomach. Floors shouldn't *move,* dammit. She was like that Greek myth guy Alice had told her about—she drew strength from touching the earth. Get her out on water or up in the air and she turned to jelly.

Not that the sea was rough, or anything. Two- to four-foot swells—that was damn near calm. But that still left her walking on a live thing, a dragon's chest breathing in and out six times a minute. And then there were the swirls of oily diesel smoke from the idling engines, and the throb of those engines through her feet, and the dead-fish smell of the rockweed at low tide . . . Kate swallowed.

Ten miles. That's all she had to survive. Ten miles, plus loading and unloading time at each end, and then she could stand on solid ground again and have a horizon that stayed where God put it. That wasn't too much to ask, was it? She scuffed at a rust blister on the deck, thinking that maybe if she sat down and stared at something that didn't move, she could fool her inner ear into thinking the world stood still.

Kate tried to think of something, *anything,* besides the slow rise and fall of the horizon. Cop work, carpentry, the bare-stone economics of Sunrise poverty that was like being nibbled to death by ducks. Alice, and the way she tied in with all of the above. Work on the old Haskell House, with that strange sense of a cat purring warm under Kate's hands as she maintained the ancient wood and stone. A woman could get to like that kind of feeling. It made her think she was important.

Cop work and Alice. Right now, those two didn't go together. Kate felt an odd dislocation there, the same sort of out-of-body experience she'd had in the hospital after the accident, when Jackie was born. She'd spent a week perched up on a shelf beside the television set, stoned out of her head. Watched doctors and nurses parade past that body down there on the hospital bed. Watched Lew appear each morning hollow-eyed and stubbled and hung-over, watched him vanish a couple of times an hour once the bars were open to return looser and looser until he staggered out the door each evening drunk enough to be a fire hazard.

Watched Alice sit next to the bed every minute Lew wasn't there, humming or singing quietly, holding a limp hand with an IV in the forearm feeding a body with nobody home. If Alice hadn't been there waiting so damn patiently, Kate never would have bothered to come down. Sometimes she thought it was the music that called her back.

Now she had the same feeling, multiplied by the miles between the ferry terminal and the Haskell House. She was *here,* watching herself walk up to the door *there.* "Along came a man with a warrant in his hand . . ." Sooner or later, DHS was going to hear about the Morgan girls. Kate hoped to be in another state when that happened. Even on a ship would be better.

The ferry gate clanged shut and locked with a thump, cutting off her escape. Well, there were two cars between her truck and the ramp, anyway, so she'd been trapped since before she shut off the ignition. Kate swallowed. Now the damned boat would actually start moving.

She pulled out her tobacco and started rolling a smoke. Maybe that would help calm her stomach. A sailor walked past, moving from the gate to the engine room hatch, noticed her makings, and pointed to stenciled letters on the side of the deckhouse. NO SMOKING. Kate swore under her breath and tossed the completed cigarette over the rail. Now they'd book her for discharge of hazardous materials into navigable waters.

Cop work and Alice. If Kate had to choose between them, which way would the old frog hop? Sometimes it wore thin, that bit about walking up to a car with your ticket book in your hand and wondering if *this* one was the dope runner with a MAC-10 tucked between his knees. Wondering if *this* was the time she picked up one of Stonefort's five resident blacks by the scruff of his neck and pitched him out of a bar that he didn't want to leave at closing time, only to have him land in the lap of a NAACP lawyer.

Hell, she was getting tired of those 3:00 A.M. calls because some maiden aunt didn't like her neighbor's cat singing in the petunias. Kate was getting too old for that shit. Alice sure rated higher on the list than Sylvia Carter complaining about Rose Leavitt's cat.

But mainly it was walking the edge every minute she was on duty. A week or two back, some brown-skin stranger had twitched his hand under his coat and her own hand had jerked to her belt. The man had hatred and fear in his eyes, and carried himself like a killer. *That* was why she'd asked him for ID, not because of the color of his skin. Turned out he was just pulling out his wallet like a nice resident alien, but if she'd been carrying, she could have shot him dead.

She'd seen a flash of herself in court on a murder charge, just like those New York cops. He'd moved like he was going for a gun. Then she'd reacted to intent and instinct, rather than rational evidence. Left her with the shakes for three days. Maybe it was time to take Alice up on her offer.

The ferry eased back from its slip, adding a rolling motion to the rise and fall of the sea. Her stomach surged, out of phase, and she started looking for the john. Head, she guessed she should call it, on board an effing ship. Fifty bucks an hour for puking didn't look quite so attractive, close up.

Alice had said that the House could be a full-time job, for a year at least. Kate had the touch, was better tuned to the House than any of the Witches in the last century. There was stuff that had been put off for generations. There were changes that the House didn't like, stuff that should be torn out and restored to the old ways or at least done right.

Kate had felt that in the pulse under her hands. Some machine-made cabinetwork that rubbed the wood's grain the wrong way, just like that cat comparison she kept making. Wires and pipes that should have run differently, aligning with the stars or the earth's magnetic field or something.

Alice wouldn't call her crazy for thinking that way, going by *feel*. All buildings had a life of their own, a soul, at least some measure of integrity to keep the roof a working distance from the cellar. The Haskell House just had more than most.

Not like this effing boat. If *it* had any soul, it was a damned mean one. Now they'd changed course and the motion was a bow-to-stern pitch with a corkscrew twist. A sailor would have called it gentle, barely noticeable. Kate's stomach had other words for it. She headed toward the side door of the deckhouse, side *hatch* probably it should be; the john would be in there. Her eyes blurred, and the kitchen counter of the House stood in front of her. It was still moving up and down and sideways, though.

Alice blocked her way. Kate's brain was disconnected, and she just brushed the phantom to one side. Alice schmalice, what *she* needed was a porcelain bowl. Kate's knuckles found cold metal and her eyes focused well enough to read LADIES on a white name-plate against grease-streaked beige walls. She followed the arrow.

The place stank, old disinfectant and other people's farts

and the peculiar menstrual-blood whiff of women's toilets when they don't get cleaned often enough. Alice shouted something from behind her, but the meaning was lost in the surge of Kate's stomach. She banged a stall door open and bent over with seconds to spare. Acid rushed up her nose and she lost sight in the sudden tears. Kate groped around for toilet paper. Her knuckles found a sharp edge instead. The new pain changed her focus and quieted her stomach.

She wiped her eyes and then her nose, standing up and blinking. Damn good thing she *had* eaten breakfast. If she'd tried this on an empty stomach, she'd still be doubled up with the dry heaves. Now, if she could get some water down, she might have peace for five or ten minutes. Until the next round.

Her knuckles dripped blood. Kate stared at them, dabbed at the blood with more toilet paper, and cussed the damned fool that had left rough edges on a *boat,* for gossakes. Bad design, bad workmanship. That kind of thing pissed her off.

Whatever it was, it had left a gash about two inches long that skipped across three fingers, with ragged skin dangling at the end of each cut like a curl of wood turned up by a chisel. Something *sharp,* then, and sticking out. Maybe a screw, with a burred head. She turned back, fumbling at her belt for the Leatherman. File, screwdriver, pliers, even an impromptu hammer—no reason to leave that ambush waiting for a fresh victim.

Red-hot pain bashed her above the left ear. She fell to her knees, blinking against blinding tears. *Forgot to duck* again, *dammit! Forty years old, you'd* think *you'd have learned how far your effing head was from the effing floor!*

She couldn't see. Her fingers explored the back of her head, expecting to find the familiar stickiness of blood or at least a swelling lump. The scalp wasn't even tender. Something burned *inside* her skull. Burst blood vessel? *Stroke?* No, she could still move everything.

The wound throbbed on her hand, pumped by her racing heartbeat. Bandages. She had the first-aid kit in her truck, stuff you'd need if you put a nail through your foot or caught sawdust in your eyes. Even some serious pain pills Alice had conjured out of the hospital when Kate strained her back, prescription stuff.

Kate fumbled for the door, crashing into the sinks and then working along the edge until she found a latch. She still couldn't see. Nothing but sparks blazing in darkness across her eyes. What the *fuck* was wrong with her head?

She mapped the corridor from memory, left and then feel for the car-deck hatch on her right. How the *hell* was she going to puzzle her way back to the truck if she couldn't *see?*

"Can I help you, ma'am?"

Must be one of the sailors, confronted with a crazy woman. Nobody else would be that polite.

"Got to get back to my truck."

"You're hurt. You're bleeding. We've got a first-aid kit on the bridge, and a certified EMT. Just calm down, everything will be okay."

Yeah, humor the stupid woman. She's hysterical. Kate could just about tell light from dark, tell which end was up. She didn't *want* to go to the bridge. Her truck felt safe. She knew where she stood with that goddamn pile of junk.

"Got my own stuff. Just let me get back to my truck." Her head *hurt.*

She felt a tug on her arm. "Just this way, ma'am. I'll get the mate to clean up that hand and bandage it. Then you can lie down. You look like you're going into shock."

He was pulling her away from the car deck and the safety of her truck. The Sovereign State of Maine *demanded* that she get help. Alice had taught her the magic words for that one.

"I refuse medical care. Got it? I *refuse* medical care. Help me to my truck." She had to fight to make the words come out straight. They tried to jam up together and fall down on her tongue. Maybe it *was* a stroke, after all.

She could feel him shaking his head in exasperation. "You're the green Dodge stake-bed, right?" The pull changed direction, turned toward safety. *God,* her head hurt.

Pain shot red streaks into the darkness around her. She stumbled, feeling a numbness spreading backward from her fingers and toes. Then she found rough wood under her hand, and she shrugged the crewman's grip off her arm.

"Leave me be."

"If you need help, just holler. We'll be watching out for you."

Damned pest. She ignored him, feeling her way across the back of her truck bed and up the passenger side. The pain eased a little as she moved forward. She still couldn't see, but she didn't need to. *Door handle, there. Passenger seat. Reach under, fumble for the flat metal case, touch-fiddle the latches. Pill bottle and water jug.*

Instead of the pill bottle, her hand found something soft, with an odd rough-smooth surface, both stiff and pliable. Her fingers closed around it and she felt warmth there. The pain and numbness eased. She could see again, sort of re-mote through a periscope with blurry water draining off the lens. She was holding a small dark bag.

Her sight cleared. The bag was a deerskin poke the size of her fist, ancient, familiar. Beadwork covered it until the skin showed only at the mouth and the drawstring tunnels. Even through tears of pain, she marveled at the skill of those patient fingers—swirling patterns flowed through the colored beads, the kind of interlocking figures she'd seen in Celtic art, made up of pure transparent colors in beads as small as pinheads, bound by invisible stitching. The work wasn't Celtic, though—she knew what it was and where she'd seen it last.

Naskeag. At least a century old. More likely two or three. Aunt Jean showed it to us, must have been thirty years ago.

TV Indians would call it a medicine pouch. Kate had no idea what name the Naskeags would use. She didn't open it, didn't wonder what might be inside. So *that* was why the truck had seemed like the only safe place in the world. She knew who had prepared the bag, chanted over it, tucked it under the seat. The warmth was love.

She held the bag against her head and felt the throbbing pain ease into the background. She felt fingers brush her forehead. Alice. But the cooling touch brought memory as well as soothing, and Kate cringed. She saw Antonio, and she saw herself snipping a lock of hair from her own head. "The finest gold ever spun," he'd said, and his tongue wove a spell that made her swallow the blatant flattery.

Hair is hair, she'd thought. *It doesn't cost a cent. It grows back. I'm not giving him my soul, or even my body. Where's the harm?*

She twisted around to look at the side mirror, and shook her head. *Damn fool.* Her fingers traced the gap above her left ear, where the pain had centered. Antonio was a drug-lord and a killer. The medicine bag told her that Bernie had been right. It told her Antonio and Alice were blood enemies.

The harm? She'd never tried to learn the things that Alice did. Kate hadn't wanted to know. All the weird stuff scared her.

That had stood between them ever since Aunt Jean had chosen Alice. Kate didn't want to fear her friend, or be afraid for her. It was that white-bearded patriarch again, the God of Wrath, hiding in Kate's childhood. "Thou shalt not suffer a witch to live." But if witchcraft didn't exist, then Alice was safe. Kate didn't *dare* believe in witches.

Some of the principles had rubbed off, though, in the years they'd known each other. Kate knew what she had done. She'd given Antonio a key to Alice, a key to the House. She wasn't sure which one was worse.

Kate kissed the small poke, spread the drawstrings, and hung her protection around her neck. It slid down inside her shirt and nestled between her breasts. Then she searched out antiseptic and gauze, and bandaged her hand. *Life goes on.* It went on the only way she knew, straight ahead. *No matter how hard it is, just do the next thing, and the next.* God knows, Alice had told her often enough that she was too bull-headed to go *around* a problem.

Her stomach twisted again, gently, just a preliminary test. *Life goes on, without Alice. She'll never forgive me. The House will never forgive me. I'm a threat to both of them.*

Now she had three reasons to stay away from Alice. That damnfool phone message and the lesbian thing. The Morgan girls. Antonio.

What I tell you three times is true.

She curled up on the passenger seat of her truck, ignoring her stomach, ignoring her hand, ignoring the tears tracking her face. The medicine bag tried to calm her, but she ignored that, too.

The ferry hooted, three deep mournful blasts. They were coming up on Ayers Island. She hadn't puked again.

Life is made of small victories. Don't think about the large defeats.

twenty-three

ELLEN AND PEGGY needed him.

Gary typed in another set of commands, hit "Enter," and watched the bank of monitors out of the corner of his eye. They continued to cycle randomly through views of the house and grounds, showing what passed for normalcy these days around the old termite mound Quincy Morgan had built in 1820 and a dozen generations had added to and remodeled in the passing years. He stood up and stretched, easing the kinks out of his back. *That* had taken much too long, with nervous sweat under his arms, and he still wondered whether Ben had followed every move. Gary knew about stealth programs that fed keystrokes to a remote computer. His father-uncle was a sly old dog, just the kind of man to set a watch on the watchers.

The security display ran through its routine, including a view of the central control console. Gary saw himself still sitting at the keyboard, dutifully studying the system specs. He smiled to himself in Real Mode. Then he sobered and shook his head. An hour wasted, when he should have been worming his way into the Pratts' security rather than his own.

That was the problem with teaching people to hack systems. Sometimes they learned more than you wanted them to. But had Ben known that Gary knew that Ben knew that Gary knew . . .

Yeah. That one's the infamous Filly-Loo bird, one of the strangest creatures in the Maine woods. Has a unique way of escaping hunters—when something scares it out of the spruce thicket, it flies in an ever-decreasing spiral until it disappears up its own ass.

Yeah, again. But computers are a kid's world. Remember the Larson cartoon. Ben is *an old dog, and that system* is *a new trick.*

And somebody had kidnapped Peggy, threatened her and Ellen. This sure as hell qualified as a case where the end justified the means.

Anyway, Gary *thought* he'd disarmed the suicide watch. He couldn't think of anything more appropriate to call it. Ben had turned obsessive since hauling his nephew-son out of the Dragon's Pool, popping out of the woodwork anytime Gary had come within smelling range of a body of water larger than a birdbath. At least the old man hadn't forced Gary to wear one of those electronic bracelets the cops used for "house arrest."

So now certain selected monitor cameras were feeding a loop into the system. Question was, what *other* tricks did Ben have up his sleeve. That little bit about the entrance Caroline had used—"Never show 'em all your cards." There must be plenty of other stuff Ben wasn't talking about.

Other stuff besides the obvious. Ellen and Peggy were gone. Somebody had stolen them from under Aunt Alice's thumb. That should have been impossible. There was worse. Ben hadn't said what, but Gary had learned to read that poker face a little better with the constant watching of the past few days. Gary had seen Ben's face when he took the call. Shock, horror, rage—something beyond simple kidnapping. Daniel—*Dad*—must have warned Ben about something, before breaking contact with the Dragon. Gary had a sick feeling in the pit of his stomach.

Ben was hatching some kind of a plan, something involving the witches and Ron Pelletier and high explosives. Dangerous mix. Ben *always* had some kind of plan. Problem was, this one didn't involve Gary.

But Gary had *three* sisters now. And the beginnings of a plan of his own, a way he might sneak Caroline inside that cave Dad had found under the Pratts' compound. Caroline, with her mix of Haskell and Morgan skills. Caroline, who could be invisible until she became too solidly, dangerously *there.*

Ben was funny. It was obvious—the old man kept tiptoeing around sex and incest. He thought Gary had fallen in love with Caroline. It wasn't that at all. Sure, she radiated "sex" on all wavelengths. From what he remembered, she hadn't been like that in high school. Maybe it was going off to college and living on her own, or the power she'd learned from Aunt Alice. Or maybe that younger Gary hadn't been tuned to the right frequency. Wasn't old enough to decode the message.

It's hitting Ben harder than it is me, he thought. *The old man is tripping over his own dick. You can almost* see *him whacking himself up side of the head, reminding himself that she's his daughter. Off-limits.*

But Gary saw her more as an Amazon princess, a tough, dangerous, competent woman who happened to be good-looking as hell. Sex didn't enter the picture—she scared him too much. If he made a pass at her, she'd whack him over the head with that broadsword, or turn him into a frog. Instead, she was an instant ally, more comforting at his back than in front of him.

And Ellen and Peggy needed him. Needed both him and

Caroline, and the help only a team with two very special sets of skills could provide.

Silence still ruled the stone tower, no roars of alarm or rage. Gary eased the heavy door back, expecting to find Ben waiting in the shadows of the hall, climbing the stone stairs, blocking the narrow, twisty tunnel. He slunk through the darkness, waiting for a hand to grab him by the collar as he slipped out of the crypt and into the green damp drizzle of the family burying ground. He'd promised Ben he wouldn't dive into the Dragon's Pool. Into. *That* was the promise.

Gary hated turning shyster, weaseling out of a contract with word-tricks, but he had to. Something horrible was happening to Ellen and Peggy, and Ben seemed to be chewing nails over a plan to stop it. Gary might be able to help. *Might,* if he could satisfy the Dragon.

He walked a zigzag pattern through the drizzle, through the coverage of certain cameras, remembering how the overlapping views were veiled by the mist. June meant rain in Stonefort, the month that fed the grass for July hay, the month of fog as moist spring air rolled up from the south and met the icy ocean of winter. This year had been drier and sunnier than usual. Now the averages were averaging out.

Shadows formed and dissolved around Gary, wraiths, gravestones and bushes and salt-stunted spruces, none of them turning into Ben. The bay appeared beneath Gary's feet, slow and gray under low clouds that grazed the cliff-top, swells rising and falling lazily against the rocks because there was no wind to drive them, gunmetal water vanishing into fog within yards in every direction.

He could barely make out the mooring from here. It bobbed with the swells, orange against gray, the home buoy that Dad used in certain winds and tides when he felt the boat would be safe without the guarding arms of Stonefort's inner harbor. Gary stared at the buoy and thought about the concrete anchor cube with its iron ring, set forty feet deep under the tide. That had been the target of a dare when he was thirteen and testing himself to prove his swelling manhood—dive to the mooring, down through the dark icy water of the bay, free-diving without mask or flippers or wet suit.

He'd followed the rockweed down the mooring chain, deeper and deeper as his ears popped with the pressure and his lips turned numb with cold. He'd touched the slimy concrete, grabbed the rust-crusted ring, torn a frond of kelp from its holdfast, and risen back from darkness into light. Into warmth, into air for his aching lungs. He looked back, now, and saw the risk as training for his heritage.

He turned and climbed down the cliff, toes searching out the remembered holds, hands shifting from nub to nub in a pattern he'd thought was natural rock. The journals said otherwise, said there were a dozen such routes up and down the cliff, ways to escape or approach the tower if an enemy held the land-side ground or had even taken the tower itself. His ancestors had known altogether too much about siege warfare.

The steel-gray water chilled his eyes. That self-made dare had been a whim of an August noon, when the air and the bay were as warm as they ever got. Now the water was about five degrees above dead winter. But Ellen and Peggy needed him. He *had* to defy Ben.

Not that Ben didn't care about the girls. It just seemed like they were abstractions to him. He guarded the son he knew, trading him for the nieces he'd never met, seen only in passing on the street, strangers seen by a stranger.

They weren't real to him. He hadn't grown up with giggles in the dark and skinned knees from roller-blading and temper-tantrums over favorite toys. He hadn't shared the hug of triumph after that first secret bicycle solo guarded by the older brother because Mom thought little Mouse was too young to throw away the training wheels, hadn't felt tears soaking his shoulder after Ellie's soccer team lost that crucial game by a single penalty kick in overtime.

Gary held those thoughts as he stripped off his shirt and laid it on the damp rocks at the base of the cliff. Piece by piece he added shoes, socks, T-shirt, until he stood shivering and clad only in goose bumps in the mist that seemed to have turned to ice. It thickened around him, as if the sea and air conspired to guard him from Ben's eyes. Gary swallowed, dreading the touch of the water as cold and clammy as a drowned corpse.

Ellen and Peggy were in danger.

He crouched down and pulled the handcuffs from his jeans pocket, the practice cuffs that had been an early lesson in Locks and Picks 101, the introductory course. Like Houdini, Ben always had picks glued to his body in unlikely places, flesh-colored metal and plastic that stood a decent chance of passing a strip search. Gary hadn't yet reached that plateau of paranoia.

On the other hand, it isn't paranoia if they actually *have* tapped your phone. He stared at the cold water. *Might as well bring it out and admit it,* he thought. *I'm scared. I don't want to dive into that stuff. What was it Dad used to say, that an unprotected man could live for about fifteen minutes in the water around here? That your brain starts to flake out on you after less than five?*

He'd barely been able to move when he got back to shore, that other time. Surface temperature was one thing, but the deep waters changed little from winter to summer. His fingers and toes had been white and too stiff to hold on to the rocks. He'd finally hooked an elbow onto something and scraped his knees raw on the barnacles, crawling out of the water into August sunshine. He'd finally stopped shivering sometime that evening, huddled under a blanket in the setting sun.

His ten-mile endurance swim had been in a nice warm lake, with a wetsuit on and the sun high overhead.

I'm scared.

He dove. He didn't feel the water when he hit. He felt the cold, instead, as if an icy hand snatched him and squeezed the air out of his lungs. Then he sputtered when the saltwater burned the back of his nose, and he kicked upward toward the light. Gary shook wet hair out of his eyes and looked around for the buoy. Thirty yards offshore, the orange plastic winked at him as it rose into sight on a swell and then disappeared again. He kicked and splashed toward it, arms and legs already awkward from the cold, the fingers of his left hand locking around the open chrome-steel cuffs.

His fingers thumped plastic, barely felt through the numbness. Gary grabbed on with both hands, hauling his shoulders above the waves, and shook his head again. His *brain* was going numb along with his hands and feet. He had to dive, had to dive *now* while he still remembered what the hell he was doing.

Practice took over. He gulped air, locked his throat, and plunged straight down. The mooring chain led him on, black and furry with weed, through gray water into shadow. He remembered the emerald glow the water had had that time before, under a clear blue sky, and briefly wished he could die in light rather than darkness. Today, the water was the fog above made liquid and menacing.

Hand over hand, he worked his way downward. Without flippers, his feet were next to worthless. His fingers slipped on the chain, greased by the thick growth of weed and stiff with cold. Something tangled his left hand and he almost threw it away before he remembered the handcuffs. They were insurance. They meant he *couldn't* chicken out.

Blackness closed in around him—he must be deeper than before, the mooring must have shifted. He swallowed against the pressure, popping his ears. That usually meant fifteen feet. He pulled the chain past his body, reeling in the bottom. His ears popped again. His hands slipped again, and he grabbed hard. He felt something grate into his flesh, like a cut without pain. *Too numb,* he thought. *Probably mussels or barnacles. Wonder how deep that cut is.*

The darkness spread in front of him, grew form, became rocks and kelp sloping off to his right into shadows of nothing. He kept pulling in the black line, hand over hand, until a black cube separated from the murk and he touched rust-scabbed iron, the mooring ring rubbed clean of weed by the constant chafing of the chain with the rise and fall of waves, the pivot of the current and the tide. His fingers wouldn't grab.

Handcuff. His brain fuzzed and sputtered, lazily. *Hook the cuff to the ring.* He fumbled at it, finally snagging the hook with one cuff like gaffing a fish. He batted at the open arm until it seemed to snap into place. *Wrist. Do something with the wrist, with the other cuff, let go and then rehook.*

He lost his grip on the chain and floated loose, drifting upward. His ears buzzed now, dark spots alternating with silver bubbles across his eyes. *Mooring ring.* He kicked back, wondering why his feet barely seemed to move him. *No fins. Negative buoyancy. Breathe out to sink.*

He sank again. His hand hooked the chain like a claw, fingers stiff and useless. *Wrist into cuff. Bash the swing-arm into place. Done. Mission accomplished. Back to the surface.*

Something held him. The chain rose up past his face to the silvery edge, curving mirrors of air against water, the edge between life and death. Gary fumbled for the button on his buoyancy compensator, trying to lift off the bottom. He couldn't find it. Couldn't find his mouthpiece, to fill his lungs and rise. Couldn't find the release on his weight belt. *Tangled in the kelp or the pot-warp of some damned ghost trap.* His brain fogged to the same dark gray as the water around him, lit by a neon sign remembered from a dive shop: THERE ARE OLD DIVERS, AND BOLD DIVERS, BUT NO OLD, BOLD DIVERS.

Something held him. His brain shivered. His lungs dove past red pain into darkness and warmth, and he felt the cold and pressure in the marrow of his bones. They burned and flowed inside his muscles, as if they wanted to escape from the mistake the rest of his body was making, escape and leave the rest of him behind like a jellyfish.

<Come to me.>

The water held a familiar scent. It wasn't the taste of his own blood, though that tinged the water around him. This was a difference in the water itself, remembered from the edge of the bay, as if a stream of fresh water flowed up from the kelp beneath him. He twisted to follow it down, his need for air forgotten. Something jerked at him again. He rolled against the pull. Sharp pain lanced through his wrist, and he was free. Free to follow that taste down past the roots of the kelp, past the rocks, into a hole that swallowed him in darkness.

The smell led him deeper, into tight spaces worn smooth by the ebb and flow of ages. His body flowed with the water, sinuous, driving, his nose sure of the way. Side passages held less fresh water, held less of the smell of warmth, tasted *different* and less welcoming. He twisted around a hairpin turn and rose and the welcome surrounded him.

A red sun glowed in the darkness, brought down beneath the sea and the rock. It woke memories in his head. He'd seen it before, seen it once and then it had hidden from him. He couldn't remember why it was important. The smell of welcome strengthened as he swam closer.

<Your strength has been proven.>

The words should mean something. They woke joy in one corner of his mind, but they didn't connect with the smooth elation of swimming free. They didn't connect with the endurance and strength he found within himself.

Other words echoed, half-remembered. "When you change, remember to change back." He fought against them. He felt complete. He was where he belonged.

<Come to me.>

He twisted, with a kick of his lower body. The red sun loomed in front of his nose, small, no bigger than his head, dripping crimson. It was injured. Blood in the water meant food. He bit at the wound, and found warmth in his mouth. He held something hard against the inside of his cheek, savory, slippery against his flesh. It was good.

The wounded sun held still. He could surface, breathe, return to feed again. He turned to the faint light of the surface, rising lazily. His body told him he could stay under much longer, but there was no need. The food wasn't deep, the water felt warm and still, no sharks or orcas threatened.

Rock ledges rose under his body, bare of weed as if they had been scoured clean by storms. He surfaced. Yellow suns shone on him from several angles, out of black sky, and he felt the wrongness of it. He had left gray sky and rain behind him when he dove.

He squirmed up on the shore, damp rock under his fur, and blinked. There was no sky. There was no wind, no fog, no rain. The water lay still behind him, rippled only by his own wake. This was a trap. He rolled over, ready to dive back into the safety of the water at the faintest threat.

"When you change, remember to change back." Ellen and Peggy needed him. That corner of his mind expanded and meaning flooded back. He remembered the fiery pain as his bones softened and flowed. The memory was the deed.

His wrist hurt.

Gary stared at his left hand, deformed and purple and already swelling. He remembered the tug of the cuff, and rolling away from the pull. *Dumb.* If he'd pulled straight back, his flipper would have slid out of the cuff. A seal's flipper was much more flexible than a man's hand, could easily have slipped out of that cuff. *If you're going to plan cute tricks like that,* remember *them!*

"You damned fool!"

It was Ben, striding angrily through the entry from the stairs. He unfurled a fleece blanket and wrapped it three times around Gary's shoulders before hugging him. Gary could feel the old man trembling with fear and relief.

Gary shrugged him off and worked his right hand free. He spat into his palm and sighed. His new Tear glowed bright crimson, red as the blood flowing from the barnacle cuts but with an inner light. He sagged with exhaustion before stiffening his knees. The joy kept him standing.

<Yes. You are a Morgan, and a child of the sea. You have found your heritage.>

He glanced from the Tear in his palm to Ben's face. "I *did* it! Now I know why Dad put that buoy there. It marks another entry. It marks the selkie path to the Dragon's Eye . . ."

His words trailed off. Pain and relief furrowed Ben's face, traced by streaks of shining water. The old man was crying.

twenty-four

—⚍—

ALICE CALMED HERSELF, staring into darkness. The House felt dangerous enough without adding her rage to the flames. That was for later, for the battle. Then she could afford to go berserk. She needed coolness and clarity now. She needed to marshal all her allies. She felt them waiting in the shadows of the cellar around her, lurking in the depths of the spring beneath her feet, circling high above the chimneys like the eagle riding his thermals. The stone of the cellar seemed to tremble like a leashed dog smelling her prey, eager to taste blood.

Again she built her small fire on the spring's altar. This time she included wood from an ash tree growing by the Morgan house, close to the windows of the room Ellen and Peggy shared. Even fresh-cut from a living tree, ash would burn hot and clean. She thanked the tree for its gift of a limb, for its protection of the girls it knew and guarded, the girls who had climbed it and hugged it close to their hearts. She touched flame to the kindling and waited until the tiny coals were ready.

"Wind of the west, I call to you. Guard the guests of this House. Guard Ellen and Peggy." She scattered a pinch of tobacco into the coals. Again the glow sent blue smoke spiraling up, straight to the chimney flue and into the sky.

"Wind of the east, I call to you. Guard the guests of this House. Guard Ellen and Peggy." A second pinch of tobacco followed the first.

Today the smoke would be invisible, rising into fog and mist. That didn't matter. The winds would taste it, the clouds would hear her plea, the waters would carry it to the waiting soil and stone. The guardians would hear.

"Wind of the south, I call to you. Guard the guests of this House. Guard Ellen and Peggy." A third pinch. "Wind of the north, I call to you. Guard the guests of this House. Guard Ellen and Peggy." A fourth.

She poured more tobacco from the palm of her right hand. It cascaded into the coals in a shower of sparks.

"Spirits of the earth, spirits of the water, spirits of the sky, I send smoke to you. I send sweet smoke to you. Guard this land. Guard the people of this land. Guard the giver of this gift. Guard us against evil. Make the sun shine into darkness, make the wind sweep the air clean, make the waters wash away the stains that lie on the land. Guard us against evil."

That was the basic ritual. Then she poured the last of the tobacco into the fire and added the other words, the words she'd hoped she'd never need to use when she'd learned them from Aunt Jean.

"Spirits of the earth, spirits of the water, spirits of the sky, I send smoke to you. I send sweet smoke to you." She swallowed, her throat tight. "Powers of this land, I call on you to harm. Powers of this land, I call on you to kill. I summon you to harm those who would cause harm. I summon you to kill those who would kill. Seek out those who stole children from this House. Seek out those who sent evil to this House. Seek out those who would gain by this evil. Find them wherever they may hide. Bring pain and death to them. Make their blood feed your roots. Make their bones sweeten your soil. Send their souls to join the stone from which they were born. May their own weapons destroy them. May the fires of the land and the waters of the sea devour them."

She paused before speaking the final words, the words she couldn't pull back once they passed her lips. "Let this thing happen. If there is evil in it, let it fall upon my own head."

It was done. She felt the smoke closing in around her, squeezing, burning in her eyes and nose, testing her. Power ebbed and flowed with her heartbeat. She heard distant screaming, curses in Naskeag, Welsh, and English, and knew that her chant had stirred more than just the powers she had summoned. The oil lamps flared like flashbulbs and then died.

She blinked back tears. The cellar lay black around her, quiet and empty. The powers had spread out into the land. She felt them hunting, as if they extended her touch throughout the ancient lands of the Naskeags. Her knees felt like ice, and she tested them with her real hands. She found cold wetness. She was kneeling in the pool, in the spring's water. She groped around her, finding handholds, and pulled herself upright. Her fingers brushed a soft bundle and she lifted it. It was heavy.

The cellar stairs groaned under her feet. She climbed into the parlor, into the bright grayness of the light, and breathed deep. It was done. She was still alive. As Kate would put it, the roof had stayed a working distance from the cellar.

She flexed her fingers, wincing at the red pits her nails had dug into her palms. *That* wasn't something she wanted to do every day. Once in a lifetime was too often. She squatted down and closed her eyes again, relishing the soothing darkness. Besides, that way she didn't have to choose between the different rooms she was seeing.

Her head hurt. Cool hands touched her forehead and the back of her neck, drawing the pain out and sending peace in its place. Caroline. She felt a breath in her ear, heard whispered words.

"You know, if you kill yourself, you won't be able to rescue those kids."

" 'M okay."

"With all due respect to my beloved aunt, that's bullshit." Alice shook her head and set the bundle on the floor. "Jus' help me get into this clown suit."

"And again I say, 'Bullshit.' You blacked out on me yesterday and again this morning. You've still got a lump on your head bigger than Glooskap's mountain. How many fingers am I holding up?"

Alice batted the hand away, rather than trying to fake a count. She chose a bundle from the three available on the three different parlor floors, carefully avoiding the question of how she could get three images out of two eyes. She fumbled with the thongs that bound it. "Help me get this open. Get it on. It'll give me strength. Block off the feedback from Kate."

"How is she? Where is she?"

"Across cold water. Safe. Alone." Alice shook her head, then winced. "Kate Rowley on a boat. You don't know how funny that is." Her tongue was working better now. Maybe her fingers would follow that example.

Between them, they undid the yellowed linen wrappings. Shimmering color spilled out, glass and shell beadwork on a doeskin base. Patterns flowed across the surfaces, forming flowers and leaves that then condensed into interlocking swastikas, left-handed and right, which swirled and drew the eyes and formed yet larger patterns. Hypnotic. Alice blinked and shook her head again, breaking the spell. She ran her fingers over the surface and backing.

The Haskell regalia—this would be the first time that Caroline had ever seen it. Preserved in the aura of the spring, it was old out of mind. The sash was all shell-work and even predated the Morgans. Museum conservators would have fits if they got their hands on this stuff. Glass-beaded Native work *couldn't* be older than the 1500s, but the sinew and linen threads that bound the patterns together would carbon-date to centuries earlier. Totally impossible.

The bundle unrolled under her fingers: vest, leggings, sash, skullcap, satchel. Chants said that the doeskin had been tanned by simple, tiresome chewing. It was as supple and smooth as velvet. Everything had been made with open side-seams and thong ties, to fit generations of women large and small. Alice could wear it and not appear ridiculous, though the vest hung down to miniskirt length and the leggings cinched around her waist. Even someone as massive as Kate could still fit inside. She'd show a lot of skin, though. Kate—that neck-pouch in her truck was part of the whole, carried some of its power. It was darker because of much handling, as it had been used for small protections through the ages.

Alice felt her headache fade as power flowed, released from the bundle. She caressed the beaded surfaces. Colors became textures under her fingertips, *feeling* of rose and lavender and indigo and emerald.

Caroline was staring at the patterns, eyes vague, almost drunken. Alice sympathized, remembering the first time Aunt Jean had shown her the ceremonial dress. It could go straight to your head.

"Help me get this stuff on. The spring says we have to get moving within an hour. Otherwise, Ellen and Peggy face some *really* nasty things."

Caroline shivered as the regalia's spell broke. She reached

out tentatively and picked up the vest, touching it as if she expected it to blow up in her hands. "You going to wear a Second Chance T-shirt under this?"

"Can't." Alice shrugged into the heavy vest, adjusted the ties, and reached for the sash. Already she felt stronger, more sure with her hands. Her headache faded into a thin memory. "Kevlar would interfere with the flow of power. Sort of acts like insulation and electricity. You have to wear cotton, wool, or linen only—natural fibers, nothing synthetic." A phantom smile flitted across her lips. "Back in the old days, you didn't wear *anything* under it. That would *really* put the preachers' noses out of joint."

Caroline stared pointedly at the open crotch of the leggings as she adjusted them over her aunt's slacks. "I can see how it might. I'd still rather have you wearing a bulletproof vest. In God we trust, but carry a backup. You know, the belt and suspenders sort of thing."

"Where's your belief in Injun magic?"

"You mean Injun magic like the Ghost Dance? Bring back the buffalo, white man falling dead like winter flies? Seems like that religion kinda vanished after Wounded Knee. Those magic shirts didn't stop the soldiers' bullets worth a damn."

Alice grimaced and nodded, then adjusted the skullcap over her hair. The gaudy yarmulke wanted to slide off every time she moved. She finally tied it down with locks of hair. "Well, *you'd* better wear your vest. I think we've got a spare that would fit Gary, as well. I know he can't wear it while he's swimming in, but use your feminine wiles to make him put it on when he's changed back."

Caroline snickered. "Feminine wiles? He isn't interested in my butt. If he won't wear the damned vest, I'll threaten to spank him. He thinks I'm his mother, not his sister. God knows, he doesn't see me as a woman." She paused. "Brother or not, I may have to do something about that."

"Well, you *do* look a lot like Lainie at your age. And he's met her. Don't be too hard on him. The poor guy's still sorting out which set of parents to believe in."

Alice stretched. The aches had vanished, and she felt ready to rassle bears. She started toward the fireplace and then stopped. She'd noticed that Caroline kept edging sideways rather than turning her back on her aunt. "Turn around."

Caroline ducked her chin like a turtle retreating into its shell. She froze for an instant as if she was going to rebel, then turned. She was wearing tan camouflage, cargo pants and baggy top, stuff that would help her disappear inside tunnels of Stonefort granite. Alice lifted the hem of the top, exposing a large black automatic tucked into the back of her niece's belt. Alice quietly removed the pistol and clip holster, a pair of spare magazines, and pushed Caroline's shoulder, turning her again.

"No gunfights. You and your brother are supposed to be mice at a cat show. Get in, get the kids and Dan, get out, don't get noticed. You know how to hide. You start shooting instead, it'll all go to hell. I've got one fight, and I won't need this for it, win or lose. Your cousin Ron takes care of the rest."

"Cousin Ron?"

"Ron Pelletier. Cousin on your mother's side. Ron's in the, um, import-export business. Competes with the Pratts. They've got a little jurisdictional dispute to arbitrate. I took the liberty of coordinating our schedules with him. Kinda suspect your daddy Ben has pulled them into *his* tangled web, as well. It's the sort of thing ol' Moriarty Morgan would do."

Caroline looked uneasy. Alice thought she knew why. "It's a small town, girl. *Everyone* is some kind of cousin of yours. Even the Pratts. Remember that before you start grabbing guns."

She took a closer look at the pistol in her hand: 9mm, Browning style. Memory nagged at her, and she tried to find the serial number. There wasn't one. Never had been. *Frigging sterile CIA special.*

"Damn. Aunt Jean was getting a little forgetful in the last few years. This was supposed to go into the bay. There are probably a couple of slugs in an evidence locker down in Augusta, waiting for a match. Where'd you find it?"

"Just picked it up, you know. Typical Maine house, guns tucked away everywhere."

"Uh-uh. I sanitized the place when the kids moved in. Come up with another one."

"Okay, so I picked the lock on the gun room. Sue me."

"Where'd you learn *that* trick? Talking with your brother through that Dragon pendant?"

"Nope. Roommate in college."

Alice decided she didn't want to ask. "I always wondered why Lainie wanted another dose of Morgan genes in the family. Maybe she was right, after all."

She checked the safety, pulled out a handkerchief and wiped the pistol for prints, and set it down on the bookshelf next to the fireplace. "This doesn't leave the parlor until we can dump it someplace safe."

Caroline's eyes narrowed. "Curiouser and curiouser. We get out of this alive, I want to hear that story. Meanwhile, what *are* you planning to carry? I assume you aren't relying on *Satyagraha* and *ahimsa*?"

"Moral force only works against moral people. No, I'm going to kill a man. If he doesn't kill me first, that is. And I think the best weapons for the job are tucked away back *here.*" She pressed a board at the end of the bookcase and one of the panels over the fireplace shifted to show a line of pale varnish. Hooking a fingernail into the edge, she swung the panel out, reached into the darkness behind the chimney, and pulled out a flat mahogany box. It was about as big as a newspaper folded in half and as deep as her palm, and she'd forgotten how *heavy* the bastard was. She set it on the mantel and shoved that felonious automatic and spare magazines back into the shadows before closing the panel. Let the dead past hide its own dead for a while.

Caroline was dripping questions all over the floor, but they wouldn't stain the carpet. She could wait. Alice slung the satchel over her shoulder, hefted the box in both hands, and marched back out through the centuries to find a place that believed in technology more advanced than the Neolithic. The parlor still thought in terms of flint axes.

She carried the box into the kitchen and set it on the table, then slid the catches aside and opened the box, revealing two antique pistols in a fitted green velvet case. A powder flask, box of caps, and other accessories filled in the space around the blued steel and walnut of the weapons. Percussion dueling pistols they were, made in London by one of the finest gunsmiths of any age, and they had been a gift from some ancestral Morgan for the defense of the House and the Woman of that day.

Probably stolen, but what the hey, who asks? They'd been kept near the spring for so long they'd become ritual weapons like some king's jeweled mace, part of the Haskell regalia. Still, like that mace, they were quite capable of killing. In fact, especially capable, when you were dealing with certain enemies.

She fitted a cap to the nipple of one pistol, cocked the hammer, and snapped it with a satisfactory bang. A second cap, with a light charge of powder, dried out the chamber and proved the action. Alice felt the House breathe that sharp sulfurous powder smoke deep into its wood and smile like a shark. It wanted *blood.* Caroline sat quietly, watching, as Alice selected a tarnished ball of silver and a second of carved apple wood from the House orchard, charged the pistol with a full load of powder and both balls, and rammed the top wad home.

"Werewolves and vampires, sterling silver bullets and a stake through the heart," Alice explained. "Old family custom. They'll also kill a man quite nicely. The wood shatters on impact and spreads out, sort of like a grenade."

She repeated the ritual with the other pistol, set both hammers at half cock, and then tucked them into their sleeves in the beaded satchel. Aunt Jean never had explained what the witches had carried in those places, before they knew of firearms. Maybe those flint hatchets. She checked the bottom of the satchel to make sure that both bundles were ready—the ancient one of herbs and strange stones and bear claws, and the modern one with her mini–EMT kit. Strangely, the House hadn't complained about that change.

She stood up and waved Caroline out. "Let's get this show on the road. You've got everything set up with Gary?"

"Yeah. The Dragon makes a really neat radio. She added some ideas of her own."

"Okay. You go in the back door, I go in the front door. We meet in the middle. There's going to be shooting and probably cops. Ignore them. Disappear. You don't have to be seen if you don't want to be. *Don't. Stop. For. Any. Thing!*"

Caroline nodded. She hugged her aunt, a fierce squeeze that admitted she was afraid they'd never meet again. *About time to introduce that kid to spirit talking,* Alice thought. *Old Aunt Molly could calm her down. Blowing up that British sloop wasn't any picnic.*

Meanwhile, "that kid" had opened the side door. But she wasn't leaving. A chill seized Alice's heart. Had the *brujo* brought the battle to *her?* No. Caroline was staring down at her feet, with a bemused expression on her face. Alice followed her gaze down to the granite steps. A tiny bundle of fur stared back at her.

"*Me!*"

Alice squatted, shaking her head. She measured the calico kitten with her eyes. The little beast must have been weaned yesterday. If she had been weaned at all, that is.

"No. Uh-uh. You're too young. You just trot back to the union hall and tell them to send out a girl who's ready to work."

"*Miaowr!*" The kitten switched her stub of a tail in an imitation of feline rage.

"Look, you little devil, this job *killed* the last queen who held it. All nine lives. Didn't they tell you that there's a war on?"

"*Me!*"

Then the kitten hopped to Alice's knee and climbed the vest's beadwork to her shoulder. A tiny nose shoved into her ear, and Alice nabbed the beast by the scruff of its neck.

"That *tickles!*" She hung the kitten in front of her nose and studied it. The kitten studied back. "This place has some special rules. You don't eat the other residents, understand? You can *play* with the mice and the crickets, but you can't *eat* them. You can't even play with the bats. They break too easily."

The kitten gazed back at her, all innocence. Well, the House had plenty of experience in training cats. Tears blurred Alice's eyes as relief flooded into her. Apparently, she didn't have to solve *every* problem by herself. The House had forgiven her. The spirits had forgiven her. She took a deep breath and swallowed the inevitable.

"Are you old enough to have figured out your name?"

She blinked at the answer in her head. "Oh, ye gods and goddesses. Little imp, you're trying to fit a size ten ego into a size one body." She looked up at her niece. "Caroline, meet Atropos. Atropos, meet Caroline."

"*Mer!*" "Pleased to meet you."

Caroline seemed vastly amused by the whole scene. Well, that might help her to face what was coming. Alice stood up and tucked the kitten into the palm of her left hand. It weighed next to nothing. *The third Fate, Atropos, she who cuts the thread of life, she who could not be turned. Oh, ye gods and goddesses!*

She stepped back into the kitchen, refilled Dixie's water dish, and shook out an estimated week's supply of dried catfood into the pan. The cat nibbled daintily at the one and lapped at the other before looking around. Alice puzzled over that for a moment, then pulled out Dixie's despised litter box from the closet and refilled it with fresh litter. The kitten jumped in and scratched around, after making it smell right.

So now the House had a defender again. A weight lifted from Alice's shoulders. She hadn't realized how much she'd feared leaving the place alone. Now she could go into battle with a clear conscience.

She did *not* lock the door behind her. There was too much chance that one of Caroline's sisters or even a cousin would have to be the next woman to open it.

At least Kate was safely out of things, across cold saltwater that shorted out most spells. The spring gave some very nasty pictures of what could happen if the big ox got caught in the crossfire.

twenty-five

—⁊⁊—

KATE THOUGHT SHE was going mad. Alice's voice kept forcing itself into her brain and she hummed along or sang with it under her breath as she worked. *That* wasn't the problem. She usually had some tune stuck in her head after visiting Alice, because Alice ran that megawatt stereo like some junkies mainlined heroin.

But mirrors should stay mirrors, reflecting the rooms around them and the people looking into them. Kate had been working in one bathroom of Keith Bauer's island hideaway, replacing a faucet washer on a Victorian sink, when she looked up straight into Alice's face in the mirror. Except it wasn't Alice. It was some ancestral Haskell in ceremonial beads holding a muzzle-loading pistol across her chest like an antique photo of Sitting Bull. Her face was set in that grim rigidity you saw in early photos, where the subject had to hold a pose for fifteen minutes in a head-brace.

Then the hallucination had faded and Kate stared into her own face. It *couldn't* have been an old photo remembered, because the scene was in color instead of the coppery silver of an antique daguerreotype. Her eyes were playing tricks on her.

Okay. She could live with that. So she got on with her work, getting the place ready for the few weeks a hard-nose corporate shyster could afford to relax away from phones and secretaries and instant access to his files. Then she'd been rewiring a floor lamp in the parlor because the mice had gotten at the cord over the winter and the bare wires had popped a fuse when she turned the power back on. The mantlepiece was one of those ornate Victorian things, white columns and carved rose garlands and an oval mirror with beveled edges crowned by a Grecian urn, and she'd glanced into it to see Alice striding through the fog and drizzle with a face like an avenging angel.

Kate had grabbed the medicine bag hanging around her neck, comparing the beadwork on it with the outfit her friend was wearing. The vision had strengthened and zoomed like a movie shot until patterned flowers filled the mirror. They matched the poke in her hand. Then Kate blinked and the mirror was a mirror once again.

Mirrors were uncanny things at the best of times. She'd taken the lamp into the kitchen and finished her chore at the counter, breathing deeply and calming her hands before she could handle a screwdriver without gouging bright scratches into the antique brass.

Now she was working outside in the cold fog, breath condensing under her nose, swearing at the mud. She really should have started in on the dining room, replacing a push-button light switch that worked only half the time and maybe rewiring the chandelier before it shorted out and burned the old place flat. She'd looked into the room and then retreated, her shoulder blades twitching like somebody had dumped an ice cube down her shirt. The sideboard was another one of those Victorian monstrosities—age-darkened oak and a mirror behind the shelf to show off both sides of your crystal and silver.

There weren't any mirrors out in the rustic gardens that led down to the bay.

She hoisted another stone back into place, rebuilding a garden wall that the freeze and thaw of fifty winters had finally torn apart. Dry-stone work of quarried granite held a bed of blueberry bushes and ferns against the slope above a path, and it was really a landscaping job that she should sub out to another crew. But that would be a minimum of half a grand, straight out of her pocket. For that kind of money, she could put on her gardening gloves.

Or just do without. The gloves slipped, muddy with the drizzle, and she tossed them to one side. She grabbed the next chunk of stone. It felt gritty, rough and cold and heavy, and images flooded out of it.

Fear and musty smells and darkness. She was trapped, but she couldn't give in to panic because Mouse was depending on her. She hugged her sister close, and whispered in her ear. "Remember what Aunt Alice taught us. People see what they expect to see. Think like a window. Think of the rock behind you. If they see a pattern that looks like the wall, they see the wall. Those African lizards do it. So can we."

Kate dropped the stone, narrowly missing her foot.

"Aunt Alice." Everybody in town called Alice Haskell "Aunt Alice," even blue-haired old biddies twice her age. That was the Emily-Post-approved etiquette for addressing the Haskell Witch.

"Mouse?" Kate had heard that nickname. Where? A small child, quick and inquisitive, you could almost see the bright eyes and twitching nose of a deer mouse poking through the leaves under a beech tree, looking for nuts. She'd been playing in front of a big house.

Kate stepped backward inside her memory, widening the view. She knew buildings better than she knew people, for all that she'd lived in Stonefort for forty years. When she thought of names, she thought of houses, like she thought of the House whenever Alice crossed her mind.

There were the Doric columns of the Frederick place, sea-captains who brought a thirst for Boston culture to the ass-end of Maine as a back-haul load for fragrant pine lumber and Stonefort granite shipped upwind to Massachusetts. There was the fake Tudor half-timber of the Pratt mansion, with dry-rot in the beam ends and a hole she'd had to patch in the eaves where squirrels had decided to make their home. The elaborate scroll-saw fretwork of the Johnsons' Gothic Revival bed-and-breakfast right off the village green that had taken her three weeks to scrape and paint. What house stood behind "Mouse" in her memories?

Not a house—a stone tower. "Mouse" was Peggy Morgan. She'd been playing tag with her brother and sister, dodging irreverently around the age-worn markers in the Morgan graveyard while Kate repointed the masonry on one of the crypts. Both Peggy and Ellen were staying with Alice. *Had* been staying with Alice, that is, a major reason why Kate couldn't go anywhere near the House.

Kate reached out toward the stone and then jerked her hand back. Why would Ellen Morgan's thoughts be trapped in cold pink granite? She was going mad.

Lightning flashed in the fog, impossible on such a still day. Kate blinked dazzle out of her eyes and waited for the thunderclap, or maybe the Voice of God. It never came. Instead, she heard the slow wash of waves down by the shore, the drip of water off the leaves, gulls crying in the gray fog against the distant grunt of the foghorn on Egg Rock. The world seemed sharp and clear and clean, as if she could cut herself on the damp spruce smell and the earthy cinnamon of the blueberry bushes. The island gripped her senses. She was going mad.

Or she was caught by magic. She wiped her hands on her jeans and clutched the beaded poke again, seeking the calm it offered. Twenty years, thirty years, she'd been like Lew Lewis. In Denial. "No, I'm not an alcoholic." "No, the world is scientific and rational. Magic doesn't exist."

Kate squatted in the drizzle, her knees too weak to hold her. Something seemed to pull the soul out of her and re-shape it before forcing it back into her body. Saul on the road to Damascus, falling on his face before the glory of the Lord: "Saul, Saul, why persecutest thou me?" At least she'd been spared the three days of blindness. Shivers ran down her spine and she squeezed the bag in her hands.

"Magic doesn't exist. Thou shalt not suffer a witch to live."

Two mutually exclusive ideas, now that she thought about them and brought them together. If magic didn't ex-ist, the things Alice did were a harmless eccentricity. An-other way the rich folks played with their money, like Tom Pratt and his antique cars.

Okay, if the Bible said using magic justified the death penalty, *somebody* sure thought it was real. But then you got into translation problems. Kate remembered that one. "Witch" should have been read as "poisoner" in the original Hebrew. And as far as she knew, no Haskell Witch had ever poisoned anybody. They tended to be more direct than that. Shot a few, blew them up, burned them alive, yes. Quibble, quibble, quibble.

Still, every case Kate knew about had been self-defense or the defense of someone else. If outside authorities had poked their noses into Stonefort business, the community always closed ranks around their Witch. "The bastard needed killing," was the common attitude.

She held the medicine bag in one hand and reached out

to the stone with the other. Her hands trembled and she found it hard to breathe. *Magic exists. It can be good or evil, just like that chunk of granite can be part of a garden wall or a weapon crushing someone's skull. Magic is a tool. I could kill someone with almost any tool in my truck. That doesn't make the tools evil.*

It's just a chunk of stone, nothing magic about it. Only a chunk of stone like any other. But her mason's brain wouldn't let that pass. It wasn't *just* a chunk of stone. It was a chunk of quarried pink granite, imported to this island of finer-grained gray stone. It was the same kind of stone that underlay Morgan Point and Pratt's Neck, Stonefort granite from those abandoned quarries the kids used for beer parties and backseat make-out passion pits. It remembered. It still touched its home. Things that had once been in contact remained in contact. And Alice said that Kate could talk to wood and stone . . .

She ran her fingers over it nervously, expecting a spark to seize her muscles. It was cold and rough and slippery-wet with lichen under the day of fog and rain. *Cold. Fear and musty smells and darkness.* Back in Ellen Morgan's thoughts, Kate ran through the scene. She didn't drop the stone this time, and Mouse answered in the darkness. *"Those men want to hurt us. You heard them talking, the things they said to that little man. The one who scares them so much."*

Kate saw the "little man" in Ellen's mind. Antonio. She broke loose from the grip of the stone, shivering with the images she'd just swallowed. She'd let Antonio into the Haskell House, and *this* was what happened. This was what was happening *now,* what *she* had caused.

No. If the stone had shown her the scene twice, it couldn't be happening *now. Now* only happened once. What she saw had to be memory or foresight.

If it was foresight, she could try to stop it.

She stood up and fumbled for a cigarette. Damn good thing she was outside—client houses were all "No-

Smoking" zones. You could smell cigarette smoke for months after the dirty deed. Funny, the trendy styles in vice. Smoking used to be perfectly acceptable but you couldn't cuss in public. Kate remembered Alice's Aunt Jean. The old woman would box your ears if you even said "darn," but she'd smoked like a chimney. She'd lived to be ninety-three or so. So much for established medical mythology.

Aunt Jean. The old woman never just lit up. Tobacco was a ritual for her as well as an addiction. She offered smoke to the spirits, the first four puffs of every cigarette. Kate turned to the west, across the bay, and closed her eyes, searching the inside of her forehead until the direction felt *right*. Whatever it was, it felt quieter in *that* direction, as if something was listening. She drew in smoke and breathed it out, gently, asking for help. She repeated the move to each compass point, east and north and south, orienting strictly by the feel inside her head. Calm settled on her, but it definitely felt like that famous calm before a storm. She could see the thunderclouds building on the horizon.

Speaking of building . . . "I could use a few blueprints here. You guys want something built, you'd better give me some plans and specs."

A loon called, out in the bay. *Some omen. Could you be a bit more specific?*

Alice and the Morgan kids—Kate had caused some kind of personal hell for them. Kate knew she damned well had to do something about it. Head straight in, bull-headed as always. That was the only way she knew. But she needed some kind of compass to give her that straight-line course.

She paced the grit walkways overlooking the surf, dragging on her cigarette. The spirits or winds or whatever weren't talking. Not unless you counted that loon.

The cigarette burned her fingers. She snuffed it out in a puddle, stripped the butt, and stowed the little ball of paper in her pocket. Lighting another, she noticed black leaves rotting in the bottom of an ornamental pool. *Have to clean that out,* she thought. *Three days work already, and I keep finding more.*

Then the black shadows wavered into smoke and firmed. They reflected a different mist, showing different trees and different rocks. Someone walked away from her through the fog and drizzle. It had to be Alice. Her back was turned, but Kate had known Alice all her life, knew that walk. Kate followed. Darkness loomed ahead, drew into lines, and became a building with a roof like drooping spruce limbs in the fog.

A second shadow detached from the bushes and stepped in behind Alice. Kate screamed a warning, but her vision was a silent movie without the piano or the captions. She couldn't touch the figures on the screen, couldn't warn Alice. The second figure crouched and took aim. Its hands jerked. Jerked twice. Alice fell. Kate screamed again, feeling her heart ripped in half.

Fire blossomed in the mist, small and then larger. The building burst outward, black smoke and orange petals of flame, and the crouching figure jumped up and ran onward into the fog. More fire blazed in Kate's shoulder and hip, and she sank down in the path. The fog thickened and went black. Then the shadows dissolved and the pool was a pool again, in need of cleaning.

Kate's hands shook too hard to hold her cigarette. Jesus Christ on a godallmighty-damned *crutch* . . . she'd *asked* for something specific. She shuddered and drew a deep breath, blinking hard in an attempt to wipe the images from the back of her eyeballs.

She looked up into the fog, trying to find a target for her terror and rage. "You didn't have to *shout*!"

God. Or gods and goddesses, if you took Alice's point of

view. Kate *knew* that building she'd seen, knew the stupid drooping curve of the eaves. It was supposed to mimic a thatched roof. That had been the carriage house at the Pratts' place. She fumbled at her belt, pulling out the hand-held radio she carried. Yes, it was still on. She turned the squelch down and got a hiss of static for her effort. It was still working.

If that explosion and fire had already happened, the radio would have been spouting calls. All Kate had heard had been routine stuff, all day. Traffic stops, license checks, cops out of the cruiser for a coffee and donut raid.

So all this crap was foresight, not memory. Alice still needed somebody to watch her back.

Kate glanced at her latest $14.95 watch: eleven twenty-five. She tried to remember the schedule for the midday ferry loop. Damn. Frigging boat would have just left the Ayers Island landing, wouldn't be back on the afternoon run until four-fifteen or so, and then she'd have to poke through the whole loop of five islands before she landed back at the Stonefort terminal.

With the fog, she hadn't been able to guess the time of her Alice nightmare, but no way was it as late as seven o'clock in the evening. That was the earliest she could hit the mainland. And the forecast for tomorrow was clear, dammit, not fog and drizzle. That image was *today.*

She had to go. She had to go *now,* or be too late.

Keith Bauer had a boat. Had two, in fact, a big-ass Hinckley ketch he moored out in the Reach and a 19-foot Boston Whaler he used as a tender and dinghy. The Hinckley hadn't even sailed up from winter storage yet, but the Boston Whaler was here, laid up in the boathouse. Kate knew that because she'd bedded it down for the winter. Wake it up, point its nose at the mainland, puke her guts out on the way . . .

Jesus Christ! If she went into the Pratt place . . . That was a shooting war she'd seen, which meant another raid. With the fire and all, no way she could get in and out without being seen. Bernie would have her badge for a tag ornament on his Harley. He'd warned her off.

Kate pulled the boathouse door open. Her feet had made some kind of decision, and she went with the flow. She dragged the tarp off the Whaler, pulled the battery down from the trickle charger, reconnected fuel lines, checked the oil in the big Honda four-stroke outboard. She reversed the fall lay-up procedure, hands working automatically while her brain dodged around her badge and Alice.

Alice was in danger. To hell with the badge.

Fresh plugs, fill the gas, fire the outboard until it caught, and then kill it because it didn't have any cooling until it was in the water. Grab a lifejacket. Check the compass on the dash; thank God the Whaler had a simple, straightforward *compass* instead of the electronic wizardry on the Hinckley. A compass she could read. GPS and radar and Loran were Greek. Open the doors and winch the boat down the rollers into the water and tie it off to the landing float that Ryan's crane had set into the water a couple of days ago.

Alice. Kate thought about the whole Alice thing. She'd nearly died when she'd seen Alice shot, seen Alice fall. That told her more than those impetuous kisses. Kisses were sex. She'd learned to tell the difference between sex and love, living with Lew Lewis.

Her feet had taken her back to the truck. She grabbed the big Colt and holster from the glove box, her lunch and soda from the passenger seat, her badge, and the blue windbreaker with POLICE in big yellow letters across the back and front. If she was going to get her ass shot off, at least she could choose which side was going to do it.

Okay. So she loved Alice. If that was an abomination before the face of the Lord, then Kate needed to swear fealty to a different Lord. Alice seemed to operate with a more accepting pantheon. Maybe it was time to go back to Sunday school.

That thought carried her through locking up and climbing back down to the float. Kate stared at the boat, her stomach doing flip-flops in anticipation. Everything she'd done up to this point was legit, caretaker work. She was *supposed* to put the boat in the water. Maybe even take it out for a test run, though nobody who knew her would believe *that*. But driving it ten miles across the Reach in dense fog and anchoring it off a cliff and abandoning it to the tide while she got into a shootout . . .

That was dancing along the edge of theft. Felony. Bauer might not choose to prosecute, but he could kill her reputation for fifty miles in every direction.

Burning her bridges behind her was one thing. Stealing Keith Bauer's boat was blowing up the abutments afterward. Between telling Bernie to take her badge and stuff it where the sun don't shine, and wiping out the web of trust necessary for caretaker work, she was incinerating more than half her income. She hoped it would at least keep her warm for a while.

How far do you take this newfound belief in witchcraft? People who let "visions" and "voices" tell them what to do usually end up in straitjackets.

As far as necessary.

Kate climbed into the boat and clutched at the railing. Her stomach somersaulted, skipping over the preliminaries. She vomited, started the engine, cast the line off from the landing stage, and vomited again. That settled her gut for long enough to turn the bow into the fog.

Aim to hit the coast to one side of the Pratts. Then you know which way to turn once you make landfall. Aim to the west. She visualized the chart in her head, the locations of Ayers Island and Pratts Neck. *Halfway between NW and WNW ought to do it. Ignore compass deviation. The State of Maine is a big target. At this range, you can't miss it.*

She rammed the throttle forward, stirring up all those Honda horses. The sea was calm enough that she didn't worry about running it full-bore, and the faster she went, the sooner she could get her feet back on solid ground. She took a swig of ginger ale.

twenty-six

—ᴍ—

GARY THROTTLED BACK on the engine and eased the wheel over, bringing *Maria* head-up into the wind. When she held station, barely idling, he made his way forward and tossed the anchor overboard into green swells.

He stood for a moment, swaying as the boat rose and fell, flexing his injured hand. Each time he changed, it got a little better. His body seemed to know how flesh and bone should be shaped, whether they started out that way or not. Maybe it was why werewolves were supposed to be so hard to kill. He sure could have used *that* trick when a slight miscalculation in the dojo had left him with two cracked ribs. As it was, it had taken him months before he could swim comfortably, and the injury had kept him out of three meets.

He made his way aft again, sure-footed along the narrow strip of decking next to the lobster boat's wheelhouse, and swung back into the open cockpit. Then he cut all power and let her drift back on the scope until the anchor snubbed her against the current.

He turned to Caroline. "Okay, Witch. Someone keeps singing in my head, sounds like Aunt Alice. What gives?"

She shook her head. "Yeah, that's her. She can't be more than a couple of miles from us, and she uses music to help weave her spells. I'm sensitive to her, and you're picking it up from me through our Tears. I think that because you wore both of them, they've become twins. Tuned together. Do me a favor, eh? Next time you settle down to make out with a girl, take your pendant *off?*"

Sisters. Gary felt a blush flooding out to the tips of his ears. Years of half-friendly sniping with Ellen and Peggy made him counterattack. "Hey, with the Haskell reputation, I'd think you'd want to take notes."

She grinned back at him. "Yeah. But you'd be doing it all *wrong.*"

Time to change the subject. "You *sure* you can handle a kayak?"

"Hey, Naskeags invented the canoe. You remember, those birch-bark things? Mom tells me I was conceived in a canoe, and came within about ten minutes of being born in one. She took me out on the lake before I could even crawl. I spent last summer kayaking Grand Canyon."

So *that* was where she got those shoulders. Still, she wasn't some freak like the Lewis kid, built like a tank so you weren't sure whether you were looking at a boy or a girl. On Caroline, muscles looked good. Even the baggy cargo pants and top didn't disguise her curves. Any man within a hundred yards knew she was a woman.

They'd made jokes in school about suiting up the Lewis girl and putting her on the football team—in a uniform and pads, no one would have known the difference. *And* she sure would have improved the team. But God help you if you said that where she could hear it. She'd decked the quarterback with one punch when he'd made some kind of lesbian joke behind her back. Of course, he *was* fighting out of his weight class.

Touchy. Jackie Lewis, that was her name, a year or so younger than him, he only knew her by sight. Mother was the town cop, bigger than the daughter. You didn't want to cross *her,* either. He'd heard stories about some cases that never made it into court. You did "hard time" right on the spot. At that, he knew kids who preferred her brand of "justice" to a juvie record.

The fog was lifting. He tried to judge visibility, making sure he'd anchored far enough down-current from the Pratts so *Maria* wouldn't attract the attention of any lookouts. They must be used to lobster boats, anyway— Dad hadn't fished these waters, but Gary recognized buoys of at least three of the Stonefort licenses. Just as long as none of them thought he was hauling *their* traps, he'd be okay.

Caroline was staring at him with an enigmatic smile, one eyebrow lifted. Gary started to blush again. He had to strip, get ready to change and swim into the cave. He *could* change with clothes on, but the result would be a royal mess. Funny—for years he'd dreamed about getting naked with a girl who looked like her, and now she had to be his *sister.* It wasn't *fair.*

She nodded and then shook her head, agreeing with his thoughts in sequence. The smile turned crooked. "You sure that both Ellen and Peggy can fit into one cockpit in this thing?" She waved at the two-man kayak they'd loaded on *Maria.*

"Yeah. Dad took them out just last month. Peggy sits between Ellen's legs. Mouse is small enough, the spray skirt fits over both of them."

They lifted the green sea-kayak over the side, keeping both ends tied off. Then Caroline winked at him and turned her back, fiddling with gear and her PFD. Gary swallowed and headed forward again.

Ben had given him a rig Dad used, bungee cords and a waterproof pack that snugged around his shoulders and across his chest and waist. Seals had shoulders, sort of, and the waistband ended up on the other side of the flippers. The bungee cords would adjust to the changing shape. According to Ben, it had stayed on Dad in both his forms.

Gary slipped off his shirt and shrugged into the harness. It felt tight around the shoulders and loose at the waist— another funny yardstick of growing up. He used to feel lost inside one of Dad's coats. Now he couldn't make the buttons meet across his chest. He still felt weird every time he looked *down* into his father's eyes.

And now he had a chance to look into them again. He finished stripping and glanced back at Caroline. She was staring at him with a Groucho Marx leer, licking her lips.

She grinned, unabashed. "Hey, it's just aesthetic appreciation. I like to look at statues, too, but I don't go to bed with them."

Gary dove over the side. His only other choice involved some kind of wisecrack about tit for tat, and even *he* couldn't stomach that pun. Besides, the air was too cold for a strip show.

The icy water took his breath away, just as it had yesterday. Changing would make it seem comfortable, but first he sculled back to the stern and treaded water for a moment. With just his head and shoulders out of the water, he could have been wearing a bathing suit. "Remember to leave that net over the side. Getting back into a boat isn't easy, and I don't know how strong Dad will be. If we don't show up in time, bug out. You know enough about running *Maria* to make it back to the town dock without us."

She nodded, solemn. He suddenly thought that he should have hugged her, just like he'd have hugged Ellen or

Mouse before going off and doing something dangerous. Touch said so much. He'd barely met her, but she *felt* like he'd known her forever. Some parts were as comfortable as an old shoe. Some parts could turn him on like a spotlight if he let them.

Some parts scared him silly.

For example, he knew what she was thinking, whether by way of their Tears or not. Right now, she felt as single-mindedly lethal as a bluefish closing in on a school of mackerel. "Remember what Aunt Alice told you. We're mice at a cat show."

She wrinkled her nose at him. "O . . . kay." She stretched the word out with her reluctance. "If I gotta."

He dove and remembered the feeling of bones and flesh flowing like warm wax. The water lost its icy grip and came alive with the touch of currents, the thousand tastes of the sea, and the strange symphony of underwater life. He'd changed a dozen times since learning how. Practice, he'd told Ben, but it was more like repeated doses of a drug. The world was so different to a seal.

He'd learned to keep his mind, though. The first time had taught him the dangers lurking down that current. "When you change, remember to change back." Aunt Alice had put her finger on the greatest threat.

Up the current. Search for the taste of fresh water and gasoline and the tang of sun-dried hemp. He'd smelled the weed, smelled the burned-rope reek when kids in school played around with drugs. He'd never tried it because of the swimming. Cigarettes, pot, booze: Any of those drugs would have cost him that state freestyle record. Even if pot didn't show up on the mandatory drug tests, smoking *anything* would have slowed him down.

He tasted iron first, old rust dripping into the water. It wasn't what he sought, but he followed it anyway, because it was a strange thing in the water. He swam quartering across the thread of it to trace the strongest line, the line that led back to its source.

Soon enough, traces of gasoline joined in and then the same taste of cut stone he'd found in the passage to the Dragon's Pool. All the flavors he sought wove their way through the symphony. A clear voice cut into the clicks and squeaks and booms of underwater life, another touch of witchcraft, Aunt Alice reaching out across the distance between them and singing the threads of her plot.

> *I AM A MAN UPON THE LAND,*
> *I AM A SILKIE ON THE SEA,*
> *AND WHEN I'M FAR AND FAR FRAE LAND,*
> *MY HOME IT IS IN SULE SKERRIE.*

Skerry—Scots, for an island or reef. So that song couldn't be about his family. He wondered if he'd ever meet another selkie, either by land or sea. The voice sang him into darkness.

Yes, all the flavors came from this shadow in the water. Black closed in around him, but loss of sight didn't mean the same thing to a seal that it did to a man. He could hunt in the deep, finding fish or crab or mussel by vibrations in the water. Find them by touch, by taste, by day or night.

He eased back to the surface, barely allowing his nostrils to break water for a breath. Ben had taped every word, every click or hiss of static from Dad's radio. Snatches had come through, his capture and the voices afterward. He'd triggered some kind of alarm, but what?

Aunt Alice's bats and cliff swallows hadn't set it off. They hadn't heard ultrasound motion-detectors, hadn't tripped any infrared beams. They'd mapped out a floating dock, a boat, a ramp, a maze of old iron overhead. That's where the taste of rust came from. He should have remembered.

Gary passed the track for a metal gate, heard rather than

seen. He rose to the surface again, not for breath but to check for light or motion before he passed into the trap. The tunnel remained as black as night, with only the rise and fall of the swells following him in from the sea.

A cave opened out around him. He followed the taste of oil and gasoline to a hull in the water, long and low and sleek, bitter with the reek of antifouling paint. He skirted its poison and slipped in between the boat and the floating dock. *Whatever* alarm system they had, it wouldn't be able to monitor that shifting space.

He thought himself back into human form, ignoring the fire of molding his bones and flesh. The chill of the dark water bit him, and he had to move fast or change again. He found a ladder on the side of the float and hooked one arm around it. His fingers turned clumsy, fumbling the straps of his pack, pulling out the IR goggles, flipping the power on, fitting them over his eyes. He slipped and caught them just short of the water. His teeth started to chatter.

The glasses showed him dying heat from the stern of the boat—it had been run this morning, but it didn't look like very long. Perhaps just maintenance—run it every day, then it would be ready and reliable if you *really* needed it. Gary filed that memory away, just in case. The craft looked like it would be a lot faster than *Maria.*

Light fixtures also glowed faintly green from remembered heat, and a door at the top of the ramp showed pale outlines where warm air leaked around the frame. He couldn't see any cameras, filtered lights bathing the cave in IR, or any suspicious boxes giving off electronic warmth. The float surged gently in the water, rising and falling with swells from the bay, and the boat thumped heavily against the bumpers. They *couldn't* have any kind of weight or motion sensors on this thing. He slithered up the ladder and lay flat on the decking.

He fumbled with the pack, pulling out the Kevlar vest,

covering it with heavy Polartec jacket and pants, staying as low as possible. He added thin gloves and neoprene booties. Warmth started to overcome the chill of the water. He sniffed, but the sea tang and musty stone told him nothing. Human noses were a waste of space, even if some of them looked cute.

<Thank you.>

<Shut up. I'm busy.>

She was looking through his eyes, hearing through his ears. At least *this* time, somebody would know for sure what happened to him.

Crawling up the ramp, he ignored the fuzzy polyester snagging on rough planking. *Get out of this alive,* with *Dad and the girls, a few hundred bucks for clothing will be cheap.* He reached up and tested the doorknob. Locked. Nobody ever said it would be easy. His fingers traced the locksets—two, *both* a key-in-knob and a deadbolt. Finks. But the door fit loosely, and swung out toward him. If he could slip the knob lockset, he could work on the deadbolt separately.

He pulled a thin strip of plastic out of one pocket—people joked about credit cards that opened any door, but that was really all you needed for some of them. The lock popped with a touch, and the door jerked toward him. Dim light flowed out from the hall beyond, followed by warm air. He ducked back, expecting to face a gun muzzle. He pulled the IR goggles off, to clear his vision.

The hall lay empty. They hadn't thrown the deadbolt.

He heard a chair scrape across rough flooring. Muttered words followed, and footsteps. The voice came clearer. "¡Puerta maldita! ¡Su madre esta puta!"

<He's cussing at the door, not you.>

<Yeah. I took Spanish, too. I think the door fits too loose, sometimes pops open on its own. Air pressure.>

A shadow loomed. Gary drew his legs under him, crouching like a coiled spring. A hand reached out for the knob and he grabbed the wrist, flowing up along it and pulling the arm. A squat man followed, brown Latino face startled and then setting into hard eagerness. Things happened out of muscle memory—Gary spinning away from the other hand, keeping his wrist hold, turning behind the man, bones cracking, hands to chin and back of head, twisting, following his opponent down to the floor.

He froze, fist just short of the man's temple. He'd done that move a hundred times before in the dojo. They always stopped at this point, just before the killing blow. The man didn't move. His head looked back over his left shoulder, farther than a head ought to turn. His eyes were open, startled, unblinking. Gary felt his stomach lurch. He remembered those crunching sounds, first the arm and then the neck. He'd just killed a man.

Totally by reflex, he'd just killed a man. His stomach clenched again.

<Look at his face.>

Caroline's voice grabbed his thoughts. Livid scratches crossed the man's cheek, barely missing one eye. The wrist he'd grabbed showed more scratches, deep ones, infected and oozing pus. The other hand was bandaged. He peeled off the tape and gauze, revealing ragged gouges that looked like the aftermath of a chainsaw.

<Dixie's teeth and claws. You just got one of the guys that grabbed Ellen and Peggy.>

Gary's brain fizzled and sputtered. He'd done that move a hundred times. He'd never hurt any of his partners. The man was dead. It had taken a second, maybe two, for Gary to kill him.

<Hey, I'm no expert. But didn't your partners know what you were going to do? They cooperated? He resisted. Save your tears for someone who deserves them.>

Now he was seeing through her eyes, her memory, the open door of the Haskell House and a black-and-white cat crawling across the floor, back broken, with flesh and blood snagged in her claws. He felt Caroline's rage and horror, and her fierce joy at the dead face under his hands. She was the Haskell legend in flesh and blood—the best friends and worst enemies you could imagine.

He clenched his jaw against the bile in his stomach. Some men deserved to die. Anyone who threatened Ellen or Mouse sure landed on that list.

<You got it, babe.>

He searched the man, coming up with a heavy gun and a ring full of keys. He tossed the gun into the pool.

<Hey, I wanted that!>

<"Mice at a cat show.">

<Yeah. But you've got damned big claws for a mouse. Aunt Alice pulled mine.>

He sensed something behind her thoughts, one of those half-smiles that implied she hadn't been *completely* declawed. Well, he couldn't do a damn thing about it now. He pulled the corpse out into the shadows and left it as a doorstop, blocking the door open for his sister.

<Best use he's ever served. Can I come in now?>

<Talk, talk, talk. Shut up. I've still got work to do.>

He peeked around the doorframe, checking for further guards. The corridor lay empty and dim, doors to either side exactly as the Haskell Air Force had mapped it out. Stronger light flowed out of an opening on the right-hand side, just where the bats had heard the hum of electronics. Ben would flat-out *drool* at the thought of having those winged mice working for the Morgans.

A security camera sat overhead on the far wall, focused on the door. Gary made a face at it and ducked into the nearest doorway. Move fast enough, odds were nobody would notice him.

The room *was* the security post, two chairs and banks of switches under indicator lights and monitors. Both chairs were empty. Gary took a deep breath and let it out. He started scanning the boards, building a map of switches and trying to fit them into the picture the bats had brought home. The system was the same make and model as the Morgans used, proving that the Pratts were no dummies. Ben had said some rude things about the "second best."

Still, it made Gary's job a lot easier. His hand flicked out and killed the video feed from the security room, then puzzled through the loop switching. *That switch, there, selects the sequence. Bingo! They don't monitor all the cameras all the time!* He cut the dead camera out of the loop, substituting an outside view. With a little luck, nobody would ask embarrassing questions.

His father's face flickered across the screen, hollow-eyed and bruised. Gary noted the camera number in the lower corner of the display: fifteen. He followed the sequence straight through. Ellen and Peggy never showed. Some of the outdoor displays looked funny, stuff that would have bothered the hell out of him if it were his own house he was guarding. Maybe Ron Pelletier was doing his bit for God and country. He flipped Dad's camera out, and three random others, adding more outside views. Someone else added a couple more—the other control center agreed with him.

A hand-lettered note caught his eye, over a bank of switches and green lights. "Always turn off photocells *before* turning on lights." *Double Bingo!*

He followed the line of switches and their engraved plastic tags—RAMP 1, DOCK 1, DOCK 2, CATWALK 1, 2, 3, TUNNEL 1, 2, 3 up to 8. The label over them said PHOTOCELLS.

Basic engineering: *Keep it simple, stupid.*

The tunnel security was photocells. Anyone coming in would need a light. Anyone going out would need a light. Waves didn't affect that, wind didn't affect that, tides didn't affect that, ice didn't affect that. Simple frigging photocells.

He switched them off. He reached over and switched on the lights. The board stayed green.

<We have liftoff! All systems *go!*>

<Hey, babe, you're smart as well as sexy. I love that in a man.>

Sisters.

twenty-seven

—⁕—

ALICE WALKED THE misted path, wet gravel squeaking under her feet. *This forest smells like Wagner,* she thought. Götterdämmerung. *The world ends in fire, igniting even the house of the gods. Everybody dies.*

But I'm getting ahead of myself. First I've got to sneak by Fafnir over there, and loot his treasure. Somebody must have warned the Pratts about impending visitors. This was the third sentry she'd seen, all armed. She drew her Tarnhelm over her head and vanished.

Vanishing wasn't hard. You're in bushes and trees, you think like a bush or tree. It was the chameleon act, changing colors to match your background. Illusions were one of the first lessons in a Witch's apprenticeship. They could save your ass. The beaded regalia made it even easier, with its swirling hypnotic figures starting out as woodland camouflage and refusing to hold still so you could focus on them. Alice hummed to herself, the clarinet statement of the theme from "Forest Murmurs," building her deception.

Nobody here but a bunch of birds and trees.

Everyone has magic. Everyone's magic works in different ways. Mine is healing, bringing the power of the Woman's spring to modern medicine. Kate is wood and stone wanting to please her and the single-minded logic of gravity. Caroline is still finding hers, but it looks like it's going to be water. Bright enough to hurt your eyes, impulsive as hell, always changing. You block her one way, before you turn your back she's broken out in another. I don't know whether that's a blessing or a curse.

Maybe it's the Morgan blood in her. Nobody is ever going to get a handhold on that girl.

Jackie? Jackie's is ice, born of cold and pain and sorrow, dead before she ever was alive. She's never loved anything but herself.

Alice concentrated on the garden, on the forest, on becoming one with it and invisible. Generations of work had transformed these spruce and stones, blueberry and rhodora and bracken, into a watercolor Japanese screen in the fog. It radiated peace.

The Pratts weren't total monsters. Their gardens reminded her of that, with such beauty and serenity. Her war was with the Peruvian *brujo*.

Pratts had lived on this land for centuries, setting their roots into the stone just as deep as the spruces, firs, and pines that ringed their home. They lived the way most of Stonefort lived, obeying those laws that they damn well pleased and ignoring the ones that got in their way. Somebody wants to buy drugs? That's his funeral. Nobody forced him. What's the *relative* difference between the hazards of pot and alcohol?

The Morgans, the Pelletiers, the Haskells: All lived the same way, hard people in a hard land. Alice had broken more laws than she could count. Kate was another example, a cop who roughed up roughnecks, did things that would leave the ACLU foaming at the mouth. Sunrise County tended to raise up that breed. Survival of the fittest. Sometimes surviving required you to be damned nasty.

She wouldn't be walking this path if she only faced Tom Pratt. Tom she knew. Tom knew her. Tom wouldn't have held Daniel Morgan locked in the cellar for weeks, drowned Maria, stolen Ellen and Peggy from the Witch's House, drained the life from three innocent old people. But Tom had screwed up royally when he hooked up with that *brujo*. Now he and his family were going to pay the price. Because of that shadowy figure in the midnight-blue Suburban.

A man slipped through the fog to her right, sensed rather than seen, a form in gray wearing a gray ski mask. So it began. She didn't know what "Rules of Engagement" Ron Pelletier had set. She didn't want to know. There were forms for this kind of thing, a *Code Duello* much like the deadly etiquette that had governed the pistols in her satchel. Whatever it was, it wouldn't be drive-by shootings and Colombian cowboys with car bombs. Those things were so crude.

She followed the path, a ghost in the fog under dripping trees. A man lay on the ground by the side of the gravel, facedown, wrists and ankles bound with duct tape and a cloth bag over his head. She touched his neck to verify that he was still alive. Muffled sounds told her that more tape gagged his mouth. "Rules of Engagement."

Her own rules were somewhat different. Maine hadn't had the death penalty in over a hundred years, but she had an enemy who deserved to die. She intended to hand down and execute that sentence.

A shout cut through the fog, muffled, followed by the silence of listening stone. "The best-laid schemes o' mice an' men gang aft agley." Was the fog helping or hindering her aims? It hid her, and the attackers, and the sentries, and the security cameras, all from each other. She hummed quietly under her breath, working her way through the forest toward the side entrance of the Pratts' house. She felt the rock pool there, drawing her—a small pool, spring-fed, with its moss and fern border and the blue flag iris edging into cattails.

Her enemy knew the power of that spring. An attack on the house would draw him there.

KATE DOUBLED OVER, racked by dry heaves, tears squeezed from her eyes and dripping. She knelt down, careful of her nonexistent balance, and reached over the side for a handful of saltwater to rinse her mouth and face. The icy seawater felt like a slap, clearing her thoughts as it stung her eyes.

She stood, weak-kneed and fuzzy-headed, swaying with the surge and fall of the boat, and tried to figure out how to get off the damned thing. She faced the Pratts' place; she knew that by the Victorian gazebo weathered gray out on a point of the cliff. She remembered that it needed shingling, with the old cedar shakes curled and split by a generation of sun and salt air. Every building in the compound needed shingling, for that matter.

But that gazebo was about fifty feet above her. She'd never looked at the place from the sea before. The cliffs were rough, they were climbable, seamed by wind and ice and the battering of the sea. She'd done worse and had no fear of heights. But they dropped straight down into the tide without any trace of a landing. She'd worked on places like this before. Tony Peterson's fifteen-bedroom summer "cottage" had a floating dock at the base of the cliff and a stairway bolted into the rock that led down to it.

She'd expected something similar. All the rich shore properties had *something* on the water. At worst, she'd figured on running aground on a cobble beach because they hadn't set the dock out yet for the summer. In spite of their reputation, though, the Pratts apparently didn't go in for boating. The only other high-rent place she knew without some kind of dock was Morgan's Castle. *That* had been designed as a fort.

Thinking along *those* lines, the gazebo was a lookout post. She couldn't tell if it was manned or not, but it didn't look quite so charming now. Pratts and Morgans—cop gossip called them two sides of the same coin, the last unhung pirates of the Spanish Main. Hell, the Morgans still had loaded cannon up on that pile of rock they called home. She remembered the flash and boom of them on Fourth of July nights, Stonefort's down-home form of fireworks.

Pirates? Well, she might as well hoist the Skull and Crossbones on Keith Bauer's Boston Whaler. She'd stolen it fair and square. Maybe she could join the club.

So why the hell was she getting in between them?

Alice.

Kate didn't need a mirror now. She saw Alice on a path somewhere up above, saw her over the sights of a pistol, falling, saw flames blooming through the fog. The magic had laid claim to Kate's mind, as if trying to lock its ownership down now that it had been allowed past the gates.

Alice had always complained about Kate's approach to problems, just plowing right straight ahead. Well, that might work here. She could ram the boat into the rock wall in front of her and jump for a handhold in that long split, follow it clear up to the crest. But that would sink the boat. A seaman could probably figure out a better way.

Her belly reminded her that she wasn't a seaman. She dipped for another handful of saltwater and rinsed her mouth and face. She blinked tears from her eyes and stared at the problem again.

How could she get ashore without wrecking the boat? If she could give the damned seasick sea serpent back, undamaged, she might not go to jail.

What would a rigger do? Those guys were the geniuses of construction, figuring out how to move huge turbines, lift houses onto new foundations without cracking the crystal in the china cabinets, stretch the reach of cranes across land that wouldn't hold man or machine. She'd watched one crew set up a slow pendulum across marshland, dropping load after load of lumber and structural steel and concrete for a house twenty feet beyond the reach of the boom, the crane operator running his winch with a feather touch to just kiss the landing at the end.

She blinked as the image changed, showed broad gray water instead of marsh.

She could do that. Set the anchor. Swing the boat out from shore on the anchor line. Power back in. Cut the motor and throw the wheel over. Time it right and the boat would just barely scrape the wall broadside before swinging back out in the current. Without power, it wouldn't hit the rocks again.

The first try came up short, at least fifteen feet out. She meant it to, getting the feel of the process. She stared at the puzzle, letting the first run settle into her muscles like a practice shot on the basketball court, figuring just how far out to shove the pendulum. Meanwhile, she checked the strap over the heavy Colt in her shoulder holster. It was firm. No point in getting up there empty handed. The cop radio at her belt stayed silent, so the shit hadn't hit the fan yet.

Her stomach calmed, going off to sulk in a corner because she was ignoring it. She swung the boat out again, farther, gauging the angle of wind and water, threw the wheel over, and blipped the throttle. This time she cut the ignition and stepped to the side, bracing against the roll.

The boat came up into the current and swung—closer, closer, closer. It paused. She shook her head. Five feet out. She wasn't *about* to jump that.

She restarted the engine and powered out again, sighting down the cliff past the gazebo, trying to gain just that plane-shaving's extra angle she needed. The fog seemed to be lifting; more trees and rocks loomed down that way, and she thought she could pick out the gray-on-gray of the steeple in the village. She chose her instant, held the wheel over, threw an extra two seconds on the power, and switched off.

The boat swung in, in, in. It paused about a foot out, a cushion of water trapped between hull and rock, and she stepped up on the gunwale and reached across. The boat dipped away under her weight and she hit the cliff like a lump of clay, full-body, and grunted as air slammed out of her lungs.

The cliff surged up and down under her. Her left hand slipped, losing skin to the coarse rock, that missing fingertip coming up short on friction. Her workboots scraped and grabbed at the rock. She felt the granite sandpaper her cheek as she slid downward. Then she stopped, attached to solid ground. Except that it was still moving. She stared at a vein of quartz, willing it to stop. It finally obliged. Then she checked on the boat.

It was swinging out on the anchor rope, obeying wind and tide, bobbing as if it was glad to be free of such a lousy sailor. *Good riddance to you, too. And your mama.* But that widening gap of seawater *did* look kind of final. Kate sniffed, searching for the smell of burning bridges mixed in with the salt and kelp. She'd better have chosen the right heap of stones, or she was going to have a long cold swim to her next choice.

Well, she wasn't going to rescue Little Nell by just lolling around on the seashore, working on her tan. Kate settled her feet and started looking for handholds. Like she'd said, she'd done this before. *Three points of support, always, hands and feet and your nose or chin if necessary.* Then she was reaching, reaching, reaching, her right foot finding nothing but smooth rock.

Hey, I could use a little help here. Alice always said *I could talk to stone. So where's the magic stairway?* One toe found a nubbin of the cliff and took her weight. She moved up on to it, grabbing a fresh handful of rock and a breath. Then she started climbing fluidly, an endless flow like a snake up the side of the cliff.

The granite seemed to like her. She couldn't tell if the stone formed handholds where she asked for them, or told her where they were so she reached right *there.* Whichever it was, she reached the top without another pause. She stopped there and knelt behind a bush, looked like a holly of some kind, not native. The Pratts had spent some serious money on landscaping over the years.

Kate flexed her left arm, checking on that stitched-up cut. No pain. She bent over and patted the rock. "Thanks, guys." A vague sense of pleasure came back, sort of like Dixie purring as you rubbed her forehead.

Now she was hearing some bit out of Alice's opera, swirling strings and the triumph of brass, big chesty blond sopranos bellowing away in stainless steel bras, selecting the fallen heroes on the field of battle. Valkyries, that was the name, the choosers of the slain.

Sounded like a messy job when you got right down to it—walking around the typical battlefield, gathering loose arms and legs, winding loops of intestine up on a reel. Then you load it all on a flying horse and carry it back across the bridge to Valhalla. Some assembly required.

The music gave her another image. They'd used the same theme for a helicopter attack in some old Vietnam War flick Jackie and her friends used to rent, must have been a dozen times. Kate couldn't remember the name, but she knew it didn't turn out well. Everybody ended up dead, bombs and fire in the jungle night. Maybe someday she'd learn to quit asking for omens.

She didn't know the Pratts' grounds all that well. The house, the garage, the gazebo, those she knew. Landscaping was someone else's job. She could get from the gazebo to the garage, though; a path connected them. She thought that was the view the pool had given her.

The radio burped static, and she switched it off. If it started yammering while she was sneaking through the woods . . .

A man lay in the gazebo, bound and gagged. Cops wouldn't use duct tape instead of cuffs. Cops wouldn't leave a prisoner behind, unsupervised. Maybe this wasn't another drug raid. If she could get in and out without being caught, maybe Bernie would never know. Maybe Kate could save Alice Haskell's witchy little butt and still keep her badge.

If she got the boat back to Keith Bauer's place undamaged. Maybe she could get her cousin John to run it across.

Maybe, maybe, maybe. Maybe she'd still be alive when the sun went down. Whoever had taken this guy out had left a silenced KG-9 lying on one of the gazebo seats, safely out of reach. That implied he, she, or it was carrying something more potent than a 9mm full auto machine pistol.

Kate started humming a dirge of her own, that old union song: "Which side are you on? Which side are you on?" The Morgans? Some other drug crew, like the Pelletier's Quebecois Mafia?

To hell with sneaking. She stood up and strode out, heading down the path toward the garage. It was a gut reaction, reading the atmosphere. If those guys were taking people down alive, they probably wouldn't shoot a cop.

Probably.

And Kate wasn't very good at sneaking, anyway. She didn't have the build for it. At least her size XXL jacket gave plenty of room to advertise POLICE at fifty paces. Anyone who shot at *that* knew what he was doing.

Trees loomed through the fog, dripping down on the shrubs and rock. Kate followed the picture in her memory, trying to fit the curve of the trail, the shadows, the shape of space, into the scene. It was close, but not a match. She tried to remember the distance from the gazebo to the old carriage house.

Pratts had something like forty acres out here, but most of it was forest. The house was set with a distant sea view, over open stone and shrubs. Make it a hundred yards of clearing, then the main house, the carriage house, and another hundred yards or two through the woods and out to the gazebo. They had a guesthouse off on the other side, tucked out of sight.

The path curved again, rounding a boulder left by the last ice age. Kate saw a shadow in the mist ahead, child-sized. It was Alice, just like in the vision, walking that remembered walk. Kate drew the Colt and held it muzzle-high and two-handed, ready to drop down on any target.

She lengthened her stride, closing on Alice. The world narrowed and clarified, every caw of the crows and mew of the gulls, every drip of fog, every whiff of pine or spruce cutting across Kate's senses like a knife.

The pictures merged, the frame in front of her eyes perfectly aligned over memory. She was twenty yards behind Alice. She could just see the edge of the garage, the Pratts' old carriage house. A bulky shadow slipped out from a dark mass of laurels and aimed its pistol. Kate notched her own sights on the back of the square form. She pulled the trigger, and the .44 magnum boomed.

The shadow jerked. Its own pistol cracked twice, and Alice stumbled. Then the figure spun and fired again, twice again, fast and instinctive from belly level. Kate felt two bullets punch into her body, low and high. The shock dropped her sights off target.

She couldn't bring them back.

Jackie! The shadow was Jackie. Halfway to the crumpled

form of Alice, Kate faced her own daughter carrying her own gun. Kate felt her knees grow weak.

The girl didn't seem surprised. She just shook her head. "Sorry, Mom. Bulletproof vest. Too bad you never bought one."

Kate tried to bring her gun back up, to fire again. The damned Dirty Harry special was too heavy. Jackie just watched, smiling slightly, keeping a firm sight picture with no sign of remorse. Kate knelt down in the path, swaying. The Colt dropped to the gravel. *Yeah,* she thought. *I never bought a bulletproof vest because there was always something* you *needed.*

Jackie turned away with a shrug, walking towards Alice, standing over her body. She raised the stolen Browning again, drawing a bead. Kate wanted to scream but couldn't find the air.

Her daughter turned back. "You know, Mom, you never really understood. You or *Aunt* Alice. You just don't have a clue how much crap I've swallowed about you two. Kids *hate* queers. I've been eating it since kindergarten."

She aimed down at Alice, staring at bloodstains spreading across the back of the beaded vest. "*Hasta la vista,* baby." The Browning cracked, Jackie's hand jerking in time with Alice's body. Kate moaned. That was all she could find strength for, but inside she keened with grief. Twenty years she'd fought against loving Alice. Now she'd never have a chance to say the words out loud.

Jackie took aim again and then shook her head. "No. Stupid bitch isn't worth another shell." She looked back at Kate. "See you around."

She turned and strode away, swapping magazines just like she'd been taught, even though there would still be a couple of rounds left. Kate slumped full-length on the gravel path, blinking against the black fog that kept washing over her. The ground was moving again, just like the waves heaving under the Boston Whaler.

She didn't want to fight them. Alice was dead.

Jackie had barely reached the garage when flames blossomed out of the windows with the hiss and whump of a gasoline explosion. She darted around the corner. Kate heard the Browning crack again, twice, just like she'd taught her daughter to shoot. A high-powered rifle blasted back: a single shot, a pause, then three more shots full auto. The heavy blasts echoed away in the fog. Silence washed back, broken by the crackling chatter of the fire.

AK-47, Kate thought, automatically. *Deputy Dawg had one out on the range for the boys to play with.*

She whimpered to herself and closed her eyes. They weren't working right, anyway. *One shot to the center of mass. If your target doesn't drop, assume body armor. Go for the head.*

Everybody dies.

twenty-eight

—ᵐ—

CAROLINE CARESSED THE water with her right blade, nestling the kayak against the cave's floating dock. That speedboat looked like some serious fun, long and low and darkly dangerous. Maybe she could steal it on the way out. Gary's spare set of lock-picks held all *sorts* of possibilities for an enterprising young woman.

Later. First, we have some other games to play. She hauled herself out of the kayak, holding the bow line in her teeth. Docks weren't the easiest way into or out of a kayak, but at least this one sat lower than the lobster boat. *And* it had a ladder. No wonder Gary had wanted that net rigged over the side. Sea kayaks posed some problems she'd never met while playing with their white-water cousins.

She tied her line off on a cleat and stood up, stretching and loosening her hips. *Time to kick ass.* She grinned to herself, showing the world some teeth—the kind of smile her friends said looked like a barracuda. She *thought* they meant it as a compliment.

<Hey, we're here to rescue people, not kick ass!>

<Buddy boy, any ass that gets in my way is going to get kicked! They *hurt* Aunt Alice!>

<Whatever happened to "Mice at a cat show?">

The ramp slanted up to a fixed landing and the door, hinges on one end and tethered rollers on the other, adjustment for the tide. It squeaked and groaned gently with each swell. Right now, the slope was low. Just past high tide, she guessed, water starting to ebb out of the basin and tunnel. She checked the line to her kayak again, making sure it wouldn't go for any little solo trips while she was busy.

Caroline stopped for a moment, staring at her hand. Her newfound brother had pointed out an oddity she'd never noticed, the slight webbing between each finger. He'd called it "The Mark," a genetic trait of the Morgans. It extended just a fraction of an inch more than normal. It extended a possibility, as well.

I bet I can do it, she thought. *I bet I can change, just like him.* She'd never met a puzzle she couldn't solve, a possibility she couldn't make real. Her aunt called Caroline's attitude hubris, pointing out that Greek tragedy was full of that kind of crap. Caroline called it self-confidence and considered it a virtue. But selkie genes were a question for another day.

Instead, she slipped her hand into the cargo pocket on her right thigh and pulled out the little .22 automatic that Aunt Alice *hadn't* caught. Caroline never *had* felt much like a mouse.

<Hey, quit goofing around. We've got problems.>

A click echoed through the cave, followed by an electric whine and the rumble of metal wheels against a track. She twisted around, tracking the sounds to their source. The sea gate was closing behind them.

She sprinted up the ramp and through two doors into something that looked like NASA Mission Control, electronic consoles and TV monitors up the yin-yang. She skidded to a stop beside Gary. The banks of switches and indicator lights confused her: green lights glowing steady, red lights blinking alarm, a few yellows scattered across the board. A loud mechanical bray filled the air, coming from a red grille up by the ceiling. FIRE ALARM, the sign next to it said.

Gary flipped toggle switches here and there as if he knew what he was doing. He glanced up at her. "They've gone into some kind of automatic lock-down mode. Look at Camera 5."

It took her a moment to decipher the displays, small digits in the lower left corner of each monitor, just a number and date/time. The image on Camera 5 seemed to be an outside view of a garage and driveway. *Big* garage—she guessed maybe an old carriage house, four arched doors with ornate iron strap hinges, a high roof with dormer windows and funny curved eaves like a thatched roof.

Flames licked out of a window to the left while black smoke poured from the one in the center, shattered as if something had exploded inside. One of the carriage doors burst outward with another explosion, and Caroline could see cars inside, blazing furiously. One looked like some kind of high-rent antique, with a big front radiator all chromed and crowned with a statue.

A body lay by one corner of the garage. Caroline's barracuda grin widened a touch. "Cousin Ron" was kicking some ass of his own. "That's our diversion."

"Yeah. But we've got to divert our butts outta here. Pretty damn soon, somebody's going to check on their buddy out by the door, and we won't give the right answer."

"How the hell are we going to get out? That gate in the tunnel's closed down!"

"Override switch." Gary pointed at the board. "We can open it from here."

She reached for the switch, but he caught her wrist. *"Don't jump the gun!* If we open it now, they might notice. Wait until we're ready to go."

Her fingers twitched. Patience was not her strong point, and that closed door felt like a noose around her neck. Gary sounded confident, but she wanted to know that the way out was clear.

"Hey!" He was staring at her other hand. "Ditch that gun. You start shooting down here, the shit will *really* hit the fan!"

"Can it, buddy! Maybe *you* can kill people with a touch, but I can't! This is *my* black belt!"

He winced and squeezed his eyes shut. "He was turning. I never thought about that in practice. I spun around behind him and he tried to follow me. I turned his head in the opposite direction." He swallowed. "The kempo was designed to work with that. I didn't *mean* to kill him!"

"Forget the bastard. He had it coming." Caroline scanned the other monitors, looking for Peggy and Ellen. An outdoor scene caught her eye, two bodies on a gravel path. One stirred, crawling toward the other.

Shit!

Aunt Alice! She froze, rage surging through her blood. *Where? That big lug* has *to be Aunt Kate!*

But she didn't have a map, nothing to show where the camera was. A quick scan of the walls didn't help. "Where the hell's Camera 6?"

"System manual on the shelf over there. We don't have time for that. Get the girls. Remember what Aunt Alice said: They're down the hall, up two flights of stairs, second door on the right. Damned place is a maze . . ."

But his voice faded behind her. Caroline was out the door. Camera 6 had to be near Camera 5, somewhere near that garage. They *had* to be numbered that way.

*   *   *

GARY SHRUGGED, EXASPERATED. *Damned uppity know-it-all!* If she'd waited half a second, he'd have tossed her the keys. Get in, get Dad and the girls, get out. *That* was the mission profile, simple as hell. Nothing in there about kicking ass. *Make them pay* after *the hostages are out!*

He switched two more monitors to outside cameras. Maybe that would cover her butt as well as his own. Then he threw the master control over to the other station and set his console on automatic mode, hoping they'd read it as the downstairs guards coming up to help. With any luck, they'd be too busy with their own problems to change his settings back.

Unplug the cameras? His brain raced down branching probabilities. *No.* A dead camera was an alarm bell, drew attention to itself. Pictures of empty corridors and empty rooms meant safety. *Cameras can't cover everything. Stay out of view whenever possible.*

He flipped the security room camera back on and ducked out into the corridor. "Third door on the left," Aunt Alice had said. That was where the bats had heard somebody. All *he* heard were his sister's footsteps clanging up a metal stair. A door slammed, heavy like armor, and left silence behind.

His fingers shook as if they were scared to open the lock. The fifth key worked. Gary eased the door open, afraid of what he'd find, checking for more guards, spotting the monitor camera, eyebrows rising at the scorched electrical outlet down by the floor. Then he saw his father.

Gary clenched his fists and squeezed his eyes shut. Then he opened them again. The scene hadn't changed. His father just slumped in a chair like a stuffed dummy, staring at the wall, glassy-eyed. Bruises covered his face and arms, fresh red and purple overlapping the yellow and green of fading injuries. Those were bad, but his father's eyes were far worse. They were blank, saying that he had given up all hope.

He'd lost weight, his arms shriveled and fingers knobby

with bones. A tray of food lay by the chair, apparently un-touched. They hadn't been starving him; he'd just stopped eating.

The room stank—no vents, unwashed bodies and vomit and a chemical toilet in one corner. Gary swallowed and stepped in front of his father's gaze. No reaction. Dad was still breathing. Gary knelt down and touched one of the bruised hands. It was warm.

"Dad?"

Those eyes didn't move, didn't focus. "They've got Ellie and Mouse."

Gary winced again. "No. Caroline's getting them out, right now. We're here to get you all out of here."

"I killed the Dragon. I can't give them the Dragon to save Ellie and Mouse."

The pendant warmed against Gary's chest, under the Po-lartec and the Kevlar vest. He reached in and pulled it out, to dangle glowing in front of his father's eyes.

"The Dragon lives, Dad. I gave my first Tear to Caroline. I can give this one to you and get another. We just have to get you home."

The dead eyes woke slightly, focusing on the crimson Tear. "Don't let him take that. Then you'll die, too. Peggy and Ellen and Gary and Daniel and Maria. All dead." He paused. "Who's Caroline?"

"Caroline Haskell, Aunt Alice's niece. She's helping me get all of you out of here."

Now his father squinted, as if trying to force thoughts through fog. "Caroline Haskell? How could *she* have a Tear? She's a Witch. The Dragon speaks only to Morgans."

"She's Ben's daughter, Dad. She's a Morgan. She's my sis-ter." Then Gary froze at the words that had slipped out. *Of all the stupid . . .*

But the faintest ghost of a smile slipped across his father's face. "Caroline Haskell . . . Ben's daughter. That sly old dog."

Maybe Dad hadn't caught the second part of that idiot speech. Gary could breathe again. He stood up and lifted his father out of the chair. "I changed, Dad. I swam in and changed back and switched the security off. Caroline is finding Ellen and Peggy. Let's get out of here." *Keep the sentences short and simple and leave the genetic grenades out of it.*

Gary tucked himself under his father's arm and eased him across the room. Close up, he smelled even worse, like week-old roadkill with vomit sauce. The corridor was still clear and quiet. Gary took a deep breath, trying to wash the prison stink out of his nose and throat. Stale mildew and damp rock were an improvement.

<Hey, you! We're out!>

Caroline didn't answer. He froze, searching his mind for her fire. That space stayed hollow. She wasn't dead; he'd have felt that. She was hiding, even from him. *About damned time!*

He shut and locked the door behind them, hoping that might slow any checkups and give a minute or two more for the escape. They hobbled down the hall together and into the security room, where he settled his father in the second chair. It sat close in under the camera, where the monitor couldn't see his face. *The top of one head looks pretty much like another.*

"You know these systems better than I do. Here's the manual. They're in a lockdown now, with a fire outside and some crazy stuff on the grounds. See if you can figure out a way to get us out without anybody noticing."

His father stared down at the manual and started turning pages. Gary mouthed a silent prayer and headed back down the hall. He didn't think the old man was in any condition to change and swim out. They *needed* that damned speedboat. Then he'd go for the girls if Caroline wasn't back.

* * *

CAROLINE SLIPPED THROUGH another door and taped the latch. *On the Eighth Day, God created duct tape to patch the fuck-ups She'd made rushing through the first six to meet deadline. Famous contractor's saying, attributed to Kate Rowley.* Caroline *had* to get out there to help Aunt Alice and Aunt Kate.

She dropped the roll back into her pocket. Pegboard covered the outside of this door, with hooks and junk hanging on it. She scanned around, getting her bearings. No windows, bare fluorescent tubes overhead. Shelves of coffee cans and jars full of springs, hinges, bolts, nails, three racks of storm windows draped with ten years' worth of dust and peeling paint, bench strewn with the guts of a stripped-down chainsaw—she'd stepped into some kind of basement storeroom or workshop. That entire wall was pegboard— the old hidden-door trick.

Not her problem. Her problem was outside, Aunt Alice and Aunt Kate bleeding on a gravel path. She stepped over to the door leading out, listening for a second and then jerking it open into a corridor that led both ways. She flipped a mental coin and headed right.

A man stepped out of an intersecting hallway. He started to say something, grunted with surprise, and lifted a gun. She fired, fired twice just like Aunt Kate had taught them for self-defense. The shots echoed like dynamite blasts in the tight hallway.

The instant froze around her. She saw the damned bullets hit, dent his jacket on the side of his chest, stop, and drop to the floor. She saw his gun rising and turning toward her. She saw the muzzle strobe orange, with sparks that lit the dim hallway. She dove for the floor and fired again, aiming for his head. He fell back around the corner. Chips of wood and plaster stung her cheek, and something thumped her chest and shoulder.

Jesus Christ and his brother Harry!

She wormed her way back to the workshop door and slipped inside. Hands shaking, she brushed her hair out of her eyes and then stared at the gun she still held. It looked pitiful all of a sudden, a useless toy. The smell of burned powder almost made her puke. She stuck one finger through a hole in her shirt, rubbing it over the Kevlar underneath, feeling the beginnings of a bruise on her left breast. Her teeth were chattering.

"Mice at a cat show." The voice was Aunt Alice in her head. That man had been one of the cats. Now Caroline knew the difference.

The hallway door creaked, a gentle touch on the knob. She froze against the pegboard, crouching, gun raised. *Pegboard—pegboard and hooks and rubber drive belts and a grease gun,* she thought. *Wrenches and rubber mallets and a spool of bulk saw chain. Nobody here but just us tools.*

The door banged open, framing two men. One low, one high, they scanned the room from corner to corner, guns held squared and ready underneath cold eyes. If they saw a target, it was dead.

Tools. Pegboard and tools. Brown pegboard with darker oil-stains like overgrown amoebas. The first two wrenches are greasy. Sloppy. The whole room needs a cleanup. Send somebody back later, after things cool down.

The top man tapped his partner on the head and they vanished from the door. A hand pulled it shut, and she heard the click of a key. *Lock down the rooms that have been checked, move on.*

She could breathe again. Her heart pounded and she thought she'd puke. Apparently it was that last detail, the greasy wrenches, that had made her illusion work. Just like a good story, was what Aunt Alice said. Make the person see what you want him to see.

"What the *hell* are you doing out here?"

Caroline froze. Nothing moved. The voice was Aunt Alice, and Caroline was back in the parlor of the House.

"Where are the kids?"

The workroom was still empty. Then reality dumped a load of bricks on her foot.

"Your job is to protect the girls, not play nurse to a dumb old woman."

She'd done it again.

She'd left Peggy and Ellen alone in the parlor, and those thugs got in and grabbed the girls. She'd left Gary because she saw Alice hurt, and forgot about the girls again. He'd tried to remind her. Several times.

Shit. Shit, shit, *shit!*

You're not here to kick ass, you're not here to provide backup for Aunt Alice, you're not here to convince your goddamn half brother that you're a sexy woman, shithead! You're here to rescue a couple of terrified children!

Caroline Haskell blows it again.

The question echoed back from her earliest memories, in a dozen exasperated voices: "Caroline Haskell, *when* are you going to learn to *think* before you *act?*"

twenty-nine

—m—

ALICE CRACKED ONE eye open, squinting around for dangerous feet. Then she risked turning her head, to check both ways. It seemed clear. She inched her knees under her belly and squatted, doing her damnedest to avoid moving her left shoulder. It wasn't hurting yet, and she'd *really* like to hold on to that condition for as long as possible.

She shook her head, trying to clear her ears. *Damn,* that pistol was loud. You got used to practicing with ear protection, you forgot . . .

I never realized she hated me. Kate and I were blind! *Even though we never actually* did *anything, everyone in town thought we were lovers. And that included Jackie's so-called "friends."*

Kids can be so cruel. They probably made life hell for her. She hated *me. Most* likely *hated both of us. So she could see me. Hate and love create ties stronger than the magic. Kate could see me because she loved me, and Jackie could see me because of her hate.*

Kate.

This was the picture she'd seen in the tourmaline crystal, Kate lying facedown on the gravel path. *Typical goddamned oracle,* she thought. *Show you a picture without telling you why. I thought I had to keep her* away . . .

Alice groped around her for the cool taste of the Pratts' spring. She drew on its power to shuffle, two knees and one hand, over to Kate's side. She settled down with her useless left hand flopped in her lap, and checked the vital signs. Breathing: shallow. Skin: cool. Pulse: weak and fast. No obvious bleeding, but Alice sure as hell didn't have the strength to turn that big ox over.

If one of those slugs had hit an artery or vein, there'd probably be enough blood to spread beyond her body. Diagnosis: unknown gunshot wounds, immediate danger of clinical shock. Stabilize the patient and wait for transport.

Well, she knew some treatments for shock that had never shown up in the *Merck Manual.* Transport was a different matter; cops wouldn't let the ambulance crew enter an active firefight.

Alice drew power from the spring and fed it through her right hand, giving warmth. Thirty feet, forty feet away from the actual pool, the thread of the earth's magic felt weak and uncertain. She measured her own reserves against her need, and fed some of the strength of her beadwork into the body beneath her hand.

Crumppp!

Alice jerked and then shook her head. Just another gastank exploding. "Fully involved," that was the fireman's term. The garage was doomed. More gunshots boomed in the forest, none close. She pulled her attention back to Kate and healing.

She paused and shook her head, ignoring the twinges waking up in her back. "My God, girl. You took a frigging *boat* to get here? If that ain't love, I don't know what is."

Then she started humming, the music that served as a focus and flow for her healing magic. Words came to her, drawn out of love and memory.

THE WATER IS WIDE, I CAN'T GET OVER, NEITHER DO I HAVE WINGS TO FLY.

Kate stirred under her hand, grunted with pain, and rolled onto one side. She opened her eyes and blinked through tears, staring up at Alice. "She's dead, Lys. I tried and tried to reach her, to talk to her, but she's dead." So the tears weren't just for pain.

Then her eyes widened with memory. *"Alice?"* Somehow she dredged up a grimace of a smile. "Old Scarecrow Collins is going to get a hell of a shock when he dies. If God goes around sending lesbian witches out to fetch the dying into heaven, that preacher-man is going to have to reset his brain."

"It'll be good for his soul. But the only place I'm taking you is Downeast General."

"Didn't know the ambulance corps hired ghosts."

"To quote Caroline's favorite author, 'I aten't dead.' " Alice could see Kate's wounds now, and sighed with relief. Right hip and left shoulder—both were places where Kate had plenty of muscle and bone to absorb the damage. Bleeding, yes, but not enough to mean anything serious by itself. The main question was, did she want to live?

Kate shook her head. "She shot you. Three times. I saw her stand over you and put a bullet in the back of your skull. Even *Jackie* isn't that bad a shot. Wasn't." She squeezed her eyes shut with a grimace, either pain or memory.

"You spoiled her aim. That last shot, I just wasn't where she thought I was. Damn near busted my eardrum, though."

"She's dead, Alice. She ran away, she shot both of us, and now she's dead. What am I going to do *now*?"

"You're going to cry, and then you're going to go on living. You're going to be a rock, same as you always are. If you don't do that 'living' part, the House is going to be really pissed. Between one thing and another, we've added considerable to your work list over the last week."

"*You* going to live, too? I *know* she didn't miss all three times."

Alice winced as her shoulder agreed. "I've got a nine-millimeter hole in my left infraspinatus muscle and scapula. Thoracic cavity is okay, and it didn't penetrate far enough to hit either of the subclavians. In other words, I'll live. I won't be using my left arm for a while. Neither will you. You want any more medical gobbledygook?"

Actually, she was lying a bit about the thoracic cavity. Kate wasn't on the "need to know" list for that one.

Whump!

Another car blowing up. *Shame about that,* she thought. *Tom Pratt had some damned fine antiques stored in that carriage house.*

Her mind was wandering. That funeral pyre for the Rolls and its sisters might satisfy Ron Pelletier. Alice had her own agenda. Tom Pratt still *owed* her, big time. Attacking the *House?* The damn fool knew better. She sat and hummed to herself, back to Wagner and the *Twilight of the Gods.* Fire . . . Dum da dum, da da *dum* . . . Wotan lifted his hands, and the magic flames sprang up around Brünnhilde.

Sparks blossomed upward from the carriage house—dry flakes of the roof caught in an updraft. *Cedar shingles,* she thought. *Almost as flammable as gasoline. But they're wet from all this fog and drizzle.*

She could see the main house from here, the dormers and hips and curves of the roof. They'd built good, wide over-hangs to protect that fake half-timbering, just like in Merry Old England. The roof under that dormer, the sheltered tri-angle where one roof rose up to meet another, the pale gray of weathered cedar was much lighter there, drier . . .

"Wind of the west, hear my cry. Wind of the east, come to my aid. I call to you. By the Spring and the House, I call to you."

She formed a swirl of the warring winds, to suck fire

from the garage roof. Orange sparks rose and spiraled in the
black smoke of the burning, then flakes, then whole shingles and then brands from the purlins and stringers underneath. Dum da dum, da da *dum* . . .

Flames, more flames, yet more flames, rising from
Siegfried's pyre to ignite the world and spread to Asgard
and Valhalla. The coals danced in the winds, following her
will across the driveway. They scattered, they fell in fire-
work cascades, but more of them drove on to lodge steaming in the damp cedar shakes of the main house roof.
Golden sparks spilled across the roof and under the dormer
eaves. They caught in the dry space waiting there. They
spread, grew into flickers, became fire. The fire fed upon itself and the wind. It climbed the slope, following heat, following fuel, following her anger up into the triangle
between the high roof and the low. Steam rolled and bled
out of the cedar. Flames climbed the dormer eave and entered hungry into the attic.

Dum da dum, da da *dum,* dum dum da dum, da dum, da
da *dum!* . . . *Gods above and below, old Wagner sure knew how to
ring down the curtain.*

Kate stirred under her hand. "Dry rot. They have dry rot
in the beams. Dry rot and carpenter ants, and they never did
a frigging thing about them. Serves the damn fools right."

Trust Kate Rowley to measure a man's character by how
he cared for his house.

Alice sagged as the fire released her, drained. Her shoulder burned as if one of those coals had landed on her back.
Spots danced in front of her eyes.

Had she drawn enough power from the Pratts' spring?
She couldn't move, couldn't leave Kate alone with her grief,
couldn't damn well *walk* anyway more than a couple of
paces max. She *had* to get that *brujo*'s attention, pull him
away from whatever Caroline and Gary were up to. She

hadn't come out here just to burn Tom Pratt's house down around his ears.

Coughs racked her, stabbing red-hot iron through her shoulder. She gagged on something and spat it out. *Blood. Red foamy blood on the pink gravel. So much for that little fib about your lung.*

Kate stared at the gob of blood. "Liar." She paused, looking around for something. "That spring over there anything like yours? Will it help?"

Alice blinked. "Might. Who told you about springs?"

"Granny Rowley. Haskells aren't the only ones who remember the old ways." Kate grunted and picked up her pistol from the gravel, tucking it into her belt instead of the shoulder holster shiny with her own blood. She forced herself to her knees and then stood, swaying like an oak half cut through. She reached down and grabbed Alice under her right armpit, lifting her to her feet.

Jee-zum! Shot twice and she still *can pick me up like a rag doll! What's it* like *to be that damned tough?*

More coughs spasmed through Alice's body, wiping out any thought. When her eyes cleared again, she was sitting by a small pool, exquisitely landscaped with cattails and rhodora, with natural ledge outcrops serving as benches backed by the blueberries and juniper that grew away from the wet. Kate lay full length on the stone, panting, her face pale. *Maybe the big lug isn't that tough, after all. Just desperate. Welcome to the club.*

Kate blinked and shook her head, as if answering Alice's thoughts. She winced and shifted her weight, trying to favor both her right hip and left shoulder at the same time. "That's Ol' Kate in a nutshell, ain't it? Always a day late and a dollar short?"

"If you hadn't been there a few minutes back, I'd probably be dead. Now hush up. I've still got work to do." Alice reached for her satchel, to set it close by her right hand. The move lit a blaze of pain across her back, and she gasped. The pool shimmered in her eyes, turning to quicksilver.

She drew power from it, calming her breathing. "In fact, why don't you just black out for a while. What you don't see, you can't testify to."

She closed her own eyes and felt for the healing and strength of this spring, sister to her own Woman's Spring. No matter that the Pratts had lived here for a dozen generations, men claiming to rule and possess the land. All springs were female—giving, nurturing. Springs were the earth goddess suckling life.

The touch eased her pain. That didn't matter. Pain wasn't the problem. She needed strength, she needed air, but most of all she needed that damned *brujo* to show up before she passed out. She yanked on the power like a bell-pull, summoning the Lord of Hell to a reckoning at his front gate.

Sirens yodeled in the distance, growing closer. Her practiced ear separated out sheriff's cars, State Patrol, and ambulance by their different cries. The volunteer fire department seemed to be slow off the mark. Middle of the day, all the guys would be at work.

A rattle of shots broke through the sirens, sounding like machine guns carrying on a South American political debate. Kate would know what they were. She could tell caliber and usually barrel length by the sound.

"Ah, *señora,* finally you come to call."

Alice blinked. He was there, across the pool, short and thin and brown, her enemy.

He bowed to her—a formal, European bow with a flourished hand. "Perhaps I have been lacking in courtesy. Should I have announced myself as a visiting member of the *asociación*—the *guild,* you would call it?"

The *brujo* looked far younger than his years. But then, she should have expected that. He glanced at Kate, a measuring look that seemed to weigh her wounds and vitality like a grocer pricing a sack of potatoes. Then he turned back to Alice.

"I believe the *inglés* would say that you are poaching. That bird is mine. But I can afford to be generous. Death drinks well this morning, and you may taste the flavor of this one. You appear to have need."

A low growl snapped her attention back to Kate. Her friend knelt on the granite ledge, hand groping for her pistol. "You goddamn *leech*! You *used* me!"

The big Colt boomed, shaking the air. Kate fought the recoil, dropped her sights back into place, and the gun roared again. The *brujo* shook his head. Alice saw splinters explode from a pine directly behind him. That .44 Mag would drop a moose, but he ignored it.

She nodded understanding. "Don't waste your powder. He isn't where you're aiming." Alice glanced up at the sky, at the brightness glowing near the zenith. The fog was lifting. "Wind of the west, hear me. Wind of the west, aid me."

The glow brightened as the west wind brought drier air and elbowed the fog aside. She searched the ground for shadows, seeking one that moved, seeking one shaped like a man. She pulled one of the dueling pistols from her satchel.

She faced her enemy, finally, with a weapon in her hands. "I would prefer *'señorita.'* The distinction is important to me."

She found her target, brought the pistol to full cock, aimed as coolly as any duelist ever had, and pulled the trigger. Smoke blasted across the spring, sulfurous blackpowder smoke like the banked clouds that used to hide the horrors of war.

The smoke drifted sideways in the breeze, slowly clearing. The *brujo* stood at one end of the pool, staring shocked at a hole in the ground in the center of his shadow. The paired silver and wooden balls nailed him in place.

She dropped her pistol and pulled its twin out of the

beaded satchel. She notched the sights on his chest, cocked the hammer, and pulled the trigger. Again, the gun leaped in her hand. Again, white smoke hid her target.

The west wind thinned the smoke and banished it, revealing the *brujo* lying still on the edge of the pool. Alice dropped the second pistol and let her hand shake for a moment, fighting back the black spots that danced across her sight. She couldn't let them win.

"Thank God, you've killed him!" Kate sounded weaker, somewhere out there beyond the smoke and fog.

"Not yet." Alice shook off the thickening fog inside her own head.

She crawled along the pool's edge, past Kate lying like a corpse. That looked too real for comfort, but Alice couldn't spare the strength. She had a job to do. They could sing their dying duet later.

Damn, wrong opera.

Alice dipped water from the spring, splashing her face. The coolness helped, but she felt it vanish in the fire of her shoulder. The Woman's Spring might have done better, but she had to fight on her enemy's own ground.

She wiped her hand before touching his wrist. He felt cold, like a toe-tagged corpse in the hospital morgue for autopsy. *No. Like a frog, cold-blooded but alive. Remember what he is.*

She made her hand colder. *Simple thermodynamics. Heat flows from an object with more energy to one with less. Damn sure I've got less energy than anything else around here. Let's get some serious energy flow going, dammit.*

<You are a fool.>

Her hand froze to his skin. Numbness crept up her wrist and forearm as her life drained down through them. Too late, she remembered that he must have done this a hundred times. She had done it only five. Four animals, including Dixie. One human, a bone-cancer patient in drug-resistant pain who had begged her for release, the Hippocratic oath be damned. Besides, she was just an RN.

<Not only a fool, but a sentimental fool. Soon to be a dead fool, *señorita*. I was prepared to respect you, but you would not accept me as your equal. *Adiós.* >

thirty

—⁓—

CAROLINE SLIPPED BACK through the hidden door, pulling the tape off the latch. She did her best to move like that damned mouse Alice was so fond of mentioning, holding the lock and releasing it with the gentlest possible touch to avoid a click. Cats could hear mice rustling in the wall three rooms away.

She set the deadbolt behind her. Someone had keys, of course, but there was no need for her to make it easy. She counted her way back down the doors, finding the one that should hide the girls. Light switch outside, flipped "off."

She leaned her forehead against cold stone, calming her thoughts and *trying* to think her actions out in advance. She whispered, half to herself and half to those remembered voices, "I'm *learning,* dammit!"

The door was locked, of course. She shuffled around in five pockets, finally found Gary's picks, and went to work. Picking the lock took forever, with the torque slipping in her sweaty fingers and her hands shaking with waste adrenaline from the shootout. Each time she gained a pin, she'd goof and lose it.

She finally noticed that the door opened out, exposing the bolt to her between the frame and lock, and she pulled her Swiss army knife from the bottomless pocket of gadgets. She dug the point into the latch bolt, shifted it an eighth of an inch, pulled the door tight to hold her gain, moved the blade over, released pressure, and gained another fraction. The fourth step moved the bolt past the striker plate, and the door lurched toward her. Crude, but results counted more than elegance.

She switched the light on and opened the door. An empty room yawned at her efforts, bare rock with the scars of quarryman's tools.

A sigh came out of the emptiness, like her own lungs daring to breathe after the gunmen closed that workshop door. Caroline echoed it, relief washing through her.

"Okay, girls, the cavalry's here! Time to bug out!"

A section of stone wall moved, then another. Ellen plastered herself against Caroline's waist, while Peggy hugged her thigh on the opposite side. Both faces felt damp through her clothing. The girls shook with fear and relief.

"No time for that. We've got to *move!*"

She hustled them toward the stairs and their brother. She *hoped* he'd kept his focus, and the way was clear.

"I'm *learning,* dammit!"

Both girls twisted around to stare at her.

"Sorry, I wasn't talking to you."

They gave her twinned "You're weird!" looks.

DANIEL STARED AT the manual and the security console in front of him, trying to force his mind to concentrate. He ached all over—a dull, diffuse throbbing from dozens of kicks and punches. His tongue kept playing with a loose tooth on the left upper side of his jaw. It was a minor thing compared to arms and legs with less strength than over-boiled spaghetti, but it kept distracting him.

Where had he lost that healthy sense of fear? Nothing seemed important anymore, nothing except sleep. He felt like an observer in his own skull. That had helped him to survive the past few days, the horror of Peggy and Ellen in the hands of those monsters. Now they had a chance to escape and he felt the same disconnection from his soul. He watched his hands flipping switches without any conscious decision, without plan or direction.

Gary had gone to the outer cave to try and start the smugglers' boat. Caroline Haskell searched for Ellen and Peggy somewhere up in the tunnels. Masked gunmen roamed the grounds overhead, and the Pratt house smoked and flamed. Alarms clanged around him. All of that should be vital to him. He didn't care.

One screen showed Alice Haskell and Kate Rowley collapsed next to a small pool—the lesbian Odd Couple, Mutt and Jeff. The *brujo* appeared, Tupash, and Alice shot him. *That* should have flooded Daniel with emotion, pure joy or release or some suitably vindictive glee, but he felt nothing. Feeling had been burned out of him, leaving foggy weakness as its ash.

Alice crawled across the screen and grabbed one wrist of the corpse. Static streaked the monitor, all of the monitors, and lights dimmed for a few seconds. Then the emergency circuits kicked in and the picture cleared. Now the monitor showed Alice and Kate lying still like corpses laid out for a wake, but even that left him untouched. He saw no sign of the Peruvian.

Daniel's eyes moved on, like they were remote cameras on a cable suspended two miles beneath the sea sending images to a dispassionate observer. Pratts and Latinos in the tunnels, Monitor 2—he shut and locked doors in front of them, aware in a distant fashion that he should be terrified of locking his daughters on the wrong side, on the side with the rapists and murderers. The caves had been set up as a shelter, a bunker, to hold a retreat. His console held master control. But Tom Pratt would have override codes. He could pass each door. Daniel only slowed them down.

Now each camera went blank as the first scouts appeared. They knew they had intruders in the cave. Daniel started killing light circuits in retaliation. Delaying tactics, nothing more.

Gary appeared in the doorway, panting, his face a study in frustration. "Damn boat has an interlock. Needs a plug-in circuit block to talk to the ignition computer. No way I can start it."

Cool, dispassionate, the shadow-Daniel weighed threats and options. "Disable it."

"I cut the battery leads and tossed them overboard. Followed up with a handful of sparkplug wires and the distributor rotor. Don't know what spares they have handy."

"Good." Gary seemed at least a foot taller and broader than Daniel remembered him. *He* knew what he was doing. The past weeks had built him up, strengthened him, at the same time that they had broken Daniel down. He'd left a boy behind in the house that long-distant afternoon. Now he saw a man. A Morgan. "Where are Ellie and Mouse? Where's Caroline?"

Gary glanced from his father to the rear wall of the room and back. He shook his head. "Quit playing games, girls. Dad needs to know where you are."

A section of granite faded into three crouching bodies. The room fuzzed around Daniel, and he blinked his eyes to clear them. By the time his head quit spinning, he was sandwiched between his daughters.

Ellen pulled back a few inches. "Daddy, you *stink*!"

She wouldn't notice *that* if the *brujo*'s threats had become actions. Warmth flooded into Daniel, starting to melt the ice. With the thaw came fear. "I'll take a bath when we're home and safe, little witch. We've got to get out of here."

Speaking of witches . . . Daniel looked from Caroline Haskell to Gary and back again. He sighed, noting Ben's face stamped on both of them, mixed with features of their different mothers. No, they couldn't have kept *that* secret from the boy. Sooner or later, even the girls would start asking difficult questions.

Sooner, if they ever met Ben.

Daniel flipped another switch and heard the answering rumble of the sea gate opening. He'd worry about explaining family secrets later—if they ever had a later. He stood up. The room spun around him, black dots swimming across his eyes.

"Dad?"

Gary's face floated in front of Daniel. "Dad? We've got to *move*! I hear people up in the tunnels."

"Weak. Haven't been eating. Won't let me sleep." Daniel blinked until the world firmed up around him. "I'll be okay. Just dizzy from standing up too fast."

Gary hustled them all out of the security room, hesitating over the master power switch. He left it on, muttering about magnetic locks that failed "open," in "safe" mode. Then he locked the door and snapped the key off in the lock. *More delaying tactics,* Daniel thought. *The boy* has *grown.*

Daniel's emotions prickled and tingled, like a foot coming awake after sitting too long in the wrong position. Something was bothering Gary, besides the current danger. Daniel saw him glance to the side as they retreated down the ramp to the float. A body lay there, crumpled, face up.

Daniel paused. He recognized the face. He reached out to Gary, touching him gently on the shoulder to hold him while the girls went ahead.

"You killed him. That bothers you."

Gary winced agreement.

"You've done the world a favor, son. He's the one who was going to get Peggy and Ellen. Rape, torture, and murder. You're old enough to know that some people aren't really human beings. They're rabid dogs on two legs. Killing them can be the simplest solution."

"But I didn't mean to do it."

"He's dead. You're alive. What would happen next if it was the other way around? That's the only choice he would have given you."

"But I didn't *mean* to do it."

"You're repeating yourself. Think back to the dojo, boy. They taught you to survive. Fights don't give you time to think. Something happens, you act. He's dead, you're alive. I like it that way."

Gary nodded, then shook his head, eyes squeezed shut. That problem wasn't going to go away with a few soothing words. Then Daniel remembered the tale the monitors had told. Maybe Alice could help. If she survived. The Haskell Witches had been practical psychotherapists for centuries. She understood about rabid dogs.

He pushed his son down the ramp, away from the corpse. Son? They'd sort that out when they didn't have a bunch of armed men at their backs. Still, with all he knew, Gary had called him "Dad." That helped feed the growing thaw inside.

Caroline stood above her kayak, feet planted on the float, coveting that speedboat. "You're *sure* you can't get it started?"

Gary shook his head, decisive. "Nope. Not today. Give me a couple of days' preparation, we could work out a bypass."

She pulled a pack of matches from a pants pocket. "Okay, where's the gas tank?" Then she spotted the filler cap beside the low deckhouse and homed in on it like a guided missile.

Gary grabbed her wrist. "Don't." She stopped and glared at him.

He glared back. "Think ahead. You've got to load the girls into the kayak, get into it yourself, and paddle out of here. Meanwhile, that boat blows up. Fills the cave with toxic smoke, dumps burning gas on the water. Dad and I have to change and swim out through all that. Think *ahead,* dammit!"

She froze, blinked, and muttered something to herself. Then she took a deep breath and shuddered. "Hey, I'm *working* on it."

He smiled and released her wrist. "You're not the only one. We knew there'd be a boat. I should have brought some kind of fuse or timer. Five minutes' delay and you could have all the fireworks your little heart desires."

It looked like the next generation of the Haskell Witches was going to be . . . entertaining. When viewed from a safe distance, that is. Like maybe across the Canadian border. *May you live in interesting times.* Daniel offered a silent prayer that Alice would live to a ripe old age.

They handed Ellen and Peggy down into the front cockpit of the kayak, and then Gary steadied it while Caroline climbed into the rear. She pushed off and turned to the sea gate with a little wave.

Gary was already peeling off his clothes and stuffing them into the waterproof backpack. Daniel started to unbutton his own shirt, wondering why his fingers trembled so much. The float rocked under him. Funny, he didn't see any waves. Then he sat down, hard.

"Dad?"

Gary's voice echoed strangely, as if he was off inside a pipe somewhere. Daniel tried to concentrate on shirt buttons, but couldn't remember why they were so urgent.

Then someone's fingers worked at his buttons, opened

zippers, tugged sleeves and trouser legs. Daniel felt blackness washing over him. He'd looked for that so hard, in the past days. Now it came when he didn't want it.

"Change, Dad. Change and swim."

He tried. He felt for the fire in his bones and muscles. The ashes were cold.

Then he felt hands again, pulling cloth over his flesh, layer after layer, more than they had taken off. He tried to help, feeble moves that probably interfered.

"You've got to hold on to the harness. Here. Put your arm through the pack."

"I can't *change*!" It should have been a cry of anguish, but it came out as a mumble.

"That's okay. I'll tow you out."

Something dragged him across the float, herky-jerky tugs and then a drop into icy water. He came up sputtering for air. He opened his eyes. The rock ceiling moved above, and he felt a powerful body warm beside him. Shouts echoed around the cave, and then shots. Water splashed close by, and Daniel barely thought to hold his breath before the sea closed over him. Cold and darkness pulled him under.

"Come *on* dammit! *Lift!*"

Daniel felt like a lump of clay. Soft, cold, slimy wet, he let hands mold him and move him. A hard edge dragged across his back and hip. He thumped down from it onto more hardness that moved. He tried to reach out, to grab something to steady his rolling body. His arm flopped around, dull and slow and uncooperative.

"Cold." He could barely mumble.

Bumps and bangs vibrated through the surface under him. *Deck,* he thought. *Stink of old herring gurry and oil and gasoline.* An engine sputtered, coughed, and growled to life, vibrating the planking under him. The pitching changed and heeled over, to surge at a new pace. He recognized the big V8 sound with the straight exhaust. Boats have personalities. No two are exactly alike. He was aboard the *Maria*.

Static squawked, followed by Gary's voice. "Five out. Repeat, five out."

Another burst of radio static, then: "Roger." It was Ben's voice, brief but jubilant. The radio fell silent.

Fingers fumbled at the layers of clothing over his chest. Wet cloth dragged away and was replaced by dry fleece. He felt warmth against his skin, a hand laid right over his heart. Heat flowed into his core. Strength came with it, and a will to live. He opened his eyes.

Caroline Haskell stared down at him, that haunting face that blended Ben's and Elaine's features. The gray light seemed to wash color from her skin. She pulled her hand back and sagged with exhaustion.

"Okay. You'll live." She reached to one side and brought back a large thermos. She poured steaming coffee into the cap and held it to his lips. It tasted like nectar, a familiar and pleasant memory; Dan swallowed, swallowed again, and drained the cup, feeling the warmth washing down into his stomach and out through his blood. She poured another cup and swigged it herself, watching him.

The aftertaste . . . "Jamaica Blue Mountain? Where the hell did you get *that?*"

"Aunt Alice has friends. And I'm not going to ask how you recognized it, because it probably involves a felony."

She stood up, bracing her free hand on the deckhouse wall and swaying as if her knees felt as weak as his did. Must have worn herself out, sprinting for *Maria* and hauling him over the side. Looked strong for a girl, though—shoulders and arms thicker than a lot of men's. Good six inches taller than Lainie, too.

Daniel summoned his own strength to look around. The

kayak lay lengthwise on the deck, rolling with the boat. Ellen and Mouse had tucked themselves into corners of the deckhouse, huddled out of the wind. They weren't dressed for a day on the water.

Caroline noticed his glance, shook herself, and knelt down to pull more fleece blankets out of a pack at her feet. She staggered again, moving across the surging deck, and sagged back against the wall after tucking warmth around the girls. She looked drained, the far end of a bad day.

A rueful smile crossed her face when she noticed his stare. "Healing takes energy. Aunt Alice is a *lot* better at it than I am."

Her glance shifted to the open back of the deckhouse. Then she stiffened and turned to Gary at the wheel. "Oh, *shit*! I thought you disabled that thing."

Daniel forced himself to hands and knees, to look out over the transom. The Pratts' speedboat showed dark against the pink cliffs, bow-on and a white bone of spray in her teeth. Thick black smoke shot with orange boiled up from the top of the cliff above it. Hounds of hell coming straight from the source. They must have had spare parts and tools right on board, and people who knew what they were doing. Made sense, for a drug-runner. You wouldn't want to call the Coast Guard for help if something broke.

thirty-one

—⁓—

THE COLD FLOWED up Alice's arm, past the elbow and into her biceps. It even cooled the flame of her wounded back. She knew that when it touched her heart, she would die. Then he would take Kate. And later Caroline, and the girls, and the rest of the Morgans, and gain the Egg of the Dawn. The Dragon's Eye. That such power should be held by such a man . . .

<NO!>

The rock seemed to shake under her, vibrating from the scream. A vise clamped around her hips, soft but unyielding, and it seemed as if the whole Stonefort peninsula was chained to it as an anchor, holding her against the tide. Warmth flowed back *into* her from that chain, the warmth of life and of the earth, and pulsed out through her hand as fire. Her back blazed again, agony like she had been crucified to the house burning behind her, and she forced the pain and heat down through her arm and palm into the wrist she held. The dead flesh warmed and sizzled and ignited.

<AIIIIEEEEEeee . . . >

Silence fell, and waited, and the world went on.

Alice gasped and stirred, feeling rock gritty against her cheek. She moved parts of herself, from the corners in, testing to see that everything was there. Fingers, toes, hands, feet, arms, legs: all present and accounted for. She felt as if the entire cast of *Riverdance* had tap-danced their finale on her back. On the other hand, that was an improvement.

She opened her eyes. Those worked, too. The pool looked pretty much as it did before. The garage still blazed, a skeleton of blackened ribs with glowing metal where its heart and lungs should be. Smoke poured from the attic and second floor of the house, above a yard curiously empty of people. She hoped they weren't all trying to sneak out the back door, right into Caroline's lap.

Speaking of laps . . . something still clamped her hips in that soft vise. She looked down. Kate lay there, the anchor that had pulled Alice back from death and then poured the energy of the whole peninsula into the *brujo*. That was the essence of Stonefort—even rock-solid straight-ahead numb-as-a-hake Kate touched the power of the land that had shaped her.

And it was Kate who had come up with that final jiujitsu move. The bastard wants power, we'll *give* him power.

Cornered, with teeth bared, *anyone* could be a Witch. Even Kate Rowley. The *brujo* hadn't realized that.

She remembered the curse she had called down. "May their own weapons destroy them. May the fires of the land and the waters of the sea devour them." She hadn't expected the result to be quite this literal.

Everything is magic. Everyone touches magic. Most people just don't see it, even when it bashes them between the eyes. Don't, or won't. The world is magic. Took Aunt Jean ten years to drum that into your head.

Alice checked pulse and breathing. Her love still lived. The bleeding had slowed. Alice untangled herself from Kate and looked around.

The *brujo* had vanished into ash. She found and pocketed the silver pistol balls, scuffed and blackened. Maybe Caroline would need them someday. She slipped her pistols back into the satchel and wormed her way out of the vest and leggings without asking too much of her abused shoulder. She studied the hole in the back of the vest for a few moments, comparing it to all the other patches that the doeskin had acquired through the centuries. She hadn't done that badly, after all. Just another repair job, and another dark stain in the soft leather. The beadwork already had drunk most of the blood.

She blinked as the trees started wavering around her. She coughed and spat out another gob of frothy pink. Even Kate's surge of power couldn't heal everything. Alice squatted down again, tucking her head between her knees until the world consented to stand still. Then she packed the regalia away and fumbled her way back to Kate's side.

Radio—Kate always carried a radio, when she was away from the truck. Alice poked around under the POLICE jacket, finding the handheld. She switched it on, and the radio spurted all the chaos of the siege that waited out beyond the trees. She hadn't heard any shots for a while.

One way she knew, to get medics into a war zone. She pulled up Kate's car number from memory, and the ten-codes memorized for ambulance work. She waited for a gap in the noise and then chanted her words of power. "Five-seven-seven to Sunrise dispatch. Ten seventy-four. Repeat, ten seventy-four. Officer down. Repeat, officer down." The radio sat silent, as if it had been stunned by her words. Then it spat a burst of static. "Five-seven-seven, this is tactical control. What's your location?"

She heard orders shouted in the background, the stuttering of other radio channels. They'd set up some kind of command post out on the road.

"Behind Tom Pratt's garage. Two casualties."

"Kate, you damned fool! What the *hell* are you doing in there?" The voice broke off, then resumed. "We'll have men there in a couple of minutes. Tactical out."

And they *would* be there. Cops never abandoned one of their own. Alice settled down by Kate's side, back to feeding gentle warmth through her hand.

"Kate, you there?"

"Maybe."

"I called you. You came over from the island. We met out here to talk to Jackie. She shot us. That's all we know."

"Got it." She lay there for a moment. "Need to get Keith Bauer's boat back out there. Can you call John Lambert?"

"Depends who's on the ambulance. I'll try."

Kate was crying again, quiet tears dripping like the mist from the trees overhead. "Lys, I can't go back to the trailer. Anytime I look at it, every room, I'll think of her. Damn place even smells of her. I couldn't stand it."

Alice sighed. Apparently a mother's love really *was* unconditional. "Plenty of room at the House. That's what it's for." She felt Kate relax, accepting the oblique answer to her unasked question.

"Lys, I love you."

A different kind of warmth flooded through Alice, settling in her belly. "I guess the boat ride kinda told me that."

GARY RAMMED THE throttle forward. The big Chevy V8 responded with a roar, digging the stern deeper into the water. Then he grabbed the mike again. "We've got company. Plan B. Plan B."

"Roger." Ben's voice again, grim this time. "Can't see you yet. Fog."

Gary dropped the mike, letting it dangle on its cord. He stared over the stern, measuring distances and relative speed. Caroline grabbed on to one of the ribs of the deckhouse roof, bracing against the bounce of the swells. She grinned for an instant, apparently immune to seasickness.

"Hey, I didn't know lobster boats could go this fast!"

Gary glanced back to her. "Dad won the Fourth of July races last year. Faster your boat goes, the more traps you can pull in a day. Then there's the macho factor. Bigger engine, bigger"—he paused, apparently remembering Ellen and Peggy huddled in their corners—"muscles."

He was measuring the distance again, wrinkling his nose at the rate of change. "Problem is, they have a planing hull and twin V8s. You got any weather-magic tucked away in your bag of tricks?"

"Why? You want more fog?"

"No. They've got radar. We need clearing, especially off towards Morgan Point."

She blinked twice, trying to figure out what *that* meant. Daniel had a glimmer, but he kept his mouth shut. Gary had the conn. He'd explain if he thought it was necessary.

Instead, she closed her eyes and started chanting, soft muscular language that flowed out into the air around them and seemed to wrap fingers into the tendrils of fog. The sky brightened, and the pale spots of blue to the west started to deepen. Daniel felt a breeze on his left cheek, the one toward the land.

She stopped, took a deep breath, and sat down suddenly, panting as if she'd run a mile in record time. Some of the words had been *close* to meaning something, but Daniel couldn't make it out. "That wasn't Naskeag."

She flashed another of her one-sided smiles. "Nope. Hopi sun chant. Hey, you guys wanted *dry*, didn't you?"

Daniel did his own calculation of time-over-distance, based on his understanding of what "Plan B" meant. He didn't like the results. He turned back to Caroline. "Can you shoot a rifle?"

Now her grin spread full-face. "University rifle team."

Somehow, he'd thought she could. "Go down into the cuddy. Locker on the right side, rear, you'll find the boat gun. Thirty-round magazines, solid-jacket rounds for sharks. We're going to need some time."

She moved, sure and catlike across the bouncing deck. Daniel turned his attention to his daughters. "You get down there, too. Lie down below waterline." That was the best he could do. Gary nodded, the captain approving his first mate's actions. The boy had grown so much . . .

Then Caroline was back, kneeling at the transom, checking and loading the rifle. "Hey, I didn't know they made these things in stainless steel." Then she did a double-take. "Selective fire?"

Daniel could almost see the cartoon question-marks floating around her head. He ignored them. She was settling down, kneeling, rifle cradled gently and rising-falling with the surge of the deck. Water spouted close by, and then something thunked into fiberglass along the starboard side. Shots rattled across the water from the speedboat, but she held fire. Good idea—he guessed the range at nearly 300 yards.

"Aim for the windscreen," Gary ordered. "Try and startle the helm, make him shear off."

She nodded. The rifle boomed—once, twice, a third time, single shots with the deliberation of a slow-fire target match. Daniel had expected her to go with full-auto instead. The speedboat slewed sideways with a rooster tail of spray, and *Maria* pulled away a little.

Then they came on again, boring straight in to cut the range. Caroline shook her head, fiddled with the rifle, and blasted out neat three-shot bursts like a combat vet. Daniel saw water spouting on either side of the speedboat, bracketing it. One or two rounds of each burst must be hitting home. More bullets hit *Maria,* shattering side windows of the deckhouse and knocking splinters from the fiberglass of the gunwale. Caroline jerked and then shook out her shirt as if ridding herself of a wasp. A spent bullet clattered to the deck. Must have been hot.

Daniel searched ahead, picking the dark stub of Morgan's Castle out of the mist. He tried to guess the range. Twenty miles from Pratts' Neck to Morgan Point by land around the bay, a little over six miles by water. They'd made a couple of miles good before they spotted the speedboat. How much more since?

That recoilless rifle had a maximum range of about 8000 yards. Effective range, less than half that . . .

He caught a flash from the top of the tower. Daniel gnawed on his thumb knuckle, hoping Ben knew what the hell he was doing. He'd always been murder on the eiders, often got a double with one shot. Still, aiming for a moving target, when each shell had to fly for miles . . .

Metal hissed over his head, and water fountained up between the boats, but off to the right. The explosion boomed back to them, mixing with the flat bang of the distant gun. Echoes rolled across the water.

The speedboat kept coming. So much for warning shots.

Daniel had started counting when the first shell landed. Right at "One thousand five," he spotted a second flash. He gnawed at that knuckle until another shell whistled overhead and water spouted beyond the black speedboat and to the left. Shot and shell-burst again echoed from the cliffs.

To make that rate of fire, Ben must have been practicing for days. The gun was supposed to have a crew, not one man loading, aiming, firing, spotting the fall, and adjusting aim. One round short, one round long . . . Daniel crossed his fingers and prayed. The speedboat held its course, narrowing the distance, trying to get too close for Ben to chance another shot.

"One thousand ten, one thousand eleven, one thousand twelve . . ."

Caroline fired again—a long burst that ended in the click of the bolt locking open. She grabbed for another magazine. Then the speedboat shattered in flame. A second blast shook the wreck, blossoming into a black mushroom laced with orange and red. *Must be the gas tank,* he thought. Bright white flashes burst and sparkled against the smoke, a string of secondary explosions, and thunder pealed back from the cliffs like the drum-roll finale of a July Fourth show.

"Jee-*zum* . . ." Gary stood at the wheel, staring back as the fire spread across the water and blazing streaks rained from the sky. The speedboat had vanished.

"Holy Mary Mother of God," Caroline whispered. "And I wanted to toss a match into *that*?"

Daniel took a deep breath and let it out slowly. "Hell of a bit of luck. That kind of show, nobody's going to go looking for funny noises from Morgan's Castle. Just echoes, that's all they were." And nobody in *Stonefort* would mention a second boat. Not even the Pratts. Not to outsiders.

He studied the smoke and dying flames. He hadn't seen a third flash from the tower, or heard another shell in the air. Caroline would have needed God's own luck to touch off that show with a rifle bullet. And the Pratts obviously had some really nasty stuff on board. Maybe they'd been worried about hijackers? Anyway, it *looked* like someone had just done a first-class job of shooting himself in the foot.

Gary throttled the engine down to a murmur and headed the bow out to sea. The thunder of war died away to the screams of outraged gulls. The cliffs faded back into mist, hiding *Maria*'s white hull from the hundreds of startled eyes on land. He glanced at his watch and then at Daniel. "How long till the Coast Guard gets here?"

"An hour for the rescue chopper, minimum." It would have been ten or fifteen minutes, before budget cuts pulled all helicopter operations back to Rockland.

Ellen poked her head out of the cuddy, looking around at

Caroline unloading the rifle, at Gary relaxing by the wheel. She climbed up on deck, followed by Mouse.

Everybody safe. Not "Everybody dies."

Daniel sagged back against the gunwale, tired but finally allowing himself to believe in life. He caught Gary's eye. "Head for the home mooring. This tide, there's a ledge you can use as a dock."

thirty-two

—ᴍ—

GARY FOLLOWED CAROLINE from room to room through
the Morgan house, tapping on a small drum that looked
about a hundred years older than God. She chanted to his
beat, slow words in Naskeag and Latin and Welsh and English, mostly names. The rest probably were titles—the
ones he could translate were. And as she chanted, a braided
rope of sweetgrass smoldered in her right hand. She waved
it gently or wafted the smoke into each corner of each room
using a turkey wing as a fan.

"Smudging," she called it. Blessing or purifying or
guarding or exorcising, he wasn't quite sure which. Maybe
it was all of them at once. Every second or third room,
something ran cold fingers across the back of his neck or
shifted one wisp of pungent smoke at right angles to the
rest, caressing an old chair or a piece of Mom's antique glass
like a familiar friend.

The drum fit perfectly between his left hand and his hip,
a hollow carved into the body and a wrap of sharkskin that
defeated the sweat slicking his wrist. The whole thing,

maple body and rough sharkskin and rawhide ties and head, was stained nearly black with the grease of centuries of hands, the soot of centuries of fires. It had seemed light when he first picked it up. Now it felt like it was made of lead.

He'd never thought about how many rooms hid under his roof, from second cellar to third attic. How many sets of stairs and tucked-away corner turrets reached only by passing through a back door forgotten behind racks of clothes in a later closet and then climbing a ladder through a hatch into ancient dust. The place had just grown, centuries of afterthoughts and additions and changes in fashion, and navigating it had grown in his head as he learned to walk and talk.

Caroline didn't seem confused by it all. Sometimes she stopped and sniffed, as if tracking down any breath of air that didn't yet carry the smoke of sweetgrass. And she wasn't in any hurry. He swiped his right sleeve across his forehead, mopping at the sweat.

"Keep drumming!" rasped into the space between two names, the second one being Aunt Jean. "Jeanne Alouette Haskell," it was, pronounced in French and sounding right that way even though he'd never heard her name as anything other than Anglicized "Aunt Jean." He barely remembered her, earliest memories as a child, a round brown wrinkled woman almost as ancient as the drum.

At least Caroline's voice sounded raw. At least this ritual was stretching *her* limits, as well. Gary concentrated on the beat, slow and soft. Easy at first, the beat had come to dominate his own heart and throb in his temples. As if the drum was beating *him*.

They'd reached Mom's room, last of the second floor. For some reason, Caroline had bypassed this level for the attics and then come back. As if she was building the jaws of a vise to squeeze something in the middle.

"You saved this one for last, didn't you?"

Now *she* swiped her sleeve across her forehead. "Aunt Alice thought it was the most likely place. Shut up and keep drumming!" Then she returned to her chant.

Place for what? But he kept his mouth shut.

She opened the door, swung the short rope of sweetgrass until its tip glowed almost to open flame, and then waved smoke into the room like a soldier tossing grenades into an enemy house before searching it. Her voice echoed in the drum, chanting, naming. Naming Haskell Witches, he finally guessed, Witches back to the dawn of time. Invoking Haskell Witches.

Then she stepped through the doorway, and he followed her into the smoke, thick and sharp and pungent, biting his nose and throat. Those things that weren't air currents teased the smoke back and forth across the room, gathering, gathering, working fingers around the right-most of Mom's three windows. The one closest to the old oak that shaded the west end of the house.

And then the smoke flowed through the closed window, through the wavy old glass rather than around the sashes and into gaps of the old wood frame, and vanished. A thin tendril rose from the end of the grass rope, glow settling back nearly to darkness, but that was all.

His half-sister's shoulders slumped, and she took a deep breath. "Done. You can stop now." Then she stepped across the room, to that last window closest to Mom's bed, to the old four-poster with lace hangings and cream silk pillowcases, and looked out. "That branch comes damn close to the house. Doesn't it bang against the wall in a high wind?"

Gary stopped drumming and flexed his fingers and wrist in the sudden silence, wrinkling his nose. He felt blisters forming on his fingertips.

He didn't need to look out the window. He knew just which branch she meant. "No. Too thick, too old, too stiff. That's another 'back door' out of the house, in case of fire or raid. Trained there, pruned and tied into place and all, a century or two ago. It's mentioned in the journals."

"Door out, door in. That's how the *brujo* got to your mother. It's guarded now."

Gary winced as things connected in his head. He knew of alarm sensors on that tree, on that branch, on that window. But Ben knew more about the alarm system than he did, more than anyone except Dad. And his parents, all *three* of them, had lived a . . . tangled . . . relationship. He knew he'd never ask *that* question.

Instead, he caught his sister's eye. "What were you afraid of?"

She wiggled her shoulders, a disturbing move that he thought she'd *designed* to catch male eyes, and then took an equally disturbing deep breath that strained her clinging sweat-damp blouse. He hoped she wasn't coaching Ellen through puberty. Lesbian Aunt Alice would be a safer choice.

But then she let the breath out as a sigh and just looked tired rather than sexy. "Some kind of GOK."

"Huh?"

"Gee Oh Kay. Geologist slang—'God Only Knows.' They use it for weird rocks. Ethnologists borrowed it for strange artifacts. Aunt Alice was afraid that Peruvian slime-ball had left some booby-traps behind."

The thought made Gary wince. "But he didn't?"

"Apparently not. Bastard seems to have had his own peculiar sense of honor. Or didn't feel like wasting time."

He wanted to get off that subject. "How's Aunt Alice doing? And Ms. Rowley?"

"They'll both live. Call her Kate. Only the girls are allowed to call her 'Aunt Kate.' But both of those damned women came within an inch of killing themselves. Not the wounds, but the witching. Used enough power to light up half the township like a Christmas tree. Blew out three breakers at the electrical co-op."

She sighed again, and this time pain crossed her face, some sort of peculiar mix of grief and anger and bone-deep weariness. Gary felt like hugging her, the kind of protective brother-hug he'd give Mouse when she skinned a knee. Caroline had been living in lounges at Sunrise General for three days now, with Elaine Haskell guarding and mothering the girls. *It takes a village to raise a child. Or a tribe . . .*

The pause stretched on, awkward, and then she glanced back at the hallway and the main stair leading down. "Speaking of invalids, how's your father? The *real* one, not ol' Balls-for-Brains Ben Morgan. I didn't want to ask in front of the girls. Or where Daniel could hear your answer."

Yes, she *could* be tactful. She just didn't usually bother.

"He's getting stronger. Gloomy. Brooding over the news from over on Pratts Neck. He managed to change this morning." Gary winced, remembering. "Took him half an hour to change back. But the Dragon gave him another Tear."

"Ouch. Suppose it wouldn't do a damn bit of good to tell him to take it easy? Just like Aunt Alice?"

"You got it."

"God, but Stonefort breeds a bunch of stiff-necked birds. *All* of us." Then she turned to the door. "Got to drop the girls off at Mom's, get back to the hospital. Before Aunt Alice witches somebody into letting her out. She's giving them a refresher course on how a nurse or doctor makes the *worst* kind of patient."

DANIEL SAT QUIETLY in his old leather armchair, just drinking in the sight of Ellie and Mouse safe in the second parlor of his home. The whole scene felt so *normal*—the girls, the dark Victorian furniture, the musty-paper smell of a wall of books blending with Caroline's sweetgrass smoke to bring up memories of *his* father and an old briar pipe.

How did Victorian décor come to dominate this place? One fifty-year period out of hundreds? Is it because the stuff is so uncomfortable you'll never use it enough to wear it out, so ugly you can't give it away?

The girls were playing a game of chess on a rosewood and holly inlay game table with a Chinese ivory chess set looted from the Philippines, not even bickering over Ellie's handicap of one bishop. Which was going to have to drop to a pawn or two, really soon. Mouse was winning. Again.

He'd have to tell them the history of that set and table sometime. But not today. He still had dark moments where he saw them in the Pratt caves, captured by monsters. By rabid dogs, like he'd told Gary. But they were safe. Unhurt.

No. *Not* unhurt. They'd lost their mother. His own feelings about Maria might be touchy, more a sense of failure than of grief, but she'd been a super mother. Raised three super kids. Now Alice and Elaine would have to finish the job. At least Lainie knew how to raise girls—look at Caroline.

Speak of the devil . . . Caroline slouched through the main hall door and dropped her sweetgrass rope into the parlor hearth, muttering Naskeag that Daniel translated as a blessing on the fire circle. Ancient words, dating back to before houses and hearths and chimneys.

She looked beat, and Gary wasn't in much better shape. Whatever they'd been doing sure drank energy. She blinked at Daniel, coming back into focus. "After the place airs out a bit, you can turn the fire alarm system back on. I'm done."

"What was *that* all about?"

"I just invited some ghosts in to watch over this place. Real ghosts, not you or your brother."

"Haskell ghosts. Okay. Some of them should know the place already. Maybe they'll show the other ones around, so we don't have to put up with ectoplasm dripping in strange places." Daniel found himself slipping into the kind of banter he'd fenced with Alice, back when she was just Alice. "You're the Haskell Witch now?"

"Temporary. Military calls it a 'brevet' promotion, do the job without drawing the pay. Aunt Alice gets out of the hospital and back on her feet, I'm busted back to 'prentice. I've wangled permission from my advisor to drop grad school for a semester, minimum. Family emergency."

Well, *that* part was true. And he'd learned enough about Caroline by now that he thought the university would bend over backward for her. They might not realize just *why* . . .

"So why are you adding guards to *this* house. Don't your ghosts have enough work back home?"

"Just following orders. Aunt Alice figures we can't protect the girls without guarding this house as well. Or protect Stonefort, either. We've just been through proof of that." Her hand crept up to her chest, over the Dragon pendant tucked into her blouse. "Besides, I've got a personal interest in some of your secrets."

Secrets. Well, she *was* a certified Morgan now, recognized and accepted by the Dragon. And knew the ancestral heap of dry rot inside and out, from years of visits and babysitting the girls. No reason why she shouldn't see *this,* as well. If she didn't *already* know it. Damned witches . . .

He pointed to Gary and waved him over to the fireplace. "Something I would have shown you, if I'd been around after you met the Dragon. Push on the far left-hand panel over the mantel, then pull out the matching panel on the right."

Caroline made a noise, choking back a laugh or something. Daniel turned to her. "You got a problem?"

"Just another old family connection, that's all."

Gary did as he was told. The second panel uncovered a gray-enameled steel face with a dial in the center. A dial with numbers up to a hundred—damned complicated combination lock, on a safe that Dan's grandfather had built from scratch. Anyone who tried to burn through the door or took more than three tries at the combination would get a rude surprise.

"Wait a couple of days and then check that safe. Combination is Elijah Morgan's birth and death years, closest gravestone to the castle, left-right-left-right." He stopped and glared at Caroline. "You Witches know about *that* one, too?"

She shook her head. "Nope. None of our business. Contrary to popular opinion, we don't stick our noses into *everything*. Don't have time."

Yeah. Give a pragmatic reason, not a moral one. That's a Haskell for you. But that's why we get along okay.

He turned back to Gary, with a sideways nod at Caroline. "I'd *suggest* you reset the combination after opening it. Remember the family motto.

"Anyway, you'll find my will in there, and Maria's, and keys to some *official* safe-deposit boxes up in Naskeag Falls. There's a bunch of legal mumbo-jumbo in the paperwork about trusts for you kids, residual estate to spouse, and a clause saying each had to survive the other by a month in order to inherit. Tax dodges. If we both are dead, the wills name Aunt Alice as guardian for the three of you. She'll be trustee, too, until each of you is twenty-one."

Gary blinked and then slid the panel closed again with a click. He turned back to Daniel. "Why? Can't you just come back alive, tell the cops you'd been held prisoner by the Pratts and escaped during the fire? And why wait?"

Well, there was a whole pile of reasons for staying dead, none of which Dan wanted to discuss in front of the girls. Maria's death, for example: Some of their fights were Sunrise County legends. The police would be *very* interested if they found out he was still alive. Then there was a hefty chunk of insurance. There was a damned persistent private investigator tracking down some Moche artifacts. There was a . . .

"Too complicated. We don't know where things stand

with the Pratts, or with Ron Pelletier. Fire, shootout, cops till hell won't have 'em. If I show up now, we'll never hear the end of it."

Caroline nodded. "Aunt Alice isn't happy with reports on the moccasin telegraph. Things they've found over at the Pratts, things they *haven't* found. She says you *don't* want to talk to the cops right now."

Damn. Alice Haskell "isn't happy." Daniel shook his head. *If Aunt Alice ain't happy, ain't* nobody *gonna be happy.* That was a fact of life in Stonefort, had been for decades. Caroline had his deepest sympathy. "Anyway, being dead is simpler. No awkward questions. And you have to wait a couple of days to give the ink time to dry." He grinned. "Don't worry—the witnesses will be legit. Besides, it's time you took over the *Maria* and ran your own lobster license."

Caroline nodded again. Studying anthropology, *she* would understand. Guardianship be damned—the license meant that Gary was a man in Stonefort, captain of the *Maria,* head of the family.

The Morgan. Seventeen had been plenty old for that, plenty old to swing a sword or buckle on a swash and climb over an enemy's gunn'l with pistols smoking in each hand and a cutlass between your teeth, back in the days of the clans.

"*And,*" he added, "we need time to move some stuff around before the executor does an inventory for inheritance tax. Otherwise, we'll be right back to those awkward questions."

He stood up. "Speaking of that wreck out in the bay, you'd better fire a memorial salute from the tower cannons. That'll cover up any nitrate residue up there. Details, boy, God is in the *details.* Use the fireworks powder—lots of trace minerals to confuse any snoopy noses. You'll find charge tables in the magazine. Just tell Eric Peterson first, over at the fire department, say Aunt Alice gave permission. He'll pass the word around."

Then Daniel stepped across to the chess game, kissed two furrowed brows, and walked out into the hall. It wasn't as if he'd never see them again.

The side door stuck a bit as usual, warping and expanding with the damp spring fogs along the shore. But if he planed it down to fit, it would rattle and leak cold air when it dried out again in the winter wind. Life in Stonefort was like that. You worked the best average you could with harsh extremes.

But this morning certainly wasn't harsh. Bright sun, sky so dark a blue you thought you might spot stars, a sea breeze to cool his face and blow the bugs away—Daniel breathed deep through his nose and savored the day. Even the bay looked serene, just long gentle rollers coming in off the Gulf of Maine, the sort of sailing that the yachties dreamed about when they planned summer cruises up from Boston or Newport in their varnished gleaming Hinckleys.

Tomorrow or next week or next month the sea would turn killer as it always did, slashing wind and bitter rain across waves pounding on sharp rock. Then the "sailors" would be hiding from its true face and wishing themselves back in safer waters.

Hiding from the powers that had molded Stonefort and its people.